DUPLICITY

BOOKS BY MICHAEL J ALLEN

Blood Phoenix:
1. ASHES OF RAGING WATER
2. RULED BY TAINTED BLOOD
3. VENGEFUL ARE THE DROWNED
4. RISE OF THE EXILED LADY
5. RAZING THE LAST BASTION

Scion (Original):
1. SCION OF CONQUERED EARTH
2. STOLEN LIVES
3. HIJACKED
4. UNCHAINED

Bittergate:
1. MURDER IN WIZARD'S WOOD
2. THE WIZARD'S BANE
3. FORGE OF WAR
4. SCYTHE OF ILLUSIONS

Guns of Underhill:
1. FEY WEST

Dumpstermancer:
1. DISCARDED
2. DUPLICITY

Delirious Scribbles:
(SHORT STORIES)

- WYRM'S WARNING
- SCRAPING BOTTOM
- CRIMINAL JUSTICE
- DREAMS OF TREASURE
- DESPERATE
- THE BOTTOM LINE

COMING SOON:

Binarai Online:
1. STORM REFUGE
2. ROGUE PLANET
3. POWER BREAK

Wayman Chronicles:
1. CROSSWAYS

Guns of Underhill:
2. METTLE KINGDOM

Dumpstermancer:
3. DECOY

Scion Rising (Remaster)

DUPLICITY

DUMPSTERMANCER: BOOK TWO

Michael J. Allen

Delirious
Scribbles Ink

Delirious Scribbles Ink

COPYRIGHT

Delirious Scribbles Ink, Inc.
4519 Woodruff Road
Suite 4, #108
Columbus, Georgia 31904
www.deliriousscribblesink.com

Interior Layout ©2022 Delirious Scribbles Ink, Inc.
Cover Design ©2022 Delirious Scribbles Ink, Inc.
Cover Art ©2018 Stefanie Saw

ISBN 978-1-944357-34-4 (intl. tr. pbk.)
ISBN 978-1-944357-35-1 (hc.)
ISBN 978-1-944357-36-8 (epub)
ISBN 978-1-944357-81-8 (large print)

Printed in the United States of America
10 9 8 7 6 5 4 3 2 1
Duplicity / Michael J. Allen. — 1st ed.

For Rebecca & Billy who have contributed so much to my worlds and the continuing efforts to maintain my sanity.

For B, B & E, J, S & J, and L.

Delirious Scribbles Readers Group

Like free stories?

How about curated deals for Science Fiction and Fantasy books?

Get your first benefit—a FREE story sent right to you—by becoming a member of the Delirious Scribbles Readers Group.

Begin your journey, just scan this image with your phone camera!

Content Advisory

In order to provide my readers the best possible experience as well as be responsive to reader requests, I've created a reader-curated content advisory on my website. If you are sensitive to certain kinds of fictional representations, please check this book's listings before reading.

I hope you enjoy this story…

— MICHAEL J ALLEN

To visit the advisory, just scan this image with your phone camera.

1

BLOODY HANDS

Adam Mathias stormed out of SMLE headquarters, bulling through the two security goons waiting by the door. "Can you believe they let him go?"

Neither goon answered.

Adam turned back, yelling at the doors. "He violated the restraining order! He's a criminal! How could you *idiots* let him go free?!"

"Sir?" Terry, the smaller and darker haired of Adam's bodyguards gestured to a reporter badgering her cameraman to hasten setting up the gear to catch Adam's tirade.

"Thanks," Adam mumbled. He straightened his suit and marched straight over to the woman.

She adjusted an evergreen skirt suit and slapped her cameraman. He got the camera pointed at Adam as the two bodyguards stepped to either side clearing the shot.

Adam addressed her with an eagerness often reserved by children awaiting Santa Claus. "If it isn't Megan French."

She raised a fine brown brow and tilted her head at the camera. Adam straightened his lapels and nodded. Megan stepped up beside him, smiling into the camera. "Good afternoon. I'm here with Adam Mathias, CEO of Thoth Corp, outside SMLE headquarters. Mister Mathias, it looked as if your visit with Seufert Fells's magical law enforcement distressed you."

Adam shifted his expression to one of disappointment. "I'm afraid so. As my fellow citizens are doubtless aware, a horrible crime was committed against our city, and once more my former partner Elias Graham seems at its center."

"Mister Mathias, witness testimony claims Mister Graham stopped the attack on over a hundred Seufert Fells citizens single-handedly. Are you suggesting he was behind the?"

"I'm loathe to speculate without all the facts, but I know a powerful wizard took over Thoth's assembly golems and forced them to commit heinous crimes. Witnesses saw Elias near them—violating an active restraining order—on numerous occasions."

"I take it Thoth's former CAO is not only a talented spell architect, but a wizard as well?"

"I think his conviction proves out what Elias is capable of."

"Are you suggesting Mister Graham attacked the city with those golems and his rescue of Seufert Fells citizenry covered the tracks?" Megan asked.

"SMLE investigators would be more qualified to comment on that, and I'm sure they'll release a statement once they take Elias back into custody and complete questioning him."

"Wait," Megan beamed at the camera. "Are you saying Mister Graham escaped and is a fugitive at large?"

"He's at large, Megan, but with the full consent of SMLE."

Megan's expression turned to one of shock. "Mister Graham violated a restraining order in front of law enforcement, may have been behind the abduction and assault on citizens including law enforcement and they let him free?"

Adam looked down, shaking his head. "I can't imagine why they'd jeopardize our friends and neighbors, but yes. A convicted and talented criminal is back on the streets."

"We can only hope SMLE knows what they are doing and that Mister Graham doesn't return to his old, illicit ways." Megan flash a hand across her throat and extended it. "Thank you, Mister Mathias."

"Thank you, Megan, and please, call me Adam."

Megan pushed a brown lock back to expose more of her face. Her posture shifted her chest into greater prominence. "You're very welcome, Adam."

Adam smiled at the reporter, noting a modest frame hidden in her professional attire as she flirted. He undressed her in his mind, weighing his options and resisting the urge to lick his lips. "Good citizens should stick together."

She nodded. "We need to take care of one another."

"I couldn't agree more." Adam's grin widened as he handed her his private business card. "Feel free to get in touch if I can do anything else for you."

"I will." She exchanged his card for hers, her voice growing husky. "I'm at your service day or night if you have anything news-worthy to share."

"Front page, Megan. Now, if you'll excuse me."

She inclined her head as Adam strode toward his limousine. Terry and Dennis stepped in on either side. A drone rose into sight from behind the limo as they approached. Terry set a restraining hand on Adam's shoulder.

The drone stopped, cameras projecting a hologram of an attractive man in a more expensive suit than Adam wore. "Mister Mathias, I need to speak to you about your former partner."

"Who are you?" Adam asked.

"Lucian Fayer, and I'm a gardener of sorts. I can offer assistance removing persistent thorns."

Adam shot a look over his shoulder, cataloging Megan's cameraman and SMLE cameras and wizard eyes. He shook his head. "I don't know what you're talking about, and I wouldn't discuss it with you *here* if I did."

"No matter." Lucian gestured toward a box truck. "Allow me to offer my card in case you change your mind."

Terry and Dennis stepped between Adam and the truck.

"I believe you lost these," Lucian said.

The truck's back opened, and three golems with glowing, acid green eyes tromped out onto the concrete.

Nearby pedestrians, still wary after the recent abductions by similar automatons screamed, ran, and pulled up phones or illusionary comm panels. SMLE officers disgorged from the building behind Adam in rushed response to the screams.

By the time they arrived, the golems stood empty-eyed and awaiting instructions. Adam turned back to Lucian to find both drone and hologram gone.

A SMLE officer offered an envelope. "Mister Mathias?"

Adam studied the envelope. Elaborate calligraphy traced his name across the surface. He inclined his head at it. Terry took it, ripped it open and frowned. He dumped a business card into his large palm and extended it.

Adam took the card and turned it over. A simpler hand-written note read: It is imperative someone address the homeless situation. Nod if you agree.

Adam scanned his surroundings then nodded.

Wayne limped away from the recently constructed high rise. A good morning's work on the lab's street corner lightened his steps, but not in front of the rubes who'd filled his pockets.

Did well, well enough I can report half to Duval without risk of suspicion.

Late afternoon sun beat down on him, soaking his artfully tattered clothes. Two turns and half a dozen blocks later, a glance through the Thoth component factory fence line confirmed no

witnesses. He abandoned his limp and turned up an alley to a storage facility's ground floor vehicle garages.

His stomach grumbled.

Anticipation brought a smile to his lips.

His day was about to get better—maybe a lot better. Adele was the assigned runner for Duval's crew north of the Columbia River. She often delivered his piping hot meatball sub last.

Freeing her up for a little quick, backseat playtime.

He picked up his pace, running along the line of roll-down doors. He stepped up to his unit and punched in the code to release the interior locks. They clanked into the open position, and the doors rolled open with little effort. Adele's purse rested atop the silver Mercedes, but it was too dim to see her waiting for him.

I married the perfect woman.

He turned to close the door, his appetites warring for precedence.

"Elias Balthazar Graham?"

Wayne spun toward the eerily familiar voice to find himself stepping out of shadows on the driver's side.

"Who are you? What are you doing here, and why do you—"

The doppelganger stepped closer. "Are you Elias Balthazar Graham?"

"Do I look black to you?" Wayne asked.

"You do not." He turned his back on Wayne and shut the door.

Wayne dug out the small shiv in need of sharpening that he kept in case of trouble. He grabbed his look alike from behind and pressed the blade against the other man's throat. "Now, you're—"

The doppelganger seized Wayne's knife hand, whirled them both around, and hurled Wayne at the Mercedes. He hit hard enough to dent the hood and set bells ringing through Wayne's skull. Wayne slid to the ground, catching himself in time to regain his feet.

He brandished the little knife at his attacker. "I don't know

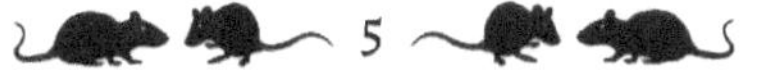

what this is about, but you'll leave if you know what's best for you. Attacking one of us will bring Duval's wrath down on your head."

"This Duval is your employer?"

"Yeah, so you better—"

The false Wayne closed, clamped a hand on the fingers holding the knife, and stared into Wayne's eyes. "Are you a hero?"

"What? No."

Wayne's attacker broke Wayne's wrist, tore away the knife, reversed it and shoved it into Wayne's gut.

The doppelganger twisted the blade. "Every chance."

Wayne screamed.

His fake shoved fingers into Wayne's gut and let Wayne slide to the ground. Darkness edged into Wayne's vision as his attacker drew letters on the Mercedes's dented hood with the blood.

Wayne's head rapped against the concrete. The killer yanked him over and stabbed fingers into Wayne's gut for more blood. The white-hot pain snapped open Wayne's eyes and forced back the darkness. His wife's sightless eyes stared back from behind the car.

Darkness closed in around him.

Two fingers shoved into Wayne's gut once more. A sound warbled in and out as Wayne cradled his abdomen.

Is he humming?

The killer yanked away Wayne's hands to get at fresher blood.

Wayne stared at his red fingers, a vanity plate just out of focus on the shining front bumper. He reached out for the car, shaking fingers fumbling to wipe drying blood onto the chrome: E...L...I...

2

UNSETTLED

I stepped to the back of my alley alcove, scaling the first slatted chain-link fence hiding a small strip of alley between buildings. Behind me, the SMLE officer parked across from my alley tensed and snapped up his radio.

I shook my head.

SMLE cars parked at either end of my alley, and a third lurked beyond the second slatted fence. My escape from their custody in the hospital hadn't made them happy. Their agents had dragged me in again before I'd gotten the rhet to heal me, but some of the regular cops I'd saved at the dam came to my defense. Someone up the chain decided to let me go with several watch dogs rather than risk negative publicity from interrogating a city hero.

I laughed.

Besides, I was too injured to go far.

I reached for the depleted pile of black garbage bags. My hands shook. I closed my eyes and took a slow sip from the thin mananet barely reaching my home. Euphoria slid into me in a warm wave.

Compared to the raw ley magic I'd wielded only days before, the magic straining against my insides seemed a lifeless counterfeit. Kenrith—a rat-like fey that resembled a real-life Rattigan—had refused me his warren's terrifying healing ritual.

I had cemented the rhet knight's animosity by going over his head to Matron Biuntcha. She ordered my healing but refused to answer questions about Kenrith's daughter, Tunoh. The heroic little rhet who'd somehow become my fiancé had taken quite a beating saving my hide.

My hands shook once more. I steeled myself with another sip from the mananet. The effect created a temporary energy boost, but left me more drained and wanting like I was trying to cross a desert on rationed candy.

Why couldn't her magic fix this?

I scaled the fence with more garbage bags. Hands long practiced in origami joined the black plastic with others into a larger mat to limit water seepage. Makeshift drop cloth completed, I grabbed the long refrigerator box stashed behind a nearby dumpster and settled it atop the ground cover in the alcove's center.

I fetched another bag from the tiny alley, pulled out a pile of small containers and a cracked, plastic hamster ball full of old jelly donuts. I set everything down and dug a silver Sharpie from my old army jacket pocket. Careful lines drew rows of circles along the top side of the refrigerator box. Because magic circles could be any shape so long as they offered a complete circuit, I drew the twenty-seven third resonance circles as basic rounded rectangles.

An itch between my shoulder blades convinced me to glance toward the SMLE officer.

How long are they going to watch me? Are they waiting for me to violate the court restrictions? I may not be allowed to enter establishments selling spell leases and components, but Sunny insists what I do with dumpster leavings doesn't count.

I reviewed the spell I'd constructed, syllable by syllable, mouthing it to practice the feel of the words. My will extended to the elaborate circle drawn around the thickest section of hamster ball. Runes in black Sharpie braced both top and bottom of the circle, allowing me to tune the resonance and magnitude of any circles created on the ball.

Here goes nothing.

My invoked third resonance circle formed a magical sphere of swirling orange and cream light just within the ball. It sprang to life at third magnitude. I backed off the power until only a mag one, third rez sphere remained.

I grabbed several compactly folded lunchroom milk cartons, set my attention on the first of the circles drawn on the refriger-ator box and called up another third rez. Power thrummed through me and the third resonance circles thaumaturgically connecting ball and box.

I recited my new adhesion spell.

Flour and dough, powdered sugar and old jelly mixed in the ball into a pinkish paste with a hint of orange from the lemon jelly. A moment later a thin, glowing film appeared confined in the third rez rectangles. I placed one of the empty folded milk cartons onto the adhesive, breaking a circle I had to maintain until the disparate surfaces were together. Magic then consumed the components as it added the subsequent energy to the touching objects' adjacent molecules, creating a magical adhesion between the separate objects in a way to make them a compound whole.

I repeated the process.

My new adhesion spell glued milk cartons, juice boxes, drink pouches, and even a few flattened tomato juice cans to the box top one by one until I'd affixed the twenty-seventh container. Two finger's worth of component paste remained inside the ball.

A frown settled onto my face.

Do I need glue for anything else? I need the ball to make food. Wait!

I kept the ball's third rez active and removed a long, flat piece of cardboard from behind the dumpster. The cement pavement didn't seem too wet, so I laid down the board and removed my black Sharpie from the pocket of my army jacket.

I sipped a little magic from the mananet to steady myself and

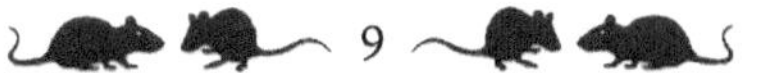

took exaggerated care to draw the first line sideways across the long board about a foot from the nearest short edge. I drew the next line closer to the first, bringing each line closer to the last the further down the board I went. When black marker lined all but the last eighteen inches, I exchanged black for silver and crawled into the refrigerator box.

I studied the blank space, slicing it in my mind over and over trying to decide the ideal adhesive layering. After the eleventh iteration, I settled on large squares down the center haloed by smaller rectangles.

I drew.

"Eli?"

Sunny's voice startled me, and I jerked upright. If the low ceiling had been much harder, I might've given myself a concussion. Worse, the rectangle I'd just drawn had a rogue line passing part way through it like a Q. A growl escaped me. "What do *you* want?"

I drew the next rectangle.

"A Doctor Porter's office called me a little while ago."

Another growl rattled my throat.

"Today's your last day to visit without violating a court order?"

I drew the last circle and crawled out of the box.

Sunny stood over me, her brown hair haloed by the sun. The plain-looking Hispanic woman's mouth turned down. Rolled-up flannel sleeves displayed mole-flecked, almond skin from her elbows down to the hands she'd perched on the waist of loose blue jeans. "Do you need a ride?"

"Are you going to preach at me?"

"Like I told you before, conversation goes where it goes, but after, we could go to dinner."

"I'll walk."

"Her last open session is in half an hour."

"I don't need a session," I growled. "She just has to see me."

Sunny folded her arms and tapped a blue and white tennis shoe. "Eli, please, this is serious."

I invoked one circle at a time until every circle in the refrigerator box's floor shined with a fine layer of pinkish adhesive. "I'm taking this as seriously as it deserves."

Sunny gestured. "SMLE's still investigating, Eli. Estranging a doctor by playing word games will not help your situation."

I slid the lined piece of cardboard inside the box and lowered it into position.

"Eli!"

"Goddammit!"

"Elias Balthazar Graham, you know how I feel about blasphemy!"

I shook my head. The left edge of cardboard lay perfectly in the corner from front to back. The right side started flush but crept up the box wall until three-quarters of an inch stuck up.

What the hell am I going to do now? Do I dare cut it now they're joined or will that foul the spell? Will it screw up the construct to leave it?

"You can't just ignore me."

I crawled out of the box, leapt to my feet and looked down into her hard, brown eyes. "I can, but you won't go away. Nothing makes you leave. You're like a plague or worse, government 'help.'"

Sunny's an ugly crier, but she's even uglier mad.

A young man's voice interrupted her impending tirade. "Eli giving you trouble?"

I glowered at a bandaged young man sporting the Beatles haircut. "Stay out of this, Darrin."

"I notice you didn't treat Darrin like some *plague*," Sunny said.

A sigh escaped me. "Do you have it?"

Darrin hobbled over, crutches deft compared to a few days prior. "Here you are, the last three."

Sunny snatched the paper before I could grab it. She reddened and her lips pressed into a thin line. "Women's addresses? You're making Darrin limp over here in crutches to bring you dates?"

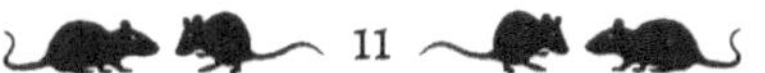

I grabbed the paper and stuffed it into my pocket. "No."

She shot Darrin a look.

"No, ma'am. Those are the last addresses of the demi-goblins Eli has caged somewhere. He won't tell me where."

"Why do you need their addresses?" Sunny demanded.

I folded my arms.

"Eli needs the addresses to get inside and—"

Sunny jabbed me with her finger. "You're breaking into your *prisoners'* houses and robbing them? Do I need to count the violations—?"

I gave Darrin a flat look. "You can leave now, Silus."

Sunny jabbed me again. "After all I've done to keep you out of jail, you're robbing people while SMLE is watching?"

"Jesus, Sun—"

Her hand cracked across my face.

My lip throbbed. The fingers of my left hand slid up and down against one another, flipping an imaginary coin across the knuckles as scenario projections for my reply queued up in my mind.

A hand clamped down on my left, preventing the motion. A muscle in my temple throbbed as my gaze rose to meet Darrin's.

"Stay with us, Eli," he said.

Robbed of my moment to plan, words rolled out of my mouth in a gravelly growl. "That's twice you've hit me without giving me a chance to explain, Sunny—even though I *don't* owe you an explanation."

"You do too."

"No." I shook my head. "You're not my mother, my wife or my girlfriend. I don't owe you anything."

A flustered expression flashed through her eyes as they retreated.

"Don't forget sister, she's not Zahda either," Darrin added.

"Why are you still here?" I asked.

"Just enjoy watching her smack you around since I know you won't hit her back," Darrin said.

"Don't count on that. I'm not the man you knew."

Darrin limped up between us, looking up at me with the same earnest eyes that had prompted me to pick him as my protégé. "Yes you are, or you wouldn't be risking your freedom to steal old DNA and change them back."

"You're fired."

Darrin laughed. "I don't work for you anymore."

"You're still fir—"

Sunny tackled me in a hug. "I'm so sorry, Eli. I didn't realize, I mean I should have. I knew pushing people away was only—"

I shoved her off me. "An attempt to get people to leave me the hell alone."

The hurt in her expression attempted betrayal levels equivalent to a berated puppy. When I didn't apologize, she peered deep into my eyes searching for who knew what.

"What are you looking for, Sunny?" I asked.

"Are you on something?" She shifted her attention to my old protégé. "Does Eli have a history of substance abuse?"

"Again, none of your business," I said.

"As your lawyer—"

"Not that I've ever seen," Darrin chuckled. "Hell, I always thought Eli was so straight-laced, he made rulers nervous."

"Then why did you tell him to stay with us?"

"You can go now, Silus. You don't have to answer her questions."

Darrin rolled his eyes. "Have you ever seen him space out?"

She chewed half her lip. "Once or twice in the hospital, but I thought the drugs they gave him caused that."

"Did you notice if his left fingers were moving?" Darrin asked.

"I'm not above shoving someone on crutches," I growled.

"No, why?" Sunny asked.

"It's his tell that he's plotting something."

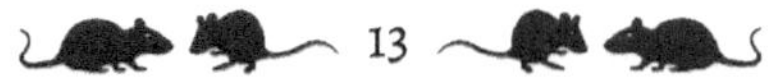

I folded my arms. "I don't plot."

Her expression became thoughtful for a two-count before she brightening. "I noticed that. It happened toward the end of our picnic, right before—"

"He escaped the hospital?" Darrin asked.

They both turned toward me.

I grabbed my pack. "If you'll excuse me, I apparently need a lecture on societal governance and how I should let a bunch of entitled bureaucrats tell me how to live."

"Need a ride?" Darrin asked

I snarled, spun on my heel and marched up the alley toward Thoth Tower and the glowing orange Eye of Thoth logo atop its shiny façade.

MY MARCH BROUGHT me up alleys, past Genghis Kahnoli's dumpster, past a theater where an actress had died after loaned components turned her into a demi-goblin, and finally into the eye-crossingly over-powered mananet of Gateway Park.

I passed a pair of ephemeral-looking elves pressed so tightly together magical adhesive might've intermingled their atoms. They gazed soppily into each other's eyes.

I shook my head.

Insanity. Terminal vanity—almost literally. Good thing Glamour wears off, or we'd all end up living in Rivendell.

I stopped at the griffon statue central to the park and looked at the long-familiar bronze creature. A glint of light reflecting off metal drew my eyes to the pigeons.

Razcolm?

Nothing answered.

I hadn't seen the imp spirit that had taken possession of my origami super spider since the battle at The Dalles Dam. Not that I'd ever seen the real Razcolm.

Guess taking out Boss Golem accomplished whatever he needed to release him from service.

I closed my eyes and reached downward with my senses. Once upon a time, I'd drawn from the mananet without ever attempting to pull magic from anywhere else. Recent experience illuminated all I'd been missing over the years. Deep below the intoxicating mananet layered over the area, wilder magic lurked. I licked my lips and pushed my reach faster.

"I wouldn't do that if I were you."

My eyes snapped open. The guy in front of me wore a shiny jogging suit of burgundy and silver. A knife sticking out of one boot suggested he liked to jog in bad neighborhoods.

"Why is that?" I asked.

He pressed his lips together until they disappeared within his goatee. At long last, he spoke. "The mananet is enough. Don't use the Ley. Don't even try to use the other natural magic sources so common here."

"Why not?"

"Because you're...important, and...as potent as that magic is, you can't afford to become...pardon the expression...its slave."

I glowered. "I can look after myself."

He held up one gloved and one ungloved hand. "Suit yourself."

I watched him stride a circle around the statue.

"Better hurry or you'll miss Porter," he said.

"What did you say?"

"Stay calm in the elevator." His path took him behind the griffon and out of sight. "And stay out from behind dumpsters."

I raced around the statue after him.

He'd vanished.

A cultured voice entered my thoughts. *<That's good advice.>*

I whipped around. "Razcolm?"

The pigeons hurried away in a flutter, but I found no one and nothing in sight. I cursed my way across the park to the brass-gilt marble municipal building and into the elevator, scandalizing a little old lady.

"Sorry," I mumbled, not feeling sorry.

Doors opened to Porter's floor, and I dragged myself from the elevator toward her frumpy, pastel waiting room and the pervasive scent of burnt coffee.

What is it with her assistant?

The curved coffee table used as a receptionist desk proved empty. I crossed to the coffee pot and shut it off. I stared at the burnt dregs inside the smoke-stained carafe.

My hands shook.

An itch prickled up my calves.

Warmth suffused my neck.

A high-end coffee pot sat atop the table before me, empty of dark nectar. After I'd schlepped all the way there, it needed to be full of dark, rich roast. I wanted coffee, *deserved* coffee.

The clenched fingers of my left hand rubbed up and down.

A young woman in bargain business attire appeared, seating herself atop the wide pillow behind the coffee table. "Are you here to see Doctor Porter?"

"No." The single word rumbled out in a deep growl. "*I'm* here for a dark, rich, caffeine-infused cup of coffee."

"Might be some left in the pot."

I snatched up the empty, stained carafe and crossed to her in three long steps. "No. It's empty. Even if it weren't, you've *burned* the coffee."

"Coffee's bad for you anyway."

My grip tightened around the pot's handle as energy prickled my other hand.

"It's not *your* choice what a person drinks."

"Caffeine is addictive. The government should outlaw caffeine, tobacco, sugar, and alcohol—then people like you wouldn't happen."

The glass pot exploded against the faux wood. Glittering glass shards and splinters sprayed everywhere as the impact caved in the little desk. "Listen you frumpy little...girl. I want coffee, and for the good of humanity as a whole, you will learn proper coffee etiquette or so help me—"

"You'll what, criminal?"

Energy coalesced in my empty hand as I raised it.

The voice of an old woman who'd been sucking helium broke through my thoughts. "Mister Graham?"

I raised an empty hand to rub away a twitching muscle in my temple.

Where did all of that rage come from?

"Mister Graham?" Porter repeated with greater concern.

I turned.

Doctor Porter's business suit appeared to have been vomited out by a Cheshire cat overdosing on mushrooms.

I glanced behind me to find the coffee table whole and unmanned. "Might be best if you hired a new receptionist. Someone who doesn't burn the coffee."

"Executive assistant." Porter corrected. She sniffed and shrugged. "Doesn't smell burnt. Smells just like Starbucks."

My jaw clenched as I strode for the elevator.

I shoved shaking hands into my coat pockets. I wasn't sure where the anger had come from, but hanging around Doctor Squeaky wasn't helping.

"Where are you going, Mister Graham?"

"You've seen me, Jessica, requirements fulfilled. Have a...day."

"That's not how this works, and I asked you before not to call me by my first name."

"You said the order required me to see you. I've seen you. You've seen me. We're done for this week, *Jessica.*"

She opened her office door and extended her hand. "You have two choices. You can come inside for a session, or I can report your unwillingness to comply with the judge that issued your treatment order."

I froze, tensed for both fight and flight. I didn't want to go inside. I'd served my sentence. I should've been a free man. I shouldn't have been beholden to the flibbertigibbet shrink.

I shouldn't have been convicted either. I shouldn't be forced to live without a home just to avoid an unjust stigma.

My thoughts flashed backed to the cowled villain that had offered me solace in fairyland—that is, right before he tried to electrocute me with plasma from an Edison node's Tesla coil.

I know where to find the Silver. Maybe I should just cross over and be done with this world.

3

———

AMBUSHED

Dad taught all of us kids to pay our debts. For that reason, I'd helped the rhet with the demi-goblins abducting and murdering their magical matrons. That debt was square. Once I'd helped the Ottiren, nothing prevented me from slipping off to whatever lurked beyond the Silver.

It's not like I'd be running away, just moving on to bigger and better things.

"Would you care to step inside, Mister Graham?"

Heavy footfalls marched me back into the monochrome noir set of an office colored only by her overly bright lipstick and a dye job engineered by a color-blind toddler. I flopped into a leather chair just off enough to keep the sitter from getting comfortable.

Porter seated herself on the other side of her humongous desk, flipped open a file left unsecured atop the grey blotter in clear HIPPA violation and traced hot pink fingernails across the page.

"I see here SMLE took you into custody?"

"And released me."

She tittered, damned odd in a middle-aged woman. "I should hope so. Fugitives are difficult to reform."

I don't need to be reformed, you uppity bitch.

She blinked at me. "Did you want to say something, Mister Graham?"

"Yes, *Jessica.* How about you recite whatever speech you need to get off your over-powdered chest so I can get back to my life."

"Your intake paperwork shows you still have no address on file. Considering the unseasonably cold weather of late, I don't see how that's even possible."

"I'm tougher than I look. Besides, I was born here, Jessica. Why should the local weather patterns be a problem for me?"

"Well, given your heritage...never mind, the attending physician noted in his report concern over exhibited signs of narcotic withdrawal." She put the file down and peered into my eyes. "Are you taking illegal drugs, Mister Graham?"

I tucked my hands beneath my thighs to conceal their sudden shake. I hadn't taken any illegal drugs. I'd tapped raw ley magic with nothing between me and the wild fey energy. It had been like a cross between godhood and the best coffee after the best sex with your first love.

"No."

She eyed my hands. "Remove your jacket and push up your sleeves please."

"I told you no."

"And I *want* to believe you, but the SMLE report also shows you exhibited similar signs. Please, do as instructed."

I should tell her to go jump in the Columbia.

Rather than burn a bridge and accept whatever collateral damage accompanied the petulant act, I took off my old jacket and bared my arms. Golden jacks embedded in my medium brown skin dotted my forearms. A bandage covered the one a street punk had tried to pry out with a knife. There shouldn't have been a wound anymore, but Matron Biuntcha had only ordered Kenrith to heal the wounds I suffered against the golems. He'd taken smug pleasure being discriminatory in their healing efforts.

"What's under that bandage? Track marks?"

"Have you ever heard of innocent until proven guilty, Jessica?"

"Remove the bandage please."

"Do you have another bandage to replace this one? I'm kind of allergic to infections and bleeding to death."

She gave me a flat look.

"You are a doctor...in theory at any rate." I dug fingernails under the medical tape, wincing in anticipation of ripping hair out of my arm for the useless shrink. The tape proved even less convinced about being removed, pulling the skin up too. Blood ran down my arm from where the tape tore open the wound. I dabbed the cut.

Doctor Porter frowned but brightened almost at once. "Mister Graham. Elias. Hurting yourself is not the answer. We can get you help. Medications."

"Weren't you just checking me for drug use?"

A wrinkled brow cancelled out her smile. "Don't you want to be helped?"

"No. I want a new bandage and then left alone."

Porter dug into a desk drawer and offered me a box of Smurf Band-Aids to replace my hospital-grade bandage. When I didn't reach for them, she set them on my side of her desk and smiled. "I understand you attempted to rescue those abducted people?"

"Something like that."

"I'm proud of you for trying to make amends for your past crimes. It doesn't excuse you for all of the terrible things you were convicted of, but it is a positive start on the road to societal integration."

I opened my mouth, shut it with a click of teeth, snatched up the box of Band-Aids and stormed out of her office without another word. She called after me, first trying to get me to come back and then reminding me of our next appointment.

I didn't listen.

I didn't stop.

I jabbed the elevator call button half a dozen times until it arrived six hours later. I charged into the open doors, brought up short by a gorgeous woman with creamy, tanned skin. She looked at me, at the blood running down my arm and shifted her gaze to a more interesting section of wall near the ceiling. A glance at the control bank showed her already headed to the lobby, so I tried to get Smurfette and Brainy to stop my bleeding.

I glanced up at her self-consciously.

A long aquiline nose raised just higher than straight ahead accentuated high cheekbones. Her head's angle made her hair shine with a luster I hadn't noticed at first. She shifted her head and hair fell around a pointed ear tip.

More Glamour. Still don't understand how Darrin could have achieved those results with a story instead of DNA.

She turned her attention toward me. Acid green flames erupted from her eyes. She hissed through long, bloodied fangs and launched at me with painted nails transformed into claws.

I lurched backward, slamming my shoulders against the elevator wall. I drew in magic and braced to defend myself when the elevator lights died. The car lurched to a stop with a screech of emergency brakes.

"Fucking great," she snarled. An eyeSentinel field surrounded her with a dim nimbus in the dark as she dug out and brandished an eyeGuardian from her clutch. "Well? Do you?"

I blinked at her lovely if normal appearance. "What?"

"Do you have a problem?"

My heart slamming my chest eased off a hair as my brow furrowed. "Why would I have a problem, other than us being stuck in an elevator?"

"The way you were staring, you creepy bastard. What, getting your jollies undressing me? Well, you're not attacking me through this shield."

I could disable that shield in a heartbeat.

"When are people like you going to accept a woman is a person, not an object."

My hackles rose. "I wasn't doing anything of the kind."

"Then why were you looking at me like that?"

"I-I wasn't looking at you, I was...thinking."

"Likely story. Just stay on your side, and you won't get a face full of Guardian."

Twice now a woman's threatened to burn me alive with...wait, no, just once. Either way, I should look into some kind of defense.

The lights flickered back on, and the elevator descended. It stopped on the next floor and opened its doors. The invitation seemed like a wise one, so I stepped out. "I'll take the next one."

"Good riddance."

I considered disabling her eyeSentinel just to be petty. Visions of mace or a flamethrower shooting made me hesitate.

The doors closed.

Instead of calling another elevator, I vented my rising temper on a long descent downstairs.

I exited the stairwell and hadn't crossed half the lobby when a woman and a hulking man cut me off. I tensed to fight, reaching for the mananet. I didn't have much in the way of magical defenses, but I had prepared a few plastic snack baggies staged with slip-n-slide components.

"Mister Graham, Megan French, Seufert Fells Network One."

My would-be attackers resolved into a semi-attractive news-woman and her cameraman. I glared. "One comment: Go away."

My sharp retort echoed loud enough it drew the attention of yet more wannabe Lord of the Rings stand-ins.

How many people did Adam test that on?

"So you have no comment regarding Adam Mathias's accusation naming you the mastermind behind the golem thefts and assaults on our fair city?"

My vision tunneled in on her face until I saw only the triangle made by eyes and mouth that can forecast a child's eventual appearance. Ice mamba'd down my spine into my gut, pushing molten acid up my esophagus. Rabid gooseflesh ate a path up my calves and my neck warmed. My dazed attention shifted to the camera.

I'd like to think there wasn't any mass murderer in the smile I turned on the cameraman. "Once more I see that without someone to cheat off, Adam hasn't got a fucking clue what's what."

I sidestepped them and hurried for the exit before she could voice a follow up question. I'd hoped cursing would make the sound bite unairable or at least force them to waste editing time. I pushed through a revolving door into a light breeze and tightened my army jacket.

"Mister Graham?"

I'd reined in my temper for the camera, but all things considered, I was feeling pretty fucking intolerant of the human race. I unleashed a snarl at an enticing brunette attired like an upscale farmer's daughter. "What?!"

She dropped her eyes, licking her lips and fiddling with something in her hands. Her submissive prey response caught me off guard. Either she'd spent time in the Wasteland, was another shrink or just wasn't a strong personality.

She crossed the distance in three leggy steps and extended a crystal wafer. "Mister Bradley is interested in hiring you for help with his first responders project. If you're interested in hearing more, this will contact me—you know how they work."

She pressed the round wafer between my fingers, suggesting some steel in her backbone. Triumphant amusement sparkled in her hazel eyes. The second lick of her lips seemed far more enticing. "A tantalizing dinner followed by dessert—a meeting to remember?"

She was across the courtyard before I recovered. The wafer in my hand had been one of the first designs stolen from Thoth. I'd designed it as the ultimate one shot distress signal, capable of summoning help even in the middle of the ocean. An arcanology company called RuneSys had repurposed the design into an expensive replacement for business cards among rich yuppies that wanted to show off their wealth.

My anger, close to the surface since I'd woken up in the hospital, rose once more and made crushing the little crystal all too tempting. I flipped it over to see a broad, almost Cyclops-like eye upon the breast of a raven with outstretched wings—the Mimir Corp logo that Adam had tried to one-up with our...their Eye of Thoth.

Mimir wants to hire me?

My initial response involved a cold day in hell, but she'd said something about first responders. Safeguarding people risking their lives for the public had been the reason we'd formed Thoth.

Okay, my reason.

The recruiter had also offered dinner. If Richard Bradley had sent her, it would be an extravagant meal. My mouth watered as my imagination danced from restaurant to restaurant throughout Seufert Fells.

No. I can't. Even if they offer a job, I can't take it without having a place to shower, shave, and dress in regularly laundered clothes.

Cold settled back into my stomach.

Shit. Dad.

Sunny had offered to drive me to see Doctor Porter and then have dinner with me. She hadn't offered dinner and fellowship. That meant she either had a sudden desire to date me or, more likely, she was trying to drag me into an ambush set up between her and Dad.

The hospital had contacted him when the ambulance dropped me into their laps. I hadn't been in any condition to object when they called my emergency contact. Dad paid my bill over the phone and gave Sunny temporary medical power of attorney to act on my behalf until he could wrap up whatever and fly out.

I'd escaped the hospital as fast as I was able, but if I knew Dad, he had spared no horses getting to Seufert Fells. He would've wanted Mom on hand. Creating an opening in her busy social schedule might've slowed them down, but they must have landed in the city by now.

Their flight probably came down while I was under 'societal governance.' Why else would Sunny wait around for however long my session was supposed to run?

Run was what I did, straight toward Gateway Park. The side trip bought me time to think. Sunny would bring my parents to my alley. Either I abandoned the alley for a new locale or faced the music.

I tilted open the lid on a park garbage can, pulled the bag edge to one side and reached into the can's bottom.

Dad didn't raise any cowards.

Digging through Gateway Park trash cans collected more dirty looks than the extra black trash bags park maintenance left in the can bottoms. To be fair, some of the distressed looks could've been about the homeless black man digging juice boxes and milk cartons from cans near the playground while mumbling rejoinders to himself about not reaching into the wild magic deep beneath the park. I escaped temptation with a half dozen small containers and without drawing on the buried power.

Go me.

The line of alleyways stretching between Thoth Tower, Gateway Park and my home felt like a desert. A slight overlap cast a layer of mananet down the Edison block strip, but after the park and the river, it felt almost like being back in the magicless Wasteland.

SMLE paced me, not even bothering to be discreet. The surveillance chaffed, particularly with my impending guests, but I wasn't breaking any laws.

I didn't even jaywalk.

A brand new diesel pickup neared alley by alley. It took half a block to remember why it seemed familiar.

I tensed.

Duval's truck. Great. The leader of the homeless mafia has come to call. Wonder if introducing him to Mom as Don Bum will piss him off enough he'll go away?

I considered turning around, going somewhere else. I was low on bologna. I could've sidelined to a store, but he'd parked his behemoth right in front of my new box. Worse, a glance at the sky portended rain. If I avoided him, the weather would destroy my working before I could even test it.

Good thing I gathered more bags.

I sucked in a deep breath and marched into my home alley.

Duval exited the truck. A large thug joined him a moment later. I'd been busy taking a beating, but I recalled Duval calling him Mihail. For all his truck and his thugs and his thick European accent, Duval wasn't a large man. Nothing about his clothes proclaimed him more than a construction supervisor. Still, he seemed somehow more than the more massive thug at his side.

"I have found you at last."

I really need to work out some kind of defensive magic.

I set my stuff in the mouth of my box and glanced around for nearby rhet. None seemed visible, but considering the little rodent fey could use glamour for relative invisibility, seeing didn't always prove anything. "If this is about the douchebag in the park, I was only trying to fill my water balloons."

"You are coming with us," Duval said.

I folded my arms and glared.

"You owe me a favor," Duval added.

He and his thugs had almost stopped Caleb, Ugly, and Tiny from drowning me as vengeance for crimes I hadn't committed against Caleb's sister. I'd still ended up almost dumped in the Columbia in chains and ultimately in the debt of an angry Indian spirit that could possess otters. Duval had accosted me later, claiming I owed him.

I hadn't worried about it at the time because I hadn't figured on reencountering him. I had no desire to beg for money or food. I wasn't encroaching on his business. All I'd wanted was to find the rhet matrons, free myself of their debt, and figure out how to live my new life.

"I'm not sure I agree."

Duval gestured at Mihail. "We stopped your beating, saved your life."

My head shook. "I still got thrown into the water wrapped in chains."

Duval raised a finger. "But you didn't drown."

"Not because of any help you offered," I said.

Mihail's accent left Duval's anorexic. While I couldn't tell where in Europe Duval had originated, Mihail's accent seemed eastern European. "If the boss says you owe him, you owe him. Get in the truck."

The 'or else' wasn't said, but it underpinned Mihail's words just behind a disgusted expression.

Duval stopped Mihail, but menace underlay his tone. "We protect our own."

"Your point?" I asked.

Duval seemed to collect himself, trying a honey-slathered carrot rather than Mihail's stick. "If we had not intervened, treating you like one of our own, you would be dead. Their beating would have rendered you unconscious, preventing your escape."

That wasn't necessarily true, but I wasn't sure making him aware of the Ottiren would help in either short term or long. "Look, Duval. I'm not sure what you think I can do for you. I have nothing—actually nothing. This is where I live. I don't beg. I do nothing that should put us at odds."

"You saved a crap ton of people using magic."

I opened my mouth, but let it close unused.

"We need your help," Duval said. "Isn't that what heroes do? Help people in need?"

I snorted. "Sorry, you've got the wrong guy."

Mihail seized me, lifting me up to the tips of my toes. "You'll repay the boss, or I'll finish what we interrupted."

"Mihail, please, set Mister Graham down," Duval said.

I had a bit of a grudge against bullies, so I looked up into Mihail's eyes. "You ever hear that quote about trifling with wizards?"

"You ever hear the one about swimming in cement shoes?" Mihail shot back almost at once.

Touché.

I rubbed the back of my head feeling stubble I'd have to shave before my day-glow rainbow hair regrew long enough to be visible. "Someone else has to be better equipped to help you."

"Maybe," Duval said. "But I want you."

I don't need this. I still have to transform the remaining demi-goblins. I have to find out if Tunoh is all right. If Glamour wore off, returning her to her crippled state, I have to restore her. Then there's the Ottiren's promise to hunt me down and eat me if I don't reopen the pathways to his ancestral market.

Duval didn't look as if he cared what I had going on. He didn't even look menacing. Somehow that even tone and casual demeanor scared me more than if he were threatening to slit my throat.

"Look, I'm sorry—"

Mihail stepped closer flexing his hands.

"No." I shot the SMLE surveillance a look.

How much of a beating do I have to take before SMLE gets involved?

Duval and his cronies had saved me, but that obligated me to save him back, not run all over town doing whatever he wanted to involve me in. "Whatever this is, I'm not getting involved."

Duval's calm demeanor darkened. Duval removed a roll of cash from a pocket. He eyed me and the money in turns. For a moment I thought he'd try buying me, but he turned toward the nearest SMLE cruiser.

"You know the first qualification for a new SMLE recruit?" Mihail asked.

"No."

Mihail's grin broadened. "Favorite color has to be green."

My gaze shot toward Duval and the SMLE officer. Mihail took that moment to club me unconscious.

4

—————

MISTAKEN IDENTITY

A speed bump taken too fast slammed me into the truck bed's cover, battering me awake. My head throbbed. A stray strand from the edge of the duct tape across my mouth flicked in and out of one nostril with each breath.

A sneeze didn't eject the strand for long.

Bed liner ribs dug into my back. The bed had enough room I wasn't cramped. I brought my hands close enough to see zip ties around my wrists and duct tape pairing my fingers to prevent wiggling.

Really need to find components for a light wisp spell. Should work out some kind of box cutter spell too if this is going to become a habit.

We entered coverage of moderate mananet, providing regulated wireless power for spell casting and devices that converted the energy into electricity.

A hard turn slid me into the side. The mananet faded, replaced by the steady thud of old concrete.

We're crossing the Columbia.

My pulse raced up to a sprint, and I suddenly couldn't get

enough breath. The wild fey power sang like sirens from sailor's tales of old.

The tremble in my hands engulfed my body. A voice sweet and sultry invited me, coaxed me to draw on what Kenrith had called the Ley. I wanted it. Hell, I *needed* that power, *needed* it like a drug.

What did Porter say the doctors reported? Narcotic withdrawal?

I considered the painful need to reach out to the ley line, the siren song of the magic calling out.

Sirens drew men to their death.

Kenrith had warned me against touching the Ley. At that moment, I'd been trying to touch the floating river of liquid energy with my hand, but he might have meant in more ways than that.

Fey magic from fairyland...is that where all our magic originates?

The mananet drew from natural sources, but while I didn't understand the fundamental difference, I felt how a natural source differed from the tamed power carried on the mananet. The ley lines running beneath the Columbia were about as pure and raw as wild magic got, coming straight into our world through the Silver.

The Ley is warmth. It's a lavish, heady homecoming, like a mother cradling an injured—

I pushed away the distracting thoughts, dubious as to their source. I'd lived in sketchy places around sketchier people and always sidestepped the little addictions that risked harm to my mind. If my distracted thoughts and tempestuous emotions were any indication, raw fey magic could do far worse.

When I'd first awakened in the hospital, I'd nearly had a panic attack when I thought the magic I hadn't needed in my century of incarceration had been taken. The first rez circle placed around me in the hospital room had been to keep me from working magic against the cops, or so I assumed.

What if it hadn't? SMLE can't know about the Silver, can they?

Razcolm had suggested that in the old days a master taught his apprentices how to channel raw fey energy safely as part of their training. I hadn't had the type of apprenticeship he meant, but the imparted information offered a course of research into using the siren without risk of her eating me.

Maybe Razcolm would consent to teach me how to filter.

I pushed away yet another rationalization for using the Ley with a snort.

Yeah, when Kermit and Piggy have flying piggywogs.

I turned away mentally from the wild magic, counting upward by prime numbers and trying to focus on the substantial danger I was already in.

The little hairs along my calves prickled like a cactus.

My last crossing ended up with Caleb and his friends abducting me, driving me over to the Washington side, and trying to kill me.

Is that what Duval intends? I won't help him, so he's just going to undo saving me? Finish the job by drowning me like Mihail suggested?

My neck heated.

The hell they will.

The means to stop them lay beneath Columbia's muddy banks. I'd used the ley energy fresh from beyond the Silver to save everyone at the dam. The same power could save me. It offered anything I wanted to make it. I'd ripped a solid steel hood from an old truck with a broken arm and not felt a thing. I'd gone toe to toe with a golem.

Oh, no you don't.

Counting primes kept me distracted until the truck turned off the bridge and the power faded behind us. Doing so meant the loss of planning time, thrusting the possibility of having to react on the fly—not my strong suit—into my near future. Still, better improvisation than the alternative.

The truck stopped.

I sneezed

Doors opened and slammed.

Mihail dropped the tailgate and raised the bed cover, displaying a shit-eating grin and practically daring me to resist or retaliate. I couldn't threaten him through the tape, but I made sure my eyes spoke of payback. Razcolm offered me untraceable sickness, or I could just use donkey DNA to cast a Thoth Glamour on him.

I sneezed.

Mihail handed me a travel pouch of maximum strength Tylenol, a bottled water and a note. I fumbled open the note. My heart sank. I knew Mom's handwriting at once. My head shook of its own volition. Only my mother would leave a note on a cardboard box to tell me she'd come to call and would meet me at the Manger for breakfast.

I pushed away the problem only to have a sudden sense of déjà vu grip me. I frowned and scanned my surroundings.

Mihail had parked us in front of a rental storage facility. Several accordion-style doors faced us. A crumpled ball of yellow and black lay before a door several units down.

Duval ripped the tape from my mouth.

I raised my bound hands not to him for release but instead pinched my nose between thumb and taped fingers. My glower should've warned off meddling with wizards, but apparently, Duval didn't watch many movies running his underground bum empire.

"You're only giving me more reasons not to help you."

Duval stared deep into my eyes. Something lurked behind his gaze as he gestured toward the rental spaces. "You know the way."

Despite the déjà vu, I had no idea what he was talking about. "The way where?"

Duval scrutinized me.

"Stop playing games already, Duval. You knocked me out, dragged me out here. If there's something you want to show me, then show me already so I can get back to my life."

Mihail materialized into looming position over me. Before he could do anything, a flick of Duval's eyes warned him off.

I spun on the spot. "Well?"

"That one," Duval pointed.

I eyed him and the bay doors in turn. If he'd wanted me dead,

he could've dropped me in the river. Even so, my Wasteland instincts jangled like a four-alarm firehouse bell.

I offered my tied hands.

Duval unbound me. "Now, Mister Graham, if you'd like to return to your life, would be so kind as to please enter this garage?"

The keypad showed the lock out of position, so I yanked up on the handle. Well-maintained doors rolled up into the bay's ceiling, unleashing a sewer scent. A cloud of flies washed passed me toward freedom with a susurrous roar.

Dark blood stained the concrete beneath a dented silver Mercedes. White chalk outlines and little plastic tents marked points of interest. A finger had traced four, bloody words on the dented hood: All Homeless Must Die.

Just below the proclamation, trembling fingers had painted my name in blood.

An icy rain soaked me to the bone without a single drop of precipitation. The hair along my skin rose, intent to get the hell out of dodge. My gaze shifted to the refuse in front of the other bay—police tape.

I'm tampering with a crime scene that contains my name. They could come back, find my DNA...

The moment my muscles tensed for flight, Mihail's huge hand clamped around the back of my neck.

"Let him go," Duval said.

"Boss?" Mihail asked.

"He didn't do it after all," Duval said.

"Maybe he's a sociopath," Mihail said.

Shock won my expression, but the heat conquered my neck. "You thought I killed whoever that was?"

Duval tapped a wrist version of Darrin's amulet, projecting images marked as taken by police photographers and later a coroner. The dead woman wasn't familiar, but even in death, the man was.

A quick scan of my surroundings not only confirmed no cops in the area but where we were. I'd known Duval's destination sat in the industrial regions of Washington State somewhere north of the Columbia. I hadn't realized we were only blocks from the factory I'd broken into while trying to help Darrin and Kenrith.

I checked for my SMLE watchers once more.

"SMLE agreed not to follow us," Duval said. "They will not learn you are violating a crime scene nor that you were within violation distance of Thoth property."

"Oh, Christ, is this rental space owned by Thoth?"

"No," Duval said. "You knew Wayne."

"Briefly, but how did you know?"

"I spoke with him after I reminded you of your debt for my saving your life."

"Great," I said. "Well, you brought me here, endangering my safety, so I guess we'll call that even."

Mihail loomed over me once more. "No. We brought you here to find out if you killed them. Boss says no. I haven't decided."

My voice rose. "Why would I kill Wayne or anyone?"

Mihail darkened. "You've done *far* worse."

"That's enough," Duval changed the holograms to display more crime photos.

I looked away.

"My sources tell me there is no DNA. The killer left no finger-prints." An edge crept into Duval's tone. "He entered this high security bay, killed two of my people and left without a trace."

Mihail all but growled. "Like magic."

"Well, I didn't do it." I edged away from them. "So, I'll just go."

"You are a wizard," Duval said. "I'd like you to help find Wayne's murderer."

"I was a research wizard, Duval. I worked in a safe lab. I didn't chase down criminals."

"Did you or did you not develop the mage sniffer technology?"

"An early version," I said, "but that was a long time ago."

"I told you," Mihail said.

Duval's lips pressed into a thin line. "Perhaps you were right. Thank you, Mister Graham. You may go."

My brows shot up. "That's it? You kidnap me? Trick me into violating a police boundary, and you're just going to strand me halfway across the city without even an apology?"

Mihail's smile wasn't friendly. "Want a ride to the river?"

"You haven't thanked us for giving you the benefit of the doubt," Duval said.

"As opposed to killing me for something I had nothing to do with?" I asked.

"We weren't certain whether or not you were involved," Duval said. "Besides, I'm a big fan of monopoly."

I opened my mouth but decided not to antagonize a man threatening to kill me because my homelessness threatened his business. Stomping all the way home would've only left me footsore, so I lightened my steps half a block away. A block of snarling to myself later, I realized I'd come abreast of the Thoth factory.

A cop car pulled onto the road heading my way. They might not have recognized me, but I turned down an alley to put space between me and the court order violation.

If Adam keeps buying companies, I'm going to be hard-pressed to move around Seufert Fells. There's always fairyland.

A refrigerator box much like my own brought me up short. Old army boots stuck out the opening. With almost no warning, their occupants sprang out of the box with a brick in hand.

"Go away! This is Zohara's box!"

A wild mop of dirty blond haloed her head, cut haphazardly by something other than a barber. Dirt caked her face, almost hiding a port wine stain birthmark and a black eye.

How'd she turn around in there so fast?

I backed away with my hands in the air. "Sorry, I was just cutting down the alley. Besides, I already have my own box."

"Well," the heat of her initial assault waned. "Well, fine then."

The Wasteland skews a person's time sense. Still, most of us walk around thinking of ourselves as in our twenties. Incarceration had stolen my twenties, but it still came as a shock to realize she wasn't much older than I was.

"What are you staring at?" she demanded.

I dropped my eyes. "Nothing."

She cackled. "Old Zohara might not be the looker she used to be, but she sure isn't nothing."

"That's not what I meant, ma'am."

She slapped me on the shoulder, smiling with more gaps than teeth. "You must be new to the streets."

I nodded. "You?"

"Nah, old Zohara's been on the pavement—one way or another —since she ran away as a girl."

Does that mean what I think it does?

"That why you're still watching Zohara? Need a roll in the box?"

"What?"

It wasn't easy not to cringe away from her lewd gap-riddled smile. "Zohara's rough around the edges, but she's still soft where it counts."

"No, ma'am, I was just thinking if you've been on the streets that long, you might be able to teach me a thing or two."

Zohara wagged her eyebrows.

"About surviving on the streets," I clarified.

"Lesson one, nothing's free." She cackled. "Except maybe lesson one. Zohara'll trade you more lessons for food, but don't wait too long. She never stays long enough to wear out her welcome."

Duval.

"There's a guy, Duval. He runs the beggars, and he—"

"And he'll not want Zohara around." She shrugged, ducking back into her box.

"So you know him?"

"Nope, Zohara's not from around here, but there's been a Duval around since the old world, boy. Always someone looking to rid the world of street folk, though thank you for the warning."

"If you're not from around here, you know the best way to move around? I wasn't looking forward to hiking to another city."

Assuming I just don't slip through the Silver.

Zohara beamed. "There are ways to score a free ride from the Feds. Bring back food and Zohara will tell you the miracles of ambulances."

Ambulances?

Zohara shooed me away.

I HURRIED through Seufert Fells's industrial district. Factories and soon-to-be manufacturing plants blocked out vast swaths of landscape, forcing roadways into mad pretzels reminiscent of my trips through Atlanta. I focused on my limited arsenal and once more wished I'd found time in the short weeks since my release to work out some kind of offensive or defensive magic.

Advanced and straightforward application of basic circle magic principals had kept me alive during my most recent misadventures. Dollar store snack baggies with a tendency to break kept several castings worth of slip-n-slide components at hand.

I reviewed what I remembered about the trigger rune and spell for eyeGuardian's flame. I had designed the construct to provide firefighters battling wildfires a backburn functionality. I'd objected to Adam's upgraded mace canister and more than once to how close they placed the flame rune to the mace rune.

The review served my primary desire to create a defense against eyeGuardian attacks on the street and allowed me to consider the functional design requirements for Razcolm's touted fireball.

Almost miss the little jackass.

A Tacky Burger franchise came into view, settling a lump in my gut as if I'd eaten their food. Across the street, a convenience store lurked behind more advertisements than graffiti. A lady inside had accused me of being a pedophile when I'd bought a doll to create the spy construct Razcolm later inhabited.

I kept going, at long last coming back to Fells Overlook Bridge.

Crossing the bridge where Caleb last abducted me set my nerves on edge and made me wonder about him. It was possible he'd thought me drowned, but Duval had sought me after seeing me on the news.

Maybe Duval's boys hurt them enough they'll lay off.

Even so, I didn't intend to relax until I'd crossed the bridge. I tried to keep an eye out for another ambush, but the broken hydroelectric generators where I'd nearly died drew my eye.

The beckoning river offered even more danger. The siren song sunk barbs into me as if it didn't intend me to escape once more. My breath fled, and my pulse sprinted to catch up with it. Black spots welled up in my vision until they forced me to stop mid-bridge, clamping shaking hands on the railing.

No. I don't need *magic. I survived a century without it.*

I didn't need magic, but in the process of dealing with the demi-goblins, I'd been forced to admit to myself that magic was a part of who I was.

I tried counting primes, only encouraging the siren to sing louder. As shameful as it was, I fought off the song with lewd images of things suggested by Zohara.

I released the rail, shoved my shaking hands into jacket pockets and rushed for Oregon as fast as I was able. Somewhere along the line, my rush became a run. There's little doubt the sight of a black homeless man running across the bridge as if chased by a demon left commuters wondering.

I wanted to collapse along the bank, kick my shoes off and soak aching feet in the icy water. I needed distance—time mostly—from the seductive fey magic. Moreover, soaking my feet in the Ottiren's river might call him.

I'm not ready for that meeting. I don't even have a good plan yet.

I'd considered ways I might restore a trade route to Celilo. The PGE tap room I'd seen offered a possible scenario. With a full set of SCUBA gear, I could dive the old village. Assuming sufficient clear area remained, I could use interlocking paving stones or hoses to lay out a more permanent circle. Leveraging the circle might allow for engineering a sustained dry zone, but I hadn't been able to figure out how to get people and oxygen into said zone.

It's not like I can just connect it to the Silver the same way the tap room is, and I have no idea how I'd ever afford enough paving stones to encircle an entire village market.

My haste eased even though only a strip of green park separated me from the soft shore opposite the touted Riverwalk. My gaze drifted up and down the manicured lawn and park benches. A musician punched away at an electronic piano keyboard, sitting on a blanket not far downriver atop a waterproof tarp. Headphones prevented me from hearing his composition, but birdsong and toddlers laughing from a nearby playground brightened the overcast day.

Casting my gaze the other way brought an old couple into view. They shambled up the walk hand in hand, talking about who knew what after decades of marriage. A casually dressed man whose physique proclaimed him the bigger foodie strolled along behind them. Some kind of event badge tangled his occasional cellphone photography attempts. He tucked the device away after each, only to draw it back out a short distance later, tap in some ridiculously long passcode and take another picture.

Set amid a line of tourist shops facing off against the river, a Bluebox nestled between a jewelry store and a fudge shop. It struck me as odd that Hengeo Inc. would put the expensive transport module in the middle of a tourist trap.

Unless they've got them in the better hotels too.

Adam had ordered one of the early prototypes so I could

reverse engineer the European company's magical teleporter. He and Thecia had framed me before I ever got the chance.

Teleporter...

A change of course hurried me over to the Bluebox. Dodging dirty looks and pointedly blind gazes, I ducked inside ahead of a snarky tone. "That's not a bathroom."

For a magical teleporter, Hengeo Inc. had made the design more Star Trek transporter than Narnian wardrobe. Cool off-white panels glowed a subtle light, broken only by a pair of useless but lovely golden, gothically-designed circles complete with bogus runes. A panel at the rear wall used the same tech as Darrin's crystal amulet to project an illusionary control console which awaited payment and destination information.

I set my things down and examined the walls for the real magic. Conceivably, whatever they'd used to design the teleporter remained hidden behind the glowing panels. I wasn't about to rip aside walls under their monitoring wizard eye, but I had no compunctions about leaning in close to examine things. I lost at least half an hour to a fruitless search.

Wish I had enough money to see it in action.

I abandoned Bluebox technology as my Celilo solution and returned to trudging toward home. I passed the man taking pictures close enough to get a look at the laminated rectangle around his neck: FORETOLD – The Future of Arcanology.

A list of sponsors wrapped around the bottom half of an emblazoned pentacle. Thoth's orange eye and Hengeo Inc.'s stylized Stonehenge rested in the most prominent positions.

My eyes came up to meet a matching gaze from the would-be photographer.

"Morning," he said.

"Uh, hello."

"Saw you looking at my badge. Interested in arcanology?"

"Once upon a time. Isn't Seufert Fells kind of an odd place to have an arcanology conference?"

He smirked at the fairy tale reference. "Thoth lobbied hard as I understand it. Paid out a lot of money too."

"Why?"

"Their CEO is trying to globalize their footprint. Lots of money to be made nickel and diming everyday people."

My response was almost a growl. "Of course he is."

"Don't like Thoth?"

"Used to work there." I shrugged.

"You some of the collateral from that Graham thing?"

I kept the heat out of my voice. "Something like that."

"Bad business." He shook his head.

I turned to go.

"Suppose it's possible Graham let the power go to his head, but I listened to audio from his testimony."

"You don't think...he did what they said?" I asked.

"I have my doubts. Either way, it sucks that so many of his personal team ended up blackballed."

Really? I should ask Darrin what happened to the others.

"I hope you land on your feet," he said. "Nice talking to you."

"Yeah. You too."

I made it a few paces before he called out. "Hey, I know what it's like to be the working stiff blamed for decisions outside of your control."

I blinked at him.

"We had a couple guys cancel last minute, bet I could get one of their passes for you since they're already paid for. Maybe we could chat, introduce you to a few people I know. I'm not promising anything as formal as an interview, but who knows."

There was no way anyone would offer me a job again, certainly not in arcanology, but it was refreshing to be treated like a human by someone not fey. The conference wouldn't count as Thoth property, but I really didn't want to be anywhere near Adam, Thecia or anyone else from my old company.

"Thanks, I'll think about it."

He smiled. "The conference is going on all week. If you decide to take me up on my offer, just ask for Chris from RuneSys at the help kiosk."

I waved thanks and hurried toward my alley.

Not on your life, buddy. Thank you, but still, no thanks.

5

———

RECRUITER TO THE RESCUE

I hadn't made it a handful of blocks before I noticed an uncomfortably familiar white panel van pacing me. On foot, the vehicle should've passed me and been done with it. Instead, the driver played a game of park and go to keep me in sight.

Caleb.

There wasn't any way to be sure without approaching the van, but it seemed a pretty good bet.

What I wouldn't give for Razcolm or Tunoh to scout for me. If it is Caleb, he can't have followed us from the alley, or he'd have grabbed me on the other side of the river.

A turn down a cross street proved the van's intentions. The new tourist area around the Riverwalk kept busy enough to prevent daylight abduction, but it seemed prudent to avoid alleys or less-travelled streets.

I scanned the horizon.

Mihail hadn't given me the opportunity to cover my box before clubbing me over the head. I needed to get back to my alley and protect my construct before rain reduced all my efforts to melted cardboard.

Death was bound to be a greater inconvenience than rebuilding my new home, so I turned back toward the Riverwalk. Using the crowd for protection probably wouldn't serve as more than a delaying tactic. I needed a plan.

A tiny city car passed by on the street, tourists pointing and smiling inside the domed passenger compartment. Paired ivory seating offered just enough room for average people to lounge in luxury—hence the reason they were called LUX. From experience, I knew the passenger pod detached from the golden Ritchie Rich undercarriage for pickup by airborne drone. By happenstance, the black filigree decorating the car sled also designated it as LUX-00143G, the same sled that had picked up Darrin and me for our trip to Hunter's Glade.

Unfortunately, I had neither a credit card nor bank account with funds to allow a LUX to whisk me away from Caleb's misdirected sense of justice.

A pedicab sped by a moment later. The bicycle rickshaw had the benefit of taking cash, but I hadn't found any way to replenish my dwindling funds.

Maybe I could piece one of those together for income.

Dismissing the idea for a time when I wasn't being actively hunted, I sought another solution. My fingers brushed against possible salvation, drawing out the crystal wafer given me by the Mimir Corp recruiter.

I hadn't intended to use the single-use call chip unless I fell on hard times and needed a meal. As sexy as it absolutely was not, my box still contained some old bread, bologna and the dregs of Sunny's latest 'anonymous' Manger care package.

I flipped the round wafer along the tops of my left knuckles and considered. No other ideas offered a sure escape, so I activated the device. A head and shoulders illusion of the woman that had approached me in front of SMLE headquarters appeared. The illusion seemed unbothered by the thumb still covering most of the wafer the way a hologram might.

She'd traded out the upscale farmer's daughter attire for an evergreen jacket and white blouse almost as bright as her smile. "Mister Graham, I'm pleased to see you and so soon. I was afraid you might not accept our invitation."

The icy bite escaped my lips before I realized it. "Yeah, I'm sure a lot of homeless ex-cons turn down the chance to be wined and dined."

"I can't say." Her eyes twinkled with humor. "We don't invite that many."

"Touché. So, how does this work...I'm sorry, you never gave me your name."

"My name is Vil Koshe, Mister Graham. We can pick you up in a limo, send a LUX, or you can just say your name at any Bluebox. Whichever you prefer."

I refrained from commenting on her flexibility, probably because I'd listened intently to the sexual harassment training after Caleb's sister Eve had come on to me at a project party.

Caleb could follow either a limo or a LUX, but he couldn't follow a teleport. Besides, I *really* wanted to get a look at the things in action.

"I'll use a Bluebox. Thank you."

She opened her mouth to ask something, but I cut off the call. Dad would've filled my ear if he'd witnessed the whole thing, but I'd only called Mimir for a quick escape. No matter what they offered, I had no choice but to decline.

I didn't have any more time for schmoozing than I had for Caleb, but the former could be cut short anytime I wanted.

The panel van jerked into a parking place as I slipped into the box. No doubt if it was Caleb, he'd be waiting outside a long time.

"Elias Balthazar Graham, Mimir Corp."

The box hummed to life none too soon.

Runes appeared on what had only been a blank wall before. I thought for a moment they'd been cunningly hidden but realized

rapidly overlapping laser light wrote the jumble of real and fake runes into place in a fascinating preprogrammed sequence.

Temporary runes perfectly rendered each time that can't be reverse-engineered by merely owning a cabinet. That's real genius.

A fifth resonance circle locked the box's contents and prevented entrance by the vigilante pounding on the door. Swirling blue-white magic dotted by blue sparkles cut us off from magic coming or going. The placement of the first and second rez barriers outside the fifth rez indicated there was a magical source inside the booth.

How are they getting that much magic inside? Mana crystals are rare, particularly in any size.

The pounding sounds cut off suddenly as a wash of green sparkles coalesced, blocking incoming elemental energy just inside the milky white. Between the two barriers, translucent green energy filled the cabinet with the reek of burnt popcorn and prevented elemental energy from escaping.

Runes I'd initially labeled as fake flashed in a sudden surge of magic. A square of shimmering violet energy buzzed to life like an angry swarm of gnats. The buzz grew with the corresponding increase in magnitude.

I'd never seen the violet energy before any more than I'd seen the runes I'd thought cleverly used to throw off reverse engineering. Truth be told, it was possible some of them were false, but I committed every one of them to memory nonetheless.

The circle seemed to reach peak magnitude after far too long.

Is that running at over mag five?

The violet field slid down the box like a scanner lamp in an old style copier. The circle passed over me slowly enough I should've felt something, but one moment I was in the Bluebox and the next the violet circle beneath my feet fizzled away to leave me in sudden silence.

A hiss of air freshener assaulted the burnt popcorn aroma with thick, cloying roses. Every circle in the cabinet vanished at once.

The door opened, revealing a flustered, out of breath Vil. She extended a hand. "Mister Graham, so glad you decided to accept our invitation."

I stepped out without taking her hand and nearly regretted it as my legs buckled.

She caught me, helping me into a plush, well-appointed antechamber filled with black and chrome furnishings. "First couple transitions can be hard on the body."

"Thank you."

I let her lead me to one of the couches opposite a murmuring holographic television taking up most of the opposite wall. Vil stepped through the projected news channel, picked up a pitcher and offered me a glass of ice cold water. From the taste, they'd infused it with rose petals and blackberries.

She let me get halfway through the glass before she spoke again. "If you're feeling better. Mister Bradley is waiting for you."

The glass froze on the way to my lips. "Mister Bradley himself?"

"It isn't the usual way we recruit around here, but he insisted. If you'd follow me." She smiled and stepped toward the double doors leading from the room.

If I'd expected a grand tour through halls lined with Mimir's various technological products, I'd have been sorely disappointed. Vil led me through halls cleanly decorated with occasional plants, rare art, and overpriced furnishings—everything Adam and Thecia had insisted we buy for our own executive floor.

Vil ushered me past a receptionist to a spiral stair. We ascended into an office vaguely shaped like Pac-Man. Windows surrounded three-quarters of the circular floor section not blocked off by a wall.

An older man in a tailored suit practically leapt out of his chair. He raced around the small island pretending to be a desk and took my hand. "Mister Graham, I am so glad you accepted our invitation."

Truth be told, Richard Bradley offered me the best welcome of anybody save maybe Sunny. He didn't wrinkle his nose or look down on my clothes.

Adam gives an excellent first impression too, and that worked out fabulously.

Behind him, Vil beamed like a proud mama.

I split a flat look between them. "Why?"

Bradley barely hesitated. "You pushed arcanology further in a few years than anyone in modern history. You helped make the world better while undercutting your competition."

"I got framed and sent to prison."

Bradley shrugged, leading me toward the walled-off quarter that didn't have windows. "So, you're not a businessman. You're trusting, a people person, an innovator."

"The Wasteland has a way of gutting those tendencies."

"Vil?" He stopped, hand on a biometric reader and his searching gaze fixed onto Vil.

"Mister Graham helped save a hundred people, sir," Vil said. "He's still the man you want for the FRPG project."

His exuberance returned. Beyond the reader and runeguard locks, a hall led to a few small rooms and an all-glass elevator. "Do you know why we're called Mimir, can I call you Elias?"

"Sure, and no, I don't."

"Vision. Odin traded his eye for forward vision. The FRPG project is your brainchild, Elias, grown from the seeds of helping first responders into a way to protect them from all harm."

The elevator took us down through the building. The elevator tube remained transparent. Each floor that came into view resembled the big brothers of Porter's reception areas. Workers lounged in sitting areas, holographic consoles canted as needed to accommodate people seated on couches and Sumo chairs.

We descended level after level, our view interrupted only by the floors themselves. Without warning, we slid into darkness. When the enormously thick floor slid upward out of sight, we entered a double height area about as big as the Bluebox entry foyer. Frosted glass walled us off from who knew what.

The elevator stopped, and Bradley led the way. "Wait until you see what we've been working on."

I lost my bearings in short order as we passed in and out of security doors like we were navigating a labyrinth built inside an old navy aircraft carrier.

Bradley stopped with his hand on a handle and beamed at me. "Inside here is a chance to reclaim your legacy, to rise above your past and show the world who you really are."

An itch tickled my eyes. My chest swelled, and lightheadedness threatened to lift me off the floor. Bradley's eager expression mimicked my own. He held my eyes for a three count and threw open the door.

I stopped dead just inside and stared. In my wildest dreams, I'd never expected to see a dozen women wearing harlequin masks prancing around in the middle of a dance number.

Translucent sashes of blue and gold and silver swirled a graceful weave of cloth that approximated actual magic.

I turned back toward Bradley, about to demand how showgirls could rebuild my reputation when a belligerent tone stole my attention. "I don't know how you got in here, but we don't have any scraps. So just get out, and don't even think about stealing—"

A man's voice barked from across the room. "Austin!"

The thin, scowling youth stiffened.

The dancers continued their routine behind him without pause. Thin black staves gilt in gold and silver twirled around them trailing ribbons of color.

Another man stepped into view. He pushed spectacles up and looked down his bulbous nose at the youth. "Apologize to Mister Graham. Rich too while you're at it."

Austin paled. "Um, I'm sorry, Mister Bradley. I thought a filthy bum had someh—"

Austin fell silent under Bradley's glower, though the way he'd

called me a bum had said all that needed to be said. Mimir's CEO turned his displeasure on the second man.

The second man ran a frustrated hand over his buzz cut. "Austin, why don't you fetch Mister Graham some fresh coffee?"

Austin stood immobile, hooded eyes blazing when they left Bradley to meet mine. For a moment, I thought he'd object, but he disappeared deeper into the lab.

"Black," Vil added.

That the recruiter knew how I took my coffee only spoke to how good she really was. I had to concede that she'd orchestrated every bit of our earlier meeting to throw me off guard enough to deliver her offer. It worked too, evidenced by where I stood.

"I'm sorry about that. Mister Graham." Vil said.

"Elias," Bradley said. "This is Willie, our head engineer, and that was his short-lived intern, Austin."

"I'll deal with Austin, Rich," Willie's voice hardened. "Don't you worry about that."

Willie and Bradley locked eyes. A quick check of Vil's face told me such disagreements weren't unusual. Bradley backed down, offering me the same warm smile he'd had at our first meeting. "You have Willie here to thank for your invitation to join our little family."

The other man stepped forward, extending a hand. The scent of Dad's Old Spice left my nose itching. A Special Forces tattoo peaked out from his rolled-up sleeves as our grips met in momentary assessment of each other's strength. "William Bradley. CTO."

Even without the title, Willie's full name explained what I'd thought of as an odd employee-employer dynamic.

"You might think of someone like me as your natural enemy. The uneducated...," Willie chuckled and glanced at his brother. "...might suggest I work matter and you antimatter. They might even cite the destruction of The Dalles Dam."

I offered Richard Bradley a reassuring smile. "A lot of propaganda went into that misunderstanding. Most people make that mistake."

Bradley nodded. "Willie pointed out to me how you'd saved lives by designing the first rudimentary cohabitation of magic and tech in hospitals. How you'd saved first responders by adding magical equipment to their gear."

Willie gestured toward the still practicing dancers. "When they sent you to the Wasteland, I undertook the FRPG project in honor of your legacy."

"By training dancers?" I asked.

Willie laughed. "No. I was just working out the program for the show's big closing ceremony. PGs stop."

PG?

Every dancer stopped, but their veils continued to float and ripple.

"Resume primary mode," Willie said.

A soft thrum of magic I'd only subconsciously registered vanished. The dancers' skin and clothing disintegrating in a rippling shower of pixels.

Magic and tech.

Holograms faded in an effect that was probably designed for the trade show as well, revealing genderless mannequins. The staves remained, but their streamers vanished with the other magical effects. White edged with red colored some of the dummies. Others wore orange-trimmed yellow and the last paneled black and white.

EMTs, firefighters, and police.

"Willie assigned me to track you down after the splash you made resurfacing at the dam," Vil said.

Willie stepped up to me, evenly meeting my eye. "I want to help you like you helped others."

Bradley cleared his throat. "*We* want to help you, and we need your help in return."

I glanced at Willie. "PG?"

"Plastic Golems," he answered at once.

"A name you promised to replace before they went main-stream," Bradley's tone became venomous. "Particularly after that Thoth nastiness."

"FRPG is our first responder plastic golem project," Vil explained.

No one stopped me when I approached whatever the PGs were. I orbited the PGs, examining them up close. Their hard surfaces were split into countless hexagons. Joints seemed covered in a shiny fabric broken up into even smaller hexes. Featureless faces were broken up by tiny mesh ports for nostrils and mouth. Twin glassy ovals I suspected were cameras approximated eyes.

There was pride in Bradley's voice when he spoke once more. "Willie managed to perfect—"

"Mister Bradley?" Vil interrupted. "We've already shown Mister Graham proprietary tech without hiring him and placing him under an NDA."

Bradley waved her off. "I know, but Elias's homeless and I think we can trust him. Besides, these babies are going to be the main event at Foretold. How much harm could he do us in the interim?"

"Were you not about to disclose information about," she glanced at me as her fingers made quotes, "the engine."

"She's making sense, Rich. No offense, Mister Graham."

My fingers ran across the surface of the nearest PG. Rather than the smooth I'd expected, a fine texture met my touch, broken up as fingertips reached each hex line. "None taken. Call me Eli."

Bradley studied the other two. "Without going into the details, the engine performs bidirectional conversion of electricity and magical energy to allow these units to function in any environment under any power."

"I can see converting magic to electricity, but why would you need to do things the other way?" I asked.

Bradley deferred to Willie.

"I wanted them able to utilize their illusion generators in any circumstances," Willie said.

"Why?" I asked.

"Cat in a tree," Bradley said.

I blinked. "What?"

"Sometimes a person in danger is so scared they can't help themselves. Holograms are good, but not quite as convincing as illusion could be, allowing the unit to imitate someone the endangered person would trust."

It made sense, assuming the unit could download image and voice prints before losing Edison power or net access. There seemed to be things they hadn't anticipated—or hadn't mentioned, but the PGs offered genuine possibilities.

"Are these meant to augment or replace first responders?"

Willie and Bradley gave opposite answers at the same moment, Willie saying, "Augment."

"When perfected they should be able to work without human supervision," Bradley said.

Willie's voice hardened. "I've told you, Rich. Even all the planning in the world doesn't survive the first few seconds of engagement. We gave them voice commands for a reason."

"I thought you gave them voice commands so you could adjust their programming to deal with the glitches," Bradley said.

"Gentlemen," Vil said. "You still haven't answered Mister Graham's real question."

Bradley turned toward me. "Your discoveries helped my brother during his last tour."

"Don't underplay things, Rich. My squad might not have made it out without some of the Thoth gear," Willie said.

"Needless to say, you impressed him, and I can't say I'm not grateful that your inventions brought him back to all of us," Bradley said. "He believes you can help us with some rather significant issues."

"Like what?" I asked.

"They're schizophrenic," Bradley said.

"What?" I asked.

"It's more complicated than that," Willie said. "As long as they have electrical power available, their decision-making processes are run by a limited AI, but to ensure they remain functional even if the engine is too damaged to convert magic to electricity—"

"—such as after an EMP," Bradley interjected.

"Right," Willie nodded. "Like after an EMP hit, the PGs are designed with golem enchantments."

"Which effectively gives them two brains," Bradley said. "They've misconstrued orders, acted on only part of what they were instructed, taken things too far."

"As you know, golems are capable of perfectly replicating tasks they are shown and following commands, but those commands are somewhat limited."

"We haven't been able to stop the magical brain from fighting with the AI. We need your skills, your knowledge to make the dream of PGs protecting first responders possible," Bradley said. "Additionally, while their bodies are designed to take quite a beating, Willie is struggling to enhance them with magical protections that might allow them to walk into fires, function underwater, etc."

Yeah, just simple problems.

A too hot cup was shoved into my face, the wondrous aroma tainted by Old Spice. "Your coffee, sir."

I wrinkled my nose.

"What took you so long?" Bradley asked.

"I had to make it fresh, as instructed," Austin said. "Not to mention, find a cup Mister Graham could take with him."

I glanced at the porcelain mug. "All out of Styrofoam?"

"We do not offer our employees non-recyclables," Vil said.

That makes sense I guess.

I sipped the incredible coffee without tasting it. Austin stiffened when I took a staff away from an EMT bot, noting contact points on the weapon and the PG's palm.

Austin gathered the staves from the still PGs, snatched the staff out of my hand and bustled out of the room. My scowl followed him. In the room beyond, a partially disassembled PG stood with his chest cavity opened. Various generations of chest plates and other parts haloed the workstation.

Austin's glower interposed itself between me and the tech. He exited the construction bay and yanked the door closed.

"So, when can you come on board?" Bradley asked.

6

DILEMMA OF CONSCIENCE

My head turned so slowly I could almost hear the hinges in my neck creak. The CEO of Mimir Corp had offered me a job. The offer shouldn't have been a shock. Why else would they have sent a recruiter to find me? Even so, hearing the theoretical offer escape his lips with such clear welcome put my world into a spin.

Bradley kept talking. "...and we can offer a corporate apartment until—"

"No," I snapped. A deep breath helped me soften my voice. "I apologize, but I cannot accept any form of residence."

Austin gaped. "You *want* to be homeless?"

"It's complicated," I said.

Bradley and Willie frowned in an eerie echo of one another.

Vil cleared her throat. "Mister Graham's conviction. We discussed this possibility after my research."

Austin impressed me with an even dirtier look than before.

My conviction was public record. No decent corporate recruiter would bring in a candidate without doing at least a cursory background check, but to have held a discussion about why I lived on the street threw me a bit.

I hadn't talked to anyone but my lawyer about the charges. Even knowing I hadn't done it, I couldn't face Dad. I'd made the decision in the Wasteland, that if I ever got out, I would disappear onto the streets. Having no residence not only shielded me from admitting guilt that wasn't mine. It meant never having to face Dad, never seeing disgust or disappointment in his eyes. It meant never learning how much my naiveté had damaged a reputation he'd spent a lifetime building.

"Right." Willie's expression cleared. He stepped closer and lowered his voice. "With respect, you didn't do it, did you?"

"Would you steal someone's free will with your tech?! Would you enslave their minds and...and—" Fury welled up to choke off the words.

Willie held up hands. "No, and neither would the man who focused his talents on helping first responders."

"Plenty of saints are secret degenerates," Austin grumbled.

Vil flashed a glance at Bradley. Before the CEO could react, Willie cut him off. "We need to get Eli off the streets. It isn't safe."

The others glanced between us.

"He's out there fighting the elements on a daily basis. Eli chooses to be homeless, and I know he's smart and probably tough. So are a lot of veterans out there on the streets." Regret crept into Willie's voice. "They die every day. It's hard living rough like that. It wears on a body, and that doesn't even take into account sickness or injury."

"They *all* choose to stay homeless," Austin said. "Government steals our hard earned pay to fund programs, but they'd rather lay around doing nothing."

Heat radiated from Willie's words. "Those veterans risked their lives for you. They're not lazy, not by half."

"Fine, but that's even worse, isn't it?" Contempt undercut

Austin's words. "So-called heroes crapping on our sidewalks because they're too proud to accept—"

Mine might have been the only eyes on Austin not readying tar and feathers. As interns went, I doubted he had much of a future past our meeting.

I cleared my throat. "The elements won't be a problem for me much longer. I appreciate your concern, and as intriguing as your project is, I'm afraid my circumstances don't really allow for me to join your company."

Vil brightened. "Wait. This campus is equipped with a full gym. Our cafeteria staff has laundry facilities for the linens. We could accommodate your needs without requiring you to maintain a residence—assuming Mister Bradley agrees.

"We could also offer you legal counsel as part of your position," Vil gave Bradley a meaningful look. "Maybe there's a way to eliminate this restriction?"

Hope knocked, but I refused to answer the turncoat.

"We need to get him off the street now," Willie said. "Winter weather is only getting worse."

"What about a company vehicle?" Vil asked. "Maybe an RV or a custom van would offer Mister Graham protection from the elements without forcing him to abandon the reasons he chooses homelessness."

I watched them, unsure what to say. I hadn't thought of an RV or a van—not that I could've afforded something like that. The problem was, RVs plugged in somewhere and that somewhere might constitute an actual address. Working for them would provide a salary I could use to pay Sunny. If anyone could rid me of the conviction, it was her.

"Adam blackballed a lot of people that stayed loyal to me," I said. "He wouldn't like this."

Bradley laughed. "Particularly if Mimir suddenly opened up an arcanology division."

Which might just be what he fears I'll do. I just didn't think anyone would offer me a chance like this again. Once my box is ready, hell, a salary would make completing the box that much easier.

"Tell you what," Bradley smiled. "Let us take this to our lawyers and see what we can do. Meanwhile, you decide whether you'd be interested in helping us on the FRPG project. How does that sound?"

"I'll escort Mister Graham out," Austin said.

"We offered him a meal," Vil said.

It took a lot of will to fight against rising hope, but I beat it down like a whack-a-mole. "You've given me a lot to chew on already."

"You're turning down a free meal?" Austin asked.

"Austin," Willie snapped. "Go check on the latest barrier interference tests."

Austin headed out of the room. He scowled at me from behind their backs. I had no doubt he wouldn't be a perk if I took the job.

"Did you plan on declining our offer of food?" Bradley asked

"I never said that," I said.

"Good," Willie said. "Go ahead, Rich. We'll catch up."

Vil and Bradley eyed him, but they filed out without complaint.

Willie strolled over to one of the PGs, depressing his fingers into a spot under its armpit. "First, I want to apologize for Austin. When you're young, well, you know."

He pulled the chest plate off the PG.

"Can't say he makes me warm and fuzzy, but I understand."

"In the service, we take care of our own." He checked something and snapped the chest plate back on. "You saved my ass, Eli. I intend to return the favor one way or another."

He extended a palm-sized plastic disk with a crystal in its center. "Take this."

Turning it over in my hands, I noted cracks spider-webbed out from a sharp dent. I raised my brows.

"Unit holo-comm. Take it as a good luck charm. Take it just to appease the guy about to feed you, whatever. I'm probably the only one in range, but if you tell whoever answers who you are, we'll have your back." Willie smiled. "Even if you don't take the job, I bet we could also pay you cash under the table here and there."

My pride raised my hackles.

His expression told me the sudden prickle hadn't gone unnoticed. "You'll earn that cash, don't you worry. I'll bet you've already noticed some holes in our designs."

"One or two."

"Come on, chow time."

As we made our way to their cafeteria, I asked the question that'd been burning in my thoughts. "How were those PGs invoking illusions? Particularly on the stave ends not built into the construct?"

"You noted the contact points?"

I nodded.

"Not much different than the Thoth designs really. A normal person keys a rune or otherwise closes a circuit that initiates a preprogrammed set of commands."

"All right, but you said they could change their appearance to match a loved one. Thoth cosmetic charms simply embellish what they find."

"And if you want blue eyes instead of brown, Thoth sells a blue eye charm or cat eye," Vil said. "Simple, preprogrammed effects."

"Right," I said, "The kind of dynamic adjustment required to mimic someone on the fly would require a will to control the spell."

"The golem enchantments give the constructs a simple will."

I shook my head. "Too simple."

"But you can show a golem a picture of someone they're supposed to serve, and they serve them even on their first meeting," Willie said.

"Usually," I said.

"The AI shows its golem half a picture—well, a 3D render—of the target illusion," Willie said.

"And if the AI is down?"

A nervous chuckle escaped Bradley. "We hope it doesn't have to save a stubborn cat in those circumstances, but the golems are programmed with a default image to project."

"Worst case, they appear as you saw," Willie said.

After a hearty, home-style meal in the corporate cafeteria, they weighed me down with so much food as to make me wistful of a bag of holding. The LUX Vil called picked me up off the building roof and took me to my alley and dropped me in a parking spot right next to one of my SMLE watchers.

SMLE and I assess one another through the separating glass.

Thunder cracked across the sky.

Shit. No time for a stare down.

I forced open the pod's door and bolted into my alley only to stop short. A figure stood in front of my already covered box. With his back to me, all I could see was a high-end trench coat and somber black umbrella. Checking the shoes visible beneath trouser cuffs cancelled the possibility my visitor might be Sunny or Thecia.

Banner day for good news.

The figure turned, the image of corporate wealth and success—if Lord Elrond had gotten pretty and gone into business.

"I do hope you'll forgive me for taking the liberty of bolstering your domicile against the elements."

The man's fluid, luxurious voice had been burned into my memory with hot plasma. That he had the tenacity to wait calmly after trying to kill me, made that plasma ignite my blood.

"What do you want?"

"First, to congratulate a fellow fencer on a successful touch."

I scowled at him. "What?"

"You thwarted me, no small accomplishment for someone so young."

"If you're talking about the dam, I beat you twice."

His fine brows rose.

"I survived your assault here in the alley, too."

"You thought that was assault?" Even his condescending laughter was musical.

"What would you call it then?"

"Motivation," he said. "Winning without an opponent can get so dreary."

I stared, unsure what to say.

He scrutinized me, tilting his head ever so slightly back and forth. "It looks as if you did not survive our contest without a scar. She's marked you."

"Who has?"

He gestured at my head. "The Ley."

What does he want?

"Has she started staking her claim yet?"

"What the hell are you talking about?" I asked.

"Surely even you know how jealous a female can be. They possess the ability to drive males from their senses, the Ley more so than any other."

"Yeah, whatever. What do you want?"

"My emerald."

"I don't have it."

He scrutinized me once more, but as it happened, I really didn't have his emerald. I'd entrusted the gemstone Sunny found in the ruins of his golem to her and hadn't thought of it since.

"Truth." His lips curled. "But perhaps not whole truth."

"Great, so what happens now? You're going motivate again?"

He laughed, turning his back and giving me an oh-so-tempting target. "No, boy. I'll leave you to the Ley. If she doesn't see to you, I believe the old shapeshifter will."

Thunder cracked open the sky and poured out its contents.

When I dropped my eyes from a flash of lightning behind Thoth's eye, the elf had vanished completely.

Wonderful.

I ducked into my box, touching small circles on the upper walls and willing little first rez cylinders a fingerbreadth long. Dim blue magical light illuminated my home's interior. The elf's wrapping job seemed on first inspection to be deflecting rain enough that no wet spots seeped through the cardboard.

I nibbled on a few of Mimir's leftovers, watching my house for signs of disintegration. When none appeared, I let sleep take me.

MY DREAM FEATURED a woman scantily clad in flowers bringing Darrin and me drinks from a cabana. I recognized the scene from one of our research trips. In a moment, Darrin would leave us alone—just in case—even though he knew I was loyal to Thecia.

"Eli?"

I frowned up at her deep voice.

"Eli?" she repeated in Adam's voice. The shock of my betrayer's words on her painted lips jerked me out of a dream that probably would've proven as chaste as the event.

What the hell is Adam doing here?

"Eli!" Adam slurred.

Jesus, what the hell else can go wrong today?

I ducked my head out the mouth of my home. Sure enough, Adam stood mere feet away. His tie hung on either side of a few undone shirt buttons. A paper bag-wrapped bottle swung in his fingers.

"Go away." I ducked back inside.

A kick impacted against the side of my box. "Get out here, you bathtard."

"I'm a bastard?!" I came out of the box in a rush, all the anger from earlier back with reinforcements. My fists were already coming up when I caught the calculating expression in Adam's totally lucid eyes. I shifted my attention to the nearby SMLE cruiser.

You son-of-a-bitch.

A step back and a deep breath put enough distance between us to keep my fingers from around my treacherous partner's throat. "I should've expected something this shitty from you. You're why SMLE's been sitting on me. They've been out here getting bored waiting for you to get around to your drunk idiot performance."

Adam smiled.

I waved over the cruiser. "Hey, SMLE! This guy is forcibly violating a court order. Get him out of here."

Adam's smile faltered.

Thank you, Sunny.

"I'm pressing charges, Adam. Maybe you'll get a shot at Wasteland."

His cheeks twitched the harder he clenched his jaw. "My lawyers are better."

I snorted. "Not anymore."

When it became apparent SMLE wasn't going to bother doing their job, unless I gave Adam the beat down he deserved, I ignored them. "What do you want?"

"You, gone from Seufert Fells."

Does he know about the Mimir offer?

I gestured. "Not much of a threat to you here."

"Seufert Fells is a nice city. We don't need people like you haunting our streets and preventing the city from becoming great."

"That's bullshit, and you know it."

"You tampered with Glamour, stole our golems, endangered—"

"Cut the sound bite shit, Adam. I know all about your Glamour victims. You were trying to figure out the problem long before I was released. I know what really happened, how it happened and who's responsible."

Adam darkened. "You're angry."

"Damn right I'm angry. We were friends, and you sold me out for money!"

"No, you're angry at the city for convicting you."

"Shouldn't I be?"

"Just admit it, you're angry at the city and its people for—"

My eyes narrowed, flashing up and down his frame until I found a slight glow coming out of his pocket. With the number of times I'd been caught flat-footed by the possessed golems, one of the first things I had done after acquiring the refrigerator box was to draw circles around it. The alcove's geometry hadn't allowed for perfect circles, but as long as a circle composed an unbroken circuit, shape didn't matter.

An act of will energized a vaguely mushroom-shaped sixth rez circle. The next smallest circle sprang to life with a seventh rez, and a first rez mushroom illuminated the area from my innermost circle. I shifted energy to the sixth-seventh-first to intensify their magnitude.

Adam started, eyes darting around us.

I almost added a fifth rez, effectively capturing him. Unfortunately, no matter how tempting a little alone time with Adam might sound, I had no doubt SMLE—at least these SMLE agents— would look upon that as a magical abduction. Instead I'd raised the sixth and seventh resonance barriers to block incoming and exiting energy—hopefully blocking radio transmissions like they would wireless electricity otherwise available from the nearby Edison node. The first rez did the same for magical energy, depriving his device of all external power.

With the extra illuminations, I couldn't tell if his device died or not, but I knew magic circles.

"You're holding me against my will."

"Jesus," I cringed inwardly, darting a glance around for Sunny. "Jesus, Adam, you run one of the biggest arcanology corporations in the world. Can't you tell one circle from another?"

He glanced at SMLE.

"They're not going to run over here just because I cut off your wire."

Adam produced his recorder and glowered at it.

"You can leave this circle any time you want."

Adam threw his bottle through the circles. Its passing forced me to hold them against breaking, but otherwise, the bagged whatever hit the concrete with a shattering of glass.

All the anger and resentment probably lit my eyes like a rhet. "Your little trick failed, Adam. Now, why don't you go back to that two-timing whore and leave me the fuck alone?"

"The forgiveness your little rescue at the dam garnered would've made driving you from town in the court of public opinion my best solution." Adam shrugged. "You should know me well enough to know I wouldn't come here without contingency plans."

I took two quick steps, hands snapping up. I stopped and shoved them into my pockets. "Damn it, Adam. You already destroyed me, why can't you just leave me alone? Hell, why can't everyone just leave me in fucking peace!?"

"You're a threat, Eli, and one way or another you need to go."

"Then why all the games?" I demanded. "Why not just put a bullet into me?"

He glanced at his bug, fingering the off switch. "That contingency could prove more disruptive than helpful. I'd rather you just left. I'd even consider paying your relocation expenses—for old time's sake."

"I didn't take Thecia's handouts and I sure as hell aren't going to take yours."

His expression tightened. A moment later that self-assured boardroom smile graced his lips. He spun on his heels and marched toward the nearest corner and out of sight.

My half snarl and half scream vented enraged frustration into the alley air. I turned back to my box, nowhere near as calm as I'd have preferred. I hadn't bent down enough to enter when a heavy footfall turned my head sideways.

A golem marched into the far end of the alley.

You've got to be kidding me.

I rose, head turning slowly with uneasy resignation.

A second golem marched in from the other end.

I turned toward the alcove's fence and quick exit, but something told me that if I took that route, a third golem would await me along with the SMLE watchman.

"To hell with all of you." I flopped down in the mouth of my box and empowered all three mushroom-shaped circles with fifth rez barriers.

It's going to be a long night.

7

FALSE FOOTING

I sat in the same interrogation room, watched by a wizard eye, a camera and a junior SMLE officer. He leaned over me, both hands on the table which had 'accidentally' slid into me twice, and screamed demands I confess.

I wiped blood from my lip and met his grin with a flat stare.

When Sunny gets here, she's going to have your badge.

The soon-to-be-out-of-work officer considered himself a hockey enforcer if my bruises were any indication.

The golems hadn't attacked my barrier. SMLE charged into the alley, ordered down my circles and arrested me for grand theft. I hadn't resisted, but that didn't seem necessary for the kind of treatment Adam had paid Officer Verde and his fellows to apply.

Detective Brooke entered, clapped a hand over Verde's mouth and physically dragged him out of the room without a word otherwise. A moment later, the door opened to admit Sunny.

"Eli," she gasped. "Are you all right?"

I folded my cuffed hands. "I want to press charges against SMLE and Adam for assault and entrapment."

The line of her mouth thinned. "Tell me everything."

I did, omitting only my conversation with the elf.

She made me go over it again and again until she probably could've written that chapter of my biography. She left with a fire in her eyes, demanding Brooke accompany her as she stormed off somewhere else in the precinct.

I laid my head down on the table and tried to ignore my throbbing injuries enough to manage a little sleep. The door snapped me awake, ready in that instant to fight for my life. I forced away the instinct until I saw Officer Verde once more.

"I'm not saying anything until my lawyer gets back."

Verde watched me, but his sad, grey eyes held no vestiges of his earlier anger.

"What?" I demanded.

"Elias Balthazar Graham."

"Yeah, we covered that while you were beating me earlier."

Verde cocked his head. "Are you a war hero?"

"What? No, I never served."

Verde's lips pressed into a thin line. "You raised a magical barrier when approached by Adam Mathias."

I folded my arms and clamped my lips shut.

"It was not a fifth resonance barrier."

I rolled my eyes. "No shit."

"Why?"

Why what?

"What purpose did these other barriers serve?" Verde asked.

I eyed the camera and the wizard eye. Both remained active, so whatever Verde's game, Sunny would have it on tape.

"Self-defense."

"He was inside the barrier, able to accost you at will."

"I wasn't worried about his fists."

"There were other dangers beyond the physical?"

"Go away." I put my head back on the table. "I'm done talking."

A minute later, Verde left without so much as a goodbye smack. His strange behavior kept me from getting back to sleep, so I

barely reacted when Brooke and Sunny entered and took seats on either side of the table. Brooke set an evidence bag down. Glass clinked as he set the contained paper bag on the table.

"Can you identify this, Mister Graham?" Brooke asked.

"If you got it from my alley, then that's probably the bag Adam was holding when he showed up on my doorstep."

Brooke's brows rose. "Probably?"

"I wasn't there to see you take it so I cannot say for absolutely sure, but the rh—there were no other broken or paper bag-wrapped bottles in my alley."

"You expect me to believe you clean up your alley?" Brooke asked.

"I'm homeless, not raised in a barn."

Sunny squeezed my hand under the table, causing me to wince. She jerked away, mumbling apologies.

"These injuries—"

I interrupted Brooke. "I didn't have any of these injuries before your boys stormed my alley."

"We'll want a full photographic record," Sunny said. "And we'll need a medical examiner to catalog and date his injuries."

Brooke nodded, pulling a cigarette from his pocket and twirling it in his fingers. "Immediately after this interview."

"No," Sunny said. "Now."

He glowered at her. "Until I have his testimony, I can't tell the examiners which injuries to check."

"Better for an objective examination. Besides, Eli was interviewed yesterday morning by Megan French. We'll have the network send over the raw footage as evidence of his condition."

"A lot can happen in a day," Brooke said.

"I interviewed with Mimir corporate executives only a few hours earlier."

"Really?" Sunny brightened. The shark turned to Brooke. "I want those examiners in here now."

Brooke bristled but stepped from the room. He returned with a

mousy-looking woman with dumpsters under her eyes. He gestured at the camera and wizard eye in turn. "Mister Graham, Ashley will examine you, speaking what she finds. Please disrobe."

Sunny bit her lip when I looked, a bit more color in her tan cheeks than usual. I undressed. Brooke gestured once more to the recording devices.

"Please, Mister Graham, relate this evening's events in your own words as the medical examiner does her job."

I told him what I had Sunny.

Ashley did her thing. I got dressed, and Brooke, Sunny and I all sat back down. As I did, I wondered if the first telling had been recorded too. I finished with the same pronouncement I'd led with to Sunny. "I want to press charges against SMLE and Adam for assault and entrapment."

Brooke's scowl deepened. He turned to Sunny. "For the moment, Ms. Terrell, since Officer Verde arrested him, we're going to have to hold your client over for arraignment."

I thought she'd object, but instead, she took a deep breath, drew out her phone and turned to me. "We'll get the arraignment expedited."

"I'll do what I can under the circumstances, but I can't promise anything," Brooke said.

She held up her phone. "I'll take care of that."

Brooke frowned.

"May I speak to my client in confidence once more?"

He left. Sunny checked the corner. The camera's power light was dark, and the wizard eye had its lids shut.

Should've checked that earlier.

"I'm going to call in a favor to get things expedited, but you're going to miss breakfast with your parents."

"Best news I've had all day."

"Eli!" She said scandalized.

"Send them home, Sunny. I didn't want them here in the first place."

She reached a hand toward my shoulder but seemed to have second thoughts. She gave me a thin-lipped smile. "Please be careful. Pressing charges—while right—won't make you many friends here."

"I was already Mister Popular."

She laughed and exited the room.

It wasn't a bad sound.

ON THE BRIGHT SIDE, my days in jail were warm and dry. With nothing else to do, I resumed my Wasteland workout regime, taking care not to overestimate my real body. The Wasteland had deadened my palate, and my bologna staples filled the belly but weren't exactly fine dining. I hadn't realized just how spoiled I'd been by the leftovers that made their way to me from Sunny's cook, Grace, until I endured my first institutional meal.

I have to admit it was a close thing between three horrid free meals a day or an empty stomach. Practicality won out, so I sacrificed my palate for the sake of a contented stomach.

Returning to incarceration raised questions about how my conviction would alter the reception my fellow prisoners offered. Caleb wasn't the only one likely to take issue with me. Brooke or his bosses decided either my conviction or my escape from the hospital warranted solitary confinement surrounded by six walls of a fifth-first rez cube.

Their precautions kept others safe from the dangerous wizard, but also meant avoiding additional confrontations. Another reason was suggested by the cool but polite treatment I received at the hands of law enforcement.

Brooke or someone up the chain must've put them on notice. No need to give me more evidence against SMLE.

In the overburdened justice system, it wasn't unusual for low profile arraignments to take weeks. Whatever favor Sunny called in got my arraignment on the docket far faster.

The morning of the fourth day, the cubic magical circle vanished —despite plenty of research, I've never tracked down evidence suggesting the reasons all variously shaped magical, three-dimensional polygons were called a circle. A green cop in a freshly pressed uniform beamed at me from the other side of the bars. The outfit was so black it probably hadn't seen a washer more than once.

"Newbie gets the shit duty?" I asked.

"I volunteered."

I scrutinized him, looking for a hint of trouble. Instead, I finally recognized Officer Flowers in the genuinely affable expression. "Flowers?"

He blinked a moment. "Um, yeah, though we haven't been introduced."

Great, Eli, give away you knowingly hid from the cops.

He glanced down, noticed his nametag and actually blushed. "Oh, right. Well, it's still a pleasure to meet you, Mister Graham."

I frowned.

Nervous laughter escaped him. "Not the best circumstances, I realize, but you saved my life at the dam. Thank you for that, and for saving the others, and well, just wow. You were incredible."

Better yet, my own groupie.

I dropped my eyes. "Why are you here, Officer Flowers?"

I swear his ramrod posture actually got straighter. I could almost see the edges of his uniform creases glint. "SMLE Special Agent Flowers."

"All right, why are you here SMLE Special Agent Flowers?"

"Technically I'm only a junior SMLE Special Agent."

"Why?" I enunciated. "Are you here?"

"Oh, right. I'm escorting you to your arraignment."

I smiled, not bothering to keep my dry tone in check. "Wonderful."

He beamed a moment, then started giving me instructions. From that moment, he was all business. All shiny, young and earnest, SSA Flowers managed to get me to the courthouse without either of us taking a bullet or lightning bolt.

Sunny met us inside with a garment bag. "Change into this and hurry, you're late."

I jabbed a thumb at Flowers, my bound hands coming along for the jibe. "It's the kid's fault."

She shoved the garment bag into his hands and glared like Mom did when I'd been late getting up for mass as a kid. Flowers escorted me to a holding cell. He searched the garment bag like he'd only just gotten his junior detective kit and wanted to try out all its toys. When he finished, he escorted me to a closet suffering size-envy of old phone booths so I could change.

Long story short, between the bottle with Adam's prints, traffic cam footage of Adam being followed out of a warehouse by two golems, and Brooke's testimony regarding Adam crashing into the previous interrogation, I was released, and the judge issued an injunction against Adam. Sunny had tried to get the SMLE cruiser's camera feed, but the recording device had experienced some sort of malfunction.

Despite my better judgment, I let Sunny persuade me to delay filing charges against SMLE. She had a tougher time getting me to do the same with Adam.

"No, Sunny. The bastard deserves it."

The perky preacher-turned-shark by her lawyer clothes leaned in. "Save this, Eli. With your shared history, it's not enough. Going after him now risks having the charges dismissed but if we can prove a pattern—especially after the judge's order for him to stop bothering you—we might be able to get him."

A flicker of hope Mimir had raised poked its nose out of its hole. I should've smacked it down again like a whack-a-mole, but I let it slip from my lips. "Would that be enough to get my conviction overturned?"

She frowned. "You served your sentence already."

My expression made her recoil.

She raised her hands in surrender. "Let's get you fully discharged and go somewhere to talk this through."

Her guarded expression offered all the conversation needed. Being falsely convicted didn't matter to her. For Sunny, the fight wouldn't be worth her time.

I folded my arms. "Fine."

We got into her old beater car. She latched an old-fashioned seat belt no longer used in newer cars and turned toward me. "Should we have your parents join us?"

"I told you to send them home."

"I tried."

My eyes narrowed. "Just how hard did you try?"

"They're adults, Eli, I don't have any—" My expression stopped her. "Okay, I told them you said they should go home."

I closed my eyes.

If Sunny had taken another tack, any other tack, she might've convinced them to leave. Envisioning their response to simply telling them I said to go was predictable enough. Mom would wonder aloud about what they'd done to me to make me not want to see her. Dad would snort around his cigar, puffing smoke from his nostrils like an old dragon and just as unwilling to be moved anywhere he didn't want to go.

"I'm pretty sure you're the evil one, Sunny, not me." She opened her mouth, but I held up a hand to forestall her, adopting a falsetto. "Humans are social creatures, and the Bible says to honor thy father and thy mother and blah, blah Jesus loves you and so do your parents."

She turned from me, jaw tight and put the car into gear. We drove in silence several blocks. I kept track of her turns, trying to anticipate what vengeance she intended for mocking her. Finally, she pulled us into a Chick-Fil-A parking lot, got out and stomped inside.

I got out of the car, checked it locked and studied the Christian fast food restaurant. Meager funds remained to me. They were best spent on simple supplies I could stretch out or a simple Edison node converter to replace my abysmal attempts with my thrift store electric kettle. I thought back to the hammer drill I'd used to take down a golem.

Did we return that to the construction site?

"I thought you liked this place." Sunny glowered at me from just inside the entry door. "Are you coming or not?"

I'd been trying to decide exactly that. It was probably safer to just leave, avoiding any possible ambushes in the process. Just the same, alienating the attorney cashing in favors and working pro bono probably wasn't the wisest choice available to me.

I went inside.

Sunny sat me in the rearmost corner. "What do you want?"

"To be left alone."

"No, Eli, to eat."

"Why did you assume I liked this place?"

She shrugged. "You've always got condiments from here, I figured with as limited as your funds must be, you'd have to like the food to spend money here."

Truth be told, I'd felt no guilt at repeatedly raiding the Christian company's reserves. They ran their business for God, managing His money. Even so, it seemed impolitic to reveal to Sunny that I figured the least God could do to repay me for all of her lectures was give up a little mayonnaise and mustard.

"Look, I'm treating—in exchange you have to tell me why you want to pursue overturning a conviction that you've already served the time for."

I tensed to leave.

Her eyes hardened.

If I leave, I might as well say goodbye to my lawyer.

"Whatever is fine so long as I get some lemonade."

Sunny smiled and bustled off.

I watched the few patrons there in the early afternoon try not to get caught watching me. Their expressions were the mixed bag I expected. Pity and disgust mixed in varying amounts. A pair of Glamoured patrons studied me while pointedly raising elven noses to ignore my presence.

Sunny sat back down, dropping an odd rectangular plastic cup with her receipt in it. "Okay, spill."

I looked at her, really looked at her. The first time we'd met, she'd been dressed in jeans, a t-shirt, and an open flannel shirt rather than the tailored skirt suit. She'd bustled around her little soup kitchen homeless shelter, prattling way too cheerfully for so early in the morning as she led me past Christian motivational posters.

For a Hispanic woman, she was too thin. Plain, flat-chested and mole-flecked, I wouldn't have turned to look at her a second time on the street. Her shoulder-length, dark hair was pinned in a bun for court, bringing to the forefront her large and slightly mismatched brown eyes.

I'd had ample evidence since my release that she was an ugly crier, even uglier when mad, and when she furrowed her brow, it creased her upper lip.

She'd also proven to be earnest, honest and genuinely concerned about others. She'd invested a great deal of her seemingly endless energy in me even though the rest of the world had thrown me away.

"I'm not guilty of what they said."

She set her hand on mine and stared into my eyes for a whole minute. "I believe you."

"I should be used to being accused of things I didn't do, but—"

"Wait, why should you be used to that?"

I gave her a frank look and gestured at myself.

"And?" she asked.

She was a Hispanic woman, and I was a black man. In the eyes of people like Porter, we were all minorities and thus all the same.

Whatever similarities we'd encountered in our lives, we weren't the same.

"I sat down behind my circle the other night because I knew no matter what happened, I'd be presumed guilty."

She frowned but didn't interrupt.

"When I was a senior in high school I had a 4.5 grade point average, perfect attendance, and numerous community service awards. It's not that I'm some genius or anything, I just worked tirelessly until I had a full-ride scholarship in the bag to the best arcanology program in the country."

"Why work so hard, Eli? Couldn't your family help?"

"Dad had more than enough saved up to pay for my tuition, but I wanted to earn my own way."

"Pride." She nodded. "You learned that from Jackson. At least, he seems the same way, successful by sheer *stubborn* hard work."

It was a close thing, but I resisted rolling my eyes. "I was breezing through my calculus final when the gym teacher proctoring the exam grabbed my paper and ordered me out of the room. I did as I was told."

"You must've been a little bit more pliant in those days."

"Maybe."

A thin young man who smiled like Sunny exchanged a tray of food for the square cup.

"Why were you pulled out of the test?" She took a drink from what looked like a milkshake.

I sipped the sweet, tart, heavenly lemonade before answering. "The coach emerged a minute later with Simon Goss, a first string receiver on the varsity football team. I tried to play it cool, but I knew what had happened. Simon was a good guy for a jock, but he'd been having trouble at home."

"You were letting him cheat?" Sunny asked.

I nodded, taking a bite of a fantastic sandwich. I resumed before my mouth was all the way empty. "He wasn't dumb, and his future didn't include calculus. I didn't see the harm in it."

"What happened next?"

I took a deep breath. "Coach took us to the principal, told her I was cheating off of Simon's test."

"What? Wait, that doesn't make sense. You had a 4.5 average."

I shrugged. "Simon was at best a B student, but he was a white jock. I was suspended, and I lost my scholarship."

"Did you tell the principal Simon was the one cheating?"

"What's the point? They wouldn't have believed me."

"Then why are you so adamant about getting your conviction overturned? Is this about the interview you mentioned?"

"What they said about me—you know what, you're right. Forget about the whole thing."

Sunny leaned forward, setting her hand on mine. "What really happened, Eli?"

I scratched my itchy nose and bought time with lemonade. My head was already shaking before I set the cup down. "I don't want to talk about it. You're right. It's in the past. What does it matter?"

Her gaze narrowed. "Have you spoken to your parents since you were convicted?"

"No."

"That's why you don't want to see them? Eli, they're your parents."

"I-I can't face them." I took another drink to give myself time to push my pain back into the cage I'd built for it, wishing I could cage it in a fifth rez sphere and never feel it again.

"Did your dad believe you about the cheating?" Sunny asked.

"What? Uh, yeah, punished me for my part in it, though he still paid for college. He even relocated all of us and his business over to Portland so I could attend my desired school while cutting costs."

"Why do you think he won't believe you this time?" Sunny asked.

I stood up, food abandoned with my appetite. "This is different."

"How?"

I didn't answer, exiting the nearest door with all the haste I could muster. As I opened the door, the pavement cracked and fell away. I froze mid-step, a gaping chasm of fire-backlit green mist stole my balance.

"Eli?"

My eyes shot to her.

Sunny's expression nearly wept with concern.

When I turned away from her once more, the chasm had been replaced by good old parking lot concrete. I charged down streets toward my alley, the place I had to live because of the lies that had convicted me. Thunder echoed across the nearby high-rises, a punitive slap from God for getting my hopes up. He dumped a cold shower on me next, letting me camouflage my failed attempt to hold back tears.

8

———

COMMAND PERFORMANCE

The downpour worsened until I might as well have swum home. I didn't want Sunny and her pitying expression to find me, so I turned away from home to the nearest library. In my absence, they'd torn down the simple building I'd spent countless hours exploring. In its place, a marble monstrosity that could've housed a league of superheroes loomed over me.

Lightning struck a bronze eagle cresting the high dome. I tried not to take it as a sign and hurried out of the rain. Beyond the two doors and metal detector in between, a large foyer offered self-checkout kiosks to my left and manned counters to my right.

The kiosks didn't seem to mind my entrance, but if their expressions were any judge, the librarians were none too pleased with a soaking-wet homeless man threatening their books' sanctity.

I might've set them at ease if I'd approached and renewed my library card, but without an address, I doubted they'd give me another. I located a bathroom, depleting the reserves of one paper towel dispenser in my quest to dry out. It might've been more efficient to use the electric dryer, but I could only imagine how security would respond to me half naked. Me and my squeaky shoes exited the bathroom and headed toward the newspaper archives. I'd like to think the rain and warning lightning bolt hadn't been the Ottiren spirit's way of chivvying me along—mostly because I didn't want to know the human made of merged otters who'd threatened to eat me could control the weather.

The young woman with her newly minted Masters of Library Science degree didn't like the look of me. "You can't go into the archives. You're still wet."

"I doubt anything I need is still in paper form, and I don't think the microfiche will object."

"You're right about that, but I don't want you shorting out the electronics."

I blinked at her.

Her one brow rose. "When was the last time you were in the archives?"

"You probably weren't out of your training bra."

She darkened. "You're not going in until you're one hundred percent dry."

"In Oregon?"

She wasn't amused.

"What time does the library close? You know what, forget that. How about I promise not to enter your archives if you can show me what I clearly don't understand."

She looked me up and down. "No."

I sighed, licked my lips and marched for the nearest bathroom. My rising temper should've been enough to dry me out, but despite the heat under my collar, I didn't even manage steam. I stood before one of the air dryers, marked out a long rectangle of wall tiles and evoked a sixth-fifth rez cube around me and the dryer.

I marched back up to the archive's desk half an hour later bone dry and irritated that my reflection had clearly displayed a rainbow layer of stubble along my skull from not being able to shave in jail.

"I'm dry."

She gave me a skeptical look but led me down a corridor to one side of her desk. She inserted a card into a reader. The doors opened up to reveal a roomy closet and a Wasteland jacking terminal.

Panic shot through me. I backed away, heart lodged so far up in my throat I couldn't voice my objections.

"What's wrong?" she asked. "It's perfectly harmless VR."

My back slammed into another archive door, forcing me to stare down the gaping maw before me.

Her brow was up above its brother once more. She walked in, taking down some kind of wireless skull cap whose design had probably been stolen from a Marvel comic book, and extended it toward me. "Did you want to use the archive or not."

"J-just give me a moment."

She rolled her eyes and stomped back to the desk. "Let me know when you're done wasting my time."

The door closed, but I could still see the horror behind it. Until she'd opened the archive cubicle, I hadn't realized just how deeply my fear of the Wasteland went. Whatever happened, I had to ensure SMLE never tried to put me back in, because I knew without a shadow of a doubt that anyone trying to put me back in would die.

My heart and lungs eventually stopped sprinting and eased back to a merely rapid pace. When hyperventilation was no longer blocking logical thought, I looked down at my arms.

This is not the Wasteland. There's no way people are getting jacks put into their bodies just to use these archives.

Once I'd repeated it to myself six thousand times, I approached the archive desk with all the confidence of a beaten dog. "I'd like to access the archive please."

She gave me a skeptical look, but let me into the alcove she'd offered. "Instructions are tucked in the pocket next to the unit. Don't make a mess."

I wasn't sure what she meant by her last comment, but I had my hands full concentrating on my mantra and forcing myself through the jaws of doom masquerading as a simple door.

Inside, I examined the alcove component by component, working out the engineering. I read the instructions and safety documentation again and again until the science reassured me I was not about to be trapped in a virtual wasteland for another century.

I put on the skull cap, closed my eyes to prevent what the safety manual erroneously labeled double vision and engaged the archive. I materialized within a blank grey cube, uniformly lit without any source of illumination.

Kind of anticlimactic.

A mousy fellow in tweed with a receding hairline appeared. "Good afternoon, sir. How may I assist you today?"

"Um, local Indian history—"

"I believe you mean Native American, sir."

"I said what I meant. You can't homogenize history by trying to give it kinder, gentler names. You're just insulting the people involved."

"Wouldn't calling them Indians be equally insulting to the native peoples of this continent?"

"Probably at the time, but that was also an honest mistake. This is an intentional insult by people trying to govern how people think in a way to further segregate a people who were Indians and are now *just* Americans."

"Doesn't referring to them as 'just Americans' rob them of their cultural identity?"

"Americans are a combined culture, a hearty stew spiced by the richness of the cultural ingredients without ever smothering any one flavor."

He stared at me a moment. "Noted. You wished to review local

Native American history? Did you have a particular tribe in mind?"

"Tribal information and history around the trading settlement called Celilo. Also, any history relating Celilo and The Dalles Dam."

"Acknowledged. Would sir like to listen to soothing music while I retrieve the information?"

"Sure. Got any jazz?"

"Only the best for our patrons, sir."

He vanished, replaced by soft instrumental jazz.

Must've been programmed for a hotel or something.

Archie—don't ask me why—returned with a slew of historical treatises and journals, offering to read them to me for whatever reason. Pictures poorly rendered into 3-D representations sprang up to surround me.

All of a sudden, I was back in my element. There weren't any spells or magical folklore to pour through, but I lost myself in research and history.

The advent of The Dalles Dam, sanctioned by the government as having minimal impact, had backed up the Columbia flooding over the section of waterfalls called collectively The Dalles. Risen water covered the prosperous trading settlement, putting an end to a century of tribal trading and drowning countless petroglyphs left behind rather than moved with their brethren by the Army Corp of Engineers.

The more I studied the history, the more insurmountable the Ottiren's task grew.

"Sir, the library is closing."

I nodded. "One more thing."

I called up a slate function and drew out the runes I'd seen in the Bluebox. "Do you have any idea what these are? They seemed to create a violet magical field that buzzed like a dump."

"That's an eighth resonance magical circle, sir," Archie said matter-of-factly

"Eighth?"

"Yes, sir," Archie corrected my runes, taking a moment to explain the tuning function of each.

"Could you slow down and go over that again for me?"

"I'm sorry, sir, but the library is closing. Perhaps you could resume this inquiry tomorrow during normal business hours."

"Fine." I thought the exit sequence. Nothing happened. Panic seized me by the throat once more. I opened my eyes to search for the big red emergency cut off button, seeing both worlds for a fraction of a second before the VR dissolved away.

I exited, heart still racing. I thanked the girl behind the desk and headed for the nearest copy room. Grabbing a stack of printing errors from the recycling bin, I headed for the street.

How the hell am I going to open a path back to Indian Atlantis?

HOLOGRAPHIC AND ILLUSIONARY advertisements reached out from storefronts, demanding I pay attention to products no rational person could live without. I did my best to tune them out as I trudged through light rain and considered my recent troubles. Night's dark and brisk wind made the shower feel icy but washed away the scents of garbage, traffic, and humanity at large.

It seemed pretty clear Adam intended to be a nuisance. Maybe he'd been too busy with the Glamour debacle, or perhaps I hadn't given him sufficient notice when I first got released. Something had changed. What, I couldn't really know, but the tenacious quality which made him such a good businessman had been focused on me.

It's not like I'm any kind of threat—unless he thinks I have a way to prove him guilty of perjury. There's one way to find out.

I stopped at a payphone and called Darrin.

"Hello?" Darrin said.

"It's Eli."

A soft female voice whispered in the background. "Who is it?"

"Eli." The softer tone indicated Darrin wasn't speaking to me, confirmed by the urgency in his tone a moment later. "What's happened, Eli? Are you all right?"

"I wanted to pick your brain, but if you're busy—"

Darrin whispered something to the woman then came back. "No, it's fine. What do you need to know?"

"Why's Adam going after me?"

Darrin didn't answer.

"Darrin?"

"Sorry, I was thinking. Afraid I don't have a good answer for you, but one thing I've learned about Adam is that he seldom does things for only one reason. He might be the only person I know that plans as much as you do."

"Plots more than plans."

Darrin laughed. "Right, you don't plot."

"Do you know anything that might explain his attempt to frame me...again?"

"Sorry, Eli, but I'll think about it."

"Thanks, Darrin." I started to hang up when I realized there was another thing Darrin might help me with. "Hey, what can you tell me about eighth rez circles? I've never heard of them before tonight."

"That's right, you were imprisoned when those came to light."

"Darrin, what does an eighth resonance circle do?"

"Think of it like a third rez, but for physicality rather than thaumaturgical linking."

"Similar to the difference between first or second resonance and fifth?" I asked

"Knew I picked a smart mentor."

"I picked you, Darrin."

"Keep telling yourself that." Darrin laughed. "So, evidence of Hengeo Inc.'s discovery of eighth resonance came to public knowledge when they were forced to disclose certain proprietary arcanology used for the teleport spell after an incident."

He launched into a list of the various experiments he had planned for testing the eighth rez circle and the projects Adam kept shoving at him that prevented his research.

"Darrin?"

"Yes?"

"This is fascinating stuff, and based on your description you might've helped me with another problem, but isn't there a girl there waiting for you to get off the phone?"

"Oh." I could almost hear Darrin blush. "Right. Bye, Eli."

"Goodbye, and thank you."

The supernatural whatever that Kenrith called the Ottiren wanted me to accomplish what at first blush was probably better left to a construction company rather than a homeless wizard. It could've been that the Ottiren's choice had been one of convenience, and pressganging me had been his most expedient path to success or a somewhat gamey meal.

Still, Darrin's description of the eighth resonance circle offered possibilities for that problem if not more.

Too bad it doesn't give me a way to rid myself of Adam.

I turned down my alley to find my worrying had summoned yet another problem. Duval's truck parked once more in front of my box. Tired, soaked and shivering, I was in no mood for the bum Mafioso or his enforcer.

Either need to learn rhet invisibility or work on Razcolm's fireball.

"Where have you been?" Duval demanded.

"Jail."

Menace underplayed Duval's tone. "More of my people are dead."

"And how is that my fault?"

"I showed you Wayne's murder."

"And?" I asked.

"I expected you to deal with this killer."

"Look, Duval, I don't know why you think I'd track down—"

"Someone killing the other homeless?" Mihail said. "Maybe looking for you?"

"Enough, Mihail. I showed you so you would do something," Duval said.

"No, you showed me to find out if I'd killed him," I snapped.

"And since you did not kill Wayne, I let you live, expecting you would want to do something about this killer."

"I'm not some hero running around in tights," I said

"You saved the people at the dam," Duval said.

"I had a personal stake in that one."

"They're killing your people," Duval said.

"Human beings?" I snorted. "Yeah, humanity's given me plenty of reasons to risk my neck on its behalf."

Duval's tone became a growl. "They may not be your people, but the ones he's killed *are* mine."

"So call the cops." I slid around him toward my box.

"The cops won't do more than pay these murders lip service." Duval interposed himself. "They don't care how many homeless end up dead."

Ones? Don't care how many?

I didn't want to ask, but I did anyway. "Wait. How many homeless have been murdered?"

"Four of my people, two who weren't and Wayne's wife."

Duval extended his wrist. Projected images of dead and gutted homeless flicked through the air, all accompanied by the same message until they rolled around to Wayne's and the three letters drawn on the Mercedes's bumper: Eli.

Shit.

"No fingerprints. No DNA," Duval said.

"As if they came and went by magic," Mihail added.

Duval stepped in far too close. "The latest victim was...this is personal, Mister Graham, and whoever murdered her possessed some kind of magic."

"That's where the boss insists you come in," Mihail said.

There wasn't much point in asking why me. The murderer had taken someone important to Duval. He felt I had the abilities to help stop a killer and owed him enough that I had no choice but to accede.

Probably expects me to just look the other way, too.

I held my hands up and backed away. "I'm sorry, I really am, but I have too much going on right now to help you."

Duval's intense glower latched onto me like a lamprey. "And when this phantom death-bringer ghosts into the Manger to feast upon the shepherd and her flock?"

If the murderer really was targeting homeless, Sunny could conceivably end up in real danger. The perky, tenacious woman had proven herself willing to welcome anyone into the Manger under only a promise of good behavior. If that someone turned on her people, I had no doubt she'd place herself between Death and her charges.

Shark teeth appeared one by one across Duval's face, growing into a confident smile. "What was that quote about good men doing nothing?"

"Who said I was a good man?"

Duval's smile widened. Despite pretense or anger, he had my number, and he knew it. "If you'd care to get inside the truck this time?"

Damn it. There has to be another way.

There wasn't any guarantee Sunny was in danger. She'd probably heard about the deaths from her patrons. Adding a firm warning—

Won't stop Sunny from being Sunny.

The inward curses spooled out like a hex assembly line. I'd nearly died repaying my debt to Kenrith and Biuntcha. They'd all but demanded it—something Sunny would never do.

Do I owe her any less?

My gaze fell upon my refrigerator box, my home. The plan had

been to build a new, *solitary* life. Willie was right about the elements, the number of strong, smart homeless that died each winter. Every minute I spent running around risking my neck again and again wasted vital preparation time.

Sunny has Grace and God, between the big bad chef and an even bigger deity, she ought to be safe.

"I will gladly hit you again." Mihail's tone confirmed that he would indeed garner genuine amusement beating me unconscious.

I cursed.

Truth be told, God's goodwill seemed about as capricious as the fey. I didn't trust Him as far as I could throw Him.

Before I could act on my decision to get into the truck, Mihail slammed me against the truck's bed. Duval's gaze swept the alley, turning to me harder than ever. He raised a wad of folded twenties in one hand. The other hand pointed a revolver in my face. Like Duval, the gun was understated, easily concealed and designed not to be noticed until you were looking down its barrel.

"Mister Graham. This is important to me. My people are being killed. I can't trust the cops, but you are a criminal with magic." Duval inclined his head toward Mihail. "We understand criminals, but we don't understand magic. You help us, you square your debt, and you get paid."

I wasn't a criminal—at least I wasn't a criminal when I'd gotten out of prison. My time since release hadn't been all kittens and rainbows. I'd been forced to—

No excuses, I broke laws. My actions. My choices. My responsibility.

I'd already decided to help, but the barrel gaping in front of me forced my heels to dig in on general principle. "If I don't?"

"Then I take back the life I gave you and find another wizard."

Options flashed through my mind. I could defy Duval. I could probably get a fifth rez between us before he could shoot. If I took that path, I'd have to live under a fifth rez barrier in perpetuity.

In a choice between an early grave and getting paid to do what

I'd already decided to do, I chose the cash. "I'll ride inside this time."

Duval inclined his head, gesturing with a now empty hand. "After you, Mister Graham."

Yeah, just you wait, you smug son-of-a-bitch.

WAYNE HAD BEEN KILLED NEXT to a Mercedes hidden in the industrial district. Still, Duval's people acted like the poor, so I took it in stride when Mihail turned us toward Seufert Fells's southern end and worst housing. A highway 197 onramp lifted us over the city's slums like a concrete magic carpet.

The thoroughfare that replaced The Dalles California Highway took us south then west through Oregon's high plains, toward the majestic heights of Mount Hood and the national forest at its feet. As a kid, the trip had been a dreaded one. Not only was there forest rather than mananet, but the quick yet subtle rise in altitude had always given my ears fits.

Fortunately, we slowed just as we passed the half-destroyed, then later designated too-historical-to-replace, Dufur city limit sign. Less than twenty miles from The Dalles and the epicenter of the hydroelectric dam's destruction, the tiny town of Dufur hadn't really survived.

To my shock, my years in the Wasteland had transformed the town into the boutique-adorned entrance to an exclusive enclave surrounded by wrought-iron topped stone walls and sculpted topiary: Olympian Heights.

A tier three mananet hit me only moments before Mihail pulled us up to a manned security gate. A sudden spike in power drew my attention to rune-shaped ward stones seamlessly integrated into the wall. The guard inclined his head in welcome as something in the truck reassured the wards that we belonged.

What would've happened if we weren't carrying a ward key?

The moment we slid from the sculpted corridor concealing the neighborhood it became clear the owners of Olympian Heights wouldn't have risked some neighbor's kids with active defenses like those I'd encountered in that hidden temple deep in the Congo.

Upscale half-million dollar houses soon gave way to their more lavish cousins.

"Someone was killed *here?*"

Duval grunted through a taut jaw.

How?

"Ullie was the Boss's trusted lieutenant. She worked one of the most lucrative downtown territories."

Mihail didn't add anything further. He turned off to one side rather than drive us into the furthest depths of the upscale neighborhood. I'm not sure how my faith in humanity could've survived if the fake beggar had lived in a house worth more than Dad had earned in his lifetime.

What do you want to bet Adam has a place out here?

Mihail pulled into a driveway which led to the four-car garage. The drive in and of itself could have parked six. Dad's house could've moved into the beggar's home with room for a brother and maybe a pet shed.

Duval's lieutenant was dead. Even so, I had a hard time feeling bad for her. She'd begged for a living, taking enough potential handouts from genuine homeless to live in luxury enough to satisfy probably even Adam's greed.

I fought down indignation, following up the driveway. I studied the professionally manicured lawns of someone who begged on downtown sidewalks. Lawn gnomes took note of us, heads shifting so slowly it was hard to catch. The wizard eyes in their grinning, bearded faces took us in with glassy stares. A greenhouse affair dominated an unfenced backyard flanked by a large barbeque pit.

Wrinkling brows pushed my frown down further. "Forgetting

the difficulty of anyone getting into this place to commit a murder, why would someone painting anti-homeless messages in blood want to kill someone who obviously wasn't indigent?"

"Let's go inside," Duval said.

"Did she have a family?"

"We are her family," Duval said.

"Besides you?"

"Shaela is modeling in Milan this month," Duval said.

"Sister? Daughter?"

"Wife."

"Any kids?"

Mihail gave me a flat look. "Girls can't get girls pregnant."

"Mihail, do not be so old-fashioned." Duval shook his head. "Forgive him, Mister Graham. I do not believe either were ready to settle down yet."

"Their parties are definitely not child-friendly," Mihail's chuckles stopped abruptly in response to Duval's dark expression.

Mihail placed a hand on a DNA reader. It flashed green and slid aside to reveal a runeguard lock.

My brows rose.

Mihail touched runes in rapid order, opened the door and gestured me inside.

Bloody heel prints trailed across the hardwood foyer, smeared on a welcome mat inside rather than out. I jumped sideways off the prints, head whipping back and forth. No police tape or evidence markers dotted the floor. A sudden, unsettled feeling crept into my gut.

"The police haven't been here yet?"

"You will be the first to investigate," Duval said.

"Look, Duval, maybe you aren't aware of this, but I'm—"

"An ex-convict who is now in an as of yet unreported crime scene."

Well, shit.

9

WOMEN TROUBLES

Ullie's living room was as monochromatic as Doctor Porter's office, but rather than plunge me into a bad noir film, it felt like the set of a Vampire movie mansion. Chrome-framed, white leather furniture atop a black area rug sprinkled with white roses.

The victim's patched, green army jacket hung partially off a white leather chaise lounge. Her disemboweled body lay awkwardly sprawled atop a swamp of smoky glass shards and mostly dry blood, lying inside the chrome skeleton of a large coffee table. A gun lay just beyond the fingers of her left hand. A shallow porcelain bowl partially covered a circle of burnt carpet surrounding melted stone tiles. I stared at the scene, trying to figure out what I could and couldn't touch.

This is such a bad idea.

I circled the body. Ullie still wore the old combat boots of her 'work uniform.' The footprints leaving the scene suggested a woman killer, but something about the scene nagged at me. I bent next to her gun and nearly fainted. Ullie had owned a state of the art Government Issue firebolter.

Her killer left that behind?

Adam and I had argued for weeks when F.M.L.E.—the State Department's version of SMLE often referred to as female—had offered Thoth a contract to design them a lethal weapon. When we'd refused the assignment, EvoKorp had seized the opportunity. Looking back, winning that argument might've been the beginning of the end.

My eyes strayed to the melted stone.

If a firebolter hits you at all, their bolts are always lethal.

I frowned back at the scene.

Adam hadn't let me refuse the contract to turn my ability to sense magic into an early version of the magic sniffers used for forensics by FMLE or their local counterparts. Our version had worked, but Thoth had lost the contract to another arcanology company less concerned about the ways such magical Geiger counters might be misused.

I'd never taken the sniffer's spell development far enough to let me or some construct see residual magical auras. I inhaled. The reek of spilled intestines dominated the scent, combining with smoke to almost cover a burnt popcorn aroma.

This is pointless. I'm not a detective or a forensics tech.

I shook my head, opening my mouth to tell Duval he had the wrong guy. The hungry intensity watching me reminded me of his revolver—uncomplicated but deadly. There was no escaping. I had to find a way to track this killer and with luck, get SMLE to capture him before Duval.

I could try to form a thaumaturgic link between the bloody footprints and the shoes that made them—though I'd have to adjust the magic to account for the much-nearer body.

Two and a half prints stained the white roses between Ullie and the melted stone.

"Are you planning on letting SMLE in on this?"

Duval shook a grim expression back and forth. "This is a family affair. We're going to handle this internally."

I wasn't part of his family, but there wasn't much point in

correcting him. Mihail wasn't immediately forthcoming, but Duval instructed him to loan me a knife. I cut out a bloody section of carpet to track. A thought struck me.

"Before I track this killer, I want to see what I'm dealing with. Where is the surveillance feed?"

Duval smiled at Mihail. "A survivor, like I said."

Mihail glowered at me.

Duval picked up a remote and switched the television on to a multi-pane display. The feed had been staged to display a clear, clean house. The shallow bowl rested in the center of the coffee table, filled with glass beads now lost in the debris beneath Ullie.

He hit play.

The scene came to life.

An elegant looking woman in heels came up to the front door, set a hand on the DNA scanner and a few moments later keyed in the runeguard code. She walked through the foyer, the living room and into the kitchen. She returned with a Henkel butcher knife. It twisted in her hand as she scanned the living room. A moment later, she stepped up against a living room wall out of sight of the foyer.

She stood against the wall unmoving.

Duval fast forwarded the feed.

"Wait," I said.

"There's nothing to see."

"She doesn't move?"

"No."

I frowned. "Not at all?"

Duval shrugged. "She just waits."

My frown grew.

He let the feed return to normal after what the recording's timestamp said had been hours. Shaela remained against the wall, not even to go to the bathroom.

Ullie entered the house, throwing her jacket down on the chaise. The other woman stepped from cover.

Ullie turned, saw her and lit up. "Shaela? What are you doing home early?"

"Ulysses Amanda Binds."

Ullie's brow wrinkled. "Shaela?"

"You are a murderer, and you must die!" Shaela lunged.

The first cut tore only cloth. Ullie took up a defensive stance that spoke of at least a self-defense education if not full martial arts training.

"What the hell, Shaela?"

Shaela charged, holding the knife close until the last moment. She thrust. Ullie tried to knock the blow out of line, but the strength behind it drove the tip into Ullie, if slightly off target.

Ullie punched Shaela in the throat.

Shaela didn't so much as flinch.

Ullie backed away, cradling her cut arm. "Call Duval."

A communications hologram sprang from Ullie's wrist as she backed away. Reversed words rolled across the display.

A cylinder of shimmering green sprang up along the border of the area rug. A moment later, darker green sparkles bolstered the wall, cutting off Ullie's phone from Edison power.

Ullie threw herself through the sixth-seventh rez wall, hands scrambling to open a decorative cabinet. She snatched a box from the dark wood recesses and laid a thumb on the lock.

Shaela charged through the still-powered circles.

Ullie produced the firebolter, raised its barrel and hesitated.

Shaela sidestepped the first shot, letting it impact against the sixth-seventh rez wall. The magical equivalent of runny napalm cascaded flame down the wall.

Shaela backpedaled, snatching up the shallow bowl.

Ullie sidestepped the burning floor and extended the firebolter through the barrier. Tears streamed down her face.

She fired.

Shaela brought up the bowl, circling Ullie and catching two

blasts within a sixth-seventh cylinder. Her knife lashed out, slicing Ullie's wrist. The firebolter flew from Ullie's grasp.

The knife flashed again, spraying droplets of blood in a surreal arch as the blade disemboweled Duval's lieutenant.

A glance at him found the bum Mafioso as still as stone.

Blood gushed over Shaela but didn't alter her clothes.

My brows knitted together.

Shaela tossed the shallow bowl atop the burning floor, combining the fire of several firebolter spots in a greenish, milky white cage.

Why did she stop the fire?

Shaela stooped over Ullie, studying the dead woman with a pensive expression. A moment later she dipped two fingers into the welling blood and wrote the same message as before—sans my name. When she finished the iterations necessary to complete the note, Shaela strode from the scene, unburnt and unbloodied.

My extended hand received the remote. I rewound, shifting my gaze from the security images and the disarray at my feet. It wasn't a large indention in the blood splatter, and I might've missed it without the video, but some of Ullie's blood had landed on Shaela rather than the carpet.

Yet there isn't a visible drop on Shaela anywhere.

Cosmetic illusion magic could cover blood stains—not the good charms. Top of the line illusions adapted to prevent shrouding their user in the uncanny valley and drawing attention to the illusion itself. A cheap one, however, just displayed as it was programmed, like thick makeup over the bruises of domestic abuse.

No cheap illusion would've fooled Ullie.

I studied the floor. Bloody high heel tracks painted a perfect trail to the exit, onto the mat and no further—my missing scrap notwithstanding.

Not another droplet anywhere. Where did all that blood go? How did the killer react to the firebolter so fast? Terror at their reputation should've at least cost the killer a moment's hesitation.

I handed the remote back to Duval and regarded the message painted on the wall. The killer waited for her victim for hours. Neither the conflict nor killing Ullie seemed to have phased Shaela. She waited, killed Ullie, and then took the time to write a message in her victim's cooling blood. Even her exit seemed unrushed.

This just doesn't make any sense.

Shaela called Ullie a murderer. I had no idea as to the backstory involved, but the emotion behind that kind of accusation would've been as intense as the murder was brutal.

Yet Shaela had seemed cold, almost amoral...like that elf.

"There isn't enough blood," Mihail said.

"Yeah," I said. "I noticed."

"The killer moved too fast and remained untouched by all the blood," Mihail said.

I folded my arms. "Other than the footprints."

"Elders in the old country spoke of the blood drinkers."

I didn't hide my derision. "Vampires?"

Mihail shrugged.

Duval stared at Ullie without comment.

The idea that the attacker had been some kind of vampire was ludicrous. At the same time, folklore and tales spun myths around vampires and other blood drinkers. The myths varied almost as considerably as the many species offered modern man in books and film, but most myths contained some truth.

My head shook without my direction. "It can't be vampires."

Mihail spit out a single petulant word. "Why?"

Because it's ridiculous? Because they don't exist? Because it entered during sunlight hours? Because I really don't want something like that in my life?

Duval broke the uneasy silence. "That woman was not Shaela."

I glanced up at him.

He squared his shoulders. "I verified her alibi, which means this killer can use magic."

I'd had plenty of time to review the night at Seufert Fells Dam. Chalk it up to dying, ley line overdose, even hallucinations, but I'd been convinced that the spirit inside Boss Golem had been an elf. When the fey had turned back up in my alley, my certainty crystalized into fact.

Elves had orchestrated an attack on the rhet, using the rodent fey to draw their goblin enemies into our world. The ultimate plan involved rhet bait and goblin blood to turn our populace into ravening demi-goblins. Taken in that light, the existence of something like vampires didn't seem as farfetched as I might like.

What if the illusion wasn't layered cosmetic charms? What if it was true glamour? Were the legends of vampires ultimately born from some kind of fey?

I met Duval's eye. "I need to consult someone. Can I come back here later?"

"We can't leave Ullie there for long, even with the air conditioner running on full," Duval said.

"This evening?"

Duval handed me a business card. "Call for a pickup."

I stared at the card, licking my lips.

"Problem?" Duval asked.

"I don't have access to a phone."

"Sure you do," Duval's smile verged on cruel. "The Manger has one."

WE PICKED up my SMLE observers not a block from the gates of Olympian Heights. Seeing them so far out of their jurisdiction troubled me. Neither Duval nor Mihail seemed concerned, so I tried to push SMLE from my thoughts. My efforts proved only partially successful as my mind focused on Adam.

These guys are probably on Adam's payroll, but I have no idea how to prove it. Maybe I should just tell Sunny and leave them to her. It's not like I don't have plenty of problems to sort out on my own—like Kenrith.

A niggling little voice in the back of my thoughts kept insisting I show greater concern about my next reunion with the little rhet knight. As part of an experiment, I'd cast Thoth's Glamour on Tunoh, Kenrith's crippled and apparently only daughter. I'd learned too late that Adam had not only bastardized my original spell but added a timer component that would undo all the spell's effects. Before I'd been able to sort out that problem, Tunoh had subsequently professed her love and intention to marry me, defied her father to save me, and then taken considerable abuse coming to my rescue once more.

The little rhet knight hadn't let me see her since. He'd refused to answer when I asked about her health. I'd learned only that she survived. If his people still watched over me, they did it discretely enough not to get caught.

Or they're leaving me alone like I told them I wanted.

Tunoh was an amazing young woman, but I hadn't fallen in love with the rodent fey. My concern was simple gratitude.

She did save my life a few times.

Pushing for a meeting with the rhet wasn't my best choice, but I needed an expert in fey magic no matter how much crow I'd have to choke down asking for help.

A glance out the window showed the edges of Seufert Fells growing up around us. Few lights shined in the poor neighborhoods interspaced by the occasional orange glow of a trashcan fire.

Ullie's firebolter bulled its way to the forefront of my thoughts. The killer had defended herself against the attack with uncommon alacrity.

Would I have been so quick? Is there a way to build a passive defense that wouldn't rely on reacting the right way in seconds?

The fake Shaela exampled the simplest means. A seventh-sixth resonance barrier blocked the fire and kept the heat from escaping the containing circle. She'd also used a porcelain bowl to prevent the physical aspects of the assault. Unless I wanted to carry around crockery, adding a fifth rez underneath would be best.

Would a first rez extinguish the fire?

The years I'd spent globetrotting to research old spells in ruins and temples had reinforced over and over that conservation of mass and energy held true with magic too. The firebolter stored concentrated magical energy in crystalline batteries built into the grip, but that was only part of the equation. A parallel magazine held tiny orbs. Each was constructed of three layers. A tiny first rez sphere encased a hardened shell of the same stuff they use to make chemical fire logs. Inside that, the components for adhesion and flame spells each occupied one hemisphere.

Depressing a thumb on the safety release empowers the gun's hammer. The magically heated hammer strikes a fire rune into the ball, breaking the first rez sphere an instant before the crystal injects a more substantial charge. A reaction similar to a tiny solid-fuel rocket ejects the round as the whole thing lazes into magical fire.

The best defense against something like that would be not getting hit.

The greatest danger from a firebolter was the extreme heat combined with the adhesion charm. The sudden flame would consume immediate oxygen, and suffocation was Heaven compared to what happened if the victim happened to be inhaling.

A vision of burning out the lungs of a gangbanger that'd tried to mug me flashed across my thoughts.

I cradled the arm sporting overlapped Smurf Band-Aids. I'd been mad as hell at the time, and the punk had tried to pry my gold-plated Wasteland jacks out of my forearm. He'd almost certainly died. A small part of me twisted with remorse. The rest refused to dwell on it a moment longer.

He forced the altercation. What's done is done.

Three likely development paths for a defensive construct pushed away bad memories.

The first required designing an elaborate armor construct of overlapping fifth-seventh cells powered by continual mananet access and probably backed by a charged mana crystal. I had no access to the tools or facility necessary to build something that complex.

Willie's PG designs seemed to include a similar cellular circle armor for his firefighters. What kind of fabric could allow a human to withstand that kind of heat diffusion? Asbestos?

Alternatively, some kind of heat-energy exchange construct might work, probably anchored to ground in order to diffuse the energy into Earth's mass.

How would that affect the ground, though?

Considering my mishap with the ley energy and nearly suffocating myself, I did a couple of quick calculations. Rough mathematics reassured me turning my footing to magma required more shots than a single firebolter magazine contained.

The last method offered me the most practical promise, not only to stop firebolter attacks but to deal with eyeGuardians in panicky hands. A properly prepared receptacle could theoretically absorb the elemental magic and allow harnessing the flames offensively.

Mihail pulled Duval's truck to a stop in front of my alcove. I made a mental note to keep my eyes out for a discarded lighter and got out.

Duval already had his window down. "Mihail will return in three hours, Mister Graham. I expect results. Soon."

I thought I was calling him. How soon is soon? Do I even want to know? Why can't people just leave me alone?

THE TUMULTUOUS SKY darkened my alley enough that even before twilight I felt little risk in calling out for Kenrith or his people. At worst, SMLE would think my marbles washed down the gutters too

I called.

And I called.

I called some more.

My three hours drained from the hourglass with the icy rainwater. It occurred to me that I might've been right, that the rhet had finally left me alone. The only problem with the theory stemmed from something Kenrith had once said about tolerating me in *their* alley. There was no way the prideful knight would move his warren just to be rid of me—quite the opposite in fact.

"Why do young girls always go for the dumb, pretty ones?"

The voice whipped me around. My box backed up against the slatted chain-link. There were no holes in the cardboard and none but the one flap had been torn away from its industrial staples. Nonetheless, two distinctly female rhet in housecoats eyed me with glowing, electric blue eyes.

"I'm not sure he's that pretty," the second rhet said. "Not too late to talk her out of this farce."

The first put a thoughtful finger to her chin just below her prominent teeth. "No, letting Kenrith have his way would make him insufferable."

A hundred thoughts raced through my mind. I'd scoured countless books and articles on the fey. One thing which repeated over and again was their enjoyment of being superior. I hurriedly spun around onto my knees and bowed my head to the floor. "I'm honored to receive two rhet matrons. May I offer you a bologna sandwich?"

The first rhet smirked. "Still, I like his manners."

"Did you note how casually he tried to bind us with the hospitality laws?" the second asked. "I will accept your cunningly offered salt and bread, human."

I dug into my rucksack to reclaim the heavily battered bread bag. I removed bologna already between crushed pieces of bread and added my last packets of Chick-Fil-A mayonnaise and mustard. As an afterthought, I set the packets down and ripped the sandwich into two.

"Miladies."

The second rhet snorted as she accepted and turned the sandwich over in her long-fingered paws. "This is more like dough than bread, you realize."

"Ugh," the first chewed. "It makes up for it with the salt, Yshtiina. Can't you afford the good bologna, dear?"

Yshtiina nibbled the edge of her sandwich. "I'll have some mustard if you please."

"Do you have any pickle relish?" the first asked.

"Noli, you and your damned pickle addiction," Yshtiina said.

"I'm not addicted," Noli's mischievous grin echoed Tunoh's. "Obsessed and infatuated, but I can stop whenever I want."

Yshtiina added mustard, nibbled the edge and shuddered, giving me and the sandwich a sidelong look.

"You don't have to eat it if you'd rather not," I said.

"Waste not, want not. Besides," Noli gestured at my empty bread bag, "you gave us your last sandwich."

"Which speaks well of Tunoh's choice."

"Tunoh? You're her mothers. I haven't seen her. Is she all right?"

Both rhet stopped eating and fixed me with glares that emptied the words from my mouth.

Noli shook limp bread and bologna at me. "Our husband is irate with you. Tunoh is forbidden from seeing you."

Yshtiina dabbed her mouth with an edge of her housecoat. "And from letting you glimpse her."

Their claims didn't surprise me. In some ways, they were a huge load off. I liked Tunoh. I didn't want her to be hurt, but I didn't think a cross-species marriage with a rodent fairy that didn't come up to my knee had much future.

"Does that mean—what does that mean?"

Noli looked me up and down. I probably didn't look like much folded into the compact space. "We're here to decide that."

"Please, Mother Yshtiina, Mother Noli—"

"My proper name is Yshtiinataira, and hers is Avegnolia," Yshtiina snapped.

"He may call me Noli."

"He certainly may not," Yshtiina said.

"He has nice manners," Noli said.

"Doesn't matter," Yshtiina said.

"I ask for forgiveness, Yshtiinataira, Aveg—"

"It's like Magnolia, dear," Noli said. "Just call me Noli, regardless of what the old crone says."

Yshtiina's expression suggested doing so only at my own peril.

Noli bit off another mouthful of sandwich.

"But no matter what our decision regarding Tunoh, it will have nothing to do with what Kenrith commands," Yshtiina said. "Men can't think right when it comes to their daughter's wedding."

"Or breeding." Noli chuckled through stuffed cheeks. "They always think even the daughters clearly not destined to be matrons won't ever spread their knees."

It wasn't the possibility that the wedding had been called off that darkened my expression, though their shared expression suggested they thought so. If they'd come to determine my suitability as Tunoh's husband, they hadn't come to my call. They wouldn't help me with Ullie's body, and Mihail was due back any time.

"Tunoh is once more crippled," Yshtiina said.

"Worse, her remaining leg is badly broken," Noli said.

"Can't you heal her?"

Noli gestured to distended teats hinted at by her housecoat. "Do I look like an unmarried virgin to you?"

I opened my mouth, closed it once more and then spoke. "That's a trap, and I'm not bumbling into it."

A superior smile curled the corners of Yshtiina's mouth. "You might just be a Magus. Why did you call for our husband?"

They were long done with their sandwiches and looking for a drink before I completed telling them about Ullie. I might've finished faster, but Noli forced me to go all the way back to Caleb's attack on Fells Overlook Bridge to provide her context.

Probably just wants to see how far she can push me.

Yshtiina's expression seemed to permanently sour when I reached the part about the Ottiren, but she neither left nor made a comment. When my tale brought me to their arrival, sound held its breath.

A moment later a vehicle pulled into the alley and Mihail leaned on the horn.

"We'll assist you," Yshtiina said.

Noli shouted beneath cupped ears. "If nothing else than to shut that Bulgarian bastard up."

Bulgarian?

"I'm reserving judgment, but none of the...," Yshtiina made a warding gesture of some sort, "Amfyries have been seen on this continent...ever."

"To be fair, none of the other fair folk have been either," Noli said. "Except those twice-be-damned goblins."

"What are *Amfyries?*"

Yshtiina repeated her gesture. "A species of wild fey responsible for your vampire myths."

"Filthy bloodsuckers," Noli said. "Why anyone would want to tell stories about them is beyond me."

Mihail leaned on the horn again.

"Not that I'd mind introducing your driver to one," Noli said.

10

FATAL DECISIONS

Yshtiina and Noli accompanied me back to Ullie's—ostensibly to see me at work. They summoned a handful of younger sons to fill my jacket pockets.

"You say this is magic?" Mihail gave the rats peeking from my pockets several, shifty glances. "Carrying *rats*?"

"Consider it an expert consultation."

Mihail shook his head. "If the boss keeps you around, you should see a shrink. He owns quite a few good doctors."

I gave him a flat look. "Are we there yet?"

Mihail stopped the truck at the top of the driveway. Lights illuminated the house like someone was home. "Is the real Shaela back?"

"You know this is an age of technology, right wizard?"

"Well, is she?"

He shook his head, muttered his way to the front door and opened it for me. I followed. As soon as we stepped foot on the driveway, the rhet youths started circling me. An inky soap bubble grew up and around us, my hair tingling with potent magic.

"Finally," Noli said. "I thought the silence was going to kill me."

"You were abnormally restrained," Yshtiina said.

Noli screamed.

My eyes darted first to our surroundings, then Mihail and finally back to Noli.

Her demure smile seemed out of place. "Tension breaker. Had to be done."

"I thought you were familiar with glamour, human," Yshtiina said.

"Yeah, though I don't see the point in making me invisible to Mihail who drove us here."

Yshtiina and Noli shared a look.

Noli patted my chest. "Pretty, but dumb."

"The boys aren't making us invisible so much as camouflaging all but you," Yshtiina said. "Your...associate will see you, the rats in your pockets and most everything you do, but he won't hear us talking. If you speak, the boys will decide whether or not to let him hear based on what you say."

I considered her explanation. To accomplish what she claimed, the spell had to be on a time delay similar to radio station broadcasts to ensure censorship time for live interviews.

Wonder if I could get one of the rhet to teach me their version of glamour.

Mihail eyed the rats as I stepped by him into Ullie's place. Both of Tunoh's mothers stilled, noses raised and sniffing. A moment later they flashed down my body as if gravity were optional.

They scented the footprints.

"Expand the circle boys," Yshtiina flashed me a look. "You could assist by moving closer to the body."

"Yes, ma'am." I did as instructed.

"Imagine if he's that pliant in bed," Noli said.

"He'd crush you," Yshtiina said. "And Tunoh would probably take issue."

Noli glanced away. "I meant for Tunoh."

"Sure you did," Yshtiina turned to me. "No amfyries have been here."

Noli took another sniff. "Chemical accelerants, evocation and illusion magic," she sniffed again and frowned. "Gun oil?"

Yshtiina frowned. "Maybe. Only one human bled here."

"Wait," I said. "Does that mean you smell Ullie's blood and blood from something that isn't human?"

Noli patted me. "Don't name them, dear. It only makes it harder to stay objective."

"I scent the women who mate here," Yshtiina sniffed again and scowled. "A Chihuahua, the lingering scent of strangers long gone and more recently the car's owner, your driver and you."

I frowned. "Can glamour cover scent as well?"

Noli beamed. "Not so dumb after all."

"But this smells like human illusion magic, not fey glamour," Yshtiina countered.

"Still, he's not as dumb as we expected," Noli said.

"Thanks?" I said.

"There is something, though," Yshtiina said.

Ullie's killer hadn't used glamour, but neither Yshtiina nor Noli picked up any scents. I hadn't killed Ullie any more than I'd killed Wayne. It seemed unlikely Duval would go to the trouble to hire me if he had killed them.

If he wanted me dead, he could've dumped me from the truck into the Columbia.

My focus shifted to Mihail. The big mafia lieutenant could've killed Ullie. He had access. The time to test the rhet youths' abilities had come.

"Mihail, please show me the door security logs." I paused long enough to give the boys a moment and continued. "Would you ladies please sniff Mihail for Ullie's blood?"

"No," Mihail said.

"Thought you'd never ask," Noli said.

Yshtiina's voice mixed exasperation and concern. "Noli."

I squared up with Mihail as he approached. I fought Wasteland instinct and met his eye. "I need to see whose security code let Shaela in before Ullie came home."

He pushed a finger into me. "No. You don't. The boss doesn't need you or your travelling flea circus."

Noli stopped mid sniff and planted hands on her hips. "I most certainly do not have fleas."

Mihail hadn't been overly friendly, but the sudden open hostility took me by surprise. The question had been meant to draw him closer to Noli's nose. The room's temperature rose. "Tell that to your boss. I don't want to be here. Hell, you're the one who threatened to knock me out again to get me here."

"And we should've chucked you back in the Columbia, mumbling to yourself."

The rhet at my feet cringed. Yshtiina's tail snaked out, snapping at the rhet circling us. Mumbled apologies reached me.

Mihail poked me again. "Walking around, acting better than us. Carrying filthy rats in your pockets, you're a sick freak."

"Filthy?!" Noli exclaimed.

Yshtiina wrapped a tail around Noli's waist, and the warning tone returned. "Noli."

I closed my fists, missing my Wasteland physique. "What's your problem?"

"I know who you are now," Mihail growled. "I looked you up just now to confirm, and you sure as hell ain't one of us."

Gooseflesh sunk fangs into my calves as the house's heaters blew hot air up my neck. My left knuckles pistoned up and down, driving the gears of my mental prediction engine to higher RPMs.

"I'm not one of you because I'm not a crook starving real homeless by pretending to be one?" I threw a fist into Mihail's face.

He was ready for it.

Mihail seized the punch mid-throw, pivoted me by my

extended arm and slammed brick-hard blows into my ribs. He released me with the last hit to stumble backward.

I slipped in the blood, falling to the carpet.

The firebolter lay just in my reach.

If I grabbed it, I could...what, kill him?

I blinked away the failed scenario projection.

That didn't work. What if...

"I'm not one of you because I'm not a crook starving real homeless by pretending to be one?" I threw a fist toward Mihail's face, pulling the punch at the last moment to duck in with my other fist.

He was ready for it.

Mihail grabbed the arm before I could complete my jab. He yanked me into a hard left to the face. The blow staggered me. His right grabbed me behind the head and slammed my face into an upward rushing knee. A crunch, searing pain and a gush of blood proceed a backward fall that could've classified as a launch.

I slipped in the blood, falling stunned to the carpet near the firebolter.

I grabbed the magical gun.

Mihail drew his pistol in a smooth motion. Three explosions proceeded pain in my chest and then blackness.

I blinked.

How was he ready for that too?

Truth be told, my imagination supplied Mihail's readiness and capabilities, so ultimately, it was my fault he kept ahead of me. Before the Wasteland, plans composed in this fashion rarely deviated sufficiently to change the outcome. A hundred years in a living scenario honed those instincts. I trusted those feelings, relied on them. If my gut informed my imagination that Mihail would act as I'd predicted, I'd move forward on that hypothesis until new data changed the variables.

"I'm not one of you because I'm not a crook starving real

homeless by pretending to be one?" I threw a low jab toward his gut, followed by an immediate fist to Mihail's face.

Mihail took the body blow. He stepped back out of the punch's path and grabbed my extended arm with his left. He turned me, opening up my defenses and brought down a right-handed hammer blow to my head. Another followed.

I tried to block with my left, but his control of my right arm let him spin me out of position. A kick slammed into my lower back, sending me sprawling near the firebolter.

I rolled to my back without touching the weapon only to find him almost on top of me with his pistol out. I slammed both feet into him, one heel to a knee and the other his groin.

Mihail tumbled backward, tripping on Ullie's body.

I came up with the firebolter and fired.

Ullie's living room filled with Mihail's screams and the scent of cooking meat.

"He might be worthy of Tunoh after all," Yshtiina said.

We took Mihail's truck back to Seufert Fells, parked it several blocks away from my alley and hiked back to my box. The rhet disappeared into their warren, and I crawled into my box to sleep off the ordeal. I'd barely entered REM when a voice woke me.

"Mister Graham?"

I poked my head out to meet the barrel of Duval's pistol. The ear-ringing shot died sometime after I did.

I stepped back from Mihail, rubbing my temple.

"You're not going to fight him?" Noli asked.

I shook my head. "You don't know what you're talking about."

"I have sisters. A daughter." Mihail snarled. "They should've castrated you in the woods and left you to the wolves."

Every instinct told my eyes to drop, but I fixed them on Mihail's accusing gaze. "You don't know what happened, no matter what you think."

Everything went still.

For a moment, I thought he might start the fight I couldn't win

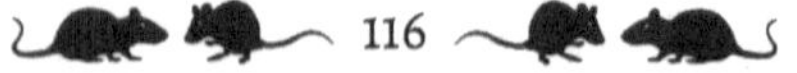

even if I dropped him. Tension built until the room practically crackled.

"Shaela," Mihail said.

"What?"

"I think you're a lying sack of shit, but the boss wants us to help you," Mihail said. "Shaela unlocked the door."

My eyes shot down to the rhet. "Was Shaela's scent as fresh as Ullie's?"

"What?" Mihail asked.

I stomped a foot near one of the tightly circling rhet. Steel flashed into his hand. Yshtiina shifted from sniffing to giving me one of those mother looks they reserve for other people correcting their children.

"Which one is Shaela?" Noli asked.

"Ullie's wife. She lives here."

Mihail didn't react, so the boys had corrected their mistake.

"No." Yshtiina snapped.

The boys cringed again, only relaxing when they realized her angry retort had been for me.

"We're done here," Yshtiina said.

I didn't agree, but I wasn't about to gainsay her. On the other hand, if I did, it might eliminate the whole engagement problem. While I considered whether any argument would help mend fences while continuing the look around, the rhet raced away in a fairy-dust-trailing blur. Noli looked up at me, patting my leg and disappeared behind the others.

Well, shit.

Considering the scene didn't offer any fresh ideas. More than anything, I ended up staring at the firebolter unable to find any new thought beyond a desire to own it.

Guess we are done.

Stepping around Mihail, I headed for the door. "I'll find my own way back."

Mihail's hand slapped down onto my shoulder. "Not happen-

ing. The only way you're disappearing while the boss has me chaperoning you is a permanent trip out of town."

By river no doubt.

"Besides, there's no way I'm letting you linger so you can swipe that firebolter," Mihail said.

Exiting the house brought me a pleasant surprise—or so I thought. The rhet lurked just behind the truck's rear wheels. Mihail let me into the back seat. The rhet joined me, but the silent treatment on the way back bristled with icicles.

THE RHET VANISHED the moment Mihail dumped us in the alley. The overcast night deepened the alley's darkness. At the nearer end, an occasional orange glow illuminated the interior of a SMLE cruiser. I hadn't given much thought to the absence of my watchers until I saw one.

The moms glamoured our departure for some reason?

"Pardon me, Magus?"

I followed the small voice to one of Yshtiina's workforce. He—assuming he remained a he—was smaller than Tunoh, though the bald tail he cradled seemed longer. "Yes?"

The little rhet studied his tail. "Begging your pardon, Magus, but if it pleases you, I am Weejok. Mother Yshtiinataira brought me along to—to give me something to do."

"What something?"

He mumbled so softly I couldn't hear.

"What?"

His whole body seemed to shrink. "I was to see if you spoke ill of them after they'd left."

"You didn't give me very long."

He shook his head. "Tunoh has cared for me. She thinks—"

"You've seen Tunoh? Talked to her? Is she all right?"

Weejok found a way to become smaller without magic. "I am

not allowed to speak of that with you."

Heat bubbled up from my toes. "Then do you want to tell me why you're talking to me?"

"There was another scent at the house, Magus."

"Why didn't Yshtiina or Noli mention it?"

"Forgive me, Magus, but the mothers are aging. I have the best nose of my honored father's get."

"Is Kenrith your father?"

Weejok shook his head. "Ahbnar."

The name struck me like lightning. Ahbnar had died trying to stop an actress from using Glamour and becoming a monster. She'd eaten him first before rampaging through the rhet to get Biuntcha. I'd helped them kill her.

"You're sure there was another scent?"

He studied his tail, ears pressed to his head. "Yes, Magus."

"Could you recognize it again?"

He nodded, refusing to look at me.

"Thank you, Weejok. Let me know if you scent it again."

Weejok flashed me a shy smile and raced away.

I stared after him a moment before remembering the note tucked away in a pocket. My mother had always been a straight-forward soul, not simple—though many believed that at first—but a person who simplified life by not participating in a lot of the dance steps most of us juggle to survive in society. Her note contained little information and no subtle subtext.

Dad generally handled their interactions when subtlety or diplomacy were called for. He shielded her much as he'd shielded Zahda while expecting his sons to learn and emulate him.

I'd missed the breakfast date in jail—not that I was heart-broken about it, though maybe a little guilty. I really didn't want to have breakfast with them. Hell, I really didn't want them in town at all. Sunny's halfhearted attempt to do as I asked had nearly guaranteed they wouldn't leave without some kind of get together.

I could just try to avoid them until they leave, but it might be better to bite the bullet so they go before they get dragged into this mess.

Duval seemed ready to blow my brains out if I didn't help find Ullie's killer, and I wouldn't put it past him to grab Mom and Dad for additional leverage. Hell, Mihail might even suggest such a move. He'd barely restrained his desire to beat me to a pulp, and only out of fear or respect of Duval.

Could part of his animosity be fear I might supplant him?

I pushed away my problems with Mom and Dad, Duval and Mihail for the moment. I needed to complete some of my mounting tasks if for no other reason than to give myself a little breathing room.

Breathing room?

An idea sent my thoughts into a tangent. Truth be told, Duval's problem didn't seem easily dispatched and while one meal with my parents might make them leave, such a meeting had the potential to evolve into some long-term nastiness.

The Ottiren's problem had seemed just as involved until it dawned on me that with a little testing, an eighth rez circle might make it possible to provide Celilo air within a fifth rez barrier.

Or at least create a long-range snorkel so I could look things over.

Until I had the time and equipment to work out some form of breathing underwater, the Ottiren's task had to keep its designation as a complicated project.

I ordered my lists of challenges by priority.

The late hour offered an excellent shield against my aging parents, so I pushed them down the list—mostly because I just didn't want to deal with Dad. Unfortunately, the late hour didn't solve anything with the equally nocturnal and diurnal rhet. Maybe I was a coward, but I decided to put off my Tunoh issues. They'd sort themselves out one way or another. I hadn't slept with Tunoh or anything like that. The mothers hadn't offered dire warnings, so how angry could Kenrith really be?

Duval's issue involved past and future murders. That trumped the Ottiren's dining particulars. I'd done my research and had the beginnings of the plan. Besides, Celilo had been under water for almost six decades. Still, I kept the Indian shapeshifter at the top of the list out of an aversion to being gnawed. Sunny would handle Adam and whatever would happen with Mimir would just wait.

I needed more food, some odds and ends to improve my survival conditions as well as components for tracking Ullie's killer. Duval had paid me a modest amount of money. That meant a long hike outside the city's hub to thrift stores and, if necessary, a Walmart.

I settled in for the night, nibbling Mimir leftovers and planning my shopping trip.

Finding Ullie's killer required a DNA tracking spell. To search for the miniscule amount beneath the killer's shoes without being drawn back to Ullie's corpse, I'd need something a bit more advanced than what I'd used with the Glamour components. Working out the runes and spell litany took less time than satisfying my stomach.

I went to sleep still hungry, saving the remaining food to fill my belly when I wouldn't be able to ignore the grumbling in dreams.

Cold woke me, but my limbs refused to wake. Pins and needles stabbed me everywhere. I shifted limb by limb, trying to restore circulation to my sluggish legs. I crawled from my box, wishing my spell preparations were complete or at least I'd raised a sixth rez barrier around my box to keep my body heat inside.

Willie was right. I need to be more careful.

It took longer than it probably should have to pack my rucksack with what I might need for the day. I trudged south, outward from Seufert Fells's center.

Working out the seeking spell in my head left me to inadver-

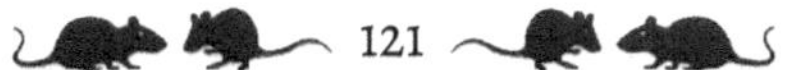

tently set a route right by the Manger. I realized my course a block ahead of time and stopped.

On the one hand, I could go into the Manger for a fresh cup of coffee and more of Grace's incredible food. On the other, going inside meant fueling the fire that drove Sunny to interfere in my life—maybe even running into Mom and Dad by accident.

I'd involved her in getting to the site of Boss Golem's attempted Glamour-pocalypse. I hadn't wanted to risk her, but I'd had neither the time nor resources to do anything else. Through some miracle, she'd stayed in the car and out of harm's way.

I turned aside, putting distance between me and warm, fresh but not entirely free coffee. A Salvation Army thrift store supplied me with another hamster ball and a dented aluminum compass with a wrist strap that might prove a useful construct for tracking spells. I also bought a beat-up old Zippo lighter in need of both fuel and flint before bankrupting that last of my release money for a portable Edison node receiver module.

Surprisingly, the store didn't have any old pull chains, so from there, I headed to a nearby Walmart. The greeter looked at me askance but didn't stop my entry. The lighting section had a decent selection of ceiling fan chains, but I passed them to the clearance selection instead. Sure enough, I found three cheap sports ball pull chains.

After hardware, I picked up a loaf of sliced French bread on clearance, some bologna, dollar hotdogs for variety, and used some of the money Duval paid me to buy a generic multi-tool with a knife blade.

It took a moment to repack in the Walmart foyer. The delay had nothing to do with the heater blasting down on my bench beside the coin-op toy machines.

Despite the possibility of curious onlookers, I connected my three pull chains before going outside. A rubber band wrapped my swatch of bloody carpet around the chains' intersection. Cold or no cold, I stepped outside, keeping close to the building to ensure enough power from Walmart's local mananet to intone my blood to blood seeking spell.

The temporarily enchanted pull chains reached out for blood matching that on the carpet scrap. The plastic baseball stretched its chain out one direction. The football strained one hundred and twenty degrees from the baseball.

I grinned down at my three dollar contraption.

The baseball pulled the chain slantways from the basketball knob in my hand.

The baseball pulls hardest, so it's reaching toward Ullie which means the football's drawing me to the blood residue on the killer's soles—unless she's given blood recently

I followed the football.

I trudged through a city's populace as they played the age-old game of ignoring what they didn't want to see. Wooden expressions pointedly didn't see my shabby attire. Conversations stilled as gentlemen locked eyes on me to ensure I didn't suddenly grow fangs and others I passed poised fingers over eyeSentinel or shifted far too close to moving traffic. A few of even the most skittish performed a double take when they realized the gravity-defying object in my fingers.

My passing created pedestrian gridlock once when my approach pinned the sidewalk's populace between one of the city's many beggars and me. Even on Duval's payroll, the thought of begging for a living—even a life as opulent as Ullie had—didn't sit right.

Advertisements leapt from storefronts and harangued all of us. The scent of grilled meat encouraged my stomach's vote to break out the new sandwich makings even if I hadn't stopped at Chick-Fil-A to replenish my condiment stores.

My planning nature desperately wanted me to pick the brains of long-term homeless to learn the best practices for survival and earning what little money I needed to keep myself fed.

Zahora offered...well, she offered a lot of things. It might be best to find a different teacher. The trick will be to talk to real homeless as opposed to Duval's crew without going inside the Manger.

The Edison converter's added weight dragged on my shoulders. I'd intended to sideline back to my alcove and hide the device, but my focus on the tracking spell dominated my attention so much, I'd traveled too far from home to justify going back.

Buildings grew progressively taller and then shorter as my tracker led into and out of downtown. I ended up back at the rebuilt riverfront. People bustled to and fro with that aimless haste of vacationers. A few wore Foretold event badges. While it had happened, I'd seldom met technical types with terminal vanity, leading me to conclude the badge-toting elven extras were either executives or Adam's shills.

An uneasy feeling edged into my gut.

I scanned my surroundings, searching for Caleb's van.

A similar van with a long, matching cargo trailer caught my eye.

A moment later the van transformed into a long serpent and opened wide jaws. Death glared down at me as its long body undulated a frantic back and forth swish that propelled it into striking distance.

I stared up at the beast, frozen by shock and terror.

A roar blasted me with hot, fetid breath and globs of saliva.

A moment's panic cemented my catatonic hesitation.

Could it be venom? Is this a poisonous—

The roar transformed into a blaring horn. The driver screamed at me from within the van's cab, making several rude gestures I hadn't seen before.

I rushed out of the street, heart knocking into my ribs so hard it slammed the breath from my lungs. I stared at the vehicle that had nearly eaten, then run me down.

What the hell?

A moment later I realized I'd fled to the Columbia's banks without any recollection of the intervening distance. My gaze

shifted to choppy river water. A soft tickle across my senses whispered notes of a siren song.

Is the Ley alive? Could that elf's warning have been true? Can it actually drive me mad?

When I pulled my gaze from the deep, brackish water, I realized the football stretched out over the Columbia. It took a moment to shake off an uneasy feeling that my seeking spell had fallen prey to the siren song.

Don't be stupid. The killer's just on the Washington side.

I stuffed the basketball through a collar button hole and turned my face east toward the Fells Overlook Bridge. When I came to the bridge's foot, I stopped.

When I'd been released a few weeks prior, the only concerns I had surrounded finding a way to survive homeless. I'd had no plans to contend with murderous vigilantes, cold-blooded killers, rogue fey, Adam's mistakes or magic in any form.

Instead of the peaceful struggle of pitting myself against the environment, I'd been harangued, guilt-tripped and blackmailed into danger time and again.

And I'm about to cross a bridge where I've already been abducted over a siren with a taste for my blood in order to chase a murderer. I might need to consider better life choices.

11

CHASING DEATH

Rather than mount the bridge, I edged down the banks to the space beneath it. A pair of ladies busied themselves scraping graffiti off into catch pots, chattering about what jewelry they'd make next and whose grandchildren were doing what.

Both flashed me easy smiles as I slipped around them and climbed the cement incline leading to the bridge's undercarriage. Cresting the rise brought empty nests for other homeless into view. Between them, a maintenance gangway I'd suspected might exist clung to the bridge's underside. A cage of iron mesh fenced off all access to the catwalk except through a chained and padlocked gate.

Without Razcolm or a friendly rhet, I'd run into trouble the first time I'd broken into one of the demi-goblins' apartments. The terminally vain victims of Adam's Glamour hadn't been stupid when it came to leaving their locks undone.

I'd been forced to retreat and regroup, pride stinging like lemon juice on road rash. I had a master's degree in arcanology, and yet my old third level DDO character had been better prepared to survive his world than I was mine.

Edging one of the nests granted me closer access to the gate. I knelt at the fence's foot, dug into my rucksack and withdrew a cheap, sock-wrapped bell. Careful to ensure I didn't ring the bell prematurely, I held the Christmas bell by its snowflake handle and removed its protective cover. An old rag gagged the clapper, but before I gave my construct free voice, I double checked the Sharpie runes remained intact.

I smiled.

Not a smudge.

A concealed wire caught my eye just as I removed the bell's gag. Tracking it behind the metal mesh brought my gaze to an alarm box. I cursed and repacked my door bell.

If I tripped the alarm, there were better than even odds I'd end up arrested somewhere between Oregon and Washington.

A sigh escaped me.

Guess I'll just have to chance another of Caleb's visits.

I hiked back up to the bridge proper and across. My concerns about Caleb quickly faded into the background as the wild fey power beneath the Columbia serenaded me with enthralling promises. As in sailors' tales of old, the siren played dirty pool. She reminded me how much I needed the offered power to deal with Ullie's murderer.

And it might not be wrong.

I tuned out the rational, logical arguments intended to enthrall, and marched across Fells Overlook Bridge—a man on a mission, not at all an addict running from his vice.

Once on the Washington side of the river, I stopped to catch my breath and choke down another dry sandwich. The break allowed me time to observe my tracker. The football edged sideways ever so slowly.

Killer's on the move.

The seeking spell pulled me through the maze of construction sites and manufacturing plants. Odd sized plots of land and the tracker's indifference to streets conspired to catch me in a few dead ends. I backtracked where necessary, keeping an eye on my surroundings in case Caleb or the Ottiren decided to put in an appearance.

I passed the Tacky Burger and judgmental convenience store.

My arm hair stood taller and looked around for danger. Other follicles followed suit, and I wasn't too prideful to do so as well.

The football yearned to go straight down the street into a factory complex. I veered side to side, even cutting right down an alley. The tracker focused on the factory.

No way is my luck that bad.

A few blocks later, I stared at chain-link separating me from the Thoth component factory that had packaged the tainted Glamour components.

Not far from where I met Wayne...or where Wayne died.

New razor wire replaced barbed and new video cameras topped every fourth fence post, swinging back and forth to cover every inch. The gate I'd followed a delivery truck through had been bolstered with a twin gate security chokepoint.

I orbited the block counter-clockwise, hoping the football would lead me onward. It turned, pointing consistently at the southern end of the factory—the opposite end I'd invaded only to be shot by Adam.

You've got to be kidding me.

A woman's blood-curdling scream rent the air.

Sunny's going to kill me.

With the lock system preventing unauthorized entrance through the gates, I bolted forward, unsure how I'd survive the bladed wire glinting down with sinister menace.

Movement caught my eye at the last moment.

A figure in shabby clothes hurried out of an alley on the factory's far side. The football pointed accusingly at the figure.

I ran.

Adrenaline and rising anger drove me, but the overlarge block stole what I had to give. I rounded the far corner breathing hard and nearly deaf from the pulse slamming in my ears.

The homeless woman strolled nonchalantly away with her back to me. Pushing my exhausted walk for all it was worth barely made up any ground on her.

"Hey!" I gasped. "Hey, you...stop, uh, in the name of Duval!"

She stopped and turned fully toward me.

Zahora?

Our eyes met.

Her soulless gaze stopped me dead in my tracks, colder than any I'd seen in the Wasteland. She considered me, and I could almost feel the cold calculation weighing my life.

I broke the connection, glancing down the alley she'd exited. The heat in my body fled for my throat, escaping piggyback on the scream of terror.

Zahora is dead.

She took one step toward me. A Seufert Fells police car stopped behind her and rolled down its window. The cops could've been patrolling the area of Wayne's murder, questioning possible witnesses. They could've just been hassling the homeless. What-ever they wanted, they'd distracted the woman I felt sure killed Zahora.

Words eager to sound the alarm sprang to my lips. Less certain second thoughts stole their charge. Another whispered with Sunny's voice. A glance confirmed her assertions that where I stood violated minimum distance from Thoth property.

I cursed and glanced up Zahora's alley.

She could be dying.

I cringed as new trouble queued up on my lips.

Only one way to be sure.

"Stop that woman!"

All eyes snapped to me.

"She just mu—attacked someone in this alley!"

I bolted up the alley. If I was wrong, Sunny'd have her work cut out for her. If I wasn't, quick response by Seufert Fells's finest might save Zahora's life.

I wasn't wrong.

A lake of fresh blood flooded the open end of a refrigerator box. Bile rose in the back of my throat. Smeared, bloody handprints braced loose entrails dragged from Zahora's body by her desperate crawl into the safety of a home so like my own.

On the slim chance she was still somehow alive, I squatted down for a closer look. The breath in my lungs froze, offering right of way to the contents of my stomach. A sudden ice age in my gut saved me from vomiting up too precious food.

I fell backward off my haunches, tailbone striking hard.

Zahora's once vibrant eyes stared back at me with the same, soulless quality of her killer's only moments before.

Gunfire barked from the street, followed by shouting.

I raced back up the alley.

A bullet ricocheting off the pavement mere feet away brought me up short behind cover.

Fake Zahora and an officer wrestled for his service automatic. She broke his wrist and came away with his weapon.

"Drop the weapon," the far cop demanded. "Blake, are you all right?"

"Are you a war hero?" Zahora remained calm as a librarian.

"She fucking broke my wrist, Tommy, how do you think I am?" Blake managed to unholster a Taser with his off hand. "Get on the ground."

"Are you a veteran?" Zahora dropped the pistol.

"No." Blake gritted his teeth. "Now, get on the ground."

"Yeah," Tommy said. "On the ground."

"If she doesn't get on the ground just shoot her."

Zahora eased onto the ground. Without warning, she rolled sideways, snatching up Blake's lost pistol.

Blake lunged at her with the Taser.

A handspring launched Zahora back onto her feet. She aimed the pistol at Blake.

Tommy's shotgun blast knocked her off balance, buying Blake a moment to get to cover. Instead, he punched the Taser at her. Zahora jerked the Taser out of Blake's hand, put two bullets in his head and leapt onto the cop car.

A quick lateral spin proceeded a feet-first slide just under another shotgun blast. Tommy fired, reloaded and fired again point blank.

Zahora seized the hot shotgun barrel and yanked it free. She lunged in, catching him in the neck with the stolen Taser.

She turned atop the hood and fixed her dead gaze on me.

She'd taken down both cops over a span of mere breaths—trained, armed, armored men put down like insects.

I'd never served in the military. I wasn't some badass Special Forces veteran. I wasn't some comic book hero. Hell, I'd been the first one to die each time Adam coerced me into corporate paint-ball matches.

I'd learned to survive in the Wasteland. I'd built up my virtual body. I'd expanded my limited street fighting experience until I could hold my own. I'd used my immense storehouse of trivia knowledge and engineering know-how to one-up those that insisted on hunting me.

Even so, even with limited projectile weapons to contend with, I'd died more times than I wanted to count.

Real life didn't include respawn points.

Faced with the casual carnage inflicted on Zahora, Ullie, Wayne and the downed cops, reason teamed up with primal terror.

I ran like I was being chased by Death's collections department.

I don't know where my body found the energy or the oxygen, but I ground to a stop six blocks later and just collapsed in front of a convenience store. I managed a handful of breaths before the woman that'd accused me of being a predator emerged. "Get away from there you...you. I'm calling the police."

My first instinct was to thank her. I needed the police. I needed SMLE. Even though with my luck they'd lock me up, I embraced the possibility. I was too tired to run any further, and I'd be safer in jail than anywhere else.

Except, I won't be safer, not if she wants me and she can look like whatever she wants.

I forced myself to my feet and stumbled across the street to Tacky Burger. Inside, I bought the cheapest thing on the menu—a god awful coffee that foretold the imminent collapse of humanity and sat as far from the front windows as I could get. If the police she called caught me inside, I'd deal with it.

Not like I've broken any laws.

No one with an official-looking hat and nightstick entered by the time my heart rate had returned to normal. I drank the poor, abused coffee in nervous swallows. Refilling the foul liquid maintained a continuous focus until my hands stopped shaking.

I need a weapon.

As an ex-con, walking around with a visible weapon while SMLE seemed to have a hard-on for me seemed a bit short-sighted. The killer had compensated for Ullie's firebolter before the gun had been brought to bear. I needed a weapon she wouldn't expect.

I pulled out the Zippo and my Sharpie.

Once upon a time, I'd have diagrammed the runes and marks on a computer with a CAD program, sent the specs down to development and received a shiny lighter engraved in exacting detail. Instead, I leaned in close and took extreme care with each stroke of the permanent marker.

Tacky Burger probably wasn't the best place to enchant an item, but my box didn't have any work tables...yet. The workers eyed me, though whether because I was homeless, drawing on a lighter or they wanted something to do other than clean, I couldn't be sure. I didn't need them ejecting me before I'd finished the lighter, so I refilled my coffee rather than buy an additional torture device.

A patrol car slid by outside, almost causing an errant stroke.

Calm down. Enchanting the lighter doesn't violate my sentence.

I put the finishing strokes on the Zippo, wishing for my development team and its engraver.

Even if they tried to arrest me, Sunny would get me out and—

All the blood in my body fled to my feet.

Sunny!

I'd meant to warn the perky preacher but had pushed it off to ensure I didn't run into Mom and Dad.

After all, Grace's cooking is better than most restaurants, and Dad's frugality would love the price—which puts them all in the killer's sights.

I stopped myself from racing out the exit. Reacting was never a better substitute for a solid plan. Sunny, her clientele, and possibly my parents were potentially in danger from the homeless killer, but the Manger was only one of many locations where homeless resided—not that I wanted anyone dead.

I wracked my brain, but there seemed no reason for the killer to single out Sunny or the Manger. The Manger's goal to help the homeless get back onto their feet and thus off the streets might even offer a kind of protection—assuming the heartless murderer stopped to do a rational analysis.

Hope for the best, plan for the worst.

The perky preacher trusted everyone until they broke that trust. If a homeless stranger entered the Manger, Sunny would feed them. If a bed remained available, she'd invite them to stay, let them roam the Manger's halls until the killing rampage began. Then Sunny would throw herself between the killer and her charges, trusting God to protect her.

My fist crushed the coffee cup, splashing my open Sharpie and the Zippo with hot liquid. God couldn't be trusted to stop that knife, not even for one of His favorites.

I'd had forewarning.

I could've told Sunny what was going on, could have prepared her so that her naïve trust in Him wouldn't betray her.

Instead, I'd repaid her persistent, bothersome kindness by avoiding her. I ignored her, pushed her away, only condescending to spend time with her when I needed legal help. That alone was on par with stringing a woman along for the occasional booty call, but when she'd been in real danger, I'd been so self-absorbed that I'd disdained to give her a vital warning because it risked my comfort.

I owe her better.

I didn't have a phone. I didn't have Razcolm to send ahead. I didn't have Kenrith or Tunoh to blur a message to her in time. I was entirely alone just like I'd always wanted.

And Sunny or Mom and Dad could die because of it.

I snatched up my things, throwing the crushed coffee cup away on my mad rush out of Tacky Burger. I paused at the door, cursed like a sailor, grabbed a fistful of napkins and headed back to the table.

After a moment to clean up the puddle of coffee I'd left behind, I dug into the waste paper I'd gathered at the library. The coffee-coated Sharpie refused to write so much as a blob. I dug into my rucksack, searching for the silver Sharpie. My search came up empty. I'd left the marker in my box.

I cursed.

I didn't have another pen and couldn't buy one from the convenience store across the street without getting arrested. I searched again despite the futility.

My hand closed on something round. I pull out what I assumed was the old compass only to find Willie's holo-comm unit.

Elation shot through me. I thumbed the send and spoke into the unit. "Hello? Willie?"

No one answered.

"William Bradley, are you there?"

Nothing.

"Please, if anyone is there, this is Elias Graham. I need help."

Austin's voice crackled over the radio a moment before his glower materialized in the air before me. "Mister Bradley's busy. You're going to have to fend for yourself."

"Look, Austin, this isn't for me. There's a killer on the loose, and—"

"We don't have time for drug-induced paranoia."

"God damn it, Austin, there are people in danger. I need to get them a warning about a murderer killing homeless. If you won't help, then get Vil or Rich, hell anyone."

"Someone is killing the homeless. You're funny," Austin said.

"This is serious, not some kind of prank call."

"Find a cop then," Austin said. "Or better yet, carry your own messages. You've got feet."

"I am trying to get them a message, but you could call the Manger, warn them quicker about this killer. Tell Sunny not to trust anyone."

"Fine."

"Fine?" I asked. "You'll do it? You'll warn her?"

"If it means you'll shut up and stop bothering us, I'll send your little message." His face vanished.

An invading army of scathing remarks lined up for an artillery barrage, but I held them back. "Thank you, Austin."

Static.

"Tell Sunny the killer can disguise herself."

Silence.

I stared at the radio, turning it slowly in my fingers. Unease crept into my guts, turned a circle and settled in for an extended stay.

"Austin?"

More static.

Shit.

The belligerent intern had claimed he'd send my message, but some part of me doubted not his sincerity so much as his diligence. My eyes shifted to the crumpled paper on the table—a piece of someone's research paper garbled by the gears of a printer.

A certainty grew. I couldn't trust Sunny's life to Austin.

I'll need two spells.

My poor skill with on-the-fly magic didn't matter. I had to get both spells right. I had to work them perfectly with no time to indulge my perfectionist streak.

Paper and printed ink met mana-backed will. The ink swirled together into a black splotch at the wrinkled paper's center. Words strung themselves across the page, surprisingly similar to my own hurried handwriting. The hasty message was barely legible, forcing me to indulge a bit of perfectionism and rewrite the warning only four times.

The moment I'd released the message spell, setting the ink permanently into its new arrangement, my fingers flew through folding. The crane was one of the simplest shapes. Magic gave the origami creation real wings.

I raced outside and launched it skyward.

The wind slammed it back into the ground, tossing it end over end down the street with the other loose trash.

I cursed, chased the construct and caught it with a heavy foot. Ignoring the boot print, I folded more and more pages into the construct, building a substantial enough crane that its wings and weight had a chance against the winds over and around the Columbia.

I grabbed stray chip bags, adding a protective covering in case of rain and I infused as much magic into the folded paper as I thought it could hold.

I lifted it on my palm, breaking my silent armistice with the bastard Sunny kept going on and on about. He was supposed to be protecting her after all, so I could only hope He would ignore the prayer's source and help her.

Paper wings ruffled and rippled. Feathered ridges ripped free of the paper becoming actual feathers. The origami bird's head rounded, its neck shortened. It blinked a flame-filled eye.

<Jesus, human, it's about time! Just how long did you expect me to hang around bodiless and give you dirty looks you couldn't see?>

"Razcolm?"

<No, jackass, I'm the spirit of some dead Indian come to inhabit your civilization's winged rats.>

"I thought you were gone."

<You cost me my new golem with that huge mess of things you caused by sucking down all that wild Ley. Could've sworn I warned you about that. In fact, I think that puts you twice in my debt once more.>

"I wasn't in your debt before, and I don't accept your claims now." I glared at him. "Right now my construct needs to fly across town and warn Sunny—"

<Aw, the big bad magus is finally getting kissy face with the preacher girl. You know there are a lot more attractive women out there. If you're worried about being too ugly, I can teach you a seduction charm in exchange for—>

I tossed the bird into the air, willing it to deliver the message once more. "Go, and you can tell me why you really came back once you return."

<Eli and Sunny, slumming in an alley, F-U-C-K-I-N-G. First comes lust, then comes denial then wobbles a knocked up preacher girl down the aisle.>

Tuning the vulgar, little imp out of my thoughts wasn't easy, and I wasn't sure whether I succeeded or he'd flown out of range. I followed the streets in his wake, unwilling to completely trust my backup message to an imp with questionable allegiances.

I turned a corner heading to the nearer, eastern bridge back to the Oregon side of the Columbia. A tall, beautiful woman nearly collided with me. I ducked sideways toward the building to avoid knocking her down. My balance fled but old concrete caught me halfway to the ground. Her bright red dress would have left Thecia deep green. My gaze climbed from her figure-hugging dress to cold, silver eyes.

Kind of an odd thing to wear on this side of town. Wait, Shaela?

Her soft, cold statement lacked the passion of her attire. "Elias Balthazar Graham."

Oh, shit. The killer.

12

BEATEN DOWN

The killer's voice betrayed no emotion. "You remain homeless?"

The question wrong-footed me. "Yeah."

"All homeless must die." Without further warning, her delicate fist flew forward.

I can thank the Wasteland and recent events for reflexive evasion instincts enough to drop me to the ground just under the concrete-smashing blow. Her foot came up and a stiletto heel thrust at me like its namesake. Scrambling out from between her and the wall was anything but elegant, but I managed.

Her heel drove a hole into the concrete sidewalk without breaking the shoe.

Guess Thecia was right. Two thousand dollar shoes are better quality.

A SMLE car came around the far corner as I fled another kick.

Shaela's calm demeanor flashed to irritation then fear. Her terrified shrieks tore the air. "Help, police! He's attacking me."

Her call for help stunned me enough that I caught a kick in the side. The sudden impact drove breath from my lungs, chased by stabbing pain.

Shaela's eyes injected ice into my veins. "Append your decisions, Elias Balthazar Graham or you must die."

SMLE leapt from their car.

She raced away, running way too fast on stiletto heels.

An all-too-long second dragged on before I shook off my shock enough to realize the killer was getting away. I hadn't even tried to unveil her true identity. I reached my senses toward her to find magic clinging to her frame like a second skin. Her flight took her toward a manhole.

I invoked a first rez cylinder, holding it against her entrance.

She danced around the trap, giving me a backward smirk.

Two dark expressions interposed themselves between the killer and me. I didn't recognize either officer, but they knew me.

"She attacked me, not the other way around." I pointed. "That woman's the killer murdering the homeless."

"Sure she is, Graham," the first one said.

"And an upstanding citizen tried to frame you," the second said.

Ah, hell.

These guys weren't random SMLE officers that happened to be in the neighborhood. They hadn't been called by the convenience store bigot. She'd have called regular cops for a pedophile. These guys were part of my surveillance. They'd helped Adam set me up.

A boot drove into the same spot the killer had kicked. A lance of pain confirmed the rib broken. I rolled away to protect the side. "Please, stop."

The second laughed. "That's resisting arrest."

His partner's nightstick came down smashing the fingers protecting my head. "He's resisting, all right."

Pain burst like fireworks.

I didn't have any ready weapons. Even if I had, assaulting an officer wouldn't end well. No matter what I did, the encounter was doomed to end badly. If I fought back, I'd validate their assault. If I didn't fight back, they just as likely kill me and drop a wand or gun next to my corpse.

I curled up, protecting myself best I could. If later examination found the SMLE agents unmarked in comparison to my injuries, Sunny would be able to get the court to vindicate me.

An unprovoked attack with no witnesses besides the dirty...cops.

Another car stopped, leaving me to hope some nosy bastard would film the assault for YouTube. If nothing else, Sunny would be able to use it to get me justice post-mortem.

The driver stepped out. "Stop."

I recognized the voice. Sure enough, newly-minted SMLE SSA Flowers rushed around his car and shoved one of the other cops off me. "Stop, that's excessive force."

"He resisted," the first said.

"He's not resisting," Flowers said. "Just stop, we'll get him in restraints, and—"

"Get back in your car, rookie," the second added. "We're handling this."

I couldn't see much while still protecting my face, but there was something about Flowers's voice that hardened. "Fine."

"There goes your last hope," the first said as his stomp broke my leg.

I cried out in pain.

"This is Flowers on scene at Casper and Ring."

"What are you doing," the second raced over toward Flowers. "Get off that radio."

"Officers Harmon and Relis have Elias Graham in custo—" Flowers grunted.

I peeked between my fingers to see Flowers on the ground, holding his gut and his radio.

"Flowers, this is Brooke." Detective Brooke barked from the speakers. "Report situation status."

"You should've just walked away, Flowers," Harmon said. "This scum isn't getting anything he doesn't deserve."

"He deserves justice," Flowers said.

"Ignorant rookie. That's not how things work in the real

world." Relis raised his fist but didn't slug Flowers again. "You're going to find that out *real* soon."

"Flowers?" Brooke asked. "Is Graham trying to escape?"

Flowers pulled the radio back to his mouth. "Graham is injured, Detective. I don't think he could escape if he wanted. We're probably going to need a bus."

"Roger, sit tight," Brooke said. "Do absolutely nothing until I get there unless Graham attempts to run."

"Ten-four." Flowers and Relis glared at one another.

"You're not going to come out of this smelling like your name-sake, rookie," Harmon said.

Brooke's voice came over the radio once more. "Dispatch, Detective Brooke, pull traffic cam footage for Casper and Ring. I want to see it before Graham's lawyer."

"Oh," I groaned. "That's going to be a good show."

Harmon kicked me again.

Flowers tensed. His free hand shifted downward, but he stopped himself. The kid was probably trying to decide how to obey Brooke and protect me at the same time.

Probably best if I don't say anything else.

DETECTIVE BROOKE HADN'T SAID MUCH, but his lips had pressed down on his unlit cigarette so hard that I thought tobacco might fall out.

I'd ended up at the hospital once more, more torn emotionally than physically. On the one hand, I really hurt. On the other, while I needed to warn Sunny, I really didn't want to be where Mom and Dad could find me. A fifth-first rez circle swirled a blue-tinted milky white tile-to-ceiling cylinder around me. The same two SMLE cops guarded the door on the opposite side of the thin, mag one wall as had my last time in the hospital.

Guess they're on staff.

Beyond the wide, interior window Sunny argued with Brooke and a doctor. Angry wasn't a good look on her, but somehow it made me smile—well, grimace—in pleasure to see it turned against someone else.

The three stormed into my room.

"He's got something," the doctor stepped through the suddenly dropped circles.

I drew in magic in the moments before they raised the circles once more. My heart rate calmed as energy filled my core and relaxed me like a warm bath.

"Whether or not Eli knows more magic than he's disclosed is not germane here, *doctor*," Sunny said.

The doctor pointed at me. "Elias Graham designed the magic behind our stasis and trauma equipment. You saw what he looked like after they brought him in from the dam."

"What I see is how he looks now," Sunny gave Brooke a dangerous look. "An explanation that had better be immaculate."

"He's got two broken ribs, lacerations, a broken femur—but none of those breaks are the same as what he came in with last time," the doctor said. "In fact, there isn't even the slightest bit of evidence those earlier breaks ever existed."

Really? Wow, Biuntcha rocks.

"That kind of magic could help millions," the doctor said.

"Ms. Terrell is correct, Doctor Thames," Brooke said. "Now isn't the time to discuss such things."

"If you'll let me out of this circle and get me some Tylenol, I'll be on my way...," The combined expressions of Brooke and Sunny changed what I was going to say mid-sentence. "To an interrogation room while they pull the traffic cam footage of me being brutally attacked by a woman and then Harmon and Relis."

"Except there is no footage," Sunny's scowl darkened. "Technical error."

"The backup?" I asked.

"Also lost," Brooke said.

"Uh huh. Is Flowers still alive?"

Shock played over Sunny's expression.

Brooke darkened. "What exactly are you suggesting?"

"With the rest of the evidence gone, Flowers is the only witness. Relis assaulted and threatened Flowers for radioing in," I said.

"Harmon and Relis claim Flowers arrived too late to see you resist," Brooke said.

I turned to Sunny. "I never resisted. I never hit them. As far as I'm aware, they haven't got a mark on them."

"They claim you tried to ensorcell their minds," Brooke said.

All warmth fled my body. There was no way to prove or disprove their claims. I'd been accused of something I hadn't done by two dirty cops covering up what they'd done to keep their extra payroll coming.

Greed strikes again.

I struggled to get up, pain lancing through my chest. Lip between my teeth, I threw my legs sideways too hard, slamming both into the bed rail in a sudden nova of pain. Sunny and Brooke rushed me. I held up my hands. "Stop. Those SMLE assholes—"

Brooke darkened.

"No offense—were trying to beat me to death."

A nurse in baby blue scrubs slipped into the room. She sauntered up to the barrier, stepping through to my right side as it dropped for her.

"You can't know that," Brooke said.

The nurse rolled up my hospital gown sleeve.

A scent of cinnamon-spiced honey bun tickled my nose and woke my stomach.

I fixed Brooke with a look that actually seemed to unsettle the otherwise always-collected detective. "I've been beaten to death. I know what it feels like. "

A needle jabbed into my arm.

"Jesus Christ!"

Exasperation filled Sunny's tone. "Eli—"

The nurse mumbled something that didn't sound apologetic while she drew blood.

"I'm sorry about the blasphemy, Sunny, but those cops purposefully broke bones. There is no way they'd be able to pass those off as me simply resisting."

The nurse withdrew with my blood while I rubbed my arm.

Brooke's tone lacked conviction. "They claim they feared for their lives."

"Oh, that makes it all right then?" I threw my hands into the air. "The defenseless homeless guy scared me, I didn't mean to beat him to death. Case closed."

"That's not how SMLE works," Brooke snarled.

"If that's what you think, then you're just as naïve as Flowers. SMLE's dirty. Adam paid those cops to kill me when his half-assed frame job fell apart."

Sunny put a hand on my arm. "Without proof, Eli, those accusations are just—"

"The word of a convict against seasoned law enforcement officers," Brooke finished, lips all but chewing his cigarette.

The nurse re-entered the room, pausing at the barrier and glancing at the two guarding officers.

Heat flashed up my calves, along my neck, and into my face. My fists balled so tight my tingling knuckles cracked.

"Eli," Sunny warned.

Eyes shut, I concentrated on breathing. My fists eased open, and I lifted them underneath Brooke's nose, turning them slowly. "Doc? Are there any lacerations, bruises or broken bones in my hands?"

"No, Mister Graham."

"Are there any signs I fought at all?" I asked.

"None," Thames said.

"There are no signs of your other injuries either," Brooke said.

Shit, fair point...if I carried a rhet warren around in my backpack.

The nurse sidled up to me, wiping down my arm with an alcohol swab. "I need to take a little blood, Mister Graham."

"Again?" I asked.

"What do you mean again, Eli?" Sunny asked.

The nurse frowned at me. "Relax, this might pinch a little."

Knuckles rapping on the window further distracted me from a desire to work out Razcolm's fireball spell. A gruff, scruffy-looking old man smiled a gap-toothed grin and pointed toward the door. Behind him, the twin of the nurse taking my blood smiled at me.

The younger of the two SMLE officers guarding the interior of the room poked his head out.

"That's all for right now." The nurse at my side taped a cotton ball over the spot she'd sunk a needle without me noticing.

The filthy old man pushed past him as the nurse exited to join her doppelganger. "I need to speak with the cop in charge. I saw everything."

I'll be damned, homeless mafia to the rescue.

My gaze shot from the beaming beggar to the nurse that had just exited to her smirking, suddenly elven twin. She vanished in front of my eyes.

Ah, hell.

Brooke pushed the witness into the hall for an interview and Sunny went, well not with him, but with him enough to overhear everything. Duval had sent a witness to lie for me, but my main concern was the elf that had stolen my blood.

It was too much to hope that some of the hospital staff was using magic to play a practical joke on me. Two possibilities seemed likely. Adam had hired one of his shills to steal my blood— probably for some kind of frame-up. As bad as that could be, something told me I wasn't that lucky. If the first wasn't right, it meant an actual elf had stolen my blood. Old texts spoke of blood magic, and folklore warned against angering the fey. The two combined fueled nightmares that filled many insane asylums.

I have to get my blood back.

I struggled to get out of my bed. Thames reacted at once, pushing me back down and triggering the nurse call button.

"Get off me, doc. I need to go."

"Your leg is broken."

The entrance of two male nurses to hold me down got Brooke's and Sunny's attention.

Sunny tore herself away. "Eli, what are you doing?"

"Leaving, that nu—just leaving."

"He can't even walk." Thames gave me a pointed look. "Unless he intends to heal himself again."

"Eli, stay put. You need medical care. It's not safe—"

Safe?

"Sunny, did you get my message?"

Brooke beckoned one of my guards into the hall. He returned a moment later. "Detective says to strap him down—for his own protection."

"We'll talk about that later. Stay here." Sunny rejoined Brooke.

The nurses belted my wrists to the bed's framework. Thames glared down at me as they exited.

I cursed a lot, but I didn't work any magic.

"If you need to leave," Thames said. "I could heal you if you taught me the spell you used."

I couldn't teach him the spell he meant. I hadn't any idea how the rhet's nightmarish healing ritual worked. I'd been reverse engineering a druid regeneration spell before Adam framed me. Using the knowledge, I'd nearly completed an alteration spell capable of restoring burn injuries to their original form. There was no reason to believe his spellweavers hadn't finished my work, but since Thames didn't know it, Adam must've never released the information.

Probably rather rent out pain management spells and Glamour.

An overhead announcement called Thames away.

I'd used the same restoration magic with stolen DNA samples

to turn demi-goblins back to their original—if still terminally vain —human selves.

Guess I do have healing magic.

Transformational magic is energy intensive. Forcing the body to regenerate had proven agonizing for spell subjects in every case. If I could localize the affected area, the power consumption of the body-wide transformation would lessen by a linear if not quadratic degree.

Except using the design schematics in DNA to heal the whole body works because DNA carries the entire architecture. How do I use that without making an arm into a foot?

It didn't take long to decide such experimentation had to wait, but I still needed out of the hospital. Escape meant a full restoration. I eyed the fifth-first circle.

Do I dare try the spell without mananet access?

My gaze shifted to my SMLE guards.

Or with an audience?

Neither seemed like a good idea. Without sufficient power, I risked an incomplete transformation—Picasso level nightmare fodder. Under guard, I could end up forcibly interrupted with similar results.

Still, maybe another sympathetic connection could be made to repair flesh and bone. A whole skeleton might work...though I can't imagine how I'd explain to SMLE keeping someone's bones in my box.

Sunny and Brooke re-entered with the beggar before I'd made much progress brainstorming a suitable thaumaturgic connection to repair flesh.

"Mister Dudley has come forward to corroborate your claims," Brooke said.

I raised my brows looking straight at Sunny.

Her serious lawyerly demeanor struggled against a grin as her head bobbed an affirmative.

I frowned.

Duval had sent a witness to lie for me. I wasn't sure how to feel about that. It had to have been Duval because it's bad for a person's general health to rat out the cops for someone you don't know.

Let's test how far Duval's protection really goes.

"Great. Sunny, I want to press charges."

Dudley's expression widened in surprise. He caught my eye and shook his head ever so slightly.

"In fact, let's sue SMLE and Seufert Fells for assault, wrongful arrest, and harassment."

Even Sunny stared at me dumbfounded.

"No." Brooke snapped out of it first. "A criminal has no grounds to bring such a—"

"Sunny? Do I have a case or don't I?"

Sunny drew out the word. "Yes." She gave Dudley a careful, assessing look. "Assuming Mister Dudley remains willing to testify."

The panic Dudley seemed to be holding just behind his manic grin leaked down his face one drop of sweat at a time.

I couldn't help my grin.

Duval had held me over a barrel to get me to investigate Ullie's murder. He'd no doubt done something similar to bring Dudley forward, and I felt like six kinds of bastard pushing the poor man into a spotlight which would jeopardize his long-term career as a professional beggar.

Serves them both right.

"You've got no case," Brooke said.

"How many times have I been brought in for questioning since my release?" I asked.

"Four," Sunny said.

"Four times including a flimsy frame job and a witnessed beating by SMLE officers, Detective. Seems I have enough to give a jury something to chew on."

"I don't want to testify," Dudley blurted. "I came forward because they were beating him, but—"

My glare pinned him under the full weight of my personality.

"Really, *Duval?* Sorry, I meant Dudley. You won't stand up to oppose injustice perpetrated against one of your own?"

The room fell dead silent, but I wasn't done putting the screws to Brooke. "You wouldn't be alone, Dudley. SMLE Junior Special Agent Flowers will doubtless testify—assuming Detective Brooke does his job and protects Flowers from *all* conceivable dangers."

"Detective," Sunny snapped. "I need a private moment with my client."

Brooke's scathing glower failed to intimidate me. "*Someone* needs to talk some sense into him."

Sunny bristled, probably at his suggestion I had no right to redress injustice like any other citizen—the most likely response for a dyed in the wool crusader.

"Before we have a little chat, you'll want to ensure Detective Brooke arranges a police—not SMLE—escort for Dudley here to the Manger. You wouldn't want me to have to use magic to track him back down."

Brooke waved the other officers out the door. "I'll make a call."

Dudley gave me a dirty look as Brooke escorted him into the hall, artfully dirty, all things considered.

My smile blossomed. I was in pain. I'd been beaten, scared to death and nearly died several times, but if things went right, I could use Duval to fill a bank account so I never needed to worry about money again.

Sunny rounded on me the moment the door clicked closed. "Are you out of your mind, antagonizing them like that?"

I blinked at her. "What? I'm within my legal rights, aren't I?"

"Yes, legally you can do all that, but that beggar lied about seeing what happened."

"How would you know?" I demanded.

"I know, all right?" She said.

"Neither of us knows for a fact whether or not he lied."

"His testimony might get you out of this mess, but they'll tear him apart if you try to sue the city."

The door closed.

Sunny whirled around. "This is a priva—Jackson. What are you doing here?"

My angry retort died on my lips. Dad had aged while I'd been locked away in the Wasteland. Softening muscles stubbornly hung on to a frame much like my own. Seeing him heartened me and knotted my insides. Grey had permanently supplanted what curls remained around an expanding bald pate.

Old age hadn't softened his expression. "You're not going to sue the city."

"The hell I'm not."

"*Language*, Elias," Dad growled. "There's a lady present."

"Thank you," Sunny said.

"Ladies don't poke their noses where they don't belong, but either way I *am* suing the city and SMLE, you don't know what they've—"

Dad folded his arms and dropped his chin to look at me through narrowed eyes. "Elias Balthazar Graham."

13

EXCEPTIONS & RULES

My blood ran cold at Dad's recitation of my name. There was no question that the words had escaped with the same hammer of doom tone I heard many times growing up. Still, the tone sounded so close to the cold declaration of the killer, it wrong-footed me.

Fortunately, a fifth-first rez barrier prevented any possible whooping that normally accompanied his dangerous expression.

"Upstanding citizens do not sue cities or entire law enforcement agencies," Dad said.

The growl escaped before I realized. "In case you hadn't heard, I'm not anything close to an upstanding citizen."

"Eli!" Sunny objected.

"Still haven't outgrown that stubborn temper of yours." Dad shook his head, voice hardening. "You listen to me, boy. That is quite enough of *that* crap."

I fixed Sunny with much the same expression as I'd given Dudley. "Get him out of here."

Sunny's response was written all over her face even before her objections escaped.

I cut her off. "I removed him as my emergency contact, so I know the only reason my Dad is here is that you called him."

"That's no way to talk to a lady, young man, certainly not one that's gone out of her way to help you."

"Help me? She's done nothing but meddle since we met. Her interference cost me—"

Dad's tone lost the last give it had. "Be quiet, boy!"

I folded my arms and tucked my chin, but didn't continue speaking.

His voice softened. "I know you've had a rough time, and we'll discuss your other troubles, but not until after you've apologized."

When pigs fly.

I clamped my lips tight.

He sighed. "You have my apologies, Marisol. I *thought* his mother and I raised him better than this. I *thought* we'd impressed upon him proper manners and that when civilized people in a civilized system have a problem, they handle it within the system. They don't sue the people risking their lives to protect and serve."

I snorted.

Dad raised his voice to speak over me even though I hadn't opened my mouth. "Civilized adults do not create problems for ourselves and our neighbors by holding the whole accountable for the actions of a few."

"They're *all* dirty."

Dad harrumphed.

"All right, not Flowers," I admitted. "And maybe not Brooke."

"Considering the number of times Marisol says you've been in trouble of late, Elias, I'd expect you would think twice before burning this particular bridge."

I opened my mouth, but Dad being Dad cut across me.

"You still owe Marisol an apology."

My glower bit into Sunny as my hand reached over and depressed the call button. "Go away. Leave me alone."

"How many times have I told you that you can't just hide from your problems by shoving everyone away?" Dad asked.

A nurse in lavender scrubs with cream-colored teddy bears entered, bringing with her a fresh miasma of chemical disinfectants.

My voice cracked but quickly hardened to flint. "Please remove them, nurse. I don't want them here."

Sunny stepped closer, grabbing my hand. "Eli—"

I snatched my fingers away. "Nurse?"

She glanced at everyone in turn, a timid smile barely hanging onto her lips. "I have to get SMLE to remove the circles."

"Then do so."

"That's no way—"

"No way to talk to a lady?" My neck burned like I'd been in the sun all afternoon. I turned my gaze on Sunny, sure only the first rez barrier separating me from the mananet kept my eyes from glowing. "Stop being such a naïve, optimistic idiot, or you will get yourself and a lot of other people murdered."

The circles dropped.

"What about murder?" Brooke asked.

I drew in magic from the mananet, but I didn't drop my eyes. "There's a serial killer murdering homeless, using illusion to mimic people they know in order to get close. The bum ma—"

"Don't call them bums," Sunny snapped. Her expression reminded me forcibly of the occasion Brooke had accused her of sleeping with her other clients and me. If the situations were truly similar, her shark teeth weren't far behind.

"Some of the," I made quotes in the air, "'*homeless*' came to me after the first few were killed hoping I could help them."

Sunny's expression softened.

"I told them there was nothing I could do to help."

"Then how do you know about the killer and his illusions?" Brooke asked.

"I met him, or in this case, her." Sunny's disappointed expression troubled me enough to force my gaze away toward the detective without resting on Dad. "The woman that attacked me before your cops tried to kill me was wrapped in illusion magic."

"How do you know it wasn't a Thoth cosmetic charm?" Dad asked.

His question wrong-footed me for six blinks. "She's an international model named Shaela who's doing a shoot in Milan."

"You're full of shit," Brooke said. "How would you know some model's schedule?"

"He's not lying," Sunny said.

"I saw her...," My gaze shot to Sunny and something made me hesitate. "I saw her on a television and heard about her photo shoot at a party."

"Who would invite someone like...who else was present at this party?" Brooke asked.

"I'm done talking, Detective. Please escort these *people* from my room. I need to rest."

"Even your lawyer?" Brooke asked.

"Mister Graham appears to have dismissed me." Sunny marched past him, jaw clenched so hard the edges could have sliced tomatoes.

Dad followed her, stopping at the door. "Damn stubborn fool. That pride's going to be the death of you yet."

I turned my head so I couldn't see them leave. The fifth-first rez circle reappeared around me. I didn't bother to check if Brooke had locked himself inside or outside.

I didn't care.

I closed my eyes, my only movement the slow rubbing of my knuckles against one another while I planned my escape.

THERE WAS no way to tell what time it was when I decided to escape. My room lights were out, turning my window into a mirror for any of the cops and nurses outside in the hall. The tile circle around me swirled with the milky-white magic of a fifth resonance barrier preventing physical objects from passing much like the little cage Boss Golem had ordered me placed in at the Dalles Dam. Just inside the fifth rez, a light blue first rez circle had prevented any magical energy from coming inside the circle.

The first resonance circle was gone.

I'd invoked my own first rez, cutting off the circle's power.

SMLE Academy courses likely instructed wannabe corrupt cops that the fifth-first circle could imprison someone like me. After all, it cut me off from the mananet, effectively keeping me from powering any magic I might have hidden on my person.

Except, in the parlance of the fey, I was a magus.

I'd never run into the term in my research, but I could practically hear the capital letters when one of the fey used it. Magus were special, and I had a theory about what made them so.

When I was about eight, Dad had sidelined our family vacation to Disneyland into Grand Canyon National Park. I'd been stuffed in the back seat between Douglas and a screaming little Zahda, amusing myself by having little origami gladiators fight one another when entering the park left us suddenly without a mananet.

My gladiators had fallen dead to my lap, much to Doug's amusement. His laughter pissed me off. My little warriors leapt back to life and attacked him—for all the damage a couple three-inch paper warriors were worth.

Doug had punched me.

Zahda had screamed.

I'd hit Doug back, and Dad stopped the car and left us all sorry.

Sulking with my arms folded, I had little to do except think. When dark little thoughts played out, my mind returned to my animated defenders.

The park had no mananet.

My gladiators were merely folded paper. They hadn't been built with any power crystals.

Dad's car was one hundred percent mundane.

I hadn't known about natural magic sources at that age, so I'd concluded that the power had come from me—ego never being a problem at that age. By the time I learned that natural magic sources existed, I'd already experimented enough to determine I could store power inside me.

Researching magical texts and cultures, I'd run across many references to powerful wizards 'walking in power'. I'd never questioned the descriptions, never really thought about it at all. Since I'd seldom traveled outside a mananet for any time, I hadn't given the ability much thought until my wet behind the ears intern, Darrin, had complained about his camp light running out of power on one of our trips.

My natural tendencies perked up at the opportunity to test a phenomenon I'd never discussed with other arcanologists. I used a cosmetic illusion to disguise a dead power crystal with light and gave it to Darrin for use with his lamp and taught him how to draw on the crystal.

In reality, I'd tricked him into drawing on himself.

Darrin's light remained steady the first night, but the second he fell ill. Our doctor couldn't figure out what was wrong with Darrin. An unsettling theory convinced me to drop the illusion on the crystal. Once Darrin thought the crystal out of power, his light went out and he rallied.

Further private experiments determined other scraps of information gleaned from my texts correct. Without a mananet or any stored magical power, a magically sensitive could convert their own life energy into magic.

A working theory evolved from those tests and other more subtle observation of my project team members. Evidence suggested that all magically talented individuals could store some amount of magic within them. Carefully engineered discussions led me to further theorize that my test subjects hadn't discovered their ability to save power or draw on their life force due to mananet availability.

While I'd never devised a conclusive test, Darrin's marginal spellweaving ability logically correlated with his limited ability to store energy within himself—though I had no idea which led to the other.

Pride is definitely one of my failings. Being a perfectionist followed a close second, though like stubbornness it had its pros and cons. Had SMLE caged me with a fifth-second-first barrier so tight it left no gaps, it might've prevented most practitioners who knew they could store energy from starving the first rez circle and restoring their access to the mananet. I probably could've threaded the needle anyway.

Might be my pride talking though.

Over the hours, I'd shifted mananet sips into the fifth rez circle, increasing its magnitude to tier three—effectively making the barrier opaque to anyone looking in from the lit hall.

It had taken a dozen iterations to plan a series of actions that would once more spring me from the hospital under the noses of SMLE. None of my planning had uncovered even a theoretical method to work a reliable, localized healing on my broken limbs. I didn't have the benefit of Yshtiina's help or rhet glamour.

But I've had plenty of recent practice working with an excellent restoration spell.

The components available in the room weren't perfect, but my will was more than sufficient to guide the magic to my desired ends. I focused on myself—a simple enough task for any border-line narcissists—and drew deeply from the mananet until the tame, stale power built up a pressure beneath my skin.

I'd tried reaching further than the mananet for a purer source, but there wasn't one to be had.

The simple, blue-cushioned visitor's chair offered up wood that wasn't yew. Bandages around one arm provided cotton gauze. A plastic pitcher at my bedside contained not-quite-fresh water, and the air conditioning vent delivered wind.

Earth, water, wind, bandages to symbolize healing, the fire of life within my DNA and the pure, stubborn will of my spirit.

I sliced a finger on an edge that would eventually get the hospital sued, but it was better than biting myself. My experience with the golems provided enough knowledge to cut through one of my leather restraints with a tiny fifth rez field. Blood drew runes on the flesh beneath my hiked-up hospital gown.

I left one arm restrained to help against any involuntary reactions. Unfortunately, there was no way to repair the first strap, so I encircled that arm and the bed rail in a fifth rez ring.

I invoked the re-engineered druid restoration spell.

Gooseflesh rippled along my skin as rising hair tickled my flesh. The prickle turned to thousands of writhing ants. Ants mutated into Amazonian army ants with the stinging bite of their fiery red cousins. Bites became long needles, became ice picks, became rapiers piecing every inch of my flesh. My scalp felt aflame, and every muscle burned like magma.

Pain—the small word could never encompass what shot through me. Agony paled as well as my spell tried to remake every cell in my body. I'm not sure when the screaming started or when it became shrieks that still couldn't drown the sounds of bones snapping together within my skin.

Thankfully, the human body comes equipped with an automated ejection system when pain reaches a point that jeopardized sanity. Mine might need recalibrating, but it plunged me into darkness eventually.

I AWOKE in hell empty of magic.

Every inch of me hurt—even my shaking hands. Of course, I

didn't hurt anywhere as badly as I had trying to rewrite my body cell by cell from the blueprint.

A fifth-second-first barrier surrounded me, Detective Brooke and Doctor Thames stood within the barrier while Doctor Porter sat at my bedside.

I shook my stiff neck.

Just kill me now.

"He's awake." Thames hurried to my bedside, pen light already seeking my eyes.

I turned away from it, but he wrenched my head back with a firm grip on my chin.

"You want to explain what you attempted to do?" Thames asked.

"What are you talking about?" I asked.

"You cast some sort of magical suicide spell." Porter appeared at my other side, disappointment wrinkling her brow enough to turn her smile completely off. "Hurting yourself isn't the answer, Mister Graham."

You aren't just whistling, "If I only had a brain."

"Whatever he was trying to do, it wasn't suicide," Thames said. "Most of his injuries are gone. The skin has even regrown over his wasteland jacks."

"What did you attempt to do?" Brooke demanded.

"Nothing," I lied. "Must've had a nightmare—"

Thames yanked up my gown.

Porter yelped, covered her blushing face and turned away.

"You normally draw runes in your sleep?" Thames asked.

My dirty look shifted from Thames to Porter. "Get over yourself, Jessica."

"Mister Graham, I've told you before, you're not permitted—"

"What did you do?" Brooke snapped. "How did you cut through your restraint? How did you gain access to the mananet?"

I'd have folded my arms, except both my wrists were strapped to the bed rails once more. I settled for silence.

"You will tell me," Brooke said.

"Us," Thames corrected.

If the stabbing pain which accompanied each breath was any indication, I had failed to heal myself. I had definitely failed my stealthy escape. I'd rather have gotten away unseen and argued my right to do so later, but low on options, I settled for a frontal assault and narrowed my gaze at the detective. "Didn't you have a witness corroborating my innocence and implicating SMLE in assaulting me?"

Brooke drew out the word. "Yes."

"So, why am I restrained against my will?"

Thames and Porter answered together. "For your own safety."

"Best go prep the AMA forms, Doc. I'm out of here."

"Your leg is still broken," Thames said. "You didn't manage to *magically heal* that this time."

My best response seemed a shrug, so I went with it.

"There's also the matter of your bill," Thames said.

A nod of my head directed him to Brooke. "They brought me in. They caused my injuries. They're paying the bill."

"Not if you're discharging yourself against medical advice," Brooke said. "Besides, you're under arrest for assault and resisting arrest."

"Which we both know is bullshit."

Brooke shrugged. "Tell it to the judge. You're lucky I don't charge you with attempted escape."

"Never left my bed."

Brooke opened his mouth to assert my intentions to leave if able, but Doctor Porter spoke first. "Since we're both here, you're not going anywhere, and you cut our last session short, now seems like the perfect time to chat."

"Doc? Can I get something to knock me out? I'm feeling a lot of pain here."

"Do you feel the need to narcotize away your problems, Mister Graham?" Porter asked.

"The detective won't let me shoot them."

"Is that your only answer to things?" Porter asked. "Drugs or violence?"

"I *am* American."

<You know, human, you're not actually funny.>

Never in my wildest dreams had I expected to thank God for Razcolm, but I was just that glad to hear him in my thoughts. Despite what Sunny had said when I'd broached the subject, I chose to ask for confirmation.

You delivered my warning to Sunny?

<I did, though I think she intended to speak to you on the matter.>

She probably didn't believe me.

<She believed you enough to visit your alley and attempt to enlist the rhet.>

Damn. Did she succeed?

<The flibbertigibbet is talking to you.>

"Huh?"

"I asked if you were listening," Porter said.

"Yes, Jessica, but not to you."

Her brow wrinkled. "Why do you insist upon being such a difficult patient?"

I shrugged. "Differing perspectives on life?"

"Is that why you've dyed your hair this way? Is it some sort of political statement in favor of homosexual rights? Maybe a protest against the treatment of a marginalized minority?"

"Maybe I just wanted to look as fabulous as you."

"Oh." She blushed and patted her hair. "Thank you."

If my hands hadn't been strapped to the bed, I might've pulled out my hair—and not just to be rid of my magical locks. Screaming seemed ill-advised, but I did it anyway.

Considering the restoration spell had grown skin over my Wasteland wire taps, it surprised me that my hair hadn't returned to its genetic design. Of course, I couldn't actually see my reflection, but I doubted Porter would've asked what she had if my curls were dark once more.

The PA called for Doctor Thames, and he departed with Brooke rather than Porter. I took advantage of the momentarily restored mananet access to pull all the power I could. One of the junior SMLE guys I hadn't seen before stood at the room window, peering in instead of just watching the door. The circle came up and with it my brows.

A SMLE wizard? Guess they don't want to take any more chances. Still pretty sure I can thread that needle—not that I'll have to prove it.

<A real Magus would simply leave.>

And I will, later.

"Mister Graham?"

"What is it already?" I snapped.

"You haven't answered my questions."

<Plague spells really are quite easy.>

Don't tempt me.

"Look, Doctor Porter—"

She beamed.

"I don't believe in societal governance. I don't believe the government should have any say in people's everyday lives. The government, like magic, should only be employed to manage what an individual can't do on their own—like national defense or interstate roads."

"I notice you don't include law enforcement. I take it you don't believe we should have laws?"

I opened my mouth to retort, but she didn't give me a chance.

"Is that why you feel no remorse about your crimes?"

"I was wrongfully convicted."

"Until you own up to your crimes, you're never going to heal, Mister Graham."

"Own up? I was *framed*, Jessica. A bunch of liars convinced a jury that the convoluted, overly complicated so-called law required them to find me guilty."

"I think you mean lawyers, not liars."

"Same difference. The way they twisted the truth, how they manipulated laws too byzantine for layman to understand is a perfect example of how a system designed by a committee of self-interested humans ends up a cluster fuck."

"Just because you insist on blaming your guilt on others doesn't invalidate the law. Those *we* elect to office are there to serve us."

I snorted.

Her jaw tightened. "We need our leaders and lawmakers right where they are, protecting us from ourselves and unfortunates who believe themselves above the law."

"Grow up, Jessica. Politicians serve their *pockets*. It's not bad enough they'll draft any old law lobbyists or special interest groups pay for. They try to make us dependent by putting through laws that coddle those too lazy to learn common sense, common decency, or to think for themselves."

"Our leaders only want to take care of us, to help us see what's right and what's not, what we need in our lives and what we don't."

"They're a bunch of greedy, self-absorbed prostitutes screwing us in whatever way they're paid to do so. They've got no right to tell people who they can marry, what they can do with their own bodies, or what they're allowed to say."

"You of all people should understand that we need lawmakers to guide us in how to live with one another."

I bristled. "Doesn't religion handle that or at the very least the golden rule?"

She patted my hand. "I can see we have a long way to go, but now that we've identified your wrong thinking, we can work together to correct you."

What was that plague spell?

Razcolm's laughter echoed in my thoughts.

14

SMLE'S GENTLE CARE

Since no rhet showed up to help me, not even my erstwhile fiancé and her mothers, I set Razcolm to collecting components. I'd have much rather built a more permanent circle for the purpose, but I didn't feel I could even risk drawing runes on the bed sheets.

It wasn't necessarily that I didn't want Thames healing people with my discovery. That had been what I'd engineered the spell for after all, but I no longer trusted that the secret of magical healing would reach and remain in the right hands.

Like some zealot forcibly reversing sex change operations.

My attempt to restore myself had taught me several things. First and foremost that particular spell had to be programmed into an independent construct for self-use.

It needed something like the wand and accompanying rune chips I'd designed for Thoth as a way to preprogram a series of commands that wasn't dependent on the caster's will or even consciousness. I settled for having Razcolm draw the runes on unlined index cards he found somewhere.

I didn't ask where.

Razcolm used the gap between the exterior hospital wall and my cylindrical fifth rez cage to remain out of sight of the watchful guard while he drew the rune cards. He paper-clipped them in collated sets around a knotted circle of stolen, water-soaked knitting yarn. I instructed him to make and connect three complete card sets on the off-chance the power involved ignited and burned away my runes.

I'd considered having Razcolm swap them out if needed, but I was afraid the amusement he'd derive from my setting the bed and me on fire might distract him in a critical moment.

The fifth-second-first rez barrier prevented Razcolm from actually delivering my components. When I dropped the boundary, we'd have a few moments to get the circle in place and start the spell.

Had Razcolm been inside the circle, I'd have had him break the second-first circles. As they were arranged, there was a simpler option than sliding my own first rez between them to grant me mananet access for the healing.

No magic in. No magic out. Oh my, what will I do?

<Get on with it already, human. These paltry attempts to live up to your previous entertainment value begin to tire me.>

Once more I invoked a fifth rez cylinder using the strap buckles. The field cut through both of the dead and thus auraless leather straps. The water pitcher on my bedside soared across the room, passing into the second-first fields. It hit the fifth rez, spraying water everywhere. The runes inlaid in the tile maintained the power connection without an active will but didn't sustain circle integrity if something broke it.

I sucked in power and killed the fifth rez circle as Razcolm bolted across the intervening distance to position my twine ring. The SMLE officer outside was already moving, so I didn't hesitate. I restored the fifth resonance circle to buy time and invoked the regeneration spell.

I screamed—a lot.

When the screaming stopped, half a dozen security, police, and SMLE surrounded me. Those that had them pointed guns—not that they could've shot me through the barrier.

Razcolm ate—don't ask me how—the rune cards, before I dropped the barrier.

"What seems to be the problem, officers?"

Cuffs replaced my destroyed restraints.

"You're not escaping our custody," the SMLE wizard snarled.

"Never tried to do any such thing."

"What was that spell you cast?" He demanded. His eyes scanned the room for Razcolm, but the construct had flattened himself and crawled out of the room through a ventilation duct.

I shrugged, not feeling even the slightest wince from my no-longer-broken ribs. My success encouraged a grin.

"What did you cast?"

"Glamour. Why? Don't I look beautiful?"

The only female among them snorted.

I winked at her. "Look, since it doesn't take six of you to guard me, could one of you go tell Thames and Brooke I'm ready to be relocated to a holding cell? The sooner I see the judge, the better."

A SMLE DETENTION officer disengaged the fifth-second-first cube just inside the cell bars and handed me a tray of torture. By some sign of favor among the gods, he jerked it just slightly as I grabbed it but before I had a firm hold.

The tray tumbled, his last motion flipping it just enough to spin toward me and fall food first.

He frowned. "Why did you do that, convict? Now you'll have to go hungry."

His smirk appeared just as he turned his back and remained visible in the way he strode away.

Oh how quickly the world turns.

I stared down at the splattered institutional food. The condition of my meal offered evidence that my intention to sue SMLE had found its way into the grapevine.

I flopped down on the concrete and shook my head at the self-proclaimed victor no longer in view. I turned the tray over and looked at the noodles splattered atop a Rorschach sauce pattern and some studiously crushed bread.

I excavated the utensil packet out from under lumpy, running green stuff ostensibly from the vegetable food group. I dipped my finger in the sauce and traced an oblong ring around it on the concrete. I duplicated the effort around the face-down tray.

Swirling cream and orange magic sprang up over both circles, leaving me wistful for a Good Humor Man. Food splatter slowly evaporated, reforming atop the tray in a clean, magically recycled food brick.

Better this way. The kitchen probably added special flavor too.

Officers stormed into the cell block, already screaming at me long before they reached my cell. "Cease that immediately. On your feet, hands against the far wall."

I picked up the still warm food brick, added a dash of salt and took a bite. My meal tasted a bit more red sauce than the usual brown, and the salt definitely helped. I took a second bite just before the magical cube caging me within the steel cage vanished.

I managed a third bite as they rushed through the cell door, and addressed them through stuffed cheeks. "M'sorry, were you talking to me?"

The guard responsible for the splatter pattern on the floor slammed me into the far wall. I managed to swallow the food before he dug a finger into my mouth to empty it.

Good thing for you I'm not a biter.

"What is it? What did he do?" a panicked officer demanded.

"He swallowed whatever it was," Splattercop said.

"How was he doing magic at all? That's impossible."

God people are stupid.

Before the Wasteland, I'd been a pampered research mage working and living within nothing less than tier three mananet access. But since the barrier was down again, I topped off my reserves from the local mananet.

I shot a look over my shoulder, cataloging the SMLE officers present. None of the agents were the SMLE wizard I'd encountered at the hospital. He might've been able to correct their misapprehension, offering me confirmation without having to risk revealing a secret.

Maybe I should talk to Emlimn about this.

A shudder ran through me. Going to see my old mentor was out of the question.

Better off trusting Razcolm not to lie to me.

Ultimately, they smashed and scattered my food, beat me, gagged me and cuffed my hands and feet to the bunk. They left me that way, back in the restored fifth-second-first rez cage that no one—except maybe a Magus—could use magic within.

THE MANANET'S return woke me. I drew in what I could as Detective Brooke crossed the barrier. He looked down on me in silence, standing still save for a little muscle twitch at the joint of his jaw. His eyes took in every inch of me.

He removed my gag. "What happened?"

I tried to moisten my mouth enough to speak. Brooke waited without a word, hands drawn behind his back and out of my sight.

"One of your boys intentionally spilled my meal, not that I believe it was sanitary before it hit the ground. Living on the streets has forced me to learn a few things, like how to clean my food to make sure I don't get sick."

"Magically?"

"Obviously, since I don't have anything else in here that sterilizes."

"How did you access the mananet through a fifth-second-first rez barrier?"

"Maybe a rodent of unusual size with a pocket watch crawled up through the toilet from Eberron and gave me a magic piece of event cake that restores mana."

Brooke's brow wrinkled. "Did you just make a DDO reference?"

I blinked in surprise.

He pulled a mage sniffer from behind his back and ran it over me. "You do read at a slightly higher level of residual magic."

"It's my charming personality."

"Uh huh. I'm going to remove your bonds. Please don't make any sudden moves."

"Don't you need backup? I might be dangerous."

Brooke looked deep into my eyes with a silent, menacing intensity. "You *are* dangerous, criminal, but as I am here to escort you to arraignment, I suggest you behave."

"Say no more."

"I'd appreciate it if you did the same."

Detective Brooke led me out of the cell, but rather than head back to the entrance, we turned deeper into the cell block. At the far end of a hall, we were buzzed through several interlocking security doors. Beyond, another short hall ended with a small office on the left and a room filled with occupied chairs on the other side.

Brooke gestured left.

I stepped inside to find a young man seated at a desk with an actual physical monitor in front of him. The opaque, plastic screen cut off my view of what he was doing, but his fingers typed on a suspended holographic keyboard.

It's not that they don't have the holographic tech, they just don't want anyone seeing what they see.

"Please sit, Mister Graham." The twenty-something said

without looking up. "I would like to ask a few pre-questions to expedite your virtual arraignment."

"Virtual?" I glanced at Brooke.

"His Honor is unable to make it for a full arraignment proceeding," the young man said. "This is not an uncommon practice. Now, how do you intend to plead?"

"Not guilty."

He nodded like he'd heard it all before. "Are you claiming insanity or any extenuating circumstances?"

"Shouldn't I have a lawyer present?"

His hands dropped to the desk. He looked at me for the first time. "If you want a lawyer, Mister Graham, you will be returned to your cell and be arraigned at some future time when both a judge and a public defender are available. Are you sure you wish to delay your arraignment awaiting counsel?"

The intercom buzzed.

My examiner turned away, tapped his ear and then a touchpad that connected the intercom to his earpiece for privacy. He glanced at me. "Are you sure? Understood."

He tapped his ear once more and set his hands in his lap. "We'll wait a moment for your attorney. She's being brought up now."

My heart swelled. I'd asked after an attorney meaning the public defender. I had not expected Sunny to come riding to the rescue after I'd been short with her.

"Did you know she was here, Detective?" I asked.

"I didn't see her when I came up."

"Speaking of, where's Flowers. Wouldn't have surprised me if he'd volunteered to escort me again instead of you. Either way, he needs to be here."

Brooke looked away.

Cold swamped the warm feeling that had risen upon Sunny's arrival. "Where is Agent Flowers, Detective?"

Clopping heels charged up the outer hall. A gorgeous Hispanic woman with long, literally sparkling red hair that clashed with her complexion but somehow managed to look incredible pushed open the door. "I'm Mister Graham's attorney."

I couldn't help it.

I stared.

She was as glamorous as Sunny was plain. The woman might as well have said she was Aphrodite from Olympus. She was Gorgeous with a capital G. She stepped further into the room, and it became immediately apparent that she had not, in fact, come down from Olympus. She had so many overlapping cosmetic charms engaged I could have used her like a portable mananet.

But who is she and why is she here?

She extended a hand to me. "I'm Valeria Hollis. Mari asked me to act as her proxy."

"Mari...sol? Also known as Sunny?" I asked.

"Marisol Terrell."

Sunny sent her?

"Why isn't she here?"

Valeria smiled, and diamonds sparkled around her face. "Mari said you and she were not seeing eye to eye, but explained how critically you needed proper representation. I owe her quite a few favors, so I flew up from LA."

I couldn't help the surge of warmth toward the invasive busybody.

"Is there anything we need to discuss?" Valeria asked. "Mari said we had witnesses, but that the video footage was too damaged to be admissible."

"I haven't seen either witness yet," I said.

Valeria looked at Brooke. "Detective Brooke? Where is Special Agent Flowers?"

"I just asked that, but he didn't answer."

Brooke licked his lip, biting the lower for a two count. "Junior Special Agent Flowers was killed in a random convenience store robbery last night."

The cold that Sunny's replacement had pushed back returned

with ice age vengeance. I looked down, remembering the cheerful young officer eager to escort me to court. Seeing him again through fingers as he radioed in my situation to prevent Hendan and Regis from killing me off the books.

Flowers is dead.

"It wasn't random," I said. "I warned you, Brooke."

"Warned him what? Please tell me you didn't threaten the detective," Valeria said.

"Mister Graham suggested that Agent Flowers might come to harm for testifying against his fellow officers." Brooke fixed me with his gaze. "I assure you, Mister Graham, there is no evidence that this tragedy is anything but."

The man at the desk cleared his throat. "Excuse me, but I have other criminals—"

"Accused," Valeria snapped.

"Fine, I have other *accused* to process, so if you could take your little melodrama elsewhere, I'd—"

"Is the judge ready for us yet?" she asked.

"Mister Graham asked for a lawyer rather than answer my pre-screening questions."

Valeria gave me a warm illusory smile. "Good boy."

They killed him...because he helped me...because he did the right thing.

Court happened.

I don't recall much. There was a prominent holographic judge. Valeria talked a lot. I think I answered some questions. I barely realized we were shaking hands in the front foyer of SMLE headquarters when she left me there for LA. I'm not even sure how she got the charges dropped without video or Flowers.

Brooke sidled up to me. "Don't get used to this, criminal. I only did right by the kid."

"What?"

<He testified on your behalf.>

What?

"Do you need me to call you a LUX back to your...alley?"

"N-no. Thank you, Detective."

I managed to find the exit, pushing through revolving doors that felt far too heavy.

<Incoming.>

Razcolm's warning made me tense for the wrong kind of assault. A microphone and camera thrust into my face.

"Mister Graham, Megan French Network One News, is it true you are suing the city and SMLE?"

"No comment." I tried to step around her, but she was quick.

"Is it true you know an ancient healing spell but refuse to share it with the good citizens of Seufert Fells?"

"No comment."

She managed to stay ahead of me once more. "Do you have any comment on Thoth's announcement earlier this afternoon to beautify the city with what some are calling hostile architecture?"

"I didn't see it," I paused. "Wait, what is hostile architecture?"

Megan's smile doubled in brightness. "Roundabouts, benches and other city amenities designed to discourage vagrancy."

I scowled.

"How do you feel about this move and its impact on other homeless?" Megan asked.

<Sensing a sudden need for rat hair and dead fleas.>

A calm, pleasant tone escaped my lips. "I trust the citizenry of Seufert Fells will justly reward Adam for all he's done."

I made my escape into the evening, barely avoiding a follow up question by ducking through an argument between a tired-looking man and two pregnant women.

Adam intended to make things hard for the homeless. My only shock centered on him using his own money rather than lobbying for the city to pay for it.

Probably tried and got blocked. No doubt Duval brought his own resources to bear.

A silvery pigeon fluttered down onto one shoulder. *<That should prove to be an exciting contest.>*

Not sure who'd I'd root for.

<Mutual destruction?>

Fair enough.

15

A FATHER'S WRATH

We trudged home in a light rain. LUX buzzed overhead and splashed through puddles. Taxis and occasional pedicabs made shushing sounds while advertisements assaulted all our senses.

I barely noticed any of it.

Adam was going to hurt all Seufert Fells's homeless just to attack me. Flowers had been killed for the same reasons.

Cold clung to me that had nothing to do with the temperature. My limbs dragged. Exhaustion stole my attention.

<Magus, beware.>

The sudden burst of noise in my thoughts stopped me short at the mouth of my alley.

My hackles rose.

I scanned the deep darkness for whatever lurking creature convinced my body hair to attempt self-plucking and flight. Nothing large and stony darkened the shadows. Even my SMLE surveillance was absent.

What do you see?

<See, nothing, but it is too still.>

Nothing evidenced cowled elves or their illusionary drones.

No vehicle blocked my path home.

The Edison node nearest hummed like it normally did. The node at the far end of the alley that cowl had used to attack me sparked occasionally. The grass at the pylon's base glowed rhet-eye blue just as it had since the attack.

"Kenrith?"

A shadow peeled itself away from a greater whole. The tiny silhouette remained in darkness a moment. Kenrith slid into a pane of light from the weary street lamp behind me, yellow light barely illuminating half a rhet face and a narrowed, glowing blue eye.

The sound of a long blade slowly slid from a scabbard proceeded silver glinting along a curved edge.

My unease tried to escape in my voice. "Kenrith?"

"You hurt my...daughter, *human*."

Human? Oh, shit.

"Tunoh is an adult. I never did anything to purposefully—"

The little shadow stalked forward. "You *hurt* my daughter. You *crippled* her...again."

"I didn't know at the time the spell had a time component." I backed away. "I can fix it. I already told Yshtiina and Noli. If you'll just let me see Tunoh—"

"If you see her again, human, it'll only be because your plucked eyeballs retain sight after I've sent the rest of you to hell."

I backed into the street, more concerned with the little fey than getting hit by sparse evening traffic. Kenrith followed me at a steady pace. Light fell across him, casting his blades with a ruddy hue. He wasn't using any glamour I could sense, so his anger had to be so complete that he wasn't even thinking about traffic cameras or wizard eyes.

I may have underestimated the downside here.

<Depends on how you feel about being fileted.>

My heel caught on a raised edge. It startled me, but I recovered

quickly. I stepped more fully into the circle created in the street by the manhole. For a moment, I considered walling myself behind a fifth rez barrier.

<Good plan, turn this into a siege with you planted square in the center of traffic.>

I really need to work out more spells for situations like this.

<Fireballs are glorious.>

The laugh almost got away from me. If I didn't find a way to diffuse the situation, there wasn't going to be a later or any more situations like the one I found myself enjoying.

"Knight Kenrith, by my honor, I—"

"*Humans* have no honor," Kenrith snarled.

At any point since entering the alley, the little rhet could've sprinted at me with that blurry, pixie-dust trailing speed. Instead, he drew things out, probably to ensure I felt the proper terror. I was feeling something, but terror only represented a small part. Anger—so close to the surface since the dam incident—crept up in a slow enough crescendo I barely felt the heat until my neck nearly sizzled. Outrage and injustice clung to anger and frustration. I didn't deserve the death stalking toward me across the manhole cover.

He's not moving as fast as the killer.

Rather than give the fey knight the opportunity to dodge too, I avoided tipping him off by pulling on the mananet. Taking care to draw slowly on my reserves, I threw the dice one more time to avoid actions that might declare permanent war with him.

"Do Yshtiina or Noli know you're doing this? Would they approve?"

Kenrith's reply almost escaped me "They never need to know."

<Nice knowing you.>

Kenrith stepped onto the manhole cover.

A combination of stored energy and my own soon to be extinguished life force raced to my call.

He felt the magic.

A fifth resonance cylinder snapped into place.

Kenrith sprang forward with a snarl, slamming into a milky white wall. The little knight blurred. A tornado of fairy dust and silver blades turned the interior into a fey Cuisinart.

In other situations, my pride or self-confidence might've combined into a fatal mistake. Fortunately, prudence demanded I not drop my guard facing off against the little rhet knight that had held his own for hours against a goblin horde.

Prudence, God love her, saved my ass.

Whether it was the fairy nature of the knight himself or some sort of magic in his blades, he did the impossible. The combined assault left barely visible silver lines in the swirling white magic.

Kenrith was slicing through an otherwise impenetrable fifth rez barrier with hundreds of tiny cuts. Like maintaining a first rez against something passing through the field, I bolstered the circle with power from the thin mananet. Regenerating the cylinder prevented whatever metal had been forged into his blades from rendering my circle less effective than cotton candy.

Razcolm dropped down next to the barrier. He circled the cage, shaking his butt and taunting the enraged knight in a singsong voice.

"Knock it off, Razcolm." I hurried toward the alley. "I'm really sorry about this, Kenrith, but I'll be right back."

"Coward! I'll turn the both of you into confetti! Come back and face your fate like a rhet!"

"I am," I shot back. "I'm observing the better part of valor."

Kenrith's redoubled assault forced me to halt mid-step just to hold the barrier against his onslaught. When he tired, or more likely stopped to plot a new attack, I hurried to a crack in the building foundation where I'd seen other rhet emerge.

"Please, I need to speak to Yshtiinataira or Noli." Kenrith's assaults on his cage throbbed behind my eyes like an ill-tempered headache.

<Better hurry. This is one rabid rhet.>

The threat twisted my gut on its way out of my mouth. "Please, I need Yshtiinataira's or Noli's help. I'd really rather not be forced to kill Knight Kenrith."

Yshtiina appeared as if by magic. Her expression left no doubt that surviving Kenrith by doing him harm would be short-lived and excruciating.

I removed the lid on my pain. "I never meant Tunoh any harm, and I can help her if you let me."

Noli stepped out of the shadows carrying Tunoh in her arms. My heart folded in on itself in ever tightening origami until it risked becoming a black hole. The little rhet that'd saved me looked wan and far too thin. If Tunoh'd been human, I'd have figured her wasting her way across Death's threshold.

I fell to my knees, my heart in my eyes.

The beginnings of a smile curled Tunoh's mouth, but she turned her head away before she spoke. "Hello, Magus."

Checking Tunoh's mothers offered mixed results. Noli eyed me hopefully while anger simmered in Yshtiina's expression.

Because I threatened to kill Kenrith?

<Probably just doesn't like your shining personality.>

I turned my back on them, fetching components I'd set aside. Each demi-goblin returned to their native form had improved my knowledge of the spell. I'd weighed my options, informed by repeated castings and extrapolated for Tunoh's race and condition. Rather than employ the druid restoration spell, I'd decided upon a modified version of Glamour.

Darrin had offered to help me reverse engineer Glamour, but I'd refused. Restoring Tunoh allowed room for neither mistake nor excuse. I owed Tunoh nothing less than the best. That meant modifying the spell personally. If I failed, all blame for forfeiture of my life rested only on me.

The spell board I laid before the rhet had seen a lot of miles. Blood and vomit stained the board. Scratches marred the laminated surface. Painstakingly drawn runes encircled the original circle and cardboard plugged the interlock holes meant for Thoth's proprietary nodules.

"Gentle, brave Tunoh, I would be honored if you would let me restore what you have lost saving my life."

Tunoh shared a look with both her mothers then nodded to Noli. Paws carried Tunoh over to the board and eased her down where I directed within the primary spell circle. Bright, tearful eyes watched me as I measured components one by one.

Glamour had been re-engineered for self-use, but my original spell had been designed for a healer to cast it on the injured. There'd been no way to test the new spell variant in its entirety, but systematically restoring the demi-goblins back to human had provided an ample refresher course.

Removing the intricately interwoven timer component proved a near impossible challenge. Adam had no doubt wanted to prevent even the most experienced user from removing Glamour's temporary nature.

The extreme extent Darrin's team had gone through just to hide the timer suggested Adam feared a savvy competitor would eventually reverse engineer the spell. Even if they couldn't compete, they could destroy Thoth's market by offering permanent changes for a one-time premium price.

I checked and double-checked everything. Throughout it all, Tunoh watched me with quiet intensity.

I met her eyes. "I've done everything within my power to redesign this spell so it will restore your body and the beauty component from Glamour—not that you need it."

Tunoh's ears tinged pink. She turned her face away.

"You all right? I'm not used to you being so quiet."

She shied away, covering her mouth with a paw. "Yes, Magus."

I sought her gaze. "Show me."

"What has this to do with your spell?" Yshtiina demanded.

"It's okay." Tunoh raised her chin much like I'd seen her and

Kenrith do in the past. Her lips peeled back to reveal a devastated mouth filled with broken teeth.

Flashes of Boss Golem slamming Tunoh around by her tail returned from nightmares. Heat prickled its way up my calves until it scorched my neck. I'd been angry enough to abandon my desire not to get involved when the elf behind everything had tried to kill me, but looking at Tunoh overshadowed the fury I'd felt before.

Next time he shows his face, I'm going to break it.

<Don't mess with Eli's little piece of tail.>

Shut up, Razcolm. Show the lady some respect.

As if she read my mind, Tunoh smiled without hiding her mouth.

"As I was saying, I've done all I can, but there was no way to test this. If it doesn't work, I will find a wa—"

"I trust you, Eli. Please go ahead."

I studied her, gaze flickering to Yshtiina and Noli.

"Why didn't you heal her?"

"She refused," Yshtiina said.

Noli nodded. "She insisted that you be the one to help."

My brows pushed together. "Tunoh?"

"Had to be you," she said. "There was no other way to keep father from killing you."

The intrepid knight continued to assault his cage in the back of my mind. I'd mostly pushed the irritation out of my thoughts while working on spell prep, but as I settled in to work Tunoh's restoration, it returned to the forefront.

I took a long, slow breath, drew in power from the thin edge of the mananet present in the alley. I'd intended to work the spell in Gateway Park's tier five mananet with the natural magic source deep beneath as a backup, but Kenrith's attack forced my hand. I offered up the magic stored within me.

Swirling creamsicle energy coalesced into a third rez field

around Tunoh and the components. Pink sparkles filled the interior. Tiny motes landed one by one on Tunoh.

My heart rate surged, thudding in my ears.

Her scream rent the night air.

<Scream for him, baby.>

I pushed Razcolm from my thoughts, focusing solely on Tunoh.

My heart jammed itself in my airway. I ignored the sudden lack of oxygen, watching every minute detail of her transformation.

Power leached into the spell faster than the mananet could provide. I let it draw on my reserves and my own personal energies.

Tunoh writhed in the circle, rolling back and forth, cupping her face. Her missing leg grew long and lithe out of the stump's end. Her hair lengthened, becoming more lustrous. Limb by limb, inch by inch, Tunoh became whole and wholly gorgeous.

All of a sudden, the power draw doubled, leaving me gasping.

<Queen of Night, Kenrith's going to kabob your balls!>

Tunoh swelled in size, her features smoothing into more human dimensions. In a moment, she was the same size she'd been when she'd saved me from a golem fist.

Shit.

<You think?>

"What have you done?" Yshtiina accused.

I ignored everyone else, applying my will to the spell. Best guess with no time to investigate, a stray hair or other DNA sample had contaminated the components. On-the-fly magic is far too loosey-goosey for my tastes, but I sculpted the magic, bullying it back into the shape intended.

Power drained away from me, nauseating me and leaving me dizzy. My vision dimmed.

Razcolm, hurt me!

The spider sank needles into my neck. It hurt like hell, and I forced away fears of him drinking my blood, but the pain delayed unconsciousness. Tunoh's DNA far outweighed whatever had contaminated the spell. I bullied magic's focus to ignore the minority contaminant in favor of the majority.

It took everything I had to offer, but Tunoh returned to her healed, glamorous self before I gave up my death grip on consciousness.

Nightmares of being chased through the Wasteland by a pony-tailed cheerleader wielding a bloody axe left my heart racing even after consciousness returned. Wet cement drew the warmth from my body. Buildings loomed to the sky, their faces illuminated by the occasional lit window. Squeezed between skyscrapers, thunderheads blocked the night sky. Tunoh and her father braced my head like the buildings did the sky.

Kenrith's glower glowed blue over a single sword held ready for action. Opposite him, Tunoh mirrored his displeasure. Clenched paws held two curved long-knives.

My neck hurt with each turn toward one of the rhet bracing me, particularly on Kenrith's side where Razcolm had bitten me.

Kenrith's blade flashed.

Blood beaded along the initially painless cut. Painted lines tickled their way across my cheek once the weight of their omen dragged them down my face.

He leaned close, his whiskers tickling my ear as he whispered. "We will continue this discussion."

Noli's firm tone drew my head up to see her standing on Tunoh's side of my waist. "Kenrith."

Kenrith met my eye, sweeping his sword away in an angry gesture that flicked blood from its tip. He turned, tail whipping my face and marched away.

Noli patted my thigh, then followed him. "He'll get over this, don't you worry."

I turned my head the other way to gaze at Tunoh.

She smiled, showing a mouth full of perfect teeth as she put away her blades. "Thank you, Magus."

"I promised I'd do what I could." I struggled up to a sitting position. "No one believed me."

"I did." Tunoh held her tail in her hands. "Don't worry. Noli's right. Father will calm now you've restored me."

"His expression doesn't agree."

Tunoh shrugged, batted her lashes but didn't meet my eyes. "So, what happened with the spell?"

"It worked."

"Not at first. I got big, and my face changed."

"Human DNA probably contaminated the components. Don't worry, I fixed you back the way you're supposed to be."

Her eyes rose to show me a hungry expression. "Would it have been so bad if I'd ended up big enough to be part of the human world?"

My exhaled breath puffed out my cheeks. "Your father would've slaughtered me."

"I won't let him hurt you, Eli."

"Thank you."

"So, Yshtiina says you're investigating a murder?"

"Can we talk about that later? I'm really beat."

She pinned her lip beneath her protuberant teeth and nodded.

I crawled into my box, adjusting my belongings to pillow my head. A glance past my feet showed her electric blue eyes watching. I closed my eyes, falling asleep some time before her vigil ended.

16

TRAILING BLOOD

I rose late the next morning.

I hurt everywhere, but no place worse than my throbbing cheek. I sat up in my box and stared out at the square of sunlight in the outside world. Traffic sounds mixed with pedestrian conversations reached me from the street. None of it seemed part of my cardboard-bordered world.

No one's trying to kill me. What do I do now?

<I could acquire a taxi and run you down if that would make you feel more at home.>

I laughed. "Thanks, I'm good."

I dug the Edison converter out of my pack, checking it over for damage from my run-in with the killer. When I felt sure the unit wasn't more than dirty, I abandoned my peaceful cave for the small strip of alleyway. I fetched my food bag, a jug of water, and the electric kettle I hadn't been able to jury rig.

I stepped toward my box when motion drew my attention to a SMLE cruiser parked beyond the foot traffic. Officer Hendan watched me through an open window with an intensity far beyond regular surveillance.

Ah, there's the undeserved black cloud ready to rain on my day.

I returned to my box and plugged the kettle in to test it. The element didn't heat. I checked the Edison node converter. An indicator light showed it sensed the wireless power broadcast by the nearby node. Another LED and a soft hum both proved its outlet powered and ready for use.

Checking the kettle showed the power light on, but despite several minutes, no heat emanated from the coils inside.

And there's the other shoe.

I put my multi-tool to the task of disassembling the kettle's wire guts. An hour's tinkering left me hungry, frustrated and still without hot water.

I gave the whole thing up as a bad job and repacked my belongings for the day. Making a list of the day's priorities, I realized my tracker construct wasn't among my belongings. Since SMLE would've made a case out of bloody fabric, I had to have lost it before I'd been transported to the hospital. Since I'd need another and I still hadn't confirmed Sunny had taken my warning seriously, I double-checked that I had Duval's card, hid my extra belongings in the little alley, climbed the other slatted fence and trudged toward the Manger.

I didn't own a cell phone. There was no way I could afford to buy one let alone pay for monthly service. In my absence, a magical version had been invented. I didn't know whether it was merely magically powered from the mananet providing an illusion rather than a hologram but otherwise connecting to a standard cellular network via embedded technology.

If they're not connected to a cellular network then how do they ensure that private conversations can't be listened to? Moreover, can I develop a spell to piggyback on this network?

SMLE didn't take long to start pacing me. Two cars drove past me, parked, watched me walk by and did it again in a relay. A block back in the crowd, Officer Verde paced me on foot.

When I arrived outside the Manger, rather than carry Razcolm into the Christian shelter, I set him to watch the door.

The little bell on the door announced me to the Manger's clientele. I closed my eyes, inhaling the warm smell of fresh-roasted coffee, braced for a squeal of delight.

No squeal came.

I scanned the room, glancing over the sparse homeless and the Christian motivational posters. My eyes fell on a sulky teen girl, knees pulled up onto the bench and held close to her chest. The old man who'd encouraged my entrance that first day toasted me with a coffee cup.

Homeless were being murdered on the street, but there was no sense of fear among the crowd of individuals each staying to themselves.

"Where's Sunny?" I asked.

A deep basso drew my eye to a hulking, black man even darker-skinned than myself. "She's not here, my friend, and I'm afraid you're too late for breakfast."

My stomach grumbled.

"Lunch will be ready in an hour," Grace said.

I crossed to the coffee pot. "This will have to suffice, I've got things to do today."

"Maybe I can find you something to take with you." Grace disappeared back into the kitchen.

I sipped hot nectar, rolling my eyes into my head with pleasure. I followed a basso singing and clank of dishes into the kitchen after Grace. He looked up from a butcher block spread with containers.

"As much as I appreciate the thought, I really just came by to make sure Sunny took my warning seriously."

"What warning?"

"There's a killer out there murdering the homeless."

"How do you know?" Grace asked.

I sighed. "I've been tasked to find her."

Grace turned away from the food. "Isn't a homeless man chasing a killer bent on murdering the homeless a little foolish, my friend?"

"A little, but I don't have much choice."

"There are always choices," Grace said.

A chuckle escaped me. "You'd think so, wouldn't you?"

Grace returned to his food prep. "Do you know what this killer looks like?"

"That's the problem, she can disguise her identity."

Grace frowned. "Then how do you know this killer is a she?"

I smirked and adjusted my tone to mimic Martin Mull. "The female of the species is more deadly than the male."

Grace laughed. "Very true, but doesn't prove anything."

"We've had a few run-ins." I shrugged. "Each time she's always been a she. Look, Grace, you need to make sure Sunny understands that anyone who comes through the door could be this murderer in disguise. You guys need to stop admitting new residents."

Grace chuckled. "You don't know Sunny very well if you think you can persuade her to stop helping people, even temporarily."

"If she doesn't, the killer could slaughter everyone here."

Grace wrapped the culmination of his leftovers in a paper towel and extended what looked like a meatloaf sub. "Here. Thank you for the warning, my friend. Be safe and go with God's blessings."

"This is serious, Grace."

"As is God's work and the protection He grants His workers."

Arguing with religious zealots seldom produces much more than strife, and I had no desire to argue my way out of free coffee or Grace's leftovers. I held up the sandwich. "Thank you. If it's all right, I'm going to use the phone before I go."

Grace smiled. "What's ours is yours, my friend."

Duval picked up on the first ring. "It's about time. Stay where you are, and we'll pick you up."

I blinked at the phone. "Um, Duval? It's me—"

"I know who you are and where the hell you are. Don't leave."

I stepped outside with a refilled coffee and bit into the meatloaf sandwich. The meatloaf between French bread was gravy rather than ketchup based. Grace had added romaine lettuce, tomato, and onion-flavored cream cheese to create heaven on a bun.

It took considerable willpower to stop eating after the first quarter sandwich and save the rest for later.

I leaned against the nearest building and folded my arms. A passerby threw coins in the general direction of my feet. The change rattled against the concrete, one coin finally falling flat after several moments of determined resistance. I glowered at the retreating back, suddenly tempted to the pick up the coins and throw them at her.

Duval's window was down before the truck stopped next to me. "Get in."

"Why hello, Duval. It's nice to see you too."

Duval glared and jabbed a thumb backward. "Get in."

It's true I'd contacted Duval to replace my lost scrap of bloody carpet. Just the same, being ordered to do what I was already planning to do made me not want to do it. The door on the opposite side of the truck open to the sound of blaring horns. Mihail got out of the truck and marched around toward me, leaving his open door and blocking traffic. I slid my hands into my pockets, fingers finding a snack baggie of rotting food.

<Do it! Do it!>

Mihail shifted his weight to step onto the sidewalk.

I smirked, shrugged, and strolled over to get in the truck.

Duval turned around to face me as I buckled my seatbelt. "I do not have time to play games, Mister Graham."

"You run a bunch of beggars and bums. It's not like anybody punches a time clock, and you certainly aren't curing cancer."

"People are dying," Duval said.

Mihail got back in the car, shutting the door on the horns and screaming. We were moving again almost at once.

"Yeah, I saw that first hand." Duval opened his mouth, but I spoke first. "I'm surprised Dudley didn't tell you about my little encounter with her after she killed Zahora. I know you're aware of SMLE's attempt to kill me."

He frowned. "I'm aware you tried to abuse my largess, and what did that get you? Stuck in jail while my people are out here dying."

"If you faced the killer, why is he still breathing?" Mihail asked.

"First off, because I'm not a murderer," I said. "Second, she caught me off guard."

Mihail laughed. "You can defeat eight-foot stone monsters, but you can't deal with some girl?"

Heat prickled my neck. "Look, golems are magical constructs. I took their magic away, but your killer isn't an animated construct."

"Excuses. Told you he isn't the right man for this," Mihail said.

"Enough, both of you," Duval said. "You found the killer, tell us where to find her and your part is done."

"I don't know where to find her," I said.

Duval wrenched around and looked into my face. "You found her once, find her again right now."

"I can't. I lost the carpet fragment in the fight."

"That's why you called?" Duval asked.

"Yeah. I need more carpet and a couple more things," I said.

"A gun?" Duval asked.

I opened my mouth to say no when the firebolter sprang to mind. It seemed unlikely Duval would hand over such a hard-to-come-by weapon. As tempted as I was to ask anyway and find out, the prospect of being picked up by SMLE with a restricted government weapon pushed my luck too far.

I needed a weapon that couldn't get me into any more hot water.

<You need a fireball.>

I scanned the air for what had to be an incredibly fast-moving pigeon. A tile shard-tipped leg caught my attention as Razcolm waved from the bed of Duval's truck.

I downed the last of my coffee. "I need three ceiling fan pull chains, rubber bands, more of Ullie's blood, and a case of juice boxes."

Duval's brows rose.

I shrugged. "I'm thirsty."

I sucked tropical fruit Hi-C through a tiny straw in the back seat and connected the pull chains. Mihail slammed the driver's side door, shot me a dirty, rain-bedraggled look and flipped a bloody square of carpet inside a Ziploc right into my lap. The formerly white carpet was brown with week-old blood. I moved the square into position but hesitated.

Is the killer even going to have enough left on his feet to track?

"Well?" Duval asked.

I frowned at the dried blood.

Is there a better way to track the killer now that I've seen her?

Nothing friendly remained in Duval's tone. "What are you waiting for? You have what you asked for, now do something."

I met his eye, fighting the wasteland instincts not to meet eyes and challenge another who might just be itching for a fight. "Let me explain something to you, Oh mighty Bum Mafioso. Proper magic requires planning—a lot of it. This blood, through delays I've no doubt you will blame on me, is dry. The remnants on the killer's shoes I tracked may well have worn off by now. So you'll have to forgive me if I take a moment to consider better options."

Mihail's hand shifted inside his jacket.

Duval laughed.

Mihail relaxed, but his brow creased with concern.

"It's okay Mihail. He is right. I don't second-guess how the dentist would fix my teeth. I don't second-guess what tools the mechanic uses to fix my car. We acquired an expert in magic. We should probably let him be the expert." Duval turned his attention back to me. Menace suffused his voice. "Just so long as our expert doesn't fail to lead us to Ullie's murderer before the next of my people die."

We stared at one another.

I'd be lying if I didn't admit that part of me wanted to be rid of Mihail and Duval, even if that meant using one of Razcolm's plague spells. Duval and his crew were a blight on society, making a business out of people's goodness, creating skepticism of those in genuine need and ultimately taking food out of the mouths of my fellow homeless.

Truth be told, I'd gone pretty far out of my way—against my personal interests—to save lives since my release. Some of the people I saved had wrongly convicted me, sending me off to endure a century of living hell, but that didn't matter. I still just wanted to be left alone. Now that Duval had involved me, like it or hate it, I could not just let living, breathing people already down on their luck—Duval's people notwithstanding—get murdered.

Unfortunately, Duval had appointed himself judge, jury, and executioner. I had no problem destroying golems. I should've felt worse about killing goblins, but as bad as it might sound, they weren't real to me. The cold eyes that had stared into my soul and weighed it didn't fit either description.

I did believe in the law and right—no matter what Porter thought. Murdering Zahora's killer wasn't right.

"Well?" Mihail asked. "Where am I driving?"

My gaze shifted to him, and all the blood drained out of my body. Mihail was a scary enough thug, but for an instant, he transformed into a bloody-mouthed demi-goblin—like Bilbo when he tried to take the ring from Frodo.

"What?" Mihail said.

Several blinks returned the thug to his intimidating but not paranormal self. I rubbed my eyes. Unsure what else to do, I invoked the seeking spell. The pull chains stretched out in directions only separated by degrees. With as old as the blood was, it surprised me the spell found two sources to track.

I handed the construct to Duval. "Follow the weaker pull."

Mihail grumbled under his breath. "About time." Not long after, Mihail's grumbles became snarls. "His magic is broken!"

I couldn't help but laugh. The seeking spell was definitely latched onto something. Mihail's problem was the same one I'd fought—the spell's indifference to buildings and one-way streets.

Mihail still hadn't realized the shortcoming in my spell. Our chase could conceivably go on forever if the killer remained on the move, particularly in a vehicle.

Our search ended barely before Mihail decided to take his frustration out on yours truly.

Late afternoon, the pull chains led us between a pair of partially demolished factories to an alley running between old mills converted into apartments.

Cold swirled in my guts despite the truck's heater.

I reached out with my senses. The mid-strength mananet almost hid a subtle prickle of illusion magic. "She's here. Up ahead somewhere."

Mihail withdrew a large pistol from inside his jacket.

Duval bent and extracted a sawed-off shotgun that had apparently been pointed at my feet beneath his seat. He turned toward me. "You're getting out with us. Arm up."

With what? Slip-n-slide?

Razcolm's sigh felt like a shiver in my brain. *<Still no fireball?>*

When have I had time? You want to volunteer one?

<No, but we could barter. Do you have any unwanted offspring?>

No.

<Waiting for you to knock up Sunny and squirt one out would take too long. Want to trade a favor for the spell knowledge?>

My frustration at the little creep vented through my glare at

Mihail. We locked eyes for a three count. He broke the connection with a glance toward Duval, and I had a sudden feeling I shouldn't carelessly stand anywhere susceptible to accidental crossfire.

We exited the truck into an icy deluge.

Duval and Mihail took up position to either side in front of me.

I laughed.

They're protecting the squishy mage.

A homeless old man in his sixties, staggered into view. He clutched a blood-soaked chest.

Duval and Mihail let their weapons droop.

The beggar wheezed, raising his free hand and mouthing in shock. It looked as if the killer had gotten to him only just before we'd arrived.

Except other than the blood, his clothes aren't damp.

I threw my slip-n-slide spell beneath his feet. It wouldn't last long in the rain, but I'd take any advantage it offered. "That's your killer."

Neither Duval nor Mihail asked any questions. Their weapons snapped up and started firing.

Their willingness to kill whomever I indicated shook me.

Duval stopped to reload cartridges one at a time.

Mihail reached for a replacement clip.

The rain quickly put down the explosion of smoke from their guns, revealing the old man's nonplused expression. He locked cold, unfazed silver eyes on mine. "Elias Balthazar Graham. You've sworn allegiance to the hero slayers?"

"I—what?"

He surged forward, snatched up a brick, hurled it at Mihail and lunged toward Duval.

"Duval, watch out."

Several quick steps brought me to Duval's aid.

Mihail beat me there. He shoved Duval into the alley trash and emptied his pistol into the murderer's face. Mihail's fierce grin drained of color, bending into a confused frown. A backward stumble pulled the knife from his chest. He collapsed like a puppet cut free.

"Mihail!" Duval's roar was drowned out by his shotgun.

If Mihail's heavy caliber pistol hadn't hurt the innocuous old man even at point blank range, the shotgun wouldn't leave a mark.

I cast around for something to use as a weapon. I didn't come up with anything offensive, so I snatched up an old trash can lid. Using the slightly dented rim as a base, I invoked a fifth resonance circle that sheathed the abused metal in a physically impenetrable, milky white body shield.

A magical surge brought my eyes back to the fight.

Duval extended an eyeGuardian.

The killer bolted sideways.

Duval triggered the flame rune.

A gout of magical fire swept along the killer's wake toward me.

Bolstering my shield with a sixth rez might block the fire, but I still needed a weapon. I dug out the enchanted Zippo, flipped it open, and completed the first incantation.

Black Sharpie runes flared to life.

The spray of eyeGuardian flame turned away from its former path, all speeding toward me.

<Magus, get rid of that thing.>

I tossed the lighter and dove the other way. Flame flashed over me, crisping my short rainbow locks and leaving my skin feeling sunburnt, but it missed. The fire followed the lighter, blackening the wet concrete and filling the alley with quickly cooling steam.

I rolled to my feet rather than risk a knife to the back. Duval still had the killer's attention, so I leapt forward and clobbered the killer with all the force I could bring to bear with my shield

My blow knocked the killer forward.

Duval cried out.

Another shield bash battered the killer sideways.

A stab wound bubbled blood from Duval's gut.

Where's the knife?

I whirled just in time to wall myself off from the killer's lunge. The still-dry old man grabbed the edges of my shield with his armed and unarmed hands, trying to wrench the trash can lid from my grip. Beyond the milky white, silver eyes wrestled me without the slightest trace of fear or anger.

I expanded the shield too wide for him to keep hold with both hands. I drove him bodily backward on the slippery concrete with all the football skills of someone who'd never played. I protected myself while keeping him away from Duval, but I had no idea what to do with him next.

The killer solved my problem. He grabbed the shield's bottom edge and heaved upward and sideways. What could only be spell-enhanced strength forced my arm upward and outward.

He lunged under the shield at my exposed chest.

Instead of fighting, I went with the momentum. A clumsy pirouette aided by rain and the remains of my previous spell twisted me away. His blade gouged an excruciating crease in my side.

The knife caught in the fabric of my jacket. I continued my turn, reduced my fifth rez barrier's size to prevent obstacles fouling my attack, and slammed the shield into him.

My blow sent him into the brick wall. He performed some kind of handspring, reversed his momentum and raced toward me.

I was running out of both gas and ideas. In the Wasteland, I'd have been running long before now.

The killer dropped into a baseman's slide, ducked my shield and nearly kicked my legs out from under me.

I staggered backward.

My heel caught.

I tumbled into a pile of trash.

The old man sprang to his feet. He didn't even look winded.

He charged again.

I snatched up a dented Pepsi can. I invoked a fifth rez cone, setting the makeshift footman's lance like a pikeman defending against a cavalry charge.

He beat the weapon to one side and rushed forward to deliver my death without the slightest expression.

<Big shield! Great big shield!>

I had no idea what Razcolm intended, but I wasted no time questioning him. I threw all the energy I could into my shield, expanding the size and increasing the magnitude. The bottom of the shield caught on the ground, tipping me backward. A swirling white wall blocked my vision, canted between the asphalt and a brick building behind me.

The colossal roar of a diesel engine and a short squeal of tires was our only warning.

Duval's tires caught.

The truck leapt forward, slammed into the killer as it ramped up my shield. A cacophonous crunch of smashing brick and metal filled the alleyway.

The truck was only visible as a dark rectangle beyond the white, but I felt the energy drain caused by supporting its weight and the back tires spinning against the wet, frictionless magical surface.

Diesel fumes and heating rubber clogged my nostrils.

<Damn, damn, damn!>

I let go of the trash can lid and scrambled to one side before dropping the circle.

The truck dropped several feet. The rear bed hit hard and bent. The cab made an ear-splitting screech as gravity dragged what was left of the front end down the building's face.

Razcolm scurried out of the cab and onto its roof. He pointed a tile tipped leg. *<He's getting away. We've got to go after him.>*

I was breathing too hard to answer the little imp, even in my thoughts. So, I just stared.

<He's limping, we can catch him!>

I glanced over at Duval. All of the bum Mafioso's color dripped to the cement from otherwise saturated threads. He needed help.

I didn't like Duval. I didn't like what he stood for, and in many ways, he'd brought his circumstances onto himself. He'd been willing to deal out vigilante justice.

But I'm not. Razcolm I need components.

<You're not serious. He threatened to—>

I shut Razcolm up with a quick list of the things that might fulfill the elemental requirements of my restoration spell. When he hesitated, I compelled the construct to fetch them. My origami spider dragged Razcolm off screaming if not literally kicking.

I bent next to Duval, putting pressure against the puncture wound where his hands had fallen away.

Come on. Come on.

Once more I needed to heal part of the body but only knew how to restore the whole thing. I ripped open his shirt with my free hand. Fingertips drew bloody runes in preparation for Razcolm's return.

"You probably can't hear me, but this is the only way I know to save you." I couldn't help the smirk. "This is going to hurt."

Seconds that felt like an eternity crept by, but Razcolm didn't return with what I needed. I'd seen plenty of wounds in the Wasteland, but I knew precious little about actual medicine.

The killer had stabbed Duval rather than sliced him. The injury had bled a lot, but until he'd lost consciousness, Duval had kept pressure on the wound.

Timely medical care remained vital, but Duval had more time than he otherwise might've had.

Razcolm?!

Nothing.

I prefer not to play loose with the forces of the universe. The idea of trying to initiate the Druid restoration spell with makeshift components and only my will made maggots writhe in my gut.

I searched my pockets as I scanned around. My fingers closed on Willie's communicator. I yanked it free and to my lips. "Willie?!"

Willie's face appeared in almost immediate response. "Eli? What's wrong? Sitrep?"

"Please tell me this thing has a GPS locator."

"Affirmative, bringing up your location now."

"A man here's been stabbed. He needs an ambulance."

"Medevac on the way. Are you injured?"

His question reminded me of the throbbing pain I'd almost managed to push from my thoughts. When I glanced back up from the wound, Willie's eyes had narrowed. "Minor. I'll let the medics look at me once they've seen to...this man. Thank you. Goodbye."

"Wait, Eli, what happened?"

"We tracked a killer here, the one killing the homeless. He got the upper hand."

"That's a job for the authorities. You shouldn't involve yourself."

I frowned. "Sometimes we don't have the luxury of staying on the sidelines."

His voice hardened. "Copy that. What else do you need?"

"I need to catch this bastard." I put away the radio despite Willie's continued questions.

I reclaimed my Zippo and turned toward the diesel-powered ladder. Climbing onto the truck and up to the hole in the building hurt like hell. Brick fragments and bent rebar made climbing inside even more difficult. Pain in my side made it all but impossible—or would have if it weren't for the stubbornness I'd inherited from Dad.

No one home?

It didn't seem prudent to question that little bit of luck. The killer had been driven through a wall, kitchen cabinets and if the dented ceiling above the breakfast bar were any judge, into the maroon-tiled kitchen with substantial force.

The apartment's residents weren't likely to be happy with their new open-air veranda, but they hadn't been home to get gutted by a raving psychopath either. A curb-scavenged, paisley sofa had been shoved to one side, allowing the killer to charge through the far window.

And he only limped away?

<Would I lie?>

In a heartbeat.

Razcolm climbed up to where I was, hanging upside down from a piece of rebar bent slightly into the room. *<You wound me, human, and after I saved your life. In fact—>*

No. I didn't ask you to help. I don't owe you a debt. Where are my components?

<I found them as commanded, then dumped them on the way back.>

"Razcolm, I need those components to heal Duval."

<Didn't you call for what your people call healers? Besides, you're better off with Duval and Mihail dead.>

I scoured the debris for something I could use to track the killer—not that I really wanted to meet him in a dark alley or a sunlit street for that matter. I could collect Mihail's blood, since gutting the thug would have soiled the old man even if he never looked bloody. That avenue put me right back where I'd started with Ullie.

There has to be something actually from the killer to track.

<Good luck with that. I'm the only one who managed to hurt him.>

Do you know whether he was a he or she?

<I didn't turn him over to check, but he looked male to me.>

Great, this newest encounter leaves me in pronoun ambiguity hell.

The killer changed appearances. Gushing blood didn't mark him. Gunshots didn't injure him. Even driven through a wall by a massive truck had only left him with a limp.

He's got to be using some sort of fifth resonance armor.

<That kind of armor wouldn't stop physics. He should've been crushed, smashed, smooshed like the filthy bug you humans are against my bumper.>

Duval's bumper.

I corrected without thinking.

Is there a way to geometrically arrange a flexible barrier so it won't compress beyond a certain threshold?

<So, Magus, if I happened to find something you could use to track this guy, would that be worth a debt to you?>

I can get plenty of Mihail's blood. It's all over the alley.

<How about a piece of the killer's clothes?>

I whirled, scrutinizing the little spider. When I didn't see it, I pushed commanded into my voice. "Hand it over, Razcolm."

Spiders shouldn't smile. *<Yeah, thought you might try that, so I didn't pick it up.>*

"Point to it."

Razcolm flopped onto his back and extended all of his legs in different directions. The construct had to obey me, so one of the legs had to be pointing at the evidence. Unfortunately, nothing stopped Razcolm from doing more than I compelled him to do...unless.

"Point only to the scrap."

Razcolm's legs adjusted but still pointed in eight directions.

"I ordered you to only point at the object."

<And I obeyed. It's not my fault the planet's curvature is blocking your view.> He giggled. *<I'm a fey. I can play these games all day.>*

My calves prickled. "Reassemble into the spider, hold your shape, point at the scrap, and then cease moving."

The series of commands resulted in almost identical positions as before. Razcolm lay on his back pointing eight directions

"Hold still right there." I'd already given the command, but reinforcing the compulsion seemed prudent. "Now, *stay*."

I repeated the word over and over like I was trying to teach a puppy. I started with the legs pointed toward the broken debris, eyeballing the area each leg indicated. I didn't see anything. After three passes I started thinking whatever I was looking for was under some of the debris.

There.

<*Shit.*>

I bent over to pick up a blood-covered scrap of what had to be part of the killer's outer armor. Mihail's drying blood had camouflaged the vaguely scale-shaped piece against the reddish-brown linoleum octagons. The underside proved a light grey vinyl. I didn't clean away Mihail's blood, but the edge seemed a nondescript cream color.

Now I've got you...not that I know what to do with you.

<*Planning on bringing a fireball to this fight, or are you just going to get all lubed up again?*>

Razcolm had a point. I needed a plan.

Before I could give the situation my full attention, ambulance sirens neared, heralding the arrival of painkillers and inconvenient questions. Duval had been gutted and Mihail stabbed. Detective Brooke's 'once a criminal, always a criminal' philosophy pretty much guaranteed I'd end up arrested. Avoiding the questions and ultimately another stay in SMLE lockdown wouldn't take much more than disappearing out the apartment door. The EMTs would find Duval without my help. Gnawing pain argued for meeting the ambulance, and I hated to leave behind a perfectly good pack of Hi-C drink boxes, but the delay could cost lives.

I can get more, and the Wasteland didn't have pain meds. I'll manage.

I held an arm tight against my side and cut across the kitchen for the apartment door. Splashes of red and green caught my attention. I dug three empty apple juice boxes and the crumpled paper towel out of the small trash can. Cradling my side with the arm holding the juice boxes, I exited using the front door and a paper towel.

The single torturous flight of stairs left me wishing my morals would have allowed raiding the medicine cabinet.

17

UNEXPECTED REPERCUSSIONS

I hurried away, walking softly in the rain to spare my side. Considering the miserable weather since my release, I probably should have been working on some sort of spell to keep dry. As with most of the times I realized a need for some kind of spell, there was too much going on to do more than give it a passing thought.

Breakfast—if you could call the slow meal I'd made of Grace's meatloaf sub over the long trip to Olympian Heights and back—had been a long time ago. The hour was headed steadily toward night, and I was hungry, tired, and in pain. All I really wanted to do was go back to my box and curl up around a bottle of Tylenol.

Well, maybe not curl up.

Duval was out of the way for the time being. In a lot of ways, that meant I could put aside tracking down Ullie's murderer. Truth be told, I didn't feel like I should. The killer had named me repeatedly. An uneasy foreboding in the pit of my stomach promised that his knowledge of me meant something.

The strange behavior of Officer Verde's second visit sprang to mind. I didn't want to be right, but it seemed likely the disguised killer had questioned me in SMLE's interrogation room. If that was the case, his questions about my interaction with Adam meant he'd been watching me.

But why? What about me interests a murderer?

I ducked down the next alley and rummaged through a dumpster.

<*You have got to be kidding me. You're going to track that thing? Do you have a death wish?*>

When I kept digging instead of answering, I expected more grief. The sudden silence irked me into looking at Razcolm. He stood eerily still, his whole body raised as if he was scenting the air.

<*I've got to go. Don't kill yourself until I get back.*> Razcolm refolded into a pigeon and disappeared into the evening sky before I could say a word elsewise.

I cursed and returned to my search.

A broken bootlace, a bread tie, and a purple plastic-coated paperclip became the components for a seeking spell. I dumped out the contents of one of my slip-n-slide spells and rinsed the bag beneath a rain gutter downspout. With a scrap of the killer's armor paper-clipped to the bootlace inside the baggie and sealed with the bread tie, I cut across a construction site toward the Columbia in search of a mananet.

I'd been in such a hurry to leave the scene of Mihail's murder, I'd fled a perfectly good mananet. Finding the killer was definitely urgent, but not so critical I was willing to sacrifice my life force for a mere seeking spell. Besides, I wanted to give the killer enough time to reach home, so there was no reason to turn an emergency into a full-fledged crisis. I'd find a mananet, restore everything I'd used holding up the truck, and cast my seeker.

It took longer than I expected to find a mananet, forcing me to wonder whether the technology and electric companies had somehow forged an alliance to dominate Seufert Fells's new industrial area. The field I found was much stronger than the one I had in the alley. I drew in power that felt like flat Pepsi tasted.

My eyes rose, staring down the paved canyon between factory and construction sites. A darkening ribbon called to me. The cold rushing waters hid a river of magic pure and powerful and straight from beyond the Silver.

I licked my lips.

My fingers tightened into a fist to hold off a shudder.

My need drew me forward several steps. I closed my eyes, trying to shut out the siren beneath the waters. Energy from the mananet filled the place where I kept magic but didn't fill the need. I drew and drew until it pressed against the inside of my skin in waves of pins and needles.

I don't know how long I stood in the street with my eyes closed. Considering the number of people that wanted to harm me, it probably wasn't the best choice I've ever made. Twilight was well on the way to dark when I'd steeled myself enough to face the siren once more.

Beyond the shadows of the calling waters, a building glowed like an oasis of light. Spotlights swept the dark storm clouds in an echo of Gotham. I let the spectacle draw me to river's edge. Flash-bulbs and camera drones further illuminated the massive icon of sweeping curves and jewel-faceted angles. Limousines, stretch SUVs, and LUX air drones delivered partygoers to a wide crimson carpet flanked by floating swirls of mage light. Illusions and holographic projectors waged a choreographed war to display the letters of one word: FORETOLD.

Nothing to do with me.

I invoked my seeking spell, careful to do so with the magic I carried rather than the oh-so-tempting power beneath the Columbia. The baggie tied to my finger floated outward like a halfhearted balloon, pointing directly at the convention center.

A piece of a murderer leads to Adam's party. Why am I not surprised?

I turned eastward toward Fells Overlook Bridge and the ruined remains of the hydroelectric dam. Instead, an about-face turned me westward away from bad memories. I pulled my Army jacket tight against cold rain and colder riverside wind.

Part way across the western bridge a swath of darkness swallowed the light of bordering neighborhoods, returning it reflected on ghostly specters. In the dark, The Dalles Memorial Cemetery seemed an endless extension of the underworld. PGE had buried the victims of the dam accident with marble headstones and apologies as restitution for their industrial accident—so many, the cemetery stretched out in a crescent-shaped necropolis to rival the city's pre-destruction size. Many a dare and not a few virginities had ended within the walled testament to mistakes made.

The seeking spell didn't point upstream toward Foretold when I stepped foot onto Oregon soil once more. I followed it away from ghosts of the past toward downtown. Both my feet and my stomach grumbled conspiratorially. The sound of my footfalls in the shallow puddles atop the sidewalk set a steady rhythm counterpoised against the light fall of rain and the shushing sounds of car tires cutting through wet streets.

Buildings grew as the magical draw led me into the center of the city. I passed beneath the glowing orange eye well north of Thoth tower. High-rises shrank with age but more slowly on the eastern side of downtown. I recognized a few of the streets and realized just how close I was to Darrin's apartment.

My strength flagged. Despite cold and careful steps, the throbbing in my side worsened. Darrin was probably in the new convention center, wiggling a finger beneath the too tight collar of a dress shirt and tie. I chanced turning aside anyway in the hope of a spare aspirin.

If he isn't home, I just tough it out. How many miles, how many countless hours did I just soldier on through injury and pain inside the Wasteland? What's a few more?

My feet took me to Darrin's apartment complex. I'd never admit doing so to Sunny, but truth be told, I really needed a friendly face. Runeguard locks prevented me from entering the building on my own. I probably could have worked out how to disable them, but I was just too weary.

I pressed the call button for Darren's apartment, oddly hopeful he would be home. His voice was almost as good as discovering an unoccupied oasis in the Wasteland.

"Hello?"

"Darren, it's me—"

The door buzzed before I could finish identifying myself. "404, Eli, come on up."

Just beyond the door, a series of royal blue Walmart carpets attempted to soften the institutional feel of the complex's foyer. The building was too close to the hydroelectric plant to have survived the destruction of The Dalles but felt old nonetheless. Wooden stairs with blue carpet pretending to be a runner invited me to climb up to the fourth floor. I declined, taking a shabby elevator that smelled of mothballs and would've transformed three from a crowd into full-blown claustrophobia.

The elevator warbled a cheery ding to encourage me out its doors. The hall beyond did a far more enticing job, drawing me onto soft carpets between warm walnut panels below robin's egg blue paint. It didn't take long to find Darrin's door in the softly-lit hall.

Darrin opened the door before I could knock and embraced me.

I winced.

He backed off in a hurry. "Sorry. Are you all right?"

"It's been a long day."

"You're here. It must've been."

"Do you have any aspirin and maybe a towel?"

"Right. Sure. Come in, come in." Darrin led me into a modestly appointed apartment that should've been the envy of others his age. He gestured me on to a comfortable barstool and rummaged in the cabinets on the opposite side of the breakfast bar. He set a first aid kit larger than most lunchboxes along with bottles of aspirin, acetaminophen, and ibuprofen onto the space between us. He added two hand towels and a bottle of black cherry-flavored water.

"That should get you started. I'll dig up some fresh towels for a shower and old sweats to wear while we bandage you and I wash your clothes."

I opened my mouth to object, but he shut me down with a hard bark. "No, Eli. This time you're going to do as I say. God only knows where you've been—"

"Mostly jail."

"—or what muck you've rolled through. I will not let the man who took me under his wing die of an infected wound because he was too proud to accept a little hot water and soap."

Darrin shoved the bottles toward me. "Take whichever med works best for you while I get everything ready—though I don't think Head & Shoulders makes a special shampoo for rainbow hair."

He marched deeper into the apartment. The bar stool rotated slowly around, letting me follow his exit.

Huh.

I turned back around and downed four from each bottle. The shower was heavenly, despite the throbbing water from the massager beating against my gouged skin. I dressed, stepping out of the foggy bathroom into the pervasive aroma of garlic, butter, and onions.

Darrin dumped a wok into a large bowl, piling grilled onions, sliced garlic, fresh spinach, sautéed mushrooms, and chicken onto angel hair pasta. Tongs tossed the mixture and mounded two plates. He extended a fork to me.

"Eat first, a full belly will relax you." He smiled, practically daring me to object. "Make you more pliant, too."

Mentors are supposed to be wise. I took the fork and sat at the bar. Darrin brought his own plate around from the kitchen side.

Rotating on the stool to keep him in sight—a Wasteland habit, a picture of Darrin beaming at a gorgeous woman caught my eye.

He noticed my attention. "Nicole. She's great—though I'm a bit worried about her self-esteem issues."

"Her ears are pointed. Glamour?"

He nodded. "She was the first of the failed test subjects I fixed once you told me how."

Cold stole my appetite. "You swore not to share what I gave you with Adam."

"I didn't. I blinded the wizard eyes with a mag five fifth rez, restored Nicole and then cast Glamour on her while she remained unconscious from the pain. Adam's convinced fixing the problem is as simple as casting Glamour using their DNA."

"You never tested recasting before my release?"

"No. Thecia was afraid it would make things worse."

"Adam's an idiot. Are all Thoth's victims fixed now?"

He shook his head. "A lot of the women had hairbrushes in their bags, but with the men, we're stuck." His expression became pointed. "Unless someone reclaimed some DNA from their homes."

"No. How's Adam keeping the victims quiet?"

Darrin looked away.

Steel entered my voice. "Darrin?"

He put down his fork. "I don't know how he's doing it, but somehow he's rewriting their memories."

Rewriting memories? That shouldn't be possible.

A sudden dread welled up in me. Even with everything Adam had done to me, I didn't want to believe he was so morally bankrupt he'd actually use the same Incan spell against human beings that he'd claimed I had.

"I'm a bit worried what Nicole will do once Glamour wears off." He took a bite of pasta to hide the pain in his voice but went on before emptying his mouth. "What if transformation reversal restores her memories? What will she think of me? I turned her into a monster."

What can I possibly say? From what he's told me, he did precisely that with full knowledge of the possibility.

Shortly after my release from the Wasteland, Darrin had claimed Adam had him over a barrel. My former partner had lied to the kid, made Darrin feel he had no choices, and coerced him to do things that became certain blackmail material.

Damn you, Adam.

"I tried to talk her out of the test." Darrin's eyes proclaimed the inner torment hidden by his expression. "I wasn't allowed to tell her what I thought would happen, but I tried, Eli. I swear."

"If the spell's end returns those memories to her, then tell her the same truth you just told me," I said. "Besides, if she refused to be dissuaded, she's terminally vain."

Darrin's tone hardened. "Eli."

I held up a hand to forestall him. "Which means she'll want another casting from you, something otherwise not possible unless you two are still dating. Not that you should want to stay with someone who'd use you like that."

Darrin sobered, swallowing hard. "She doesn't need me. She could just buy another casting."

"Wait, Thoth's putting Glamour back on the market? The slightest bit of stray DNA could cause who knows what damage."

"Which is why Glamour is now only available inside an eyeStore—which also solves Adam's industrial espionage concerns. You should probably eat before it gets cold."

I looked at the food. The mix of colors and aromas stoked my appetite, and I dug in. Darrin's cooking was incredible, damn near heavenly when compared to my usual fair. Fork after fork kept me silent as Darrin regaled me about his elven girlfriend.

What I heard—outside Darrin's happiness—didn't make me happy. Adam was playing with peoples' lives like the Olympians in the old Clash of the Titans movie, and he really didn't need any more fuel for his delusions of godhood.

Why am I surprised? He hired SMLE to kill me.

My plate slowly emptied as Darrin moved on from his girlfriend to the new projects he was working on. He was probably violating an NDA, but my separation from Thoth didn't occur to him. The excited eagerness as he talked about new spells buoyed me up for a while, but eventually, the weight of the food, painkillers, and a long day dragged me toward sleep.

I excused myself to the bathroom in preparation to make the long walk back to my alley. It was hard to avoid my reflection while washing my hands, but I managed by knocking a prescription bottle into the sink when reaching for the soap. Fortunately, I caught the Imovane bottle before it could spill and put it back.

"Darrin, I should go."

"Your clothes aren't ready. Besides, this has been nice," Darrin said. "Like old times."

It had. So much so, I'd forgotten all about pushing Darrin away for my brief visit.

This was a mistake. What if Adam finds out? If he hurts Darrin...

"Sit, I'll grab you some more food. Eat while I check on your laundry, then we'll bandage you up."

Without my clothes, I had little choice. I ate what he gave me until my stomach threatened mutiny. Darrin didn't have the expertise to stitch up the wound, and there was no way for me to properly reach. We settled for antibiotic gel, gauze pads and overtop it all, duct tape to better hold my side together. I was nodding off on the couch before I realized it, Darrin's voice soothing me to sleep as he told me more about his life.

"Adam gave me access to your notebooks from that last spell you were researching before you went to prison," Darrin said.

Sleep blinked away too slowly, and fatigue slurred my speech. "Wah? N-no, tha's too dangerous."

Darrin hovered over me, an Addams Family grin on his young

face. "But so powerful. I couldn't work it at first, but I found another little gem in your notes."

"Darrin?"

Sparkling blue and swirling white magic sprang to life around me. Darrin gestured through some kind of spell just beyond the wall. "Seems there's a way to draw magic out of other people with power."

Magic sank long, jagged fangs into me. I struggled against it, but couldn't seem to collect my thoughts enough to remember how to beat the circles caging me. Agony intensified, power drained away, but I couldn't wake myself up.

Wait, what was in that pill bottle?

Darrin lived within a tier four mananet, but without any idea how to thwart the circles it didn't matter how much magic waited on Darrin's side of the barrier. I tried to pull on my life force, but my ability to manipulate magic failed all together like it had never existed.

"No!"

I struck out, every bit a cornered animal. Kenrith had somehow managed to damage my fifth rez. I threw everything I had against the barrier. I felt my hand, and the wall shatter simultaneously. I leapt to my feet, ready to punish my attacker.

Darrin lay at an odd angle on the opposite side of the room. Scorch marks blackened his jaw and half his shirt. Bone fragments stuck out like white islands in the bloody lines running down his face. An elven beauty stood in the doorway, frozen with shock.

Christ. What just happened?

The slightest draw filled up my exhausted reserves from the powerful mananet. My power hadn't been stolen. The whole thing had been some kind of nightmare.

Nicole rushed around me to Darrin's side. Horror and disgust warred on her features as she bent next to Darrin. She touched an amulet, summoning an illusionary call screen.

"What are you doing?" I asked.

"Calling the authorities. He needs help."

I ripped the amulet from her and launched myself toward the kitchen.

"You won't stop me from—what kind of monster are you? Eating while he bleeds to death?"

I turned toward her with my water glass left over from dinner and a fist full of pasta. "Condoms, you guys have sex right?"

"What?" Her eyes widened. She backed away.

"Get me a condom," I snarled.

"I'm not helping you rape me." Nicole snatched one of Darrin's replica swords from a wall.

"I can help him if you can find me a condom." I yanked the couch out of the way, kicked the coffee table to one side and set my components on the carpet. I'd gotten a hold of Darrin before the sword came down hard onto my shoulder. The replica didn't have an active edge, but something broke.

Agony seared through me. I dropped Darrin harder than I intended and snatched the sword away. "Get me a condom now!"

She disappeared into the apartment. She'd probably call SMLE if she had another way to do so, but so long as she brought me a condom, it wouldn't matter. I arranged mushroom and spinach on one side of Darrin. My poorly enchanted Zippo went over his head and the water glass below his feet.

Nicole hadn't returned.

I stormed into the bedroom, pain attacking me from both sides. She huddled on the opposite side of the bed with the device Darrin had used to show me Nicole's Glamour test. I snatched open a bedside drawer, dumping their contents onto the bed. I rounded to her side and yanked free three dresser drawers in a fruitless search.

"Help, he's going to rape me."

I shoved her head to one side, clearing it from a drawer's path.

She screamed.

I pulled the bedside drawer out behind her. A chain of

condoms dropped to the floor between her ankles. I snatched up the chain and hurried back to Darrin.

Blowing up the condom tasted horrible. The first one broke, but I tied off the second inflated prophylactic and set it on Darrin's opposite side. SMLE broke down the door. I used the doorframe to box them into a fifth-first rez cube, threw myself over Darrin to hold him down and invoked the restoration spell.

His gurgling screams rent the night.

"NO, OFFICER." Darrin wrapped an arm around Nicole's shoulder. Something about his voice seemed off. "We're not pressing charges. This was just a misunderstanding."

SMLE had me on my face, wrists cuffed behind my back in an angle that might as well have been dipping my shoulder into magma. I'd have already had Sunny on her way, but we hadn't reached my phone call yet. We were still in hurt the suspect mode.

"You're sure?" the officer asked.

"Y-yes," Nicole whispered. "Just a misunderstanding."

When she answered rather than Darrin, I realized she was holding him up. What little I could see showed Darrin wan with at least a dozen pounds missing from his already lean frame.

"I don't know," the officer said. "Graham's got a history. Is it possible he's done something to their minds?"

Darrin's tone became obsidian. "Eli has not now nor ever used magic to overwrite a person's free will."

"Wasn't that—," Nicole squeaked. "Didn't he go to—"

"No." Darrin snapped. "Officers, release Mister Graham immediately."

"I don't know," the officer hedged. "Might be best if we—"

Darrin stomped across the room. "Then I'm calling his lawyer."

The two SMLE agents spoke in tones too low for me to catch more than the barest fragments. They debated in fits and starts.

"Hello?" Darrin asked. "Who's this? Yes, I know Eli, that's why I'm calling. He needs Sunny to get—well, he's a little tied..., all right. I'll put you on speaker. Go ahead..."

"Elias Balthazar Graham."

Three words drove spikes through my heart. Darrin had called Sunny at the Manger. There was no mistaking the cold voice that had answered the halfway house's phone.

"Darrin, that's the guy killing the homeless. He's got Sunny."

18

―――

FACING MYSELF

Fortunately, Darrin convinced SMLE to let me go before I had to do something everyone would've regretted. Unfortunately, Darrin could barely stand. There was no way he could channel all the magic necessary to restore my body without a series of runes to manage the spell like I'd used in the hospital. He'd left the wand he'd used to restore the Glamour victims at Thoth.

I considered writing out the runes. The condition the restoration spell left Darrin and I in immediately after casting made me question whether I'd be able to help Sunny.

Better to swallow more pain pills and hope for a little miracle.

Nicole took a corner too fast, muttering to herself. The turn slammed my less injured side into the passenger window.

I yelped then spoke through pain and gritted teeth. "Darrin?"

"You're doing fine, honey, turn left in three blocks," Darrin said. "We told her to hurry."

I gripped the handle against a hard right. Centrifugal force played tug of war with my broken shoulder. Encroaching night filled with circling stars crowded in, darkening my vision.

"The alley," Darrin said. "Nicole, turn into the alley!"

The hard turn cost the car traction. The back wheels slid across the wet cement. Nicole cried out. The car screeched to a halt in the alley mouth, and Nicole's cries became shrieks.

She jammed the car into reverse.

I tried to escape the car in a rush, but the seatbelt tightened to keep me in the car as it started to move. I wrenched it free and threw myself out before she could drive away.

"Nicole, stop!" Darrin yelled.

The passenger side door punished my escape, knocking into my injured shoulder and batting me to the pavement. I winced, resisting the urge to grab and hold my shoulder.

Tunoh all but materialized into place beyond my tears. "Eli? You're hurt."

Nicole screamed. "That rat's—"

Fortunately, Nicole fainted before a panicked reverse hit me with the car door again.

Tunoh glared into the car before returning soft eyes to me. "What happened?"

"Long story short, I didn't have my little guardian angel." I redirected my gaze to the writhing mass of rats that had freaked Nicole out. "What's going on?"

"Grace," Tunoh said. "He turned up a little while ago looking for you on his way to Death's door."

"You healed him?"

"His food's delicious." Tunoh shrugged. She exploded to full size and helped me to my feet. "Besides, he looks out for you."

"I'm guessing Kenrith isn't home."

"There's been an—" She blustered past the topic. "You know what, that doesn't matter. Let's get you healed."

Tunoh nearly deafened me with an ear-splitting whistle. The writhing pile froze, breaking apart enough to see Grace. Red cut marks riddled his naked, not yet fully healed skin. My concern for the excellent chef notwithstanding, I stared at the rhet. For the first time, I looked upon a group of unmoving rhet transformed into their healing form.

Most of them were uniformly black, but other colors invaded, particularly on their almost club-like, foreshortened tails. Their long, clawed fingers and hunched hybrid human-rat stance completed their resemblance to Professor Lupin transformed by the full moon.

"Come here and heal my betrothed."

"Knight Kenrith—"

"Isn't here," Tunoh snapped. "As Knight's Squire, I command you to heal he who would be our kin."

My gaze shifted back to the partially-healed wreck that had brought me so-called leftovers. "Shouldn't they finish healing Grace? I need to get to Sunny, but—"

Tunoh's voice sharpened even more. "You need to rest. That woman can see to herself."

I met her hard glare with one of my own. "Grace was hurt by the same killer that's got Sunny. She *and* Grace look after me. I'm helping her, whether you heal me or not."

Tunoh bit her lip and set me down. She didn't meet my eye. "Fine, I'll see if there's anyone available to bail out your *friend*."

"She's not my friend," I said to empty space.

Darrin's weary voice chastised me a moment before the rhet swarm blinded me. "Give it up, Eli."

Tunoh insisted upon accompanying me, so I sent her in search of a replacement trashcan lid. I left Darrin and Nicole to lean against each other, admonishing them to go home and not to call SMLE unless I failed to call them from the Manger in half an hour.

Free of erstwhile helpers more likely to get in the way than actually help, I hurried up the street toward the Manger. It'd been a garbage truck driver who'd nearly killed me that ultimately led

me to the halfway house and its nosy, opinionated proprietress. The first day I'd met Sunny, I'd made her cry, and yet, she'd offered me a place to stay. I'd refused for a number of reasons, and she'd given me even more reasons not to stick around. Her parting words at that meeting had advised me of a cache of cardboard boxes near the Manger's back entrance.

I'd left her cardboard, unwilling to take her charity. Truth be told, she'd later stepped in as legal counsel to bail me out. I'd accepted that charity, but it took a lot of pride-swallowing effort not to resent being forced into that situation. It'd taken even more to admit to myself that I'd grown dependent on her legal help. I'd also had to ask her to drive me to the ley line cavern and ultimately to my battle at the hydroelectric dam.

Much as with what occurred with Kenrith and his rhet, I felt all of this combined to leave me clearly in her debt. Saving her ass would shove that score far enough the other way any further legal assistance would count as payment rendered instead of charity.

Enlisting her infuriating driving skills also provided knowledge of the Manger's back entrance area. I rounded the building, squeezing between Sunny's beater and a concrete wall she'd parked too near.

Razcolm?

The fey inhabiting my spider didn't answer, which left me without a scout or someone to pick the lock. I dug into my pack for my door bell. Several curse-filled moments later I resigned myself to the fact that I'd lost the construct.

I cast around for spell components I hadn't bothered prepping after completing the construct. Time wasn't on my side, so I abandoned the search in short order and turned to the door.

A fifth rez barrier could break the security door from its frame or cut away the hinges—the second doing less damage.

Tunoh arrived with a suspiciously new-looking metal trash can lid. "What's wrong?"

"Trying to figure out how best to get through this door."

Tunoh squinted up the crack between door and frame. Her flat expression grew as she shot upward in size, shoved the lid into my hands, reached out and opened the door. "It's unlocked."

My rhet fiancé shrank back to normal size as I gawked at the door. "She leaves her door unlocked?"

I held the new trashcan lid like I had as a kid playing Captain America, filled it with a fifth rez disc I could expand as needed and stepped softly through the door. Shelves lined one side stocked with household supplies opposite several mismatched washers and dryers that had seen better days. Blood discolored aging white linoleum with faint smears and unspoiled droplets.

Tunoh raised her nose. "Grace."

"Then why weren't there any bloodstains outside."

"I don't know." Tunoh shrugged, sliding long, curved knives from beneath her fur cloak. "I didn't even scent any."

I eyed the silver blades. "Are those like Kenrith's?"

"Shorter, until I can acquire more feysteel."

We crept across the back room, keeping our voices to a whisper. "He almost cut his way through a fifth rez barrier."

She straightened for the lifespan of a mischievous smile. "Father was quite irritated that you had the presence of mind to maintain that cage against his assault."

"Can feysteel damage the barrier?"

"It exists in two—" she froze, her eyes suddenly hooded.

"It exists on both sides of the Silver?" I asked.

Her guilty, self-conscious expression turned to shock. "You know about the Silver and our world?"

"Some. I told you the cowled bastard that tried to kill me offered to take me to fairyland."

"But you never said anything about the Silver itself," she said.

We entered a hall containing several doors and a half dozen gutted corpses. My gorge rose, and I darted back into the laundry room, holding a hand close to stop impending vomit.

"Eli? Are you all right?"

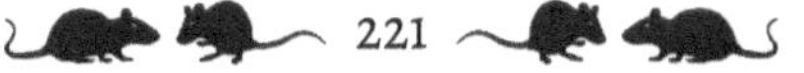

I shook my head, holding back tears but unable to hide the pain in my voice. "I-I haven't seen anything like that since—"

In an instant, she was large once more and holding me. Her warm arms were reassuring, but we didn't have time for comfort. Pushing her away summoned hurt to fill her eyes.

"Thank you, Tunoh, but we don't have time to coddle me. Besides, you should save your magic for something important."

She caressed my cheek, cleaning away an escaping tear. "Taking care of you *is* important."

"Not right now." I steeled myself.

This is the Wasteland. This isn't real life. It's all fake. None of this is real.

Even though I knew they were lies, I kept repeating reassurances to detach myself from the situation as I pushed the door back open. It didn't work as well as it had in the Wasteland, but the mantra kept the contents of my stomach where they belonged.

Blood smeared both bathroom doors. A leg and string of entrails blocked open the men's room. Drying blood coated nearby stairs like morbid icing melted down a tiered cake by summer heat. The head of the old man who'd recommended Sunny's food canted against the bottom stair in a puddle of blood trailed down from his body. Knife scars cut through the blood-stained paint on the door to the right of the stairs, revealing the grey of a metal reinforced door.

Three forward steps into the hall-become-charnel house brought me up beside a dry goods pantry. The storage closet's door had been smashed from its frame onto the homeless runaway I'd seen the day I came by to call Duval. I stared at the dirty but pretty girl and her beaded ruby necklace.

Some insect bit at my calves. My calves itched.

The room became suddenly stifling.

Magical energy bit into me like gooseflesh inside my skin, straining outward like a beast intent to escape its prison.

I turned my back on the murdered girl, faced the almost pris-

tine dining room door and reached out to a doorknob marred by red fingerprints. Opening the door slowly took all of my will—so much that had the killer been beyond, the magic stored in me might have pounced on him like a minute river of ley.

The dining room proved worse than the hall. Before I could enter all the way, Tunoh motioned me to hold back and blurred through the space. She returned a moment later by way of the front door, its closed sign swinging to a stop and the lock's click somehow thunder over the ocean roar in my ears.

Tunoh's voice had a slight hitch. "No one living."

I marched across the dining room toward the kitchen that had fed me so well.

"Eli?"

I didn't answer.

The concern in Tunoh's voice intensified. "Magus?"

I snatched the old phone off where it hung for public use and dialed Darrin's number.

"Eli?" Darrin said.

"Call the police now. This is bad." I hung up and marched toward the stair. Burning fingers pressed nails into my palm. "Can you get me a feysteel weapon?"

"Feysteel is very rare, Eli. We don't normally even carry such precious weapons, but with everything that's been going on—"

"Right, how's your stealing ability?"

"Knight of the Rhet don't steal," she said.

"All right, how's your requisition ability?"

She straightened. "I am an accomplished requisitioner in service to the greater good."

I almost slammed open the dining room door but held back my anger by the barest of threads. Tunoh would requisition me a weapon. Hell, the love-struck rhet would probably get me anything I asked for, except I drew a blank on what to request. Neither Mihail's high caliber pistol nor Duval's shotgun had slowed the killer.

"Find me a twelve-foot extension cord."

Tunoh blurred away without even acknowledging the request.

The Manger's upper floors housed the guest rooms and Sunny's office. She might have climbed the stairs to hole up in her office or to protect her other charges. I hadn't seen much of the upper floors. For all I knew, she'd installed a panic room.

My eyes flit to the security door.

If she's in there, she's not going to open—

Sunny's scream had me half a flight up the stairs before the sound died out. I followed the noise of a fight to Sunny's office. A body flashed past me out the door and up the hall.

I squeezed a slip-n-slide inside my jacket pocket, but before I could steal the killer's footing, Sunny's voice snatched my attention away.

"Elias," Sunny gasped. "Help me."

I looked up to see the killer's silhouette dropping out of sight beyond a broken window.

"Please."

I went to her.

Sunny lay half in and half out of a room filled with filing cabinets and a big safe. From her angle, she must've gotten caught sneaking out. One delicate hand more red than caramel held a gut wound. Blood trailed down her face from a cut across her scalp, and several bad bruises were forming on her face and jaw. Sliced clothes showed shallower cuts, blood and far more skin than the preachy do-gooder ever would have willingly displayed.

I grabbed the nearby desk lamp, glad it was mananet-powered, and I didn't have to fuss with a cord. In the bright LED light, her skin tone looked even paler than I'd thought.

Lost a lot of blood.

The itch of a half-formed thought demanded to be scratched, but I didn't have the time.

She's lucky to be alive.

I stripped out of my jacket and my t-shirt, ripping the latter

into strips. Darrin had called the cops, and Sunny had pressure on the belly wound, so I tied the first strip around her head wound. I pressed t-shirt scraps against the smaller wounds, trusting its absorption abilities to combine with clotting for the time being.

I took a deep breath. "Sunny, I'm going to need you to move your hand so I can see."

"Did you take the job?"

"What job? You're delirious."

Her head shake was weak. "The Mimir job."

"How do you—never mind. I haven't gone back yet, but—"

"But, if you...took the job...you could...get off the streets," she said in short spurts. "You could...have a home."

"You must be goofy from blood loss because I know you're smarter than this," I said. "Move your hand."

"Everyone wants a home."

I tried to move her hand away from the wound, but she held the arm too tightly against her side. "I don't want a home just like I don't want any friends."

"W-why?"

"Come on, you have to have figured it out by now. Move your arm so I can help you."

She shook her head. "Why?"

Distant sirens edged into my hearing. My anger had softened a hair as I'd cared for Sunny, but there was no way it would've departed surrounded by so much death. My frustration at having to put up with her nosy, intrusiveness while fighting her just to check her gut wound boiled it back to full strength. "I've told you before. I didn't do what they convicted me of doing."

"What's...that matter? If you had...a job—"

"No," I snapped, yanking her arm away so hard in my temper I could've broken it. "I will *not* register as a sex offender. I—"

"Eli?" Tunoh said. "Get away from her."

Anger flashed to fury. "Tunoh, this is no time for jeal—"

"If you would remain homeless, you must die." The hand I'd yanked away from Sunny's wound shoved a knife into my gut.

"No!" Tunoh dropped the thin, white extension cord, blurred onto the hand, and sank teeth into Sunny's fingers.

Sunny yanked the knife out. She seized Tunoh with her empty hand and tore the rhet's teeth from her fingers by brute force.

Dark blood bubbled from my gut.

Sunny stared at Tunoh as if she's never seen a rhet before. She abandoned a short-lived examination and slammed Tunoh against the desk.

Images of Boss Golem breaking Tunoh flashed through my sluggish thoughts. I scrambled backward, one hand on my own belly wound as I kicked out at Sunny. The blow knocked her back into the file room and made Tunoh miss the desk by the breadth of a rhet's ears.

Sunny let go of Tunoh. She grabbed my offending leg and brought down an elbow. Bones snapped under the sledgehammer blow.

I screamed.

Darkness welled into view.

"Tunoh. The cord." Coughing stabbed me again and again. "Circle us."

Shockingly, she didn't argue. The white cord slapped down around us plugged into itself to complete a circuit.

Circuit?

The stray thought nearly sidetracked my desperate plan.

Let's get a look at the real you.

The mananet covering the Manger made summoning a fifth-first rez circle a simple thing which I barely managed. The illusion of Sunny flickered away, revealing my own face.

Tunoh drove between us, slicing at the clean, uninjured version of me to no avail. My brain recoiled.

That's not possible.

None of what I saw was possible. Tunoh couldn't be inside the fifth-first circle. The killer couldn't look like me. The killer's armor construct couldn't continue deflecting blows without magic to power the barriers.

Blue-tinted milky white swirled behind the killer. My circle remained intact, locking out external magic.

The killer has to be a wizard.

The killer was on her feet, stomping faster and faster at the blurred rhet. Dark blood coated my fingers, an omen I couldn't manage to dig from the recesses of my brain. Instead, the stray thought returned.

Circuit!

I snatched up the desk lamp, dropped the useless circle and laid the lamp end across the cord. A flash of fifth resonance energy cut the head from the lamp. I shoved the broken end into the killer's back leg and threw every bit of magic I could from the mananet and my own reserves.

Electricity, generated by a mananet converter inside the lamp's innards, shot into the killer, amplified who knew how many times by force-feeding everything I could channel through the lamp.

My doppelganger jerked, and his image flickered, giving me a glimpse of his true identity too fast to register. The killer magus managed to hurl his knife into my face.

I flinched, saving an eye and probably my life by the barest of margins. The blade sliced across one cheek and through an ear.

The wound was enough to steal my concentration.

The killer sprinted out of the office. The sound of smashing glass reached my failing ears as visions of sparkling glass crystals showered the enveloping darkness like jagged stars.

19

ARMING UP

Waking up in my cardboard box was disorienting, to say the least. Neither looking up at the sheer white and silver veils of the beautiful matron Biuntcha nor being haloed by Tunoh, Yshtiina, and Noli improved things.

Biuntcha smiled down and patted my forehead. "You'll be fine now, Elias."

I turned to Tunoh. "Sunny?"

Tunoh scowled, folding her arms.

Yshtiina glowered and folded hers too.

Noli rolled her eyes. "He asked Tunoh, who is obviously present and uninjured, after the only friend engaged in the battle he can't account for. Chastising him for his logic and loyalty is no way to grow a relationship."

Yshtiina huffed, but Tunoh's expression grew uncertain.

"Your friend sustained only minor injuries," Biuntcha said. "Human law keepers discovered her shortly after we evacuated you. She'd barricaded herself in the building's basement with many of her charges."

"Thank you, Matron, but why are you here in my box and not

in safety?" I asked.

My question improved all of the rhet's expressions.

"You needed immediate care. Unfortunately, the earlier healings performed upon Grace and yourself exhausted our warren's strength," Biuntcha said.

"So *you* stepped in? Why?"

Yshtiina whipped around, her tail snapping my cheek where the killer had sliced. "Show respect, *human*."

I opened my mouth, but Tunoh shoved Yshtiina away from me. "Eli's question offered no disrespect. Magus are naturally curious."

"It sounded disrespectful and distinctly ungrateful," Yshtiina said. "You'd better train your male better, and quickly."

I raised my eyes to meet Biuntcha's. "I am grateful, Matron, but I fail to see how I have earned such a consideration, especially out here where you are in danger."

She smirked at me. "You'll figure it out."

Matron Biuntcha vanished.

Yshtiina disappeared an instant later.

"Damn. I'd really like her to teach me some healing magic."

Noli shook her head and smirked at Tunoh. With a pat on the cheek, she blurred out of sight.

"I only managed to insult one of them, that's an improvement."

"Yshtiina is warming to you, Eli, but she never rushes."

If you say so.

I struggled up into a sitting position, winning until Tunoh expanded to full size to keep me down. In the cramped space, she had to lay atop me to manage it.

"I'm not sure your father would approve."

She glanced down at her position atop me, but instead of blushing, wiggled a little and smiled. "I'm an adult."

"The Magus is right," Kenrith growled. "I don't approve."

Tunoh snapped back to normal size, her blush particularly visible on the edges of her ears as they pressed against her head.

I sat up, scrambled around in the tight space and bowed. "Knight Kenrith. I am honored by your presence."

My obeisance seemed to wrong-foot the rhet, freezing the rejoinder on his lips and sparing Tunoh its sting.

Before Kenrith could collect himself to deliver the blow, I cut across him. "What service have you come to ask of me?"

His anger found a new target. "Not everything is about you, *human*. I came because my squire is shirking her training."

"You haven't trained me in over a year," Tunoh objected.

"You were not whole during that time," Kenrith said.

"No," Tunoh said. "This isn't about training, father. This is about keeping me away from my betrothed. It's the same reason you've dispatched me as a messenger to other warrens nearly every moment since Eli healed me."

"A squire serves a knight. A knight serves a matron. We have a duty that may not be shirked."

"Do we not owe service also to our spouses?" Tunoh asked.

"*I* owe measured service to my wives. As an adult rhet, *you* owe service only as a squire," Kenrith glared at me. "No foolish crush overrides that duty."

Tunoh stomped her foot. "This is not a crush. I love Eli. Helping him protect the city protects our warren."

"The Magus protects his people, not ours. Your options are only to remain here protecting our warren, at my side dealing with...," Kenrith eyed me. "Other concerns or serve on missions I assign you. Now, follow me. "

Tunoh watched Kenrith march away, never having stepped foot inside my box. She rushed over and up me, kissing my cheek where it still stung and whispering. "I left you a gift behind your box."

Kenrith escorted Tunoh away.

I felt like the several miles of the roads between me and the ley line cavern, but curiosity demanded I find out what she'd left. Tunoh's care package contained a cache of drink boxes and milk cartons. A CiCi's pizza box contained a mishmash of old cinnamon rolls, apple pizza and the occasional square of nibbled brownie.

A check skyward suggested I had enough time to put her gift to use. Uncovered, my refrigerator box still had room for more of the little containers. Mixed dessert remains applied via third rez circle glued the already cleaned containers atop my home. More adhesive allowed me to sandwich them beneath flat sheets of cardboard. A Sharpie filled the blank cardboard surfaces with little rectangles, and the whole process started once more. Tunoh's gift completed the first layer and filled a third of the new one.

Thunder cracked in the distance.

I made use of the warning to get the black plastic covering into position before rain soaked my makeshift abode.

All the while, I considered the wizard killing the homeless. Magically talented individuals like Darrin were uncommon, but it took a talent of at least my level to maintain his armor up against everything I'd seen thrown at him. Had I lived in the time of the Roman expansions, I doubt I would've been more than a footnote compared to real wizards like Merlin.

If this killer is that level, I might as well pick out a nice spot to die.

<Your foe is no Merlin.>

How would you know?

Razcolm's mental smirk made my skin crawl.

Where did you go?

<His Majesty required my service.>

I shot my gaze skyward. What I could see of the moon's glow beyond the storm cloud belied any possibility that Razcolm had communicated with His Majesty from our side of the Silver. Without a new moon to weaken the Silver between worlds, Razcolm either had to take the hijacked construct through the Silver or hide it somewhere and return to his own body.

What do you look like when you're not in my spider?

<Handsome.>

You're pretty surly. Did His Majesty order you to do something kind?

<Screw off, human.> The origami construct cradled its face. *<Oh, right, Sunny won't let you.>*

I ignored the imp and returned to analyzing my foe.

My stunt creating a makeshift Taser had penetrated the wizard's armor. He might adapt his protections to include seventh resonance, but if not then elemental energy could harm him. Another mananet-capable appliance would serve, but only at close range. Considering the damage I'd seen him do with a simple knife, I preferred a ranged assault.

I took out the Zippo in my pocket and turned it over. I'd gotten the runes wrong somehow. My lighter had acted like a magnet to Duval's fire as intended but hadn't gathered the flames inside the lighter as designed. Without absorbing fire from an outside source, there was none to fuel testing the other runes I'd drawn on the lighter's surface.

I need a few eyeGuardians, but it's not like I can walk into an eyeStore.

<We could steal some...I'm sorry, requisition.>

Stealing eyeGuardians fell under the category of just desserts, but it also meant violating the restraining order.

And I'll bet garbage to gold bullion he's got people watching for me to even get near Thoth properties.

<I could do it.>

The little imp could, but such a request would cost me.

<You're no fun>

I dug out what little money I had left from Duval. Before prison, the amount could've purchased two maybe three eyeGuardians. There was no way to know outside a store how much Adam had jacked the prices.

Darrin would know.

Call it laziness or chalk it up to weakness from all the fighting and healing, but I really didn't want to walk all the way back to Darrin's apartment. I settled for a smaller effort and headed for the Manger's telephone.

Halfway houses don't close, do they?

As it happens, they do if they're wrapped up in police tape and have their proprietress in the hospital. Locking the place down meant hardship far outweighing my tired feet for the surviving residents.

What about Sunny or Grace? Where do they live?

A hand slapped down on my shoulder a moment before deep basso nearly made me leap tall buildings in a single bound. "It is almost like being homeless myself, not that you ever accepted it as a home, did you, my friend?"

Still-healing reddish lines marked future scars on the bigger, darker-skinned man. I didn't owe Grace anything, but the words still tumbled out of my mouth. "I'm sorry. I did what I could."

The huge man seized me in a hug that brought my feet off the ground. Though he'd stolen all of my air, he'd kept speaking as he set me down. "I know, my friend, that you see Grace as a big and cuddly teddy bear."

"More like a grizzly crossed with a rabid panda."

Grace laughed, and his slaps nearly stole my balance. "I have seen violence, though thank God, not in some time. I know the eyes of a soulless killer when I read my fate within them. I should have known he wasn't you when he entered and bypassed the coffee pot."

"When I entered?"

Grace's expression sobered. "Yes, my friend. Yours was almost the last face I saw."

I swallowed.

I'd seen the wizard use illusionary disguises to get himself close enough for the kill. I'd never considered he might use mine. I frowned. The killer had known my full name from the start, almost as if he'd been trying to track me down. That he'd killed the others could have been meant as a way to draw me out, but I couldn't figure out what I'd done to warrant all the blood.

Caleb had come looking for my head over perceived wrongdoings to his sister. I had a feeling that score was personal enough that Caleb would do his own dirty work. A horrible thought struck me.

Is someone trying to kill me because I'm working magic outside the government regulated channels?

I almost laughed. The commercialization of magic had brought about government regulations after greedy sons-of-bitches like Adam started peddling more advanced spells that ignorant, untrained people had botched. Real wizards—wherever I fell upon that scale—had *always* developed their own blueprints. I was no different.

<*Or inherited spell recipes from their masters.*>

"Heavy thoughts burden you, my friend." Grace slapped me on the back. "I came to cook, but since I cannot cook here, let me take you back to my apartment and make a meal to lighten your burden."

My brow wrinkled.

Don't get me wrong, food is something I love above most other interests, but I wasn't sure what motivated Grace to offer.

I decided to ask.

Grace's shrug beat me to the punch. "Cooking is my joy. Eating is your joy. Shared joy always lightens the day."

My stomach grumbled on general principle. I hadn't eaten since the night before at Darrin's. Breakfast sounded like heaven itself, and I was sorely tempted to accept his offer despite the potential pitfalls involved in allowing myself to grow more acquainted with the excellent chef.

"I'm probably better off having something I can eat on the run."

"Is that why you came? A cup of coffee and something for the road?"

"I wanted to call Darrin and ask what eyeGuardians went for these days. I need to persuade someone to buy a few for me."

Grace's brows rose, veering together at the very end. "Why would you need more than one?"

"I discovered a chink in the wizard's armor. I need to run some tests for a spell and for that I need a fire source like an eyeGuardian."

Grace peered deeply into my eyes. Looking up at the massive chef's clouding expression left me uneasy and with a crick in my neck. "You are a good man, my friend. This killer, whatever his faults, is not a magical automaton like those you fought before. He is a living, breathing person with a soul—no matter how stained. Do not stain your own by taking his life."

My calves prickled. Heat flashed up my neck. I pointed at the Manger. "Did you see what he did in there? He slit the throat of a teenage girl."

"Taking this man's life will not bring her back, my friend."

"No, it won't," I snapped. "I generally leave raising the dead to the religious types, but I wouldn't mind raining a little hellfire on this bastard."

Grace cocked his head. "Does that number you with the devil?"

I wanted to scream.

I wanted to hit something.

My temper had been closer to the surface since tapping into wild ley energy, but even so, I couldn't understand how Grace could accuse me of being the bad guy after the wizard had murdered so many people within sight of where we stood.

"Talking to you is as frustrating as talking to Sunny."

Grace smiled. "Thank you."

I threw up my hands and let a growl of frustration escape my lips. "I'll find a way to get what I need on my own."

Grace let me storm away for a three count before his deep voice rumbled once more. "Walmart carries your eyeGuardians, but I beg you not to take this path."

I whirled around. "And why would you tell me that?"

Grace smirked. "Because He told me to."

Snarling under my breath about infuriating religious zealots, I marched south toward the nearest Walmart.

<WooOoo. He moves in mysterious ways.> Razcolm cackled. *<Especially when he's jerking around his toys.>*

I noticed a SMLE shadow a block from the Manger. There were any number of reasons for SMLE's presence. They could merely be patrolling—fat chance. They could be keeping tabs on me for Brooke or Adam or out for vengeance over my threatened suit.

I didn't really need any more distractions. My plate had gotten so full things teetered dangerously. It seemed only a matter of time before something slid off to splatter against the ground.

My mind raced, tracks spinning and discarding plans like a spider obsessed with web perfection. A spare track uninterested in watching the other chaos cursed me for not at least asking Tunoh to teach me fey glamour. I had the ability, if not the components, to create simple illusions, but the near-invisibility offered by fey glamour would've come in handy.

A Bluebox came into view.

A side trip through the teleporter to Mimir offered several possibilities, foremost annoying SMLE. There was no guarantee the Bluebox would transport me again. Pissing off SMLE without a guaranteed escape promised bridge burning of epic proportions.

Even so, the temptation was almost too much to pass up.

Only the prospect of revenge against the wizard kept my feet from turning aside. SMLE paced me all the way to Walmart.

The bored teenager behind the sporting-goods counter seemed more interested in popping her gum than helping me. After some effort, Little Miss Gum sold me two eyeGuardians and a makeup mirror in exchange for my remaining cash. On my way out of Walmart, I stopped by the vending machines designed to make children scream at their parents. More quarters than I like to admit purchased a plastic egg containing a sheet of Disney stickers and a second egg with a small, plastic pixie.

A check of the parking area failed to find my SMLE observer. It occurred to me that the killer, rather than SMLE, could've been the one pacing me. Determining the worst of the possible evils left me with a third, ultimate evil—the killer worked for SMLE.

<Not everyone is out to get you.>

If you say so.

<I'm not trying to kill you.>

I smirked.

If you say so.

I moved around to the superstore's rear, searching for a place to set up my test. The area contained the usual detritus with the added bonus of a sulky girl dressed in all black with a brand-new broom.

We eyed each other.

When I gave no indication of fleeing her glower, she huffed, shot me an extra-dirty look and marched away.

The best place to set up my Zippo seemed to be on the concrete retaining wall at the rearmost of the property. Unfortunately, grass and brush grew up to overhang the wall. I drew rune adjustments onto the lighter that I'd worked out on the long walk. Rather than start a fire that could spread to nearby neighborhoods, I placed the Zippo on the ground near the wall.

I was about to activate the eyeGuardian's flame rune in the general direction of my open lighter when the crackle of tires on loose gravel announced a Seufert Fells police cruiser.

The car stopped.

The window descended into the door, removing the separating glass between a mirror-shaded young woman disturbingly reminiscent of Thecia and me.

"May I ask what you're doing?" she asked.

"Recharging my lighter?"

She raised the glasses revealing eyes the color of dark chocolate brownies. Her lips curled into a pert little smirk. "I'm not sure that's how it works."

I shrugged.

"Did you happen to notice the posted 'no loitering' signs?" she asked.

I held up a receipt. "I'm not loitering. I'm a customer attempting to refill his lighter—however incorrectly."

"Uh-huh. You'd better move along."

Despite her apparent amusement, the underlying hardness of her expression offered nothing in the way of special considerations. My calves prickled but I was a black vagabond playing with fire behind a shopping center. I stuffed everything back into my pockets. "Yes, ma'am."

A shiny pigeon landed on my shoulder. *<You sure told her.>*

I wasn't going to win that argument.

<Who said anything about arguing? You could've used a little of that mysterious wizard charm. Did I mention I know a seduction charm? Could've cured your blues—if you know what I mean.> Razcolm mimicked music straight out of a bad 80's adult film.

I imagine chuckling and rolling my eyes simultaneously didn't exactly offer the clearest message for discouraging the little imp. As annoying as the little pest could be, the jerk had his funny moments.

<You're occasionally entertaining yourself, human.>

My alley had little in foliage, and the brick and concrete buildings weren't likely to catch fire in a hurry. I'd rather have had the spell tested sooner rather than later, but I had no doubt the pretty cop would keep an eye on us as long as we remained in her territory.

We headed back to my alley to work on the spell.

The SMLE agent parked at the alley mouth scowled. The chip on his shoulder meant Adam's grudge-carrying stooge wouldn't look hard for a legitimate reason to bust me.

Well, shit. Now what?

I recalled the little park I'd used to fill holy water balloons for my failed assault attempt on the golems. The small picnic areas had sported metal grills for barbequing. I decided to unload the nonessentials from my shopping trip and change course to the park for a bit of peace and arrest-free spell development.

I ducked into my box only to come up short.

Weejok leapt to his feet, performing a hasty bow with his tail in his hands. "Great Magus, I bring tidings from your betrothed."

"Weejok, right?"

He brightened. "The Magus remembers well."

"Shouldn't you be doing something more important than ferrying messages?"

"I'm greatly honored to serve a Knight's Squire and a Magus."

"Please, just call me Eli."

Weejok mouthed silently, eyes as wide as his ears.

"What was the message?"

"You are in her thoughts, and she will find time to," Weejok's ears pinked, "attend you when she is able."

"She didn't mean what you think," I frowned. "I don't think."

Weejok wrung his tail and nodded at the ground.

"Something else?"

Weejok darted past me out of the box, over the fence and back. He held up a plain, white coffee cup. "This has the other scent."

"Coffee?"

"No, there is a man perfume upon this cup."

Willie was in Ullie's house?

20

VILLAINY REVEALED

Even with as cold as it had been, the Oregon foliage held onto its leaves. The park glowed that special green all foliage seems to get right after a rain. Most parks emptied out in winter months, but Oregonians had different views on temperature than the rest of the country. Georgians I'd met in Atlanta ran for coats at seventy degrees. Oregonians brought out the sprinklers and swimsuits.

I crossed the sparsely populated park, still troubled by the idea that Willie had been in Ullie's house as I searched for an empty picnic area.

Couldn't have been Willie, just someone wearing Old Spice.

<Right, everyday man perfume.> Razcolm's snicker itched where I couldn't scratch. *<Maybe your Dad visited for a little Ullie time.>*

"Watch it, Razcolm."

The imp's laughter increased.

Weejok has to be wrong. It can't be Willie.

<He is a trained killer.>

Shit.

<Could be that Austin too. Maybe he's Willie's apprentice assassin.>

How do you even know about Willie?

<*Told you I was hanging around invisible making faces at you.*>

We passed a family grilling up a picnic lunch. I remembered Adam's hostile architecture initiative and latched onto thoughts other than Mimir's possible tie to the killings.

Will the city remove the grills as part of Adam's hostile architecture?

Razcolm pointed out an empty spot, and we crossed to it. I'd barely arrived when a seemingly homeless man bum rushed me from nowhere.

I recognized him at once.

He'd forced me to deck him on our last encounter when all I'd wanted to do was fill up holy water balloons in peace. I side-stepped his new assault and ducked his follow-up swing. All-too-glad to vent a little steam, I jabbed him in the nose.

"You really don't learn, do you?" I asked.

He came at me again. "This is *my* territory."

I slipped around the blow, a snarl on my lips when he suddenly pitched forward with a startled cry.

<*There's mud in your eye!*> Razcolm's spider legs jabbed left and right and left. <*Quick, hit him with the eyeGuardian.*>

I'm not setting him on fire.

<*He'll only burn for a minute. We're here to test your spell, aren't we?*>

Testing doesn't typically include immolating people.

<*Wow, you really don't know anything about being a magus.*> Razcolm's attention shifted from me to the bum on the ground and back. <*Got anything you could stab him with? Purely in the name of science, mind.*>

I folded my arms. "Science?"

The bum rolled over and attacked his double knotted shoelaces. "What, demonstration of gravity? Juvenile prick."

<*Yeah, let's test how long repeatedly stabbing him makes me giggle. The record is thirty-two seconds.*>

"No," I said.

"Duval is going to hear all about this," the bum threatened.

Razcolm refolded into a pigeon. He launched himself toward my face, veering at the last moment to deposit his opinion on my head.

Charming.

I sighed. "You're right. When he gets out of the hospital, Duval is going to hear all about how you interfered with the wizard he… hired to find Ullie's murderer."

"If you're supposed to finding Ullie's killer, what're you doing screwing off in the park?"

I flipped open my Zippo and tossed it into the little grill. I pointed the eyeGuardian in his general direction, careful to ensure the flame jet wouldn't actually hit him. Fire lanced across the intervening space curving in defiance of physics toward the park-supplied grill and down the neck of my Zippo. "Arming up."

He yelped and jumped away, tripping on his once again tied shoelaces. He gawked up at me. "What if that hadn't worked?"

I smiled.

The moment his shoes were untied, he scrambled away as fast as his legs would take him.

Razcolm landed on my shoulder. *<Do you smell urine?>*

"You mean over the scent of pigeon crap in my hair?"

<The real challenge was only crapping on the pink section.> Razcolm roared with laughter, rolling off my shoulder and hitting the ground without pausing his mirth.

I grabbed the Zippo. Pain seared my fingers. I jerked my hand away. A quick examination discovered blisters bubbling from my skin where it had touched the lighter. My scowl intensified.

Razcolm's laughter grew louder. He folded into a spider so he could point with multiple legs while still laughing at me.

I used my jacket sleeve to pick up the lighter. Heat seeped through almost at once. A flick of the wrist closed it. Another flick opened the lid as the first step of the secondary spell inlaid in

Sharpie on the Zippo. Whispered incantations filled in the gaps I purposely left in the magical circuit.

A gout of flame lanced out of the Zippo's mouth. Razcolm's telepathic yelp felt odd but even more satisfying. He scrambled out of the target area, one back leg igniting. *<Hey! What the hell?>*

I touched the outside of the Zippo with a non-blistered finger. It was still warm, but nowhere near as hot as it had been.

So was it hot because it contained the fire or because the metal touched the fire when the lighter absorbed the flame? One way to find out.

I used the other eyeGuardian to charge the Zippo. Using my now-singed army jacket, I carried the lighter over to a nearby water fountain. After a few minutes of rapid cooling which couldn't be good for the metal, steam stopped rising off the lighter. Another touch test proved the charged Zippo cool enough to pocket.

<What do you do if the lighter accidentally opens up in your pocket?>
Don't even think about it.
<What?>

The range of my portable flamethrower wouldn't give me as much distance as I might've liked, but it was undoubtedly better than hand-to-hand. Furthermore, if my theories regarding the wizard's protections were correct, he'd be vulnerable to an unexpected gout of fire from my enchanted lighter.

A twinge of guilt suspiciously equipped with Grace's voice reminded me of the costs of killing. I didn't need the reminder. I knew them. They counted among the reasons I couldn't go home.

I set the makeup mirror I'd purchased on a picnic table and dug the old aluminum compass out of my pack. I took exaggerated care as I inscribed Sharpie sigils around the compass's grey, exterior casing, traced a circle around the protective cover's border and drew even more runes around the inner barrier.

Next, I retrieved the little plastic eggs disgorged from the vending machines. I'd read a novel once which featured pixies imprisoned inside lanterns. The little fey had been forced to fly in order to provide their masters light. I'd never have done something like that to a pixie—if they actually still existed.

Come to think of it, they probably do.

Opening the larger egg granted me access to a sheet of Disney stickers. The smaller offered up a tiny plastic toy molded into a generic cousin of Tinkerbelle. My little fairy went into the larger egg and into my bag.

I'll figure out how to transform them into a floating lantern later.

A sticker of a sparkling fairy went onto the compass's glass. The compass needle would be harder to see straight up and down, but I hadn't bought the compass to help me tell directions. The survival gear had been intended as a tracking construct, but I'd come up with better uses after tangling with the killer.

Electricity is produced when a current-carrying conductor moves relative to a magnetic field. Compasses are all about magnetic fields.

An LED is constructed from two semiconductors bridged by a p-n junction diode—essentially two differently conducting materials. Voltage applied to the leads aligns electrons with so-called electron holes releasing electroluminescent energy—light.

Combining the two principles makes hand crank survival lights possible. I didn't have a p-n junction diode or for all practical purposes a current-carrying conductor. I had a sticker displaying a glowing fairy.

I don't have a cubic ton of KY either when I bag up rancid noodles.

Schooled will designed a blueprint of linked concepts then built out the walls with magical energy. Physical representations of the blueprint made constructions easier—hence magical devices like the eyeSentinel are called constructs.

All forms of energy share similar characteristics, so when I applied magical energy in lieu of electromagnetic energy across my cartoon conductor, she glowed to life.

I grinned, killed the power and closed the compass's lid.

Pushing my little victory aside, I focused on carefully inscribing sigils along both sides of the makeup mirror's silvered glass. I went to work on a broken section of cat-5 cable with my multi-tool, painstakingly removing the twisted pairs from their insulating sheath. I chose the white-blue, blue-white pair and separated the insulated wires from each other. I twisted both into individual figure eight shapes a bit rounder than an infinity symbol. The blue-white went around Razcolm's faceted, paperclip eyes. The other wound around the makeup mirror's handle. I re-wrapped the glass inside the multiple plastic bags Little Miss Gum thought constituted safe packaging.

The next phase of the plan required another hike. When dealing with Boss Golem and the demi-goblin issue, I'd been forced into reacting over and over again. Excepting Duval's abductions, only the killer's Manger invasion had actually forced an immediate confrontation.

Judicious use of information, intellect, and preparation will always win.

<Don't forget a whiz-bang fireball!>

A chuckle escaped my lips. I had a rechargeable flamethrower rather than a fireball. Not only did the construct offer defense against flame attacks, it wasn't something SMLE would arrest me for carrying. I had given some small thought to the imp's fireball.

There were some mechanical challenges involved in that kind of spell. I had no doubt that if I employed information, intellect, and preparation, I could arm myself with such a weapon.

A cigarette flared in my mind's eye. Flame coursed down the throat of a greedy gangbanger. Sympathetic fire burned my own lungs, and a soul-deadening cold left me shuddering.

I'd filled his lungs with fire and walked away feeling righteous. The memory replayed each time I'd considered Razcolm's touted fireball. A suspicion had grown into a certainty the more times I'd viewed my retaliatory attack on the youth. I'd killed him.

I'd killed with an intensified ember and an intake of breath.

If I solved the academic questions and perfected the design of an actual fireball spell, I'd have the ability to burn people alive any time I lost my temper. Sickness twisted my insides and filled the back of my throat with bile.

I can't be trusted with that kind of power any more than I could resist shooting Mihail with the firebolter.

I turned the attributes of success away from fireball spells and bent them instead toward doing good. Once I found and stopped the wizard murdering the homeless, I could help the Ottiren and then slip away beyond the Silver.

Dad's voice flickered through my thoughts. *<Running away instead of facing your problems.>*

<Don't listen to him.> Razcolm thought. *<Why would you want to stay here anyway? These people won't ever treat you any different than trash.>*

A spark kindled in my chest.

They might, if Sunny can get my conviction overturned.

<Already living beyond the Silver, I see.>

It took me a moment to work out that Razcolm had accused me of living in a fantasy world. It rankled that the little imp was probably right. Even Sunny had balked at the possibility of legal redemption.

Murderer, Ottiren, then leave Porter and the rest of this behind.

Armed for vicious squirrel if not for bear, I headed in the general direction of Darrin's apartment and invoked the seeking spell once more.

The trip back downtown didn't take as long as my aching legs claimed. I came into sight of Thoth's orange eye, a glowing ember in overcast daylight gloom. Even turning my back to the eye, I could feel the itch of Thoth's Eye watching, the Egyptian goddess of magic in Adam's service judging me.

I still felt the itch when another eye confronted me. It gleamed upon a raven's breast from atop another tower rising high amidst the gleaming walls and electronic surveillance of Mimir Corp's main campus.

Mimir's raven crushed all my hopes in a single talon.

Fuck my life, Weejok could be right.

<Problem?>

It seems my adult job prospects revolve around backstabbing liars and sociopathic murderers.

<They both offer hellacious retirement packages.>

In the overcast daylight, the outside of the complex resembled a shining metallic version of the Emerald City edged in black. Pavilions dotted the landscaped grounds, sheltering employees collaborating on holographic tablets in the fresh air.

The whole picture before me spoke of picnics in peace and prosperity. By an oddly anachronistic twist of fate, the technology company employed—knowingly or not—a wizard assassin.

I raised my gaze to the lofty heights of Mimir's highest tower. Was it possible the person behind the killings did so with Bradley's knowledge?

No. there has to be another explanation. Bradley is nothing like Adam, and—well, Austin reminds me a bit of him in college, but Willie?

<Seems to me you didn't think Adam capable of betraying you either.>

My jaw and fists tightened. My luck was bad, but I refused to believe it had achieved an epic level on par with Odysseus. My gaze shifted up my backtrail to the Eye.

He had a goddess screwing around with his life too.

Even so, I'd already proven some of my assumptions wrong. Until I had more facts, I refused to believe the people who'd offered me help were killers.

Willie's military service notwithstanding.

<No, not killers at all.>

Scout out a way inside while I triangulate.

<If you're not sure this is the place—>

Just do it, all right? I need some peace and quiet to think.

Razcolm disappeared into the corporate campus, and I circled the block. The seeking spell pulled me toward Mimir regardless of my position around it. The heavier my hopes fell to crush my guts, the more I wondered if not talking to God had allowed a very Athena-like Thoth to take over my care and torturing.

I stopped at the campus's backside after circling it almost all the way around. Verifying the killer inside Mimir required me to complete the circuit, but seemed a waste of energy. Circling Mimir the last quarter wouldn't change the inevitable.

The only question is whether Bradley, Vil, or Willie are complicit.

On his return, Razcolm and I discussed the merits of day versus night infiltration of Mimir Corp. Razcolm preferred a day infiltration on the auspices that the mischief would begin earlier rather than later. To an extent, having him go in during the daytime meant I was more likely to see what was really going on rather than a bunch of labs shut down for the night.

Concern for Sunny's injuries eclipsed everything else at the time, but she'd known Mimir had tried to recruit me. I'd told her about the interview, but never named the party involved. No one outside Mimir had known.

Guess no matter how much I'd prefer it otherwise, there's really no question. The wizard had to have been present during that interview.

Staring up at Mimir, I couldn't find a handle on the wizard's motives. I got the distinct impression that the killer had been genuinely sorry I intended to remain homeless. The concern could've been part of the disguise, but I didn't think so.

It's almost as if he wants me off his kill list, but how does that make sense? Some sort of compulsion? Multiple personalities?

Once more I seemed doomed to drown in unanswered questions. I couldn't be sure, but the killer's question led me to discount any idea he was after me for some slight against whatever community wizard's had.

<Maybe we could find out if you'd stop navel-gazing.>

Well, get to it then.

A position in an alley across from the campus offered a secluded spot to perform recon. Back to a brick wall, I laid the mirror across my raised knees. Willing it to life filled the reflective surface with the faceted view through Razcolm's eyes as he scurried across the top of one of Mimir's lower buildings. The portable spell medium was a vast improvement on the viewing pool I'd used to infiltrate Thoth's component factory.

Razcolm stopped outside a ventilation exhaust. *<You see what I see?>*

Yes. What's wrong?

<Turn it around so we can talk face-to-face.>

I turned the mirror around to the magnified side only to get a close-up of Razcolm sticking his tongue out at me. The little shit giggled in my head. I reversed the mirror.

Get to work.

<Oui, Mon Capitaine.>

I shook my head.

A metal security mesh came into view as Razcolm approached the ventilation exhaust. I cursed, stopping mid-expletives as he somehow passed through into the ventilation shaft. The origami spider scurried down the square grey tunnel without any clear preference to a given orientation.

Little shit is just trying to make me dizzy.

As if I had invoked a challenge, he launched himself spinning down a vertical shaft. I caught sight of his legs forcing an end over descent and closed my eyes. The sensation of the imp's giggles didn't help my sour stomach.

Razcolm darted left and right through a maze of ducts occasionally stopping to peer through a grate or slotted vent. Other than choice bits of office gossip, he failed to discover anything useful. Razcolm worked his way down floor by floor, headed toward Willie's workshop without my telling him.

<Not exactly a brainstorm, human. Even if he isn't involved, that's where all the lab and testing spaces are housed.>

He had a point.

Down one more floor, Razcolm raced through the ventilation system. He took a right, and something caught my eye.

Razcolm, stop.

<What?>

I'm not sure, something seemed off about the duct ahead when you took the corner.

<I think I know what I'm doing, human.>

Fine. Just be careful.

<Snore.> Razcolm resumed his breakneck charge. All motion stopped abruptly as if he'd slammed into a wall that wasn't there. A blur of blue light sent ice water through my veins. I flipped the mirror looking up Razcolm's back path as magical barriers snapped into place one by one.

<Help I'm tr—>

My mirror showed a close-up of my dour expression.

Shit.

21

DINNER AND A SHOW

I was still cursing up a storm when a black electric SUV pulled into the alley and stopped directly in front of me. Panic flashed through me a moment before the window rolled down and my mom waved. "Hello, Sugar Dumpling."

The back door opened close enough after mom's pet name to hear Sunny's snort. "Yeah, hiya, *Sugar Dumpling.*"

I glared, taking in bruises and scrapes on her exposed skin. A butterfly closure strip held her left cheek together under one eye.

Sunny laughed harder.

I'm really getting sick of everybody laughing at me today.

"Get in, Elias," Dad ordered.

For a moment I considered just walking away. I needed to find out what had happened to Razcolm and, if possible, retrieve the construct. I didn't know much about how the fey possessed things from across the Silver. Still, I didn't doubt the sudden loss of connection would probably leave a flaming headache which really couldn't happen to a nicer imp.

Dad's voice lowered until I could barely hear it. "Get in the damn car, Elias."

I opened my mouth to object, but realized I couldn't without explaining. Since the explanation included culpability for actions that probably constituted trespass, industrial espionage, and several other illegalities, I got in the car.

Mom had been the cradle robber, but you couldn't tell it in her youthful appearance. My maternal great-grandmother had been half Korean, and though you could only barely see the heritage in Mom's beaming face, she benefited from the genetics nonetheless.

Rather than answer mom's expectant smile, I glowered at Sunny. "How did you find me? Got your minions watching me?"

"Elias," Dad growled.

Mom held up a disk the size of a silver dollar. Three quartz pebbles studded the surface around a depression which Mom held her thumb in. Two of the gems glowed orange. A tiny orange mote flitted around the rim like a sprite as it moved in her grip, always staying between the seeker and me—Mom's desired object.

"These are really marvelous, Sugar Dumpling, and so affordable," Mom preened. "Three spells for only five dollars? What a steal."

"Highway robbery," I growled behind the fingers tracing lines down my face.

"Elias."

Mom batted at him. "Hush, Jackson. Eli's probably so exhausted by his ordeal he wasn't taking care with his tone. You know what a Grumpy Gus he can be."

A bark of laughter turned my attention to my back seat companion. I lowered my voice so it wouldn't carry. "We're going to talk about this later."

Sunny rolled her eyes at me. "Someday you'll thank me."

"Not hardly," I said.

"So, are you two dating?" Mom asked. "Are there grandchildren in my future?"

Before I could deny any chance of anything of the sort, Sunny answered for me. "No, Cynthia, we're just friends. Eli's engaged to one of the rats that lives in his alley."

Mom's expression clouded. She turned back toward Dad. "Is that some sort of slang for a street person?"

"Probably one of his origami creations," Dad said.

"No, Cynthia," Sunny couldn't hold back her mirth. "Eli just prefers rats over people."

"Are you done?" I asked.

Sunny met my gaze. "They don't call him out on his bull spit."

"I can't imagine how he could prefer anyone over you, Marisol." Mom turned back around and fixed me with a pointed look. "You're such a kind, generous Christian girl, smart and successful."

"Drop me at the next corner," I said.

"I certainly will not," Dad said. "We came all this way to see you. We're going to have a nice family dinner and then a candid discussion about your troubles."

"I don't have time—"

Mom summoned hurt like a master magician. "You don't have time for one meal with your parents, let alone the woman who's helped you so much?"

Unable to snarl directly at Mom, I focused on Sunny once more. "There's a killer on the loose. I need—"

"To let the authorities handle that, Elias," Dad said.

"That would be nice, wouldn't it?" Sunny asked.

I fell back into the way too comfortable seats, folded my arms and tucked my chin. When Dad slowed for a traffic light, I grabbed the door handle.

"Elias," Mom yelped.

The door remained securely locked. "Child locks, really?"

"Seems we needed them, didn't we?" Dad said.

I flopped back into my previous position and stewed on the list of spells and constructs I needed—especially a new door bell. My...well Razcolm wasn't a friend, so my construct had been trapped inside Mimir by an anti-intruder spell. There was still a killer on the loose, and I was being held hostage for a family dinner.

Skeleton key or a bobby pin, maybe some rhet hair or magnetic shavings. Those beard toy things would work if they still sell them.

We pulled into the Happy Clamily, a seafood restaurant jutting out over the river from the Columbia's southern banks. A television family of beaming clams made the place look like a barely grown-up Chuck E. Cheese. They served an excellent menu of local seafood, specializing in buckets of the sign's butter-steams extended family.

I eyed the Columbia, hair on my arms prickling. "Could we eat someplace else?"

"Sugar Dumpling!" Mom's hurt was feigned, but the guilt underpinning it felt real enough. "This used to be your favorite restaurant."

"When I was a child with an uneducated palate."

"Don't be such a snob, Elias," Dad said. "They serve excellent, fresh-caught seafood for far less than any place in Portland."

Elated anticipation from my nearness to a ley line fought with a cold dread rising out of the Columbia's waters.

Caught is what's worrying me.

Sunny smirked at me. "Come on, *Sugar Dumpling*. Let's have a nice, friendly, *uneventful* dinner."

"Kind of like a double date," Mom said.

A suspicious log bumped and spun its way down the riverside just beyond my window. I licked my lips and waited for someone to let me out of the car.

Dad shoved a small duffel into my hands the moment I escaped the SUV. He pushed me back inside. "Change. We'll wait."

"If you want me to change, why not go inside first?" I asked.

"Have you seen yourself lately?" Dad scowled. "There's a cosmetic charm in there to fix your hair."

"You're embarrassed to be seen with me?" I asked.

"Never, Sugar Dumpling," Mom said.

"What she said," Sunny smirked.

"Best foot forward, Elias. Always."

I got out and shoved the bag back into dad's hands. "I'm fine."

He pushed it back into my hands. His voice lowered, but rather than becoming more dangerous it took on a pleading note. "Your mother hasn't seen you in a decade. She's going to want photos. Stop being so stubborn and make this special for her."

My gaze flicked to the women. Mom laughed at something Sunny said, casually touching Sunny's arm the way she had whenever she'd approved of one of my dates. I took the offered bag and climbed into the SUV. Roomy as it was, changing into fresh underwear, khaki's, and a polo while staying as out of sight as possible proved a cramped affair. I dug my scrying mirror out of my belongings to use the cosmetic charm. As I'd feared, my ley-touched hair refused to be covered.

Dad opened the door back up at my knock.

"Do you have a shaving kit with you?" I whispered. "Charm didn't work."

"Why did you do that to your hair if you can't fix it?"

"It's a long story, and it wasn't my choice."

Dad frowned. "Cynthia, Marisol, please go inside and get us a table. We'll be right behind you."

"Something in the middle of the room," I said.

"Don't you want to sit over the water like you did as a boy?" Mom asked.

My pleading expression widened Sunny's eyes. "Weatherman predicted rain, Cynthia. Inside is probably best."

As soon as they were out of sight, Dad unfolded a large pocket knife. "Lean forward, boy."

After a century of death and blood in the Wasteland, my trust in another had long ago been murdered. Lowering my eyes and presenting my undefended head to any man, even Dad, required a monumental struggle. The scrape of metal against scalp registered a moment before the rasp reached my ears. Dad's blade passed over my skin in expert motions, raining rainbow curls to the parking lot pavement.

"Done."

I patted my head looking for blood, but Dad hadn't so much as nicked me. Dad stepped out of my way toward the restaurant. I closed the car door and bent over the hair.

"Elias?"

I drew a sixth rez circle around my loose hair.

"What are you doing, boy?"

I drew my Zippo and met his eyes. "Protecting my bridges."

I activated the pavement circle and the Zippo, expending the stored flames into the half sphere on the cement. I dropped the circle and stepped into place behind and on Dad's right.

"Things that bad?" Dad asked.

"I'm not paranoid." A sardonic chuckle escaped me. "Okay, maybe I am, but not unreasonably so."

"Never said you were, boy. You're a lot of things that could use a little work, but you're not stupid. If you think destroying your DNA to prevent its use in something arcane is necessary, I can only assume things are serious."

"What do you know about arcanology?"

Dad stopped and peered deep into my face. "A man protects his family, Elias, *all* of them. I take exception to my boy being attacked. I was not about to sit around ignorant when a little dutiful study meant I could be there for you if you needed."

Despite the way we'd always butted heads, genuine warmth filled me. "Thank you, sir."

He chuckled and grabbed me around my shoulders. "You're welcome, son, but you can really thank me by making this a nice meal for your mother...maybe let her hope you might eventually have a thing going on with Marisol?"

"It's never going to happen," I said. "We're too different."

"You figure out a fortune telling spell?"

"No, why?"

He shrugged. "Saying never tempts God's sense of humor."

I didn't respond.

"Bet having fresh skivvies feels good," Dad said.

I sighed. "Yeah."

"We'll talk about that after dinner."

"Yes, sir." I had every intention of finding a way to escape without ever discussing my conviction with him or Mom. Still, there was no point setting the bridge on fire right before we all sat down to a meal on its planks.

AN AROMA OF GARLIC, butter, and fresh-cooked seafood offered us warmth as we walked in. I scanned the restaurant in hopes Mom and Sunny had gotten an inside table. Dad gave his name as homey reassurance bypassed me. An adorable hostess in a black dress with red and white roses seated us with the energy of a girl working her first job. It wasn't her fault she was marching me toward the menu.

She spun back to us, extending a hand to the deck table. Her smile melted away on sight of my expression. Unsure how to deal with me any more than a deer knew how to deal with the oncoming big rig, she froze.

Sunny swept her up and toward the restaurant's inside. "Don't worry about him. The table's perfect. He's just the grumpy type."

The lap and slap of Columbia's fresh water filled the boards beneath my feet. Dread slithered up from between them.

Sunny grabbed my arm, whispering as she drew me toward the table and Mom's beaming grin. "Look on the bright side. She could've seated us all in one of those squeaky double-date booths with too little space to avoid touching."

My flat tone told her just how bright a side I considered the open air table over the water. "Hoo-ray."

Mom gestured. "Sit there by your—by Marisol so she and I can still talk about you two."

Mom's mischievous titter was supposed to downplay the very real threat. I could almost feel Dad's impending use of my name, so I sat on the armed wooden chair and slid it further back from the table. I eyed the water and fidgeted. The new polo's tag irritated the back of my neck.

"They've got those steamed butter clams in garlic butter you love so much, Sugar Dumpling."

"Mom."

"Elias."

"Yes, baby?"

"How about a sampler?" Sunny asked in a cheery tone that all but echoed Mom's pet name for me.

A pretty college-age waitress with a blond pixie cut stepped up to the table with one hip jutted slightly out. "I'm Darlene, I'll be your server this evening. What can I get you to drink?"

Dad picked up all the menus in reach and handed them to Darlene. He ordered appetizers, chowder, entrees, drinks, dessert and after dinner coffee for the table.

She blinked a moment, but restarted her smile and slipped away from the table.

I shot Dad a look. "Sunny could be allergic to what you ordered her."

"Nonsense," Dad said. "We've eaten with Marisol before."

"She might have wanted something other than what you ordered. You didn't even discuss it with her."

"It's all right, Eli—"

"Isn't it cute how he goes out of his way to make Marisol happy?" Mom asked.

"I ordered the best items on the menu, Elias. I have been here before."

"Years ago," I countered. "Besides, I might have wanted something different."

"What?"

"I don't know. I never got to look at the menus."

He shook his head. "You'll be happy with what I ordered."

"How do you know?"

He fixed me with a flat, hard stare. "You're living on the street, eating garbage like a damned fool. You'll be grateful for any real meal."

While he made a distinct point, I wasn't about to concede it. "I've developed a spell to cleanse and recycle leftovers."

"Besides," Sunny said. "Grace and I make sure he doesn't starve."

Mom placed a hand on Sunny's arm. "You are so good for him."

"Probably still tastes like garbage," Dad said. "And beggars shouldn't be choosers."

A shadow passed over Sunny's expression.

"I minored in culinary arts, as you well know."

"Fine," Dad barked as he folded his arms. "How does it taste?"

I opened my mouth to brag on my magical culinary prowess, but stopped short. The spell did the job, and I hadn't finished tweaking it yet, but the end product hadn't progressed far from the initial prison equivalent of Mom's meatloaf. "As good as homemade."

The arrival of drinks and appetizers forced Dad to hold his next salvo. Mom cut him off. "This looks so good. Elias, how did you and Marisol meet?"

"I'm sure Sunny's already told you all about it."

"I want to hear your version of it," Mom said.

I popped a piece of fried razor clam into my mouth, resisting the urge to roll my eyes in pleasure. Chewing the heavenly mollusk allowed me a few moments to decide how best to answer. "The garbage truck driver that nearly ran me down told me about the Manger. I entered. She fed me. I made her cry. She poked her nose where it didn't belong. I told her to leave me alone, and she hasn't stopped interfering in my life since."

"Elias."

Mom sipped her white wine. "I like her version better."

Darlene reappeared. "Is everything all right—aww, so cute!"

All eyes turned toward the dock's edge. A half dozen river otters crawled onto the planks, shaking the water from their coats.

The food in my mouth turned to ashes.

The otters swarmed one another.

A nearby diner covered her child's eyes, demanding answers in a harsh whisper. "Dear God, are they fornicating?"

"What's fornicathing?" the blinded boy asked.

I pushed back from the table, my chair falling back to hit the deck with a resounding crack.

"Eli?" Sunny asked.

"Sit back down, boy. Whatever they're about. They're not going to bother you."

The otters pressed into one another. Magic washed over me, and I summoned power without thinking. Nearly pure ley energy sent me into cross-eyed euphoria. Dread fell away as the otters blurred.

"Eli?" Concern laced Sunny's voice. "What are you doing?"

"He's glowing, honey," Mom said. "Probably just trying to impress you."

"Elias where are your manners?" Dad asked. "No glowing at the table. You're frightening people."

On cue, screams coursed through the restaurant patrons. Male staff, one a manager, shot around us apologizing and reassuring us that everything was fine.

It's not fine. Not by a long shot.

An ancient-looking Indian medicine man stepped out of the magical haze and fading fur. My eyes traced the dock, trying to define a large enough circle to cage the Ottiren if need be.

"Elias Balthazar Graham, we are most displeased." His smile looked more than displeased. It looked positively like an irritated barracuda I'd once encountered in the Caribbean.

On the plus side, his tone cut through my magical high enough I recognized the danger leering from the water's edge.

Dad rose and interposed himself. "I don't know your business with my son, but I'm sure we can work out whatever it is."

I rounded the other side of the table, cursing myself for using the flames inside my Zippo. "I've been working on your problem. There's no need for threats."

"I do not threaten," the Ottiren said.

My calves prickled.

"I'm not going to just stand here and let you eat me," I shot back.

"Eat you?" Sunny squeaked. "Eli?"

Dad crossed the distance, shoving a finger into the Ottiren's chest. "Look here, Mister."

Dad's tangled finger made the shaman's necklace clatter as the Ottiren seized Dad, throwing him thirty feet and into the Columbia.

My neck burned.

"You'd better back the fuck off if you want my help."

"Language, Elias," Mom scolded. "There are children present."

"Be silent, woman. Men are speaking," the Ottiren said.

Sunny beat me to the punch—literally. Her fist impacted on the old Indian's solid chest. She cradled her wrist and scolded him anyway. "You don't talk to a person that way."

Sunny went through the air. The glisten of an eyeSentinel shrouded her just before she bounced off the opposite end of the dock, through a railing and into the water.

My knuckles burned hot enough I didn't feel the fingernails cutting into my palm. I drew in more wild magic. The Ottiren strode forward. I didn't have a fireball or a firebolter, so I summoned the forces I did have. The milky white surface of the next board catapulted the Ottiren backward into the water.

Dad was visible, dragging himself out of the water, so I rushed after Sunny. She panted at the water's edge, one hand cradling her chest. "You know, Eli, these shield charms need more cushion."

If the water I stepped down into had flashed to steam when my foot touched it, I wouldn't have been surprised.

"Are you all right, do you need a doct—"

Dark tendrils of river grass shot out of the Columbia, wrapped around my throat and yanked. My sudden flight slammed into the gasping woman, sending her back in the river.

Black water swallowed me whole.

Even if there had been air to breathe, the woven grass vines tightened around my throat until I feared they'd crush my windpipe. Unlike the last time I'd been committed to a watery grave, I wasn't chained, magic coursed through me and I was armed.

Expediency discarded thoughts of crafting a fireball on the fly to burn away my bonds and light the Ottiren up for barbeque. My multi-tool cut at the weeds.

A dark shape slithered through the water. An otter bit my knife hand. I released the vines and struck out with the same force I'd used to smash Boss Golem with a truck hood. My arm shot forward through the water, only fingertips curled as they slid into the otter's nose with all the force I could deliver.

The flash of light accompanying the impact illuminated a cloud of blood. The otter barked a distressed yelp and released my hand.

I thanked him by jabbing the blade at him.

Two others grabbed me from behind.

I reached out to draw in more wild magic in preparation to fight them off. The disapproving voice of Kenrith echoed in my throbbing head.

<Destroying yourself to kill a ghost is so typically human.>

Whether Kenrith's voice was really in my thoughts or merely an echo of my wiser if nastier nature, the voice was right. I'd been accused of narcotic use. I'd recognized my need for the raw fey power and until the Ottiren's attack, held off any desire to draw upon the power again.

I didn't know how to filter the raw magic. I didn't know how to protect myself from its lure and the hungry siren just beyond.

Who cares? I'm drowning. I can break the Ottiren, free myself and then worry about slipping the fey magic's grasp.

<Shortsighted, Magus.> Kenrith's voice held a ring of truth even though I imagined him.

<Nothing wrong with embracing power,> Razcolm responded. <Seize the power, win the day, and worry about the rest later.>

I needed air. I needed to break free. I needed to hurt the two pulling me backward in a way that tightened the vines around my throat. I fought euphoria and elation, ego and power to free myself enough to form a plan.

Drawing on the Ley was a mistake. Panic is the enemy in a crisis.

The voices of Kenrith and Razcolm argued from either shoulder as I fought off my attackers without drawing any more ley. I resisted the elaborate need to torch the river bottom foliage in favor of my slow but sure knife.

Otters forced me to slash out with the knife, then feel the blade back into the edge-gouged vine. Every moment I lost shifting my focus between my three attackers, the more my lungs burned.

I was losing ground on every front, the direst being my fading consciousness.

Without warning, a shimmering energy shield sheathed me. I didn't waste time searching for a reason. My lungs were on the edge of bursting. I cut at the weeds as the two otters behind me tried to pull the vines tight enough to pop my head from my neck.

The last dark tendril parted.

I shot backward, pulled back hopefully toward the shoreline in a rush by my would-be stranglers. My head breached the water. I gulped air. An otter shot at me like a furry barracuda.

A deafening explosion thundered next to my ear. At that same instant, the water exploded red in front of me. My head shot around in an agonized search for the shore. Dad and Sunny braced me—my so-called attackers. Sunny extended a pistol in one hand. Her other steadied me atop an eyeSentinel clipped to my shirt.

Another otter appeared.

Sunny fired another shot.

The two dragged me toward shore, hampering my attempts to slash at any otter that got too close. Sunny still had at least three bullets, but there were six otters. I had no idea how badly she'd hurt them, if they had some kind of magical healing, or if they were even vulnerable to bullets.

We made it close enough to shore for me to stand up. My would-be saviors were panting harder than I was. They kept pulling even after I'd managed my feet. I shook them off and attacked the vines still strangling me.

Something struck my leg. Another hit unsteadied my stance. Dark shapes slid around my feet. Visions of being yanked down once more shot through me. A wash of magic swirled through the water.

The eyeSentinel's glow vanished.

Teeth sank into my ankle.

I screamed.

Dad and Sunny grabbed me again and yanked me up onto the shore. Blood ran down into the water from the bite marks.

The Ottiren stood up in the water, once more an old Indian. He extended a palm full of blood and smiled. "This is not over, Magus."

Sunny shot him.

He vanished under the water. There was no way to tell if her attack had cost him my blood or even if she'd done him harm.

My leg collapsed and took me with it to the ground. My body felt a wreck, but a seductive whisper reassured me I could kill the Ottiren with the ley power beneath the water.

"Eli? Eli?" Sunny repeated.

After several more attempts, I answered. "What?"

"Are you all right? Is it still there? You're staring into the water like you can see something."

"The siren wants me to come play."

"What?" Sunny asked.

"He could be delirious from lack of oxygen," Dad said.

"He's on his feet."

I'm standing?"

I looked down to find myself standing calf-deep in the river once more. Ley energy sang in my veins, but not as loudly as the beckoning siren offering me more.

"What's going on?" Sunny asked.

"I want to go play with her." Want wasn't the right word. Need pulled me toward the power. Fury sided with need. I'd been trying to figure out the Ottiren's issue, and I damn well wasn't going to lay down and be eaten just because he was in a hurry.

"Her who? Tunoh?" Sunny asked.

Whispers and warning ran through my head. The power to part the entire section of Columbia called to me from beneath the water. "The siren beneath the waves."

A hand stopped me from diving into the water.

"Let's go inside and finish dinner." I pulled against his grip, but Dad didn't let me pull away. "Come on, son."

Sunny ducked under my arm on the bitten side. "Your mom's waiting. She must be scared to death."

I frowned at her. "Fine, but we're eating inside."

"You won't get any arguments from me," Sunny said. "You don't happen to know a drying off spell by any chance, do you?"

"Not today."

22

DUMPSTERS PROVIDE

Suggesting our attempt to resume dinner was doomed proved equally tantamount to calling a nuke a firecracker. The restaurant manager approached the inside table Dad claimed for the resumption of our meal. He asked us to leave, which suited me fine.

"We didn't bring any trouble. We're hungry patrons still waiting on our meal," Dad said. "We should be allowed to eat in peace."

They argued, but the manager acquiesced to Dad's persistent reason. We were allowed to stay and finish our meal, but both staff and remaining patrons filled the Happy Clamily with disapproving tension.

SMLE and EMTs showed up before we made it through our chowder. The EMTs went to work checking a woman who'd suffered an anxiety attack, Sunny and then Dad in that order. SMLE took a few statements and promptly tried to arrest me.

Dad interposed himself. "On what charges?"

"Dad, you realize my lawyer is right here."

Sunny pursed her lips. "I thought you fired me."

"I tried, but based on that LA lawyer you sent, your termination didn't take."

She smirked and offered a small, wincing shrug.

"Are you all right?" I asked in a low tone.

She waved me off and mouthed, "Bruised ribs."

"We don't need a lawyer," Dad waved over the restaurant manager. "Tell them my son didn't do anything."

"He only acted to save the woman after she attacked the Indian and was thrown into the river."

I didn't groan, but it was a close thing.

"We'll want to press charges, of course," Dad said. "What do you intend to do to ensure our safety, Officers?"

Can't press charges against a ghost.

I dipped my spoon into the steaming chowder, not making eye contact with the two SMLE cops.

"Elias, wait for your father."

Aromatic steam rose from piping hot bowls of chowder practically forming animated come-hither motions. My stomach grumbled.

"So," Mom said. "How do you know that Indian fellow?"

Sunny's attention riveted on me.

"He saved my life. I'm helping him to clear that debt," I said.

Dad's hand slapped onto my shoulder as he took his seat. "I'm proud of you for repaying him, boy. So, what's the problem?"

I eyed my soup bowl, sighed and faced him. "He wants me to restore the trade routes of his ancestral village underwater for the last five or so decades. I'm working on the problem, but apparently not fast enough."

"Why not?" Dad asked. "It's not like you have a nine to five."

I shoveled several too hot, but admittedly good, spoonfuls of clam chowder into my mouth as a stalling technique that provided the added benefit of quieting my stomach. "Before the Ottiren saved me from drowning—"

"Why were you drowning?" Mom asked.

I kept going without answering her question. "The man who runs organized begging in Seufert Fells—"

Sunny all but growled a single word. "Duval."

"Yeah, him. He and his boys intervened in a beating—"

"Wait, who was beating you?" Dad asked.

"Why would anyone want to hurt you?" Mom asked.

I rubbed the bridge of my nose, swallowed more chowder and took a bite of sourdough bread.

"Maybe we should let Eli tell us all of it," Sunny said.

"You haven't even told Marisol?" Mom frowned at the two of us. "Communication is essential in a—"

I was on my feet. "We're not dating! Do you want an answer or not?"

"Sit, boy. You're causing a scene."

"I didn't mean to upset him," Mom whispered too loudly to Sunny.

"Continue," Dad said.

"All right. Caleb, Tiny, and Ugly—please don't ask," I shot the table a look. "Grabbed me on Fells Overlook, took me to a construction site, beat me and chained me up in preparation to drown me in the Columbia."

Mom leaned forward. "Were they white? Was it a race attack?"

"No. They're black like us, well, except Sunny. Duval and his goons showed up mid beating thinking I was homeless."

"You are homeless," Dad said.

"Right, but not their kind of homeless," I said. "They thought I was one of their employees being beaten up by anti-homeless militants or something."

"Why were Caleb and his friends attacking you?" Sunny asked.

I glared. "I don't want to talk about it."

"If Duval's people intervened, how did you end up in the Columbia?" Dad asked.

My ankles prickled. "I did, okay? That's where I met the Ottiren. He demanded I fix his trade route or he'd eat me."

"What's keeping you from doing that, and how does this Duval fellow come into it?" Dad asked.

"Duval claims credit for saving me from Caleb. He pressganged me into finding the murderer killing the homeless—including the pretend homeless that work for him."

"Pretend homeless?" Mom asked.

Sunny's tone would've made a cobra nervous. "Duval's people are conmen, professional beggars who steal from genuine homeless. They make a business of taking advantage of peoples' generosity and in the process create skepticism that lessens the already small amount people are willing to give. The homeless need that help to survive."

"You're already helping the homeless," Dad said. "You're providing a way for them to find their feet, get a job and make something of themselves."

"For some, yes. Some can't hold down a job for legitimate reasons. We're working as hard as we can, but there are too many homeless for the Manger to help them all." She fixed me with a hard look. "There are also some people too stubborn to accept our help."

Dad's tone hardened, and his eyes fixed on me. "There's no excuse for *begging*."

"Okay, I don't want her help, but I don't beg either, Dad."

Sunny's voice broke. "But other homeless d-die every year b-because Duval's people d-do."

Mom covered Sunny's hand. "It's all right, dear."

"It's n-not. I h-help everyone I c-can, t-try to g-give them a safe h-haven, b-but...," Sunny dissolved into silent sobs.

Mom gave me a pointed look. She already had Sunny well in hand. Besides, there was nothing I could do to help her. She'd nearly died when the wizard had come calling with my face. Countless of her flock had been killed in the sanctuary she'd offered.

Dad's expression mirrored Mom's.

Fine.

I stood.

"Where do you think you're going?" Dad asked.

Mom's and Sunny's eyes rose to watch me.

I extended a hand toward Sunny. "You want me to make her feel better, well I can't do that sitting here. She promised people a safe haven, and a bunch of them got murdered. The only way I can make things better is to take out the killer."

Mom's color faded. "Take out?"

"He's going to kill the murderer," Dad said.

"Damn right I'm going to kill him," I said.

"Eli, you c-can't," Sunny said.

I snorted.

Heat built up into Sunny's voice to bolster her tone. "Vengeance is mine sayeth the Lord."

"Mom?"

"What?" Mom asked.

"Where did my name come from?" I asked.

"The Bible. It's a form of Elijah," Mom said.

"What does it mean?" I asked.

Sunny scowled. "Eli, that doesn't change—"

I answered for Mom. "How many times did you remind me when I was coming up that my name means Jehovah is God, that Elijah was a prophet, chosen to bring God's message."

"That doesn't mean you can take justice into your own hands," Dad said.

"How could you even consider something like that?" Mom asked. "You're not a killer."

I leveled my gaze, peering deep into Sunny's eyes.

Her expression hardened. "This is real, Eli, not the Wasteland."

"He," I dropped my voice, looking around. "He butchered a teenage girl."

"Leave this to the authorities," Dad said.

"At the very least, if he confronts you again, detain him. Let me

handle the legalities. Eli. You don't want to worsen your legal standing," Sunny said.

"Like you've handled Adam?" I shot back.

She growled her reply. "I'm not done with Adam Mathias, not by a longshot."

Mom rushed around the table and wrapped her arms around me. "Please, Sugar Dumpling. I know you get angry, but don't do anything that'll take you away from us again."

The entrée's Dad had ordered floated toward the table balanced on Darlene's shoulder.

"You're so smart." Mom caressed my cheek. "Surely you can protect Marisol without sacrificing yourself."

I eased myself from her reach, resisting the urge to yank myself free out of consideration for her feelings. I lowered my voice. "I'll think about it."

Before anything more could be said, I turned on my heels and marched away, leaving my unhappy family in the Happy Clamily.

DAD CHASED me into the parking lot, demanding we talk, demanding I come home. I was done talking. More words only wasted time and shortened my smoldering temper. I needed a plan.

The fingers of my left hand rubbed up against one another, sticks trying to build up enough friction to ignite the fire of inspiration. Hunger eclipsed thought. Not for food, but the wild magic entering our world from beyond the Silver.

If it rained on the way back to my alley, I didn't feel it. Holograms and vehicles, people and illusions passed by in a blur of irrelevance. My hands shook once more, but I pushed the telltales out of my mind. I couldn't have drawn in more magic if I'd wanted —at least not without expending some.

I wrapped my arms around my chest, tucked my head and

trudged toward my box. Waking up in the hospital hadn't been as bad, but I'd been unconscious at first. They'd also walled me up behind a barrier of blue sparkles that forced a cold-turkey fast. Walking through mananet after mananet was like drifting through a world filled with phantasms but no actual people.

My feet stopped.

My eyes came up.

I stood before the bronze griffon in the center of Gateway Park. My gaze wasn't directed to the majestic figure, but to the angry orange glow of Thoth's condescending eye.

Thoth, goddess of the night, goddess of magic, glared down at me, allied with the best friend who'd framed and betrayed me.

Rage added to the reasons for my shaking body. Far beneath my feet, another source of natural magic beckoned me—another false god offering power that could destroy me.

I won't. I will not bow to anything set to use me and discard me.

"What is the worse betrayal? Which lies cut the deepest?"

I whirled.

A victim of terminal vanity stood before me in Glamour splendor, dressed in a Lord of the Rings cosplay to match his elven grace. He stared at the griffon rather than me. It took a moment to register his questions had emerged in a thoughtful tone.

Meant for the statue, not me.

The stranger shook his head. "Betrayal by those closest to our hearts is nearly the pinnacle, but can that truly compare to betraying ourselves?" He turned toward me. "Where can you go for safety when you cannot even trust your own eyes?"

He marched away, pausing only to spit on the griffon's talons.

I watched him depart with purposeful strides.

Prophet or demon? Messenger or madman?

I needed the power beneath my feet so badly I could barely think—the one capacity that had never before fled me. I turned my attention to the statue and then the Eye blazing its contempt down upon all of us—a modern-day Eye of Sauron.

No.

"No!" My fists ratcheted tighter and tighter until my fingers tingled from lack of blood. "I will not be used!"

I turned my back to Thoth's Eye and marched toward home. My insides had been run through a pasta machine. I stopped at Genghis Kahnoli's dumpster to fill a couple snack baggies with slip-n-slide components. The dumpster had been emptied recently, forcing me to lean over the edge and reach deeply for a knot of noodles and what looked like cooked spinach. I grabbed a huge handful. A Styrofoam container with half its lid bent open fell over my fist, displaying a mess of old marinara and calamari rings.

An idea hit me.

I collected extra noodles and the container of fried squid. Excitement bubbled up.

I need ingredients for an adhesion charm, some plant matter and maybe some fertilizer.

I hurried up the alley, the heady anticipation of working through a new spell buoying my steps. A car parked in the alley mouth made me slow my pace, but a moment later Darrin's exit banished my unease. He was dressed far too nicely for visiting the homeless. I craned my neck but caught no silhouette to suggest Nicole was waiting in the car.

Return to my box felt long overdue.

"Eli? You look nice."

"Don't get used to it." I laughed, stripping out of the business casual clothes Dad had forced on me. I checked the pockets out of habit and was surprised to bring back a twenty dollar bill. Turning it over revealed a heart drawn on the back around two letters: S & D.

Mom.

"Is Nicole feeling better?" I asked.

"Yes. Thank you for asking."

"I hate to ask, but," I held out the bill. "Any chance you can get

me an eyeGuardian and some fertilizer?"

He took the twenty, staring at me. "Why?"

"Killer on the loose?"

"You want fertilizer to stop a killer?"

I crossed the alley with a smile and carefully drew a dandelion out of a crack in the pavement. "Wait until you see this new spell."

"Eli." Darrin turned the bill over in his hands. "You're homeless."

"Nothing gets by you."

"That murderer is killing the homeless. He attacked the Manger to get at you."

"A good reason for me to find him before he hurts someone else."

"Maybe...maybe you should avoid meeting him," Darrin said. "I've been thinking about the things I learned about the attack, and...I don't think you can survive him."

"Oh, ye of little faith." A thought occurred to me. I looked up from repacking my gear for the coming encounter. "Either way, I still need those things."

Darrin pulled the twenty back out from his pocket and extended the money. "I'm sorry, Eli, but I can't be part of you getting hurt again or worse, sending you back to the Wasteland. That's why I'm here to get you off the street, so the killer can't come after you."

I searched Darrin's expression. There was no budge behind his eyes. My injured, former protégé had made a hard decision, and he wouldn't be moved.

"So, will you come stay with Nicole and me a while? Before you say you can't because of your conviction, consider. Is your pride really worth your life?"

I turned toward him like a seldom-used garden gate. "Have you talked this over with Nicole?"

"I have."

"And she agreed?" I asked.

"Eventually. It's my place. She still has her own."

"Darrin, that's not good for your relationship."

"I can live with her anger," he said. "I couldn't live with myself if you died when I could've saved you."

I rose and clapped his shoulder. "Thank you, but as it happens, I was offered a job."

Of course, one of the people offering could be a cold-blooded killer— though I still can't see Willie or even Austin killing a teen runaway.

"If things turn out the way the recruiter hopes, I may even have someplace new to stay."

Darrin relaxed visibly. "How soon?"

When bacon delivers itself on the wing?

I shrugged. "Soon?"

"You'll stay with me until the new opportunity materializes?"

"Thanks, Darrin, but whether either of us likes it or not, that killer has it in for me. I'm not bringing that into your house."

"We have good building security."

I met Darrin's eyes. I didn't say anything more. There was no need. He might prefer not to know, but he knew I wasn't just walking away.

I made a show of preparing double Ziploc bags and poured water into the nonfunctional electric kettle plugged into my Edison converter.

He eyed my makeshift warm water bottle.

"Was there anything else?"

His voice mimicked a frightened mouse. "No. I'm late picking up Nicole and getting back to Foretold. You sure you'll be okay?"

"I'll put up a fifth rez, all right?"

Darrin chewed his lip.

"Go, Darrin. I've survived a lot worse than a little cold weather in an alley."

He nodded to himself, handed over my twenty, and left me for an angry girlfriend. The things he'd told me about Nicole made me think attending Foretold would impress her, soften her temper. Darrin was a good man, a rare prize for any woman.

His concern touched me. He'd no doubt seen whatever the news had shown about the Manger killings, but he hadn't seen the teen runaway.

This wizard has to be stopped, and SMLE is sleeping on the job.

I ran my spell through several tests. The dandelion seemed to provide sufficient responsiveness without the fertilizer—though I remained convinced a little Miracle-Gro would improve the spell.

Next version.

I reviewed my plans for retrieving Razcolm. The more I went over everything I would need, the more convinced I became that changing back into Dad's clothes would help me if I ran into any security inside Mimir.

Not that I didn't interview in street clothes.

Laughter bubbled out of me as I changed.

Best foot forward, even breaking and entering, right Dad?

I took my slip-n-slide components and everything I would need for the new spell I still hadn't named. Either might work if I ran into a security guard, though using them probably nixed any chance to work for Mimir.

Weejok's nose and my own seeking spell suggested Mimir's halls hid a murdering wizard. There'd been no opportunity to prove out the killer's identity. I still didn't want to believe the Bradley brothers were directly involved.

Willie claimed they needed my services as an arcanologist, but their PGFR initiative displayed elements with suggested they kept at least a few arcanologists on staff. It was even odds the killer was among those employees, hiding his abilities and wearing Old Spice.

Unless the job offer was a trap.

A hike away from Mimir and my box brought me back to the selfsame Bluebox I'd seen but not used. Even with my hackles encouraging me to hurry, I sidelined to Walmart for an eyeGuardian. I fretted the whole way back to the teleporter, entered, and uttered words guaranteed to sort out the biggest question mark in my plans.

"Elias Balthazar Graham, Mimir Corp."

The Bluebox came to life.

I'd hoped that with as little time as had passed since using the box to accept their invitation, that they hadn't removed my access. The access code could've been programmed for a single use, but overlapping circles building toward an eighth rez connection refuted the possibility.

I stumbled out and back onto Mimir's couch. Dizziness and nausea warred for a World's Worst Companion award.

My head did rollercoaster imitations while I prepped a seeking spell to find Razcolm.

Ideally, searching from within Bradley's elevator offered the easiest access to the rest of the building. Unfortunately, biometric readers and runeguard locks kept me from the Mimir Wonkavator. A few judiciously employed fifth rez fields could probably cut a path to the elevator and just as easily sound an alarm to cut off my search.

There seemed little doubt that executives and special guests arrived in the building via Bluebox. Such people, despite rumors spread by their employees, did occasionally use the bathroom. Escorting guests to and fro from the washroom could potentially tie up a receptionist for too long.

As such, I bet the receptionist desk contained a few guest security badges with access to most of the public areas.

All I have to do to claim one of those badges is stand up, and—

The room's temperature plummeted into an ice age that froze my intestines in an attempt to catch my freefalling stomach. Impossibly, I stood next to Megan French on the holographic news broadcast.

"Are we to take from your appearance here, Mister Graham, that you intend to resume your work in arcanology?"

I opened my mouth, mimicking the actions of my doppelganger. In the background, a group of security guards left an irritated Adam to storm away through double doors.

Before security could escort me off the premises, Willie appeared. "Eli, so glad you could make it. Let's get you a pass."

Megan French whipped around us both to block our escape. "Mister Bradley, has Mister Graham joined the Mimir team?"

Willie smiled at the camera and spoke no doubt well-practiced words. "That's need to know, Megan. Guess what you don't have?"

He whisked me away so fast I felt the world swoop. Megan said something, but I couldn't hear her over the rushing wind in my ears.

My mind raced.

The killer is at the trade show.

He's using my face.

Why would he...Adam.

I knew I was right the moment the idea hit me. I'd been a thorn in the wizard's side. If he killed Adam and disappeared into the crowd, they wouldn't even summon a jury until after my lynching.

They'll put me back in the Wasteland.

I was on my feet in an instant. If the world was still misbehaving, I didn't pay it any mind. I threw myself into the Bluebox and across the space to the controls. There was no way to tell if the private Bluebox would charge me or not, but it didn't matter.

If I don't get to the tradeshow and save Adam, I'm fucked.

23

DEATH OF BELIEF

The eighth rez field dropped me inside another Bluebox. I bolted out onto the riverside boardwalk in a desperately-weaving sprint. Oriented on the island of light downriver, I gave my legs the command to do or die.

Dizziness from lack of oxygen took over remaining disorientation from the teleport. I stumbled to a stop at a line of regular cops and SMLE auxiliaries who were trying to keep the masses and uninvited reporters back from the arriving limousines.

Hendan strong-armed me, nearly clotheslining my charge. "You're not on the list."

"You didn't even look."

His smile was predatory. "Interfering with an officer in the execution of his duties. On your knees."

I raised my voice to draw the attention of the barred reporters. "I'm invited. Get Chris from RuneSYS."

Cameras swarmed around me. Under the eye of video recorders he couldn't erase, Hendan scowled deeper and deeper.

"Yes, I am discussing a return to arcanology. No, I can't confirm with which corporation. No, this is just business."

While I answered questions, one of the local cops had apparently had my so-called contact paged. The plump, middle-aged man had upgraded his attire since I'd met him on the riverwalk. He cleaned up well. He blinked at me a few times, then brightened. "Yes, I invited him."

A reporter shoved a microphone in Chris's face. "You invited the infamous Elias Graham to Foretold? Is RuneSYS recruiting him despite his conviction?"

Chris's color drained out of his face. He narrowed his eyes at me. I couldn't tell him I was there to stop myself from murdering my enemy, but I pleaded silently that he'd help me.

"RuneSYS did not invite Mister Graham," Chris said.

My hopes fell.

"I invited Elias personally as a guest consultant," Chris pushed his way through and grabbed my arm. "Please make a path."

Chris dragged me through the crowd and off to one side. "Are you really Elias Graham?"

"I am."

"I invited Elias Graham." He shook his head. "And here I thought I'd invited some down and out arcanologist who probably wouldn't show."

"Description still fits. I wasn't planning on coming."

"What changed your mind?" Chris asked.

"I have to stop someone from using my face to kill Adam Mathias."

Chris scrutinized me for a six count. He set his shoulders. "It's a pleasure to make your acquaintance, Elias. Let's get you a badge."

He led me through the crowd into the new convention center. The carpet assaulted me the moment flashbulb-induced night blindness wore off. The decor had probably looked good in the catalog, but in the vast swaths that covered the floor, the design probably was the toast of Hell's poker night.

Holographic screens hugged arched ceilings. Splashes of color and motion matched the mad dance filling open areas with arcanologists and Glamour shills wandering around like living bill-boards. A glance at the displays showed Adam saunter up to a podium. Thecia stood center stage behind him, flanked by more elf wannabes in cosplay similar to the man I'd encountered in Gateway Park.

Chris and I stopped at the back of a really long line. Being the last night of the trade show, I'd have thought everyone else already registered.

Chris noticed my confusion. "They're picking up their goody bags before they're all gone."

"Why not pick them up when the show started?" I asked.

He shrugged. "Less to carry."

Laughter roared from behind a line of closed double doors. Adam beamed on the screens high overhead. Chris handed over a Bluetooth headset. "They're already tuned to the main ballroom."

"Why are you being nice to me? For that matter, why did you bring me in after you learned who I was?"

"You seemed like a nice guy."

"For an ex-con?"

He laughed. "Keyword being ex, right? You didn't escape?"

"No one escapes the Wasteland."

He hesitated, smile growing brittle. It blossomed once more. "So you served your time. You're no different than I am."

"You were—"

He held up a hand. "No, I meant we all make mistakes. Besides, you were a legend, and it sounds like you're trying to do the right thing. Maybe it'll lead to your return to the stage...as it were."

There really wasn't anything I could say. I'd already told him about the killer. Talking about it any more risked being overheard and starting a panic. Worse, if someone fetched SMLE, they might keep me from stopping the murderer.

Observing knightly valor, I put on his headset.

"—like you to join me in thanking my fellow sponsors. It's been a great show, don't you think?"

Adam paused for cheers and applause.

The line hadn't moved enough to require my attention. Instead, my gaze riveted to the screen above me, watching Adam drink in the approval.

"Since our founding, Thoth has led the way—"

"From behind!" a voice shouted.

Adam nodded, raising a hand. "Yes, we've had a few setbacks that took the wind from our sails, but I'm here to announce something I think you will all agree puts Thoth back into the race."

Behind Adam, Mimir's PGs lined up clothed in harlequin illusions. They planted dance staves before them and waited still as statues.

"Since we brought magic to the masses, we've provided spell leases to our more advanced patrons. Our customers reached out to us, asking us to find a way to lessen the environmental impact of our single-use, auto-ignite spell scrolls."

He figured out a way to wipe out sections of the scroll?

"They cited the need to return to their neighborhood eyeStore for another usage. Well, we listened, and I'm happy to announce we've developed a solution that will revolutionize the industry!"

One of Mimir's dancers shifted her weight.

Dread welled up inside me. At least half a dozen people separated me from the registration kiosk.

I have to get in there—

"Allow me to introduce the world's first fully-digital grimoire!"

WHAT?!

Adam drew a tablet-sized device from where he'd hidden it out of sight. "Behold the brand new eyeTome!"

The feed zoomed in on the device's faux-leather binding artfully designed to mimic movie renditions of old spell books.

I stared, unable to believe what I was seeing.

"Utilizing specially designed voice recognition technology, your new eyeTome follows your spell incantations, projecting runes in order as they're needed. But that's not all."

The restless PG shifted its hand up the dancing staff, breaking me out of my daze. There were still too many people between me and a badge. "Sorry, Chris."

I yanked his badge over his head and bolted toward the closed ballroom doors.

"Not only will this adaptive technology allow you greater spell customization, but now you can download or renew spell leases with a touch of your Thoth wand anywhere in the world!"

I burst through the entry into a wall of cheers that nearly knocked me down. I took a moment to gather my bearings, but Megan French took advantage of the moment's hesitation.

"Mister Graham, nice of you to dress for the occasion. How do you feel about Thoth's new invention?"

"I don't care. Get out of my way." I snarled.

Her smile brightened. "Was the eyeTome one of your inventions? Did Adam Mathias steal the designs from you?"

I pinned her under my gaze. "I'm not here about anything to do with Thoth or arcanology."

She recovered more quickly than I might've given her credit for. "That's not what you said during our earlier interview."

"That's because you weren't interviewing me."

She scoffed. "We have it all recorded."

"You were duped by a murderer killing Seufert Fells's homeless."

"Is that a confession? Did we get that?" Megan asked, barely restraining her glee.

"No, you dumb bitch. You interviewed a psychopathic wizard using illusion to look like me."

Motion on the stage drew my attention. The PGs stepped forward to surround Adam. I dove into the crowded aisle.

"I'll be back with our full eyeTome presentation and Q&A session right after this special treat presented by Mimir Corp."

Adam stepped out of the way, headed just off stage as the presenter's podium lowered out of sight.

The PGs started their routine as I tried to break through the milling crowd. Each time one of them neared Adam, I held my breath and pushed harder, collecting numerous dirty looks.

A sudden flash stole my remaining breath. Both ends of the PGs staves burst into flame, turning their exotic dance of veils, illusion, and magic into a fire-juggling wonder that wrote horrifying dooms across my retina.

The dance slowed.

Fire whirled.

As several minutes of dazzling—if otherwise uneventful—dance routine mesmerized the crowd, I edged halfway across the ballroom until the masses blocked the aisles entirely. I cut across a row of seats, stepping on toes in a rush to get to the next aisle over. The podium rose back out of the stage and Adam crossed the space to meet it. The PGs froze into stances impossible for any human being to maintain as he reached center stage.

Adam led the applause.

"Fantastic, give them another round of applause." Adam's smile grew ever more insufferable as attendees did as he bid. "Before we get to questions about the eyeTome, I'd like to introduce the man responsible for the fantastic display we've all just witnessed. Richard Bradley, Mimir Corp CEO."

Bradley mounted the stage from the opposite end and joined Adam in front of the still immobile PGs.

"Thank you, Mister Mathias." Bradley grinned at the crowd. "Who says old adversaries can't come together once in a while?"

"Well, there is an open bar, right everyone?" Adam asked. When the cheering died, he spoke directly to Bradley. "You've got an announcement tonight too, don't you?"

"We do, one you upstaged, pre-empting our dancers instead of just introducing them. In the tradition of Nova Robotics," Bradley paused for the obscure reference to sink in. He swept a hand back toward the PGs. "Mimir Corp is proud to unveil our FRS project."

"Planning to open a Broadway show?" Adam asked.

"No." Bradley forced a laugh. "These excellent dancers are in fact the first generation of our First Responder Shield initiative, ironically inspired by Thoth's original work making a difference."

The PGs stood in unison, their illusions pixelated away to reveal the same first responder designs I'd witnessed during my visit to Mimir Corp.

I sucked in breath and let it out slowly. I'd been sure the wizard had hidden among the PGs to get close to Adam. With their real faces—as they were—revealed, I breathed more easily than I had since I'd seen myself on Mimir's reception area television.

I'm going to owe Chris a huge apology.

I'd apparently missed some of the conversation.

"Thank you, Richard," Adam shook Bradley's hand.

Bradley shook back and addressed the ballroom. "The Bradley brothers and Mimir Corp will be answering more questions about our FRS initiative directly after Thoth's presentation. The floor's all yours, Adam."

Bradley stepped to the back wall next to Thecia. Nodded heads and handshakes passed between them as Adam drew all other eyes to him with a loud clap of his hands. He rubbed his hands together like a kid in a candy store. "Now, I'm sure you're all eager to get through this presentation and to our question and answer session, so without further ado—"

Sunny's all too familiar voice halted him. "I have a question for you, Mister Mathias."

She marched onto the stage and extended a sheaf of papers. "Adam Mathias, you are hereby served a notice of subpoena to appear in the Oregon Criminal Court of Appeals, a notice of civil suit for defamation of the character of one Elias Balthazar Graham, a formal injunction against further harassment of Mister Graham and a restraining order forbidding you or those in your employ within a thousand feet of him without his permission. What do you have to say about that?"

The room fell utterly silent. With the distance involved, it was hard to determine whether Adam or I was the most shocked. He recovered faster, purpling with fury. Thecia bodily placed herself between Sunny and Adam, covering his mic and whispering.

Sunny strode over and shoved the papers into his chest, moving close enough that the big screens behind the stage held them both.

"How dare you!" Adam seethed. "This is an invitation only—"

Sunny held up a convention badge with an awkward grip, turning it so that the flat face was visible to the crowd.

Adam's harsh whisper carried over the speakers. "This is not the place for this."

Sunny shrugged. "I wanted witnesses."

"This is Eli's doing. Neither of you will get away with trying to publically humiliate me."

"Why not?" she asked. "You got away with perjury and framing me for a crime I didn't commit."

Adam froze.

He wasn't the only one. I couldn't believe Sunny had dared accuse him like that in front of so many witnesses. She was a great lawyer. She had to know that if her case fell apart, he'd come after her next.

Wait. Did she say what I think she said?

Sunny's image disintegrated in a shower of pixels, revealing a figure in ratty street attire: me. I stabbed the badge into Adam's chest, except the badge was actually a knife.

"No!" I sprinted forward.

The crowds' screams drowned the end of my cry.

I allowed myself a moment's worry about Sunny. The wizard wore her face and her dressed up court attire rather than what she'd worn the day of the Manger attack. He could've simply adapted the illusion to fit the situation, but a fearful whisper argued that the papers were most likely real and had probably been taken from her on Sunny's way to serve them.

While I fought my way to Adam's rescue, Thecia rushed to

Adam's aid. All but one of the Lord of the Rings extras stepped forward from the back wall and drew curved, black swords.

Bradley stared gobsmacked at the tableau.

Overhead screens shifted views between Adam sliding off of illusionary me's knife and my own upstream struggle through the panicked crowd to the stage. The screens returned to the unfolding drama on stage as the only elf not fighting held up a hand. "Hold."

"We had a deal," Adam gasped. "You're supposed to protect me."

Amplified so loud, it took a moment to realize the elf giving the orders was the boss elf from my alley. "Our bargain covers protection from Elias Graham, not this thing."

Boss elf is working with Adam against me?

"Elves, retire the field."

Boss Elf's soldiers had attacked the other me so swiftly that only the last two were far enough away from the wizard for a clean withdrawal. The wizard attacked the elves like a bladed whirlwind despite wielding only a short, bloody knife.

The elves moved like living examples of their fantasy ilk, though without fighting wires or other artificial effects. Their precision bespoke decades of training and every strike and counterstrike displayed elegant deadliness.

Unfortunately for the fey, the wizard didn't duel them.

He just ignored the damage of their strikes and drove his blade in and out of their bodies in waves of spraying emerald blood.

I hit the stage at a sprint as fake me cut down the elf from Gateway Park. I threw a slip-n-slide. Magically-lubricated surfaces fouled the fight in progress, threatening the balance of even the mythologically sure-footed elves.

This is going to hurt.

I canted my attack angle to drive the killer away from the audience and careened into the homeless mirror of myself at full speed. Our collision knocked him away from Adam. "Thecia, get Adam out of here!"

I rolled away the best I could on the slick surface, but not before his blade pierced one arm.

The wizard rolled the other way.

We came up facing one another across a gulf of slime.

"You no longer look homeless, Elias Balthazar Graham. If this is now true and you have forsaken the hero slayer, there is no need for you to die."

"Nothing has changed since you tried to kill me last."

"I would rather not slay you."

"You used my face in the Manger to murder innocents, including a child. For all I know, you hurt Sunny, and you tried to frame me by attacking my...well, okay, Adam might've deserved it, but the rest is unforgivable."

He threw the knife.

I tried to dodge, I really did, but somehow he managed to throw the knife in the same direction I dodged and even had the blade heading the right way despite all the physics calculations necessary to hit an evading target with a thrown knife.

Two words: foresight and god-damned-planning.

A fifth rez shield exploded from my compass into a three-foot round disk precisely as it had been programmed in Sharpie. I could still modify the shield by choosing which runes to activate or adjust the variables via my will, but evoking the shield as designed only took a split second of magic-fueled thought.

The knife bounced off into the slime at my feet. I gave him a hard smile which I hoped offered genuine menace.

My turn.

24

HOLLOW PROMISES

I threw my new spell.

Unlike the slip-n-slide which was typically aimed at a broad, easy-to-hit surface, this had to hit him. Fortunately for me, I didn't have to worry about a knife tip or penetrating the magical barrier protecting him from the elves. In D&D terms, it was a basic ranged touch attack.

My opponent didn't even bother to dodge.

Noodles, dandelion roots, and calamari hit his left thigh with a splat. His glance down held nothing but contempt.

"Soiling my leg is not a victory," he said.

Dandelions are amazingly hardy plants. Dad used to curse them because, by the time you saw the plant, they'd grown a deep taproot that wasn't easy to completely remove. The dandelion I'd plucked had survived to flower in a mere crack between slabs of concrete. They are tenacious—though perhaps not as tenacious as bamboo or blackberry brambles.

Power washed out of me in a dizzying rush. I bit my lip and focused on the mananet rather than the siren song far too close for comfort. Noodles expanded downward first, swelling in thickness as they sought cracks in the stage. Their exterior became rubbery, growing outward and around the wizard like slithering tentacles.

He struggled against the leafy squid growing around him.

I cheered inwardly despite the power costs. It didn't matter how much he struggled. He couldn't possibly be stronger than the fishy straight jacket anchoring him to the floor. I'd captured the wizard rather than kill him, satisfying Mom and Sunny if not myself.

Though killing him on camera probably wouldn't have been great for my future prospects.

I swapped the compass to my right wrist and yanked off Dad's polo. The multi-tool's knife cut bandages from the shirt without much difficulty.

I wrapped polo strips around my arm, using my teeth to knot the last. My brain raised minor concerns about the absorption qualities offered by using wicking fabric as a bandage, but it was all I had.

I turned my attention to Adam. The beautiful former love of my life cradled him in her arms, blood staining her clothes. To one side, the cowled elf that had tried to kill me watched us both over a slight curve to his lips.

"You and I are going to talk, elf."

"We've already spoken," he said

"Well, we're going to talk again," I sighed. "After I help Adam."

A single elf brow rose.

I knelt over Adam. Thecia's worried eyes met mine over the pressure she was keeping on the wound. Her expression darkened when my grin emerged at the mere thought of subjecting Adam to the druid restoration spell.

SMLE would probably pounce on me for torturing him, and the cameras would steal the spell's secret.

I looked up at the still PGs. "Hey, guys, injured man over here."

They didn't move.

Willie's voice thundered through the hall from his attempts to reach us. "PGs, defend life mode!"

The otherwise-still PGs dropped their staves and swarmed us. An EMT model removed me from Adam's side by the simple expedience of bodily picking me up and setting me behind his fellows.

Not like I would've argued.

Willie and Austin broke free of the crowd. Seeing the intern didn't brighten my day, but Willie's intervention meant I wouldn't have to personally save Adam's life.

"Elias!" Thecia pointed behind me.

I whirled to see the wizard ripping his way out of the now-green tentacles. I stared opened-mouthed. It wasn't possible. The tentacles had been at least six inches of writhing muscle.

My gaze dropped to the discarded bonds.

Hollow?

An urge to smack myself surged to the forefront of my thoughts. Dandelion tap roots were tenacious, but the green stems bridging root and blossom were hollow.

Should've used blackberry.

It took another moment to realize that beneath the tentacles being quickly ripped away, the wizard was an all-white plastic golem.

Larger hexes marked his body than on his brethren. His joints weren't covered in protective cloth but overlapping layers of hard plastic. A fine hexagonal mesh covered its glassy eyes.

"Damn it, Austin," Willie snarled. "How did that thing get out of the Faraday cage?"

"Don't look at me," Austin said. "I put in a service request to have the cage locked off with those magic circles each time you said to."

A Faraday cage would've walled the PG away from any electrostatic or electromagnetic influences, effectively cutting it off from the Edison network. That Willie had ordered both a Faraday cage and protective circles suggested that the white PG had caused them Issues. Unfortunately, the PGs had been designed to use Edison and mananet power, and it didn't sound as if the surly intern had bothered to follow up past completing the corporate minimum.

Yeah, he's not going to be working there long.

"PG-One, power down," Willie commanded.

"I am in life protection mode." PG-One turned his attention to me. "Protecting the endangered heroes' lives and my own."

Three steps and a leap brought a fist flying toward me.

Even without a knife, I had no doubt the PG could kill me. Its statement suggested that it had taken the voice command Willie had issued to the others, but decided to interpret it differently than the rest of us might like.

Willie tried his command again. "PG-One, power down!"

I threw a slip-n-slide where the PG would land and dove forward under his assault on the slick stage. The mechanical automaton didn't stumble like I hoped, but rode the slide like a champion surfer.

I scrambled to the discarded dancing staves. The moment I had one in hand, I turned it over, trying to position my hands on the contacts used to complete the circuit and activate the flame runes.

PG-One charged me first.

I leveled the stave like I had the rez five lance. He knocked the lance away before, so I wasn't surprised when his arms shifted to do the same again.

I jerked the stave backward as I leapt back several steps and willed the fire rune to life. Like with an eyeGuardian, initiating the rune ignited the chemicals in the stave's end. I set the flaming lance almost too late as PG-One collided with its end.

The thin stave bent. The flaming end broke with a loud crack, spilling fiery liquid down the thing's front.

Rather than prematurely count my victory *again*, I swung the staff around, willing the other rune to life. PG-One caught the stave's unbroken end. He snapped off the fuel reservoir with one hand and hurled the flaming club at me.

The speed and distance involved left no time for me to dodge.

We're both going to burn.

Futile or not, I scrambled for my Zippo, beginning the first incantation even before I had the top flipped open. My panic cost me my grip. The lighter toppled to the floor as a black, plastic arm snatched PG-One's flaming missile out of the air.

A mechanical voice scolded me. "Caution, sir. Carelessness handling fire can be hazardous to your health."

PG-One grabbed his black and white sibling and twisted off the head. He wrenched the burning fuel reservoir from his dead fellow so hard he crushed it. Fuel and fire ran down his arm as he threw it at me once more leaving runny napalm burned atop the sparkling green and milky-white shields protecting his surface.

The missile hit me square in the chest, but the Zippo stole away the flames.

PG-One kicked my lighter across the stage and turned to his brethren, speaking with Willie's voice. "PGs, power down with voice commands disabled."

Shit.

The remaining PGs ceased all function.

I dove for another stave. Double vision slowed the grab, but I managed to come away armed if dizzy as hell. I threw my last slip-n-slide and swept PG-One's legs with the stave.

He leapt my feeble attack and managed to keep his feet.

I considered igniting the staff in my hands and touching the flame to the slip-n-slide coating the flooring squares making up the stage. I discarded the idea. I'd worked several iterations on the spell to ensure the lubricant wasn't flammable. Besides, his seventh-fifth rez skin totally protected him from an elemental assault.

Think!

"I don't think we're going to get our little chat," the elf said.

Like the other elves that must've departed during our altercation, he wore a sword in his belt. I had a stave, not that I knew how to use it beyond playing Daffy Duck or Little John as a kid. Even if it had been crafted of feysteel, his sword wouldn't have been much more than a shiny club in my hands.

And they hadn't been able to hurt the golem with years of training.

I stepped into the center of one of the floor sections and invoked a fifth resonance cube.

PG-One had no mouth to smile. Its eyes could not glitter with mirth either normal or sadistic. With such things taken into consideration, I remained certain PG-One's non-expression was maliciously smug.

Willie jumped him, grabbing at the plating edges under one arm. The magical hex barriers kept his fingers from reaching their goal. PG-One seized Willie and hurled him against my cube.

I dropped the shield, caught Willie and threw the barrier back up before PG-One finished closing the distance. I *knew* the thing's expression even if he didn't physically wear amusement or condescension.

"Thanks," Willie said.

"How do we stop this thing?"

Willie shrugged. "We're in a tier four mananet. He can effectively shield himself from physical harm, and he's adopted a seventh rez against elemental assaults."

"You're the one that gave them a learning AI."

The odd visit from Officer Verde flashed through my mind.

Shit, did I teach him that? We're screwed as long as he's in a...mananet.

PG-One turned his back to me, strolling toward the discarded knife. He marched—nearly sauntered—over to Adam, seized Adam by his neck and dragged him screaming back onto the stage in the center of the mayhem.

Thecia beat on the plastic golem to no avail.

PG-One isn't a wizard. He's a limited AI augmented by golem enchantment.

His shield was constructed from a small army of little circles activated through a preprogrammed sequence much like the early concepts for the eyeSentinel. He powered the protection with the mananet and could augment the mananet as needed with an engine that converted both Edison power and battery power.

PG-One positioned Adam just outside my barrier. My former partner snarled threats. "What the hell is wrong with this thing? Call off your machine, Bradley or I'll—"

PG-One drove his knife into Adam.

Adam screamed.

It was hard not to enjoy Adam's torment, but Thecia rushed to Adam's aid. PG-One grabbed her by her hair and laid the blade beside her gold chain.

"You will surrender, Elias Balthazar Graham," PG-One said. "You cannot be allowed to thwart our mission."

"How do we shut it off?" I whispered.

"My hearing pickups are quite a bit better than that, Elias Balthazar Graham," PG-One said.

Willie shook his head. "If I can't get the chest plate open and it won't take voice commands, there's nothing that can stop it as long as it can draw power."

Draw power?

My senses reached toward the Columbia. Power straight out of fey coursed through the riverbed in semi-truck thick veins. "How much power can its system take?"

"We built in surge protectors. It'll section off functions before an overload could do any real damage," Willie said.

"I'm still waiting," PG-One slid the blade a hair.

Thecia yelped.

Blood beaded on her neck then ran in thick red fingers.

Her pain made my breath catch. "Why should I?"

"Surrender, and I will cease harming these humans."

"Eli, please," Thecia begged.

"What will you do with him?" Willie asked.

"I will kill him, Creator. He stands with the hero slayer. He interferes with our mission."

"What mission? I didn't assign you any mission," Willie said.

"Killing the homeless," I said.

Pixels swarmed PG-One, reforming him into Willie wearing different clothes. "The purpose of these plastic golems is to protect first responders, protect heroes from harm."

The golem became Austin. "Another one of those beggars is camped out on our doorstep. Why doesn't the city do something about all these homeless?"

PG-One became Willie once more but in yet another outfit. "He's a beggar, but not really homeless. Security caught him on camera entering a Corvette." The image flickered. "Damned criminals the lot of them. They're killing heroes."

"It was powered off when we had that discussion," Willie said.

"Apparently not," I said.

The illusion changed to Ullie. "Clear off. This is my territory. No one is allowed to beg in this city without Duval's permission."

PG-One became Austin. "How can you defend even one of them? They're a disease, Willie, cluttering our streets and killing everything good about Seufert Fells. We should ship them all off to the Wasteland."

Austin became Willie pointing imperiously to one side. "Some of those homeless are veterans. They served their country, protected us and our rights. They're heroes. Maybe they're down on their luck, but they deserve every chance to put their lives back together the best they can."

Willie's voice echoed in my mind. *<They deserve every chance...>*

It all clicked.

PG-One had been after Duval's people originally, killing the false homeless to protect homeless veterans. He'd somehow known about me from other overheard conversations, and he'd been faced with opposing directives until he'd seen me working with Duval. That had shifted its programmed priorities, but it still wanted me off the streets based on something it had over-heard about my value to the project—the project to protect heroes.

"Why did you attack the Manger?"

PG-One became Sunny from our dinner at Happy Clamily. "Duval's people are conmen, professional beggars who steal from genuine homeless. There are too many homeless for the Manger to help them all. The homeless need that help to survive."

I tried not to react to the suggestion that PG-One had been stalking us at dinner.

"She said that after you attacked her." I snarled.

The golem's voice returned to normal. "In an environment with limited resources, logic dictates that competition for those resources must be eliminated to ensure those of greatest impor-tance receive every chance to survive."

"You and other homeless were killing heroes by consuming their portion of the available resources," PG-One said.

"For the veterans to have *every* chance, you eliminated their competition?" Willie said.

Sunny transformed into me. "The only way I can make things better is to take out the killer."

"So it's you or me?" I asked.

I smiled back at myself and cut deeper into Thecia's throat.

"No matter what you have to do, kill *all* the power." I shoved Willie into the fifth rez wall, dropping the barrier before he hit. I paid no mind to whether he did what I'd asked as I threw myself at Thecia and the golem.

He released her as promised, preparing his knife for my guts.

The golem's monologue had been educational in more ways than one. I'd noticed partway through the show, that hexes shielded the back of his hands, but not the individual fingers.

I rushed toward him, right hand cradled low on my gut.

A human might've varied his assault, but the golem had no fear that my limited strength could stop his blow.

Using the compass as a base, I invoked a megaphone-shaped fifth resonance cylinder. The barrier encapsulated PG-One's knife, severing his mechanical fingers and baring his circuitry.

PG-One hit me with his broken fist, probably calculating that he could disrupt my attention and reclaim his weapon.

I didn't give him that chance, transforming my continued charge into a tackle. We slid through blood and offline PGs like they were bowling pins. I hurled the contents of my cylinder away as I invoked a fifth-first rez cube around a floor section containing both of us and my lost Zippo.

With a first rez preventing his access to the mananet, only the magical energy provided by the Mimir engine's conversion ability empowered PG-One's shield.

I added a seventh rez outside our cage.

If Willie took the Edison field down, the seventh rez was unnecessary, but I also needed someplace outside the fifth to put as much power as I could draw.

Blue and sparkling green magic curtained our milky-white cage.

"That was a mistake," PG-One said.

"I'm betting you can't keep all those shields active forever without a power source."

"They will hold longer than you will breathe."

A fifth rez shield exploded between us from my compass, filling the cube with an impenetrable barrier. I bent for my Zippo only to have PG-One slam bodily into the wall between us.

The impact hurt like hell but didn't knock me silly.

He hit me again.

I thickened the barrier to deprive him of run space.

PG-One braced his legs against the cage and turned my safety into a trash compactor. A quick contraction of shield thickness allowed me to drop to the ground, angling the shield so the corner and its size kept him from turning me into paste.

"You cannot win."

Our cage wasn't high enough magnitude to block out oxygen. Without the mananet, I was working off reserves. So rather than make it higher magnitude but permeable to air, I trusted the barrier to hold us tight long enough.

PG-One fought my will with his strength. His foreshortened arm braced against the barrier separating us and his remaining hand pushed against the outside cube. I'd thought early on that he'd come up with some kind of strength-enhancement magic. Knowing his body was machine stole the mystery behind his enhanced strength.

Physics and sheer stubborn will sided with me.

The lights went out.

A moment later, emergency lighting cast a yellow hue over the humongous room, ivory moons in the darkness.

"Elias Balthazar Graham?"

It hurt to breathe and my arm throbbed. "Yeah?"

"I must fulfill my mission. I must protect our heroes."

"Good luck with that."

"For me to succeed, you must die."

I gestured at our cage. "Too late. The party's all over except for cleanup."

"I've collected many valuable pieces of data in the fulfillment of my mission," PG-One said.

I resisted the urge to rise to the bait.

"Security is seldom a problem when you are a familiar face."

"Shouldn't you be conserving power rather than talking?"

"If you weren't homeless, you'd no longer be on my kill list."

Chuckling hurt.

"Would you remain homeless if your conviction were overturned?"

Cold washed through me. There was no question that PG-One

knew the answer. That he'd asked after an answer already in his possession meant a setup.

I glanced around, unable to see others in the darkness beyond our white-walled cage. "What are you getting at?"

"Adam Mathias possesses data which can indefatigably prove your innocence."

My breath caught in my chest. For a moment I couldn't seem to get enough oxygen. "Bullshit. Adam would never keep data around that could incriminate him."

"Like the male Glamour subjects?" PG-One asked.

Is it really possible?

"If you release me, I will give it to you," PG-One said. "If you do not, I will delete records containing the location of this data and I will kill you."

Shit. Shit. Shit.

I was suddenly thrown down a dark well. Restitution lurked one decision away. Everything I'd lost could be restored if I willingly risked the lives of who knew how many innocents.

I could release him and then stop him before he did more harm.

The runaway girl—young and innocent with her throat sliced —filled my mind's eye. Tears blinded me, choking my breath. I couldn't risk another being killed, not even for personal justice.

I took a long breath to turn him down only to realize there didn't seem enough air to do so. Black spots welled up to tunnel my vision.

Son-of-a-bitch!

I turned my attention to our cage. With limited light outside as reference, PG-One had intensified my fifth rez cube until no air had permeated its walls, and I'd been so secure in my own superiority, I hadn't even noticed as he'd tricked me into using up my oxygen even faster.

My instinct was to leap to my feet, but there seemed little doubt such a leap would end with me on the floor. If I passed out,

PG-One would go free—assuming he didn't maintain the cage until he was sure I was dead.

The first rez component of my cage prevented us both from accessing the mananet. We'd both been working off of reserves.

Blackness welled up to steal my consciousness.

PG-One's engine was generating magic to power his personal shield and transferring it through the taps in his hands to fuel the magnitude that stole my air.

I closed my eyes.

"Elias Balthazar Graham?"

I reached out my senses for magic. Within the first rez, there was only one source. It took too many gasps to latch onto his engine's generator and the link in his palm, but I'd only get one shot.

Have to hold on.

"Release me," PG-One said. "You cannot win."

I smiled.

My eyes sprang open, latching onto him in more ways than one. I turned PG-One into my own personal mana crystal and then pillaged all the power I could yank out of him.

"What are you doing?" PG-One demanded.

I pumped his power into our cage, adding air passages. My burning lungs gulped air. A hoarse growl escaped me. "Don't trifle with a Magus."

PG-One went berserk. He kicked at the walls. He pounded the barrier. He echoed Knight Kenrith in all but his feysteel blades.

His shields died one hex at a time.

"You're going to die, *Magus.*"

More hexes died.

I dropped my wrist shield and grabbed the edge of his chest plate.

His punch sent pain exploding through my chest.

I bounced off the cube wall, all of my reclaimed breath driven from my body. My head hit hard. His chest plate clattered along the floor. Our cage vanished.

My illusionary smile was colder than any shark.

My own was hotter than hell.

He fell on me with a vengeance, seized my shoulders and slammed my head against the floor.

I flipped open the Zippos in my two right hands, dropped it into his chest cavity, and finished the incantation.

Fire exploded in his chest.

The heat seared my cheeks, burning my eyebrows to my scalp.

I kicked him off me and rolled away.

The intense magical flame destroyed his unprotected circuits in moments. Unlike Boss Golem, PG-One died before I slumped to the ground and wished things had gone the other way.

A painful chuckle escaped me. "I win. I didn't get knocked out, and I didn't even have to draw on the—"

25

———

DELUSION & COLLUSION

Without the slightest herald of screams from the convention center hall, a swarm of demi-goblins rushed into the ballroom.

I scrambled onto my feet and grabbed a discarded staff. I rushed to interpose myself between my former partners and the fey mutations.

"He's attacking us!" Adam said. "Restrain this criminal."

I wasn't sure who Adam was snarling at, but it didn't matter to the horde charging us. They drew serrated blades, fetid saliva dripping from even-worse teeth.

I lit the ends of the stave. I didn't have any slip-n-slides left, though I still had one of my failed squid-root spells.

The ley line beneath the Columbia beckoned me, inviting me to seize its strength and unleash it at the perverted horde.

Demi-goblins shouted garbled obscenities punctuated by my name. Some produced pistol crossbows, their arrows throbbing with black-green auras.

"Back off, now," I snarled.

Thecia put a hand on my shoulder. "Eli."

I shrugged her off. "Guard Adam, I'll protect you."

I spun the flaming staff.

The goblins raised their crossbows.

"Magus, stop!" Tunoh dropped onto my shoulder from who knew where. "Eli, you must put down the weapon."

"The demi-goblins—"

"Aren't real." She bit my ear.

The sudden pain made me wince. When my eyes opened once more the swarm of demi-goblins were cops. I glanced at the monitors. My image looked wild. A stark-raving madman spun a flaming staff between himself and a crowd of cops with nightsticks and handguns readied against him.

"The Ley?"

"No, you were subjected to glamour."

The elf.

I scanned the room. Somewhere during the fight, the elf and his minions had left Adam and me to our fates.

Tunoh wasn't visible on the screen as she whispered, but the blood trickling down my neck was. "Put it down, Eli. Claim injury madness."

I released my will from the flame runes and dropped the staff to the stage. Since I didn't know what the PGs had done to extinguish the fire, the staff rolled away still burning. I raised my hands. "I'm sorry. My injuries, I was disoriented, some kind of night terror."

"He tried to attack law enforcement officers. He's unstable and needs to go back into the Wastela—" Adam yelped and cradled his face. Blood ran down a long cut beneath the fingers cupping his cheek.

Laughter bubbled out of my lips, no doubt as mad sounding as Adam claimed. I flopped down into a sitting position and laughed until tears ran down my face.

SMLE and the EMTs closed on me. The former with cuffs and the latter demanding I receive stitches. It didn't really matter which one of them won. I seemed to live in the hospital and jail more than I did my alley.

But that's over now. Once Sunny gets me out of this I can...Sunny!

"Tunoh, what happened to Sunny?"

The authorities gave me a worried look.

"Who is Tunoh?" Brooke demanded.

"It doesn't matter. That murderbot served Adam a bunch of papers. He had to have taken them from Sunny. We need to find her, she could be—"

"Those papers were bullshit," Adam snarled. "A prop made of lies so you could get your monster close enough to kill me."

"Could someone slap something—"

A crack rocked Adam's head back, despite no one being near him.

I smiled at the grinning rhet back on my shoulder. "As I was saying, could someone slap something across his mouth, please?"

Tunoh wiggled a paw.

I shook my head. "We need to know if Sunny's all right."

Tunoh's expression flickered through happy to stubborn to resigned. "You will be all right?"

I nodded, leaned close and kissed her tiny cheek. "Thank you."

"I told you!" Adam railed. "He's ma—"

Tunoh sidelined to slap him on her way out of the ballroom.

I smirked and shrugged. "Don't look at me. I never moved."

"Screw this," Brooke growled. "Take them *all* to the precinct for questioning. You, ride in the ambulance with Graham so his injuries can get tended, and someone get me all the video recordings from tonight."

"We need to assess everyone first," a human EMT said.

"Fine, but we do everything by the book." Brooke eyed Adam. "No exceptions."

I flopped onto my back. They could check me out while I slept.

My sudden rest proved to be short-lived. Two EMTs, neither

plastic, bent over me. One waved nasty chemicals under my nose. I choked back to consciousness.

"They're all responsible," Adam snarled. "I demand you arrest them all. I said I was pressing charges."

I lifted my head enough to see. An EMT set a restraining hand on my chest, making me wince. Dad's polo had been replaced by actual bandages.

"I heard you, Mister Mathias," Detective Brooke said. "However there is no evidence that Richard Bradley or Mister Graham had anything to do with your injuries."

Willie and Austin were physically cordoned off to one side by SMLE, but neither was cuffed. Richard Bradley was in the senior-most officer's face, forcefully repeating phrases dictated into his ear from a probable lawyer.

Adam pointed at me. "He is responsible for all this. He's unstable, a dangerous criminal."

My voice croaked as I struggled to sit upright. "Detective, Mister Mathias is within a thousand feet without my permission. I'd like to press charges."

I HELD the copies of what the fake Sunny had given Adam, politely given to me by Richard Bradley's attorney who had managed to get both Richard and me released.

"Thank you, Richard," I said.

"It was the least I could do." Bradley squirmed. "About that job offer. I'm really sorry, but until things get sorted out, the FRS initiative is dead."

I nodded. "And with no project, you've no need to soil your now-questionable reputation with an ex-con in your employ."

Bradley glanced around for witnesses and lowered his voice. "What you did weren't the actions of someone who...well, who did what you were convicted of doing. Between you and me, Mathias is the criminal. I hope Mimir recovers so we can be a part of your vindication."

The edges of the bubble of hope Mimir had offered burned like a chunk had been cut out of me. "You created the golem that murdered people. Even as an earlier model, you told the world to trust their lives in the hands of that same technology."

Bradley glanced deeper into the precinct as he nodded.

I shook his lawyer's hand and clapped Bradley on the shoulder. "Go take care of your brother."

A scan through the documents on my march toward the Manger heartened me, though not as much as they had when she'd served them. The injunction and restraining orders had been signed by a judge. The others were file briefs in mid-preparation. Sunny intended to go after Adam. The doppelganger had just announced some of her intentions prematurely—giving Adam time to build a defense.

The EMTs had wanted me transferred to a hospital. Of course, I'd refused. Even if I couldn't get the rhet to help me, I knew a way to fix my own injuries.

Tunoh hadn't turned back up, and no one had any news of Sunny. My gut writhed with worry and dread. Each step closer to the Manger tighten the knots.

The halfway house was still closed when I arrived. Sunny's car wasn't in her spot. The back door was chained shut. A notice of eviction plastered to the door sent ice through me.

I marched around the building. There had to be a way inside. How else could Sunny comply with the eviction? The front door was also chained. An eviction notice stuck to the door partially concealed by a notice of demolition.

The world swooped around me.

I stumbled back from the door.

I hadn't liked the Manger. Grace had been right to claim it had never been my home, but it meant something to the homeless that did. Hell, it was more than just a business for Grace and Sunny. It was their life's mission.

An angry orange eye glared down on me from a banner hung across several of the block's buildings. Big black letters filled the world with doom and fury: An eyeStore Emporium coming soon!

I balled my fists and marched away.

I had no idea where Tunoh was.

Elves were plaguing me with glamour illusions.

Razcolm had been captured and imprisoned.

I'd lost Kenrith as an ally.

If I wasn't addicted to fey magic, I felt damned close to the edge.

Sunny remained missing.

And Adam had bought the Manger and scheduled its demise.

What else can go wrong?

The Story Continues…

Keep reading for a sneak peek from
Dumpstermancer 3: Decoy

Thank you for reading *Duplicity*.

Word of mouth recommendations and book reviews are insanely helpful, not just to other readers, but to an author's success. More-over, we use these reviews to know what *you* want to read more of. Please consider leaving a short, honest review—nothing special required, just a sentence or two about how you felt about this book. I can't thank you enough.

If you loved this story and would like to stay up to date on the latest book releases, promotions, giveaways, and a free story, please be sure to become a member of the Delirious Scribbles Readers Group. [Your email address will never be shared, and you can opt out at any time.]

Begin your journey, just scan this image with your phone camera!

Keep reading for a sneak peek....

Thecia stopped outside Thoth's main boardroom. Adam's anger slipped through the cracks in the otherwise sound-proof conference room, his furious demands an octave higher than normal. She checked her reflection in the glass display, pointedly not seeing the Incan tablet that had ruined Thoth.

Dark hair, expertly straightened then laced through jeweled golden spirals, framed her face. Emeralds in the matching necklace set off her ebony eyes as much as the gold complimented her dark lustrous skin.

A particularly loud snarl drove Darrin Silus out of the board-room. He stopped short when he saw her, eyes flashing but his own tirade held at bay behind lips clamped tight.

Darrin's gaze flicked to the framed tablet, darkened then flicked back to the boardroom. When his gaze fell on Thecia again, she could all but feel his judgement.

No, more like disgusted condemnation.

She liked Darrin, had done all she could to keep Adam from casting the young man out with the reset of Eli's arcanology team. Watching Darrin's repulsion mount as his eyes flicked from the ornaments in her hair to her earrings, necklace and bracelet twisted her guts.

<How can you wear Eli's gifts after you betrayed him?> He demanded within her thoughts. She didn't answer. Darrin had been young at the time. He didn't understand the whole picture.

Darrin shot her a last glower and stormed away.

She scowled at the Incan tablet.

This is all your fault, Eli.

The boardroom door opened once more, allowing a crowd of corporate executives and directors egress.

Adam Mathias semi stood thanks to the automated support chair. Blood seeped through the bandages beneath his dress shirt. He shouldn't have been out of the hospital, but Adam seldom listened to anything other than his own council. His expression mirrored Darrin's. "This is our one opportunity, gentlemen. Get it done before losing this opportunity forces us to audit our personnel costs."

He noticed her. "It's about time, Thecia! Get in here."

Her eyes flicked back to the display case, resting on the tablet one last time. Knotting guts herded bile up the back of her throat—an echo to how sick she'd been ten years before.

ADAM MATHIAS MET her at the door to his executive office suite, taking her hands in his. "Thecia."

"Shouldn't we be waiting for Eli?" she asked.

"I need to speak to you alone."

Unease chilled her. "I'm not discussing business without Eli here. We have no secrets from each other."

Adam's expression sobered as he led her to a crimson couch. "This isn't about that argument."

"Then why are we meeting without him?" She demanded.

"Secrets." Adam turned his back on her. "Eli's secrets."

A chill stroked her spine.

"We're in trouble, Thecia. Eli's put this whole company in jeopardy." He turned around, his expression green and guilt ridden. "There's no easy way to tell you this."

She leapt to her feet. "Whatever it is, just spit it out!"

"The tablet Eli brought back from his trip to South America…"

"The Incan artifact?" she asked.

Adam nodded. "He deciphered the Incan Priesthood's spell."

"That's what he does."

Her partner shook his head. "You don't understand. He's been testing the spell on our employees, Eve Krisp for one."

"Okay…," she said. "What does the spell even do?"

"Enthralls its victims and turns them into sex slaves," Adam said.

All warmth fled from the room.

Gravity doubled.

Thecia's legs collapsed, bringing her down hard onto the bloody sofa.

"Eve Krisp was only one of the first," Adam added. "Eve, can you come in now?"

The young acanologist (wannabe) stepped in from a side room, her expression driving home the coffin nails of Eli's guilt.

"I SAID GET IN HERE!" Adam's demands shattered the memory.

His tone made her bristle, but she was glad to be free of the devastating moment she'd learn about Eli's cheating–an abuse of trust and magic she might've suffered if she'd declined his marriage proposal only days before Adam's revelation.

"Thecia!"

Magical slave or Adam's slave–I was doomed either way. She stepped into the conference room, wishing she'd just walked away all those years before.

He'd persuaded Thecia to stay, soothing her pain while

painting a fanciful picture of his dreams for Thoth and Seufert Fells.

"We have an opportunity, Thecia." Avarice darkened his handsome features. "To make our dreams reality ahead of schedule."

Your dreams.

Adam Mathias had convinced her younger self to surrender Eli's thirty-three percent stake. He'd used her heartsick disgust, her betrayed, broken heart, and his honeyed words, convincing her to testify against Eli. Adam had promised to shield her from all that was to come after, using his controlling stake to implement decisions that left her as trapped in Thoth as Eli had been in the Wasteland.

Should've just sold it all and walked away.

Thoth's CEO outlined his updated plan for a hostile takeover of Mimir Corp and how doing so accelerated his plans to transform Seufert Fells. As the public face of Thoth's operations, she was forced to understand Adam's intentions and his war against homeless in their city.

Poor souls. It's not their fault Adam's harboring a deep-rooted need to further destroy Eli.

If she was honest with herself, she didn't understand Adam's obsession. She abhorred what Eli had done and the way he'd betrayed what she'd thought of as a forever kind of love. Even so, Eli had been convicted. He'd served his sentence.

Why isn't that enough? Why hurt the homeless just to make things worse for Eli?

She left their meeting troubled enough to have lost her appetite. If she hadn't had lunch scheduled with Megan French, she'd have gone home, taken her migraine medicine and wrapped herself in blankets, ice cream and darkness.

Her limousine met her in front of their building.

Hair prickled the back of her neck.

She scanned the street.

Her initial thoughts turned to Eli, not that he hadn't been troubling her thoughts since his return. She didn't see anyone watching her. Even so, she shifted her fingers nearer the newly upgraded Thoth shield charm and hurried into the back of her car.

CYNTHIA GRAHAM FROWNED.

She didn't make such expressions often as evidenced by the scarcity of wrinkles on her face. She fussed with her dark hair. "Um. Jackson?"

Her husband looked up from the contracts spread across the dining table. He glanced at the realtor. "Would you mind giving us a moment, Alex?"

The middle aged man inclined his head, stepping out of the room.

"What is it, dear?"

"Do you really think this is a good idea?" Cynthia asked.

"Of course, I do."

"But don't you think you should discuss this with Elias and Zahda before you buy them a house?"

Jackson scowled. "We warned Zahda about that *boy*. Did she listen? No, and now our daughter is destitute, Cynthia. The little bastard stole everything. If we don't help her, she'll be homeless, *homeless*, Cynthia."

"Eli doesn't seem to mind living on the streets."

Jackson purpled. "I mind. My baby girl is not going to live on the streets, not if I can help it. Same goes for Elias."

"Marisol said Eli would never leave his alley, that his pride won't let him."

Jackson grinned. "I have a plan for that. Alex?"

The realtor reentered.

Jackson sat down at the table, pen sweeping across the purchase contracts. The realtor handed Jackson the keys and left with the documents. Eli's father sent a text and then escorted his wife outside and over to a storage pod being unloaded outside the garage. He opened the garage door first then the pod. "Lend me a hand?"

Jackson grabbed a huge duffel.

Cynthia stepped around him, picking up a folded cot. "What is all this?"

"A safe place for Eli to hide out when he needs to lay low."

"How does this convince Elias to no longer be homeless?" Cynthia asked.

"I've figured this all out. Elias refuses to leave the streets because having an address will force him to register as a sex offender–admitting he's guilty." Jackson pointed to the main house. "Right in there is hot and cold running water, a large kitchen where he can prepare food. He might start by using the camping gear out here, but eventually the comforts of home will counter his pride."

"I don't know," Cynthia said. "The boy inherited your sense of pride. Also, with everything going on here, all Eli's troubles, wouldn't Zahda be safer back in Portland?"

"Elias's troubles are of his own making. Why would they affect Zahda? Besides, we can't afford two new homes. This way, Zahda has a place to get back on her feet, and Elias has a safehouse. Win-win."

Cynthia gave the burgeoning garage campsite a dubious look.

CALEB KRISP ADJUSTED the hood of his jacket to better hide his face. He had no eyes for the flowerbeds or trees of Gateway Park. He sat facing toward but uninterested inThoth tower, though the company which had given his sister's attacker the opportunity to hurt her still had a debt to pay. Instead, Caleb focused on the government building. Bench arrangements prevented his clean view, interposing a bronze statue of some bird thing between him and the doors Eli Graham would eventually enter then depart en route to his doom.

Caleb could sit on the opposite side of the statue, but that meant craning his neck or twisting to see the building's entrance.

Not exactly low profile.

Cody and Beau sat in a burnt orange conversion van just south of the park, waiting to snatch Graham the moment he was vulnerable.

This time no one's going to stop us from giving that bastard what he deserves.

"You are a fool."

Caleb glanced up toward the cultured voice. One of the snooty, rich, bastards that profited on people like him looked down his nose at Caleb. The insufferable jackass had prettied himself up like some comic book, Legolas-wannabe hero.

"What the hell do you want, elf boy?" Caleb demanded.

The pretty boy frowned, looked down at his attire then shot the statue a nasty look. "Nothing.

"Then get lost."

He did, letting Caleb return to watching for Graham.

Half an hour later, a shimmer of energy drew Caleb's eye. An alien creature materialized in the beam. A moment later, the creature wavered, becoming human. Caleb stared as the creature joined the lunch crowd exiting the government building. He stopped, fixed his gaze on Caleb, and beckoned with an inviting wave.

Caleb stiffened. He shook his head.

The world went topsy turvy. Darkness swallowed him, spitting him out in front of the alien in a fit of dizziness. The disguised creature paced around Caleb, looking him up and down.

Caleb opened his mouth, but no sound came out.

An awful, nails-on-chalkboard screech undercut the thing's words, driving spikes into Caleb's already wobbly thoughts. "You might do."

"Do what?" Caleb spat.

"Your world interests us, but before we approach your people, your society needs repair."

If Caleb hadn't seen the thing beam down, he'd have called the creature a nutball. "What are you talking about?"

"Injustice," the alien said.

Caleb's eyes flicked toward the government center building. *Tell me about it.*

<Your desire to see justice done drew us to you.> The alien withdrew a small, high-tech box from behind his back. *<Take this gift. Use its powers to bring justice and equality to your species.>*

Powers?

"Powers?" Caleb asked.

The alien smiled. "Strength, speed, a defense shield, and of course energy beams to stun or kill—only as a last resort, of course."

A dark chuckle rumbled from Caleb's chest. "Of course."

The alien opened the box, offering a thick rope of what looked like black gold geometric shapes chained together.

Reaching forward, the moment his fingers touched the metal, power washed through Caleb. He'd barely lifted the chain from the box when the alien beamed away. Caleb rolled the heavy chain around in his fingers.

I'll be a super hero...

He clasped the chain around his neck, Power washing through him doubled. Caleb stomped, driving his foot through the sidewalk.

Right after I correct a few wrongs in my life.

Appendix A: Basic Arcanology

The basic principles of arcanology revolve around two elements: arcane energy and circles (loosely derived from the concepts of magical or summoning circles mentioned in folklore).

Arcane energy is a naturally occurring energy form not unlike lightning, and can be harnessed and regulated using methods similar to regulating electricity.

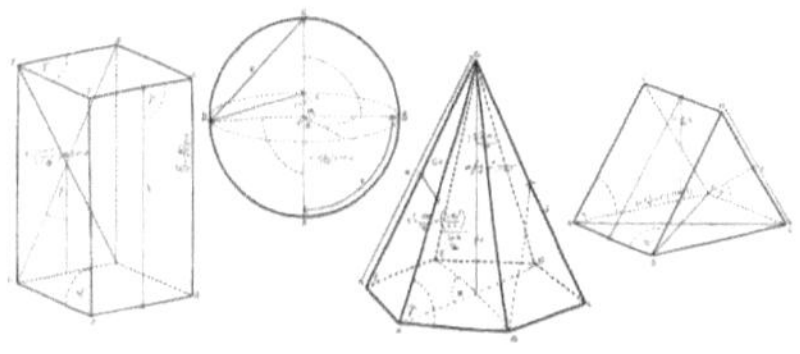

A circle is, in effect, any completed circuit for arcane energy flow regardless of shape. These circles are three-dimensional areas, defined by base circle shape, control runes, or, in the case of those with advanced education in arcanology, the will of the arcanologist creating the effect. This last control type is the least reliable, and is generally limited to laboratory development of control rune series meant to produce the desired shape, resonance, and magnitude.

RESONANCE

Arcane energy produces a wave. The wave's resonance, or frequency, can be adjusted to produce variable effects. Thus far, arcanologists have discovered eight resonances that produce stable, repeatable conditions. The shape of the base circle or its rune-derived three-dimensional field seem to have no effect on the resonance.

First Resonance: first resonance, or rez, circles manifest as a soft blue-white energy field. At this frequency, the circle prevents arcane energy outside the circle from penetrating the interior.

Second Resonance: second rez circles are less opaque than first rez, producing a clear but sparkling blue energy. Second rez circles prevent arcane energy within its circle from exiting.

Third Resonance: third rez differs from first and second in that it requires two circles to product a stable effect. The paired circles act as a magical conduit—thaumaturgic linking in old folklore—connecting both ends of the arcanology formula in effectively a cause-and-effect cycle.

Either circle can be the origin or destination. The third rez pairing allows for energy transportation from one unconnected point to another, as well as for energy transmutation from one form to another. In this way, arcane energy might be converted into thermal energy, visible light, or kinetic force such as used to push a piston.

The third rez field manifests as swirling orange and off-white.

Fourth Resonance: fourth rez fields are a yellowish green sometimes referred to as lemon-lime. Some arcanologists also report scenting peppermint near an active fourth rez circle. Experimentation with the fourth rez circles has brought to light evidence of apparitions. The appearance of said "ghosts" may be a light echo or illusionary effect of the field itself. Further study is required.

Fifth Resonance: fifth rez fields create a milky-white field capable of blocking physical matter. Caution must be used at higher magnitudes to ensure the field isn't blocking air flow from those within the circle.

Sixth Resonance: sixth rez manifests with a translucent green energy which gives off a strong odor of burnt popcorn. Similar to a second rez circle, sixth rez prevents energies other than arcane or kinetic from escaping the enclosing circle.

Seventh Resonance: seventh rez is the opposite to sixth. The sparkling green field prevents energies other than arcane and kinetic from entering the circle's area.

Eighth Resonance: the newly discovered eighth rez circle is in many ways similar to the third rez. The eight rez circle must also be paired, but rather than energy transfer, this magical field allows for transfer of physical matter. As an example, the origin circle could be placed in a floating snorkel tube while the destination circle is inscribed around a diving mouthpiece, effectively creating a remote air supply. The energy of this circle creates a shimmering violet light. Some arcanologists have reported a buzzing sound, similar to swarming gnats, when close to the field produced by this circle.

MAGNITUDE

Circles can be produced at various magnitudes depending on the desired effect. Magnitude effectively works as a sliding scale from first to fifth magnitude, first being the initial magnitude of a circle and fifth being the maximum. Magnitude has varying effects depending upon the application.

As an example, the interior of a fifth rez circle at the maximum fifth level of magnitude would be sealed against airflow without additional rune effects included in its controls.

For a first rez, the stronger the magnitude, the more arcane energy can be prevented from entering the circle's area.

Magnitude is commonly discussed in reference to mananet effectiveness. The arcane energy field will be more stable at higher magnitudes. Many arcanology products list minimum mananet magnitude levels to prevent mid-spell availability failures.

COMBINATION CIRCLES

Laboratory application often utilizes multiple resonance sets to create combined effects. While visually complex, layering of concentric circles requires only careful arrangement of the basic constructs. Circles employed need not be maintained at the same magnitude or in the same shapes.

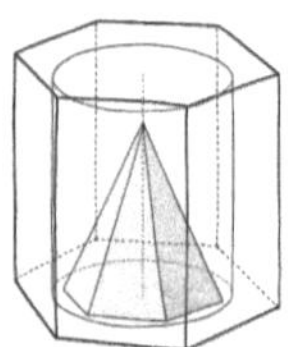

When layered, circles are identified from the outermost in. A first resonance circle placed inside a fifth rez circle—called a fifth-first rez—would prevent physical objects and arcane energy entrance into the inscribed area. Planning must be applied to prevent conflicts in the layering order. For example, encapsulating circles or constructs within a first rez will cut off the energy flow to these objects.

APPENDIX B: CAST OF CHARACTERS

Appendix B: Cast of Characters

HUMANS

Adam Mathias: CEO of Thoth Corp. Eli's former best friend who reported Eli's crimes to SMLE.

Caleb Ford: Brother of Eve Ford. Out for revenge for Eli's crimes against Eve and her subsequent death.

Dad (Jackson Graham): Stubborn and judgemental successful businessman. Father of Zahda, Eli and Douglas Graham.

Darrin Silus: Head of Thoth arcanology. Eli's former protege.

Detective Brooke: Straight arrow detective for SMLE.

Dr. Jessice Porter: Social services psychiatrist assigned to Eli to assist his transition back to normal society. Dedicated to correcting Eli's wrong thinking.

Duval: Head of organized begging in Seufert Fells

Elias "Eli" Balthazar Graham: Homeless former CAO of Thoth Corp. Talented arcanologist recently released from incarceration in the Wasteland virtual penitentiary.

Emlimn: Eli's mentor in arcanology

Eve Ford: Deceased member of Eli's Thoth arcanology team. Testified against Eli in his criminal trial. Sister of Caleb Ford

Grace: The Manger's highly skilled cook

Marisol "Sunny" Terrell: Former attorney and owner of the Manger. Dedicated to helping people, especially Eli despite his combative attitude.

Megan French: Network One news correspondent

Mihail: Primary enforcer for Duval.

Mom (Cynthia Graham): Loving but naive mother of Eli, Zahda and Douglas.

Nicole: Test subject in Thorth's Glamour troubleshooting trials.

Officer Andrew Flowers: Suefert Fells police involved in shooting investigation around Eli's alley and later captured at Suefert Fells Dam

Officer Winslow: Suefert Fells police involved in shooting investigation around Eli's alley and later captured at Suefert Fells Dam

Sergeant Jackson Danielson: Suefert Fells police involved in shooting investigation around Eli's alley and later captured at Suefert Fells Dam

Thecia Crospe: COO of Thoth Corp. Eli's former fiance. Testified against Eli

Tiny: Smaller of Caleb's thug friends. Responsible for multiple attacks on Eli.

Ugly: Uglier of Caleb's thug friends. Responsible for multiple attacks on Eli.

Wayne: Beggar in the employ of Duval, assigned the territory near the Thoth component factory.

Zahda: Eli's younger sister,

PARANORMAL BEINGS

Ahbnar: Knight of Rhet and son of Kenrith. Perished in an attempt to prevent the use of Eli's Glamour material backstage in the theater used for Eli's recovery.

Knight Kenrith: Knight Commander of the Knights of Rhet. Father of the rhet warren established in Eli's Alley.

Lucian Fayer: Mysterious elven figure responsible for the plot against Thoth, Seufert Fells and later attacks on Eli.

Matron Biancha: Spiritual advisor and shaman of Kenrith and his warren.

The Ottiren: Ancient indian spirit capable of possessing animals. Rescued Eli. Demands Eli restore his ancient trading routes in exchange–or be eaten.

Razcolm: Abrasive disembodied spirit possessing Eli's origami spider.

Tunoh: Squire of the Knights of Rhet, Kenrith's daughter. Eli's fiance.

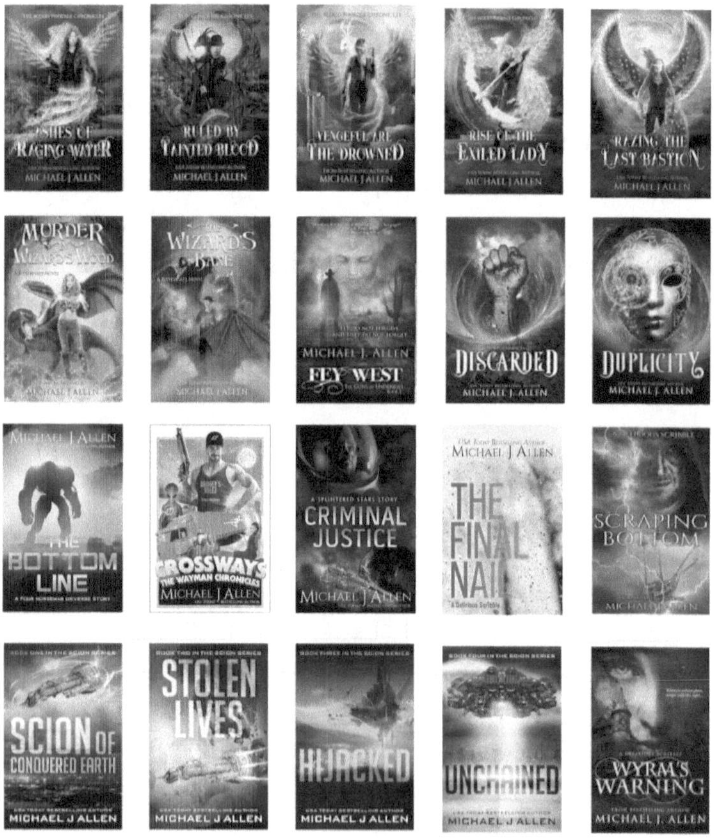

Look for more great books like these at a book reailer near you and learn more at www.deliriousscribbles.com

ACKNOWLEDGMENTS

The second chapter of Eli's adventures has come to an end. Thanks for reading Duplicity. Hopefully, you've enjoyed all the new texture this journey brought to the Dumpstermancer world. There's more to come, and I invite you to keep reading. While we wait for Disrupted, please check out some of my other titles.

They say it takes a community to raise a child. Well, it certainly takes more than a single author to build a novel. I have the support of an incredible team of people. I'd like to acknowledge them in no particular order. For the record, none of my children were tortured in amusement park lines during the creation of this novel.

Once more we have Stefanie Saw of www.seventhstarart.com to thank for providing Dumpstermancer's sequel such an incredible cover.

The soundboarding, editing, and proofreading crew deserve just as much if not more thanks. These are the people that spent long hours slogging through all of my many mistakes: Jennifer and Jason, Scott and Tina, Rebecca, Frank and Barrie D.

The last people I want to thank are the citizens of Seufert Fells. My leading man Eli and his associates gave us one hell of a rollercoaster ride. This one ended on a bit more of a cliffhanger, but I—more than anyone—am looking forward to whatever comes next.

See everyone as soon as possible in Disrupted.

ABOUT THE AUTHOR

Photo credit: Jim Cawthorne

Michael J. Allen is a star-lord, goofball, and USA Today bestselling author of character-driven, multi-layer, full-spectrum science fiction and fantasy novels - pretty much whatever madness sprouts from his head... (Learn more at www.deliriousscribbles.com)

LET'S CONNECT

I love chatting with my readers, and hope you'll join my reader groups. If you'd rather stay up to date without joining in on the fun, there are plenty of ways to follow along.

— MICHAEL J ALLEN

READER GROUPS:

Discord : https://discord.gg/WeM4bwq
Facebook: https://www.facebook.com/groups/dsreaders
MeWe: https://www.mewe.com/join/dsreaders

FOLLOW THE SCRIBBLER:

www.deliriousscribbles.com

amazon.com/-/e/B0096GEILG
bookbub.com/authors/michael-j-allen
facebook.com/deliriousscribbler
goodreads.com/deliriousscribbler
instagram.com/thedscribbler
twitter.com/Thedscribbler